A Crafter
Hooks a Killer

Also available by Holly Quinn

A Crafter Knits a Clue

A Crafter Hooks a Killer

A HANDCRAFTED MYSTERY

Holly Quinn

CROOKED
LANE

NEW YORK

PUBLISHER'S NOTE: The recipes contained in this book are to be followed exactly as written. The publisher is not responsible for your specific health or allergy needs that may require medical supervision. The publisher is not responsible for any adverse reaction to the recipes contained in this book.

Published in the United States by Crooked Lane Books, an imprint of The Quick Brown Fox & Company LLC.

Crooked Lane Books and its logo are trademarks of The Quick Brown Fox & Company LLC.

Library of Congress Catalog-in-Publication data available upon request.

ISBN (hardcover): 978-1-64385-012-2
ISBN (ePub): 978-1-64385-013-9
ISBN (ePDF): 978-1-64385-014-6

Cover illustration by Ben Perini
Book design by Jennifer Canzone

Printed in the United States.

www.crookedlanebooks.com

Crooked Lane Books
34 West 27th St., 10th Floor
New York, NY 10001

First Edition: June 2019

10 9 8 7 6 5 4 3 2 1

Jennifer—because libraries are relevant and essential...and community matters. Rock on, you're killing it. (I mean that with true admiration.)

Chapter One

The early summer sun warmed Samantha Kane's shoulders as she tacked the advertisement to the outside display window in front of Community Craft. The air was warm and dry outside her storefront; not humid *yet*. She wished the summer would stay this picture-perfect temperature, but she knew it wouldn't last. She couldn't complain, as it sure beat the cloudy winters of Wisconsin that seemed to roll on endlessly.

The smell of sweet alyssum wafted on the subtle breeze from the recently planted oversized terra-cotta pot placed strategically by the front door to welcome her local customers. Dainty white flowers, contrasted with deep-blue lobelia, spilled generously over the sides and encircled orange and pink geraniums. Samantha wished she were on a long, leisurely stroll with her golden retriever, Bara, to view the flower beds set in the freshly tilled soil along the river walk. Instead, she was stuck indoors on this beautiful June day working at her craft store, where members of the community sold their handcrafted wares. Hopefully the dry air would hold and she could sneak away from the store as soon as her sister Ellie came to work later in the afternoon.

"Sammy!"

The urgent cry swiftly caught the shop owner's attention. Samantha dropped the Scotch tape to the cement sidewalk. Her auburn ponytail swung and slapped her hard in the face as she turned abruptly in the direction of the yelling of her nickname.

"Oh Marilyn, you startled me! Is everything okay? You all right?" Sammy's round hazel eyes widened as she searched her harried next-door neighbor for signs of distress. The owner of the Sweet Tooth Bakery approached at a rapid pace.

"No. I'm absolutely *not* all right." The baker fanned her overheated plump red cheeks with one hand, sending flour falling like snow. If only it *had* been snow and not flour, it might have cooled off the agitated baker. "*Sammy!* I've gone and burned the cupcakes for the book signing!"

Sammy tilted her head back and laughed. Her eyes crinkled like half-moons when her amusement transformed into a large smile. "You have four days before the book signing; no need to get your panties in a knot." She pointed to the newly attached advertisement on the window, then leaned over to pluck the Scotch tape from the ground. "With all your bellowing, Marilyn, I thought something tragic had happened. I'm just hanging the sign with the time and details of the event now. If you made the dessert today, wouldn't it be stale by Saturday afternoon anyway?" Sammy's pencil-thin eyebrows came together in a frown.

"Yes, but this was the sample batch. I wanted you to taste-test them first. These cupcakes must be ab-so-lutely perfect! They're for Jane Johnson's book signing, after all. *The* Jane Johnson!" Her chubby fingers came together in air quotes. "I still can't believe she's coming here to little ole Heartsford! Well. I guess that will put us on the map for sure." Marilyn placed her hand atop her large round bosom, transferring the remnants of flour to her chest. "And I've gone and ruined the sample!" The baker shook her hairnet-covered head in disgust.

"You've plenty of time to bake another batch." Sammy waved her off casually. "No need to fret just yet. I'm the one hosting the signing for her latest book, *and* I'm going to be interviewed for her next book, *Behind the Seams: A Journey of Why We Love to Craft*. If you can imagine the preparation on my end. I have so much left to organize, and I also have to clean the store." Sammy began ticking off a mental list of what needed to be tackled first.

"Well. I suppose you're right . . . I'll have time to try again." The baker must have sensed she wouldn't receive any sympathy from her neighbor, so she quickly changed the subject—to digging for dirt. "Has Jane Johnson made it to town yet? Where's she staying? I heard a rumor that she's booked a room at Pine Haven Bed and Breakfast. Annabelle saw a stretch limo driving in that direction! Have you already met her?" Marilyn placed her hands on her overrun hips, demanding answers.

"Aren't you full of questions today?" Sammy laughed and rolled her eyes.

Just then, Sammy and Marilyn's attention was diverted to Main Street by the sound of a honking horn, causing the two to check and see who was pulling up to park beside the sidewalk. Sammy was relieved to have a reprieve from the baker's demands of juicy gossip. She wasn't sure how private the bestselling author was, and she didn't want to offend the new guest to their hometown by spreading needless information.

"Hi, Mayor Allen!" Sammy waved to the mayor of Hearts-ford as he stepped from his newly washed black SUV, drops of water still visible on the Toyota.

His hand rose in a friendly wave as he stopped momentarily to greet the women. "Be-a-u-tiful day, Sunshine Sam! And Marilyn, good afternoon to you. Connie will stop in soon to order a few of your famous strawberry pies. The wife and I love to indulge this time of year on your seasonal sweet treats."

The mayor tipped his silver head, which shone in the sun like mounded strands of glitter, to regard the baker before looking both ways, crossing the street, and stepping inside Liquid Joy for his daily afternoon caffeine pick-me-up. Although Sammy was trying to cut down on her daily caffeine intake, iced coffee did sound delicious. Her mouth began to thirst for the cool, creamy liquid.

"Sunshine Sam? Why, I wasn't aware the mayor had a *special* name for you, Samantha Kane. Why doesn't he call you Sammy like the rest of us?" Marilyn searched her with inquisitive eyes.

"He's called me that ever since I was a kid hanging out with his daughter, Kate." Sammy explained. Although she didn't think it needed an explanation. Everyone in town knew she had taken over the mayor's deceased daughter's store, Community Craft, after a tractor accident took her life far too soon. Everyone knew she and Kate had been best friends since childhood. Why wouldn't Kate's father have a nickname for her? Suddenly Sammy was weary of Marilyn's inquisitive nature.

"You'd better get back into that kitchen quick," Sammy urged. "You're right, those cupcakes have to be perfect. Good luck with the next batch. I can't tell you how much I look forward to that sample. And it sounds like the mayor is licking his lips for a few of your strawberry pies. You'd better get back to work. Busy, busy!" Sammy moved closer to the front door of her shop. "I should get a move on and get back to work too. Have a great afternoon, Marilyn," she said as she dismissed the baker and swung open the door to retreat to the safety of Community Craft.

Bara lifted his golden head as Sammy approached. Her golden retriever's bed sat directly beside the cash register on the right-hand wall toward the back of the store. He wasn't a guard dog but rather a welcome furry face that made the customers smile and linger to pet him. When Sammy stopped to scratch his head, he lifted his weary body from its comfortable position and stretched his hind legs.

"Oh, the life you have," she said to the dog. The tinkle of the bell on the front door alerted them both that a customer had entered. Bara, so accustomed to the sound after spending years in the store by the register, didn't go and greet the customer but instead slumped lazily back to his original position. Sammy shook her head at him and smiled.

"Hello."

Sammy's eyes lifted from her lazy dog to the newcomer. She instantly knew it was *not* one of her regular customers. A real live celebrity had officially stepped inside Community Craft.

Jane Johnson held out a manicured hand in greeting. "You must be Samantha Kane?"

The bestselling author stood about Sammy's height—barely over five feet. Her hair was cropped short in a wispy blonde cut and was obviously sprayed in place to perfection. Her azure eyes were friendly and alert and held an air of mystery. Jane's casual dress surprised Sammy, as she had always seen the celebrity dressed to the nines on TV. Although, even in her sleeveless navy blouse and white cropped pants, she looked as though she had just stepped from a cruise ship and not Main Street in a small farm town.

For a moment, Sammy was speechless. If only Kate had been alive to witness the bestselling author in the craft world standing right here. The woman who was the *queen* of all crafts, hobbies, and home, standing just arm's length away. The one all the fiber artisans in her store aspired to be. The one who had been interviewed on HGTV sharing her crochet talent. The one with her own monthly magazine. *And* numerous bestselling books!

Sammy reached for the author's hand and shook it gently in greeting. She could feel her mouth moving and the words tumbling out. "I'm Samantha Kane. Most people call me Sammy. Only my mother calls me Samantha. And lately she's been calling me Sam, unless of course we've had words—then she's back to calling me Samantha. But she lives in Arizona with my dad now that the Wisconsin winters have become too brutal for them . . . They're flying in for a visit this week. Actually, Mom should be here for the book signing." Sammy could feel the flush rising from her neck to her cheeks. "I'm rambling. Sorry."

The author smiled. Sammy wanted to crawl under the rug. Or hide under Bara's dog bed. Even Bara seemed to shake his head. Why was she acting like an idiot? Sammy justified the nervous energy as a normal reaction. After all, it was rare to have anyone of stature here in Heartsford, never mind her store. She could barely feel her feet on the ground, and she suddenly felt uncharacteristically befuddled.

"So, this is Community Craft. I've heard so much about this place." Jane turned from Sammy's gaze and fingered a hand-dyed aqua silk scarf that hung close to her touch.

"The one and only," Sammy said, before sneaking slow yoga breaths that her cousin Heidi had taught her to calm her jittery excitement. She really needed to relax. Right now. Breathe in . . . one . . . two . . . three . . .

"I've been actively researching the original owner. I was so sorry to hear about the loss of Kate Allen. Her tragic and early death led me to seek out the communal bonds she nurtured in this store. Very special and unique, from what I've gathered thus far in researching my next book, *Behind the Seams*. Very rare indeed."

This comment from the famous author instantly stirred Sammy from her awkward stance. "Thank you," she said sincerely. "Kate was the brains behind all of this, and of course she encouraged a sense of community and kindness that I've tried to keep alive. We don't just create and sell handcrafted items here. We hold many community fund-raisers and the like. Whatever the people of Heartsford need, we're here to build each other up, work together, and lift each other's burdens."

"Yes, it's that very nature of community spirit and what you all do to support each other in this town that so intrigued me. I find it very unusual nowadays, don't you think? That's what inspired me to visit Heartsford, to be honest; news has traveled. I had to come see and experience this place firsthand. Do people actually live in *genuine* community anymore? Seems to me people are so preoccupied with their own lives and social media that they don't reach out personally anymore . . . Everyone is so isolated.

The idea of returning to the old-fashioned hooking circle certainly fascinates me. Or maybe I'm just not privy to that type of lifestyle, as my life is so different now. It seems because I spend the bulk of my time in the public eye, people have a way of treating me as if I'm above all that. But I'm not, you know. I'm really not. I'd love an afternoon working my hands through some yarn while chatting with other women. I wonder why people seem to think I wouldn't enjoy that anymore?"

Sammy remained silent. She was surprised the author had disclosed so much of her inner thoughts.

Sammy then noticed Jane's eyes scanning the space to take in her surroundings, and she pointed a finger to a room enclosed in glass on the opposite side of the open-concept store. "And what's that room?"

"Oh, that's our craft room. We hold art classes and host meetings for various fund-raisers and community events in that space. We keep it open, as people tend to get involved when they see things happening back there. We actually hold our monthly book club there, too, when the community room at the library is otherwise occupied."

Jane nodded. "Inventive idea." Sammy thought for a moment that the author seemed honestly impressed.

"I think it will be too small to host the book signing in that enclosed room, though, as we're expecting a very large turnout. Heck, the whole town will probably show. I'll have to move a few things around and have a table set up for you here. Maybe on the back wall . . ." Sammy's voice trailed off as her attention diverted and her eyes pinballed around the room, seeking the perfect location to host the book signing for the author's previous best-seller, *Hooked for Life: Crocheting Through the Generations*.

At that moment, the back door of Community Craft opened and Sammy's sister Ellie rushed into the room. "Sorry I'm late," Ellie said without raising her eyes. She stepped behind the register and dropped her oversized purse to the floor behind the expansive polished wooden counter.

"You're an hour *early*," Sammy corrected, pointing to the clock that hung behind the cash register.

When Ellie finally raised her hazel eyes to argue the fact, it was obvious the time wasn't her only surprise. "Jane Johnson! You're here! In the flesh!" Ellie blurted, her voice raised to an unusual octave. Sammy's sister suddenly bubbled over with excitement.

Sammy couldn't help but let out a nervous giggle. She clearly wasn't the only one who was star-struck.

"Yes, in the flesh." Jane shrugged, nonplussed. She seemed mildly uncomfortable with the two sisters gawking at her and quickly redirected the subject. "You two look so much alike. I'm guessing you're related?" Her watery blue eyes danced between the two of them.

Ellie touched her shoulder-length russet hair and twirled it nervously.

"Sisters," Sammy and Ellie said simultaneously, and the two shared a grin.

"But her hair has never been as red as mine. Sammy will have natural blonde highlights by the end of the summer if she spends any time outdoors. I'll just end up with a face full of freckles and hair like Raggedy Ann." Ellie regarded her sister. "But I was lucky to at least get a little more height from my father's side of the family."

Sammy smirked and nudged her sister playfully.

The author smiled. "Can I set up a time to interview you, Samantha? I'm only in town a few days. I'll be leaving right after the book signing on Saturday. I have so much I'd like to discuss with you for my latest manuscript before I leave."

"Absolutely! When would you like to meet?"

"Whenever you have time. How about now? I was thinking of visiting that lovely coffee shop across the street. Can I pull you away? Or is this a bad time?"

Annabelle Larson, owner of the Yarn Barn, suddenly approached out of nowhere, interrupting the three women, and rushed toward the counter at record speed. "Jane Johnson! Oh, what an honor!" Sammy must have missed seeing her gregarious neighbor enter the store in all the excitement. She knew her work neighbor was a bit miffed that Sammy had been chosen as an interview subject for the book and not her. Annabelle had assumed owning the yarn store would make her a shoo-in, but the famous author was more interested in the history of Community Craft than crochet or any other fiber art, apparently. Annabelle snapped her mint gum annoyingly as her eyes bored into the author with curiosity. "Are you going to be here awhile? I'll go run and grab my cell phone for a selfie! Or maybe you'd like to come see my shop too? The Yarn Barn . . . It's just a few doors down. Please come over and take a peek! Wait until you see all the natural fibers I sell. It'll make you drool, I promise!"

Before Annabelle could finish listing the merits of her store, another customer who had overheard barged toward the author, nearly knocking her off her feet. Jane seemed suddenly overwhelmed. Sammy wondered if she was tired from her journey to Heartsford and suddenly felt protective of the new guest to her store. She stepped between the author and the overexcited crowd of fans, which was growing by the minute.

"Yes, ladies, and she'll be here again on Saturday to meet with you," Sammy said firmly as she raised a hand to block the lookie-loos. "But for now, she has to be on her way. I'm sure Ms. Johnson has prior engagements to tend to at the moment."

Sammy protectively ushered the author toward the back exit of the store. When the two reached the safety of the door, Sammy turned to apologize for their collective behavior. "I'm sorry about that. We don't have many famous people pass through our area. I apologize if we're all a little overzealous."

"Oh, it's perfectly all right. I'm quite used to it. I'm afraid I'm still suffering a bit of jet lag. I've spent the last few days crossing the country in airports and hotels. After a few long days of travel, I think I might need some fresh air."

Sammy nodded. It was then that she noticed the dark shadows under the author's eyes, concealed under heavy makeup.

Jane continued, "But I do want to meet with you soon. Would you like to walk with me? I have some rather sensitive information I need to discuss with you. I'd really like it to be a private conversation, if that's possible. Is there a place we can talk?" The author searched Sammy's eyes with growing intensity. "I'm thinking the coffee shop across the street probably isn't the best place?"

"I have a thought," Sammy suggested. "Why don't you follow the trail down along the river walk?" Sammy pointed across the expansive parking lot behind Community Craft to where the trail began. "This time of day, it's usually quiet. There's a set of stairs that will take you to a bench by the dam where the waterfall cascades. A very soothing spot. And private, too. I'll go pick us up an iced coffee or tea from Liquid Joy and meet you there. How does that sound? It'll give you a few moments to catch your breath and regroup. I'll join you in about twenty minutes or so. Would that work?"

"Sure. Sounds perfect. And I'd love an iced coffee; that sounds wonderful. Thank you so much, Samantha. I'll meet you there, then." Jane was about to step out the back entrance when she stopped, turned, and reached for Sammy's wrist with sudden urgency. "I uncovered some rather sensitive information in my research regarding the previous owner of Community Craft. I have something to tell you . . . something that could change everything. Please come alone." The bestselling author released Sammy's arm and was out the door in an instant, leaving an air of mystery in her wake.

Chapter Two

S ammy stood at the glass back door staring into the almost vacant parking lot, completely dumbfounded. For the life of her, she couldn't understand what Jane Johnson had meant. *She wants to tell me something that could change everything? Something about Kate?*

Sammy's cousin Heidi, who was more like a sister or a close friend than a cousin, suddenly disrupted her reverie and pushed through the back door, waking her from her confused mental state. Heidi's dyed blonde hair was braided from the left side across the back of her head and fell loosely to her right shoulder. She was wearing a pale-blue tank top that hugged her perky breasts (which Sammy envied, as she had none to speak of) and matching nylon shorts. Sammy also envied her cousin's tall lean legs and sculpted arms. But Sammy didn't exactly put in the effort of a disciplined exercise routine like her cousin did. She could only blame herself for not sticking to a workout plan and eating far too many "samples" from Marilyn's Sweet Tooth Bakery.

Heidi plucked her earbud out of one ear. "I just finished my run, and you'll *never* guess who I saw entering the trail as I was jogging over here."

Sammy crushed her cousin's excitement with one swift comment. "Jane Johnson."

"How did you know?" Heidi's dimples faded and her face fell flat.

"Not working at the hospital today?" Sammy changed the subject as she wondered why Heidi wasn't in her typical nurse scrubs. She was also envious that her cousin was playing hooky on this beautiful summer day.

"They've changed my schedule to twelve-hour shifts, on and off days. I've moved out of the ER and onto the hospital floors. It's just a trial period while Natalie is on maternity leave. I swear, that woman pops out babies like a Pez dispenser."

"Are you happy with the change?"

"Never mind that; back to my original question." Heidi flung her slender hands to curved hips. "How did you know the best-selling author of all that's good and crafty is in town already? I thought you said the book signing isn't until Saturday."

"Jane's in town a few days early to do research for her next book. She's interested in the back story of how Community Craft began. Actually, I'm off to Liquid Joy to buy us an iced coffee and meet her under the bridge for an interview for her next book. She's interviewing me because she's impressed with what Kate created here in our little town."

Heidi's mouth dropped in awe. "You're already on a first-name basis?"

Sammy playfully looped her arm through her cousin's and led her over to the cash register, where Ellie was giving a customer a brown-handled paper bag and a smile before the patron left the store.

"Hey, Heidi," Ellie said, after the customer exited through the front door onto Main Street. "Little Missy here is going to hang with a well-known celebrity. Can you believe it?"

"I heard!"

Heidi hopped up to sit atop the polished wooden counter between them. No way could Sammy ever sit on the counter. Her legs wouldn't allow her to reach, even with a jump.

Sammy moved swiftly into the office behind the register counter to retrieve some cash from her purse locked inside the office desk. She shoved a few crumpled bills into her faded jeans pocket. She had already wasted enough time lollygagging; Jane Johnson was waiting. But she did want to give the poor woman a moment's peace to catch her breath before the interview, too.

After closing the drawer and locking her purse back in place, Sammy stepped from the office. She stopped momentarily to wait for Heidi and Ellie to halt their chatting back and forth about the bestselling author. Even if she tried, she couldn't get a word in edgewise.

The two finally acknowledged her presence, and Heidi said, "Don't you need to go meet the craft queen? What are you standing around here for?"

"Yeah, get going!" Ellie chimed in.

"You *guys*," Sammy huffed. "I was waiting for you two to stop clucking like hens, because I wanted to tell you something before I go meet with her. That celebrity you two can't stop chitchatting about said something weird at the back door before she left the store. It's really got me wondering. She grabbed me by the arm and said she had to tell me something about Kate. Something that would change everything. I wonder what she meant by that?" Sammy said pensively, biting the edge of her fingernail. "What do you guys think?"

"Well, you're never going to find out standing here talking to us beauties," Heidi said with a raised, manicured eyebrow.

"Unless . . . you think this is a job for S.H.E.," Ellie added jokingly, and the two cousins exchanged a wink.

S.H.E. was the childhood club the three had formed: *S* for Samantha, *H* for Heidi, and *E* for Ellie. Even though Heidi and Ellie were two years older than Sam, the three had created an imaginary detective agency in grade school that had bound them together. They had even used their sleuthing skills recently as adults to assist in solving the murder of Ingrid Wilson. In Sammy's humble opinion, the case would still have been unsolved if it hadn't been for S.H.E.

"Yeah, I'm sure Tim would just *love* that. Us three getting involved in nosing around about nothing," Heidi said sarcastically, referring to her boyfriend, who worked as a patrol officer for the Heartsford Police Department.

Sammy tapped the palm of her hand on the top of the polished wooden counter twice. "Okay, then. I guess I'm off. You two chickens cluck about what you think she meant, and I'll tell you when I get back which one of you gumshoes got it right. Thanks for minding the store, Ellie. I'll be back in a heartbeat, I'm sure," she said as she moved with purpose out the front door to cross the street to Liquid Joy. A moment of guilt passed through her brain for not bringing Bara along, but she decided it would be a bad idea. Twice yesterday she'd had to stop while he chased through the dog park after the multiple squirrels and chipmunks that crossed his trail. Not only that, he'd probably end up playing in the river and getting soaked. Then everyone at the store would have to smell wet dog all day. No thank you. She needed to stay focused for the interview anyway. *Later.* She promised herself to take her dog for a walk later.

After collecting the iced coffees and briefly stopping to talk with Douglas—the owner of Liquid Joy—about providing coffee to pair with Marilyn's cupcakes for the upcoming book signing, Sammy retreated across the street. Instead of walking along the sidewalk to a side street off Main, she took the shortcut and headed down the narrow alleyway that connected Community Craft with a historical building from the early 1900s, which now held the recently opened Live and Let Dye hair and nail salon on the main floor and a Farmers Insurance office on the second floor. Both of them were turning out to be great business neighbors. Sammy was happy to see the empty offices filled and the downtown thriving.

The air remained dry and warm. Sammy soaked up the sunshine and reveled in the unusual lack of humidity. After crossing the expansive parking lot and weaving through the few parked cars left in the lot, she headed down the worn dirt path that led to the river's edge. A canopy of maple and oak trees shaded the entrance to the footpath, and a breeze chilled her skin, causing Sammy to want to rub her bare arms with her hands. Unfortunately, with a coffee dripping with condensation in each hand, she'd have to wait. Sometimes the cooler air swooping down from Canada refused to give up, even in early June. When she finally reached the river's edge, where the purple bearded irises greeted her, she took the route that closely wound along the river. Once again, she was warmed by the sun's rays.

The river walk was quiet, as expected at that time of day, until she reached the library, up on the hill, on the right side of the path, where patrons moved to and fro in the neighboring parking lot. A few years back, the library had been demolished and a new building erected that the surrounding counties drooled over. The architecture mimicked that of Frank Lloyd Wright, a Wisconsin native. The building had become a vibrant focal point in the town as others traveled from neighboring communities to visit. Not just to borrow books, but to view the architecture or attend a gathering in the richly decorated community room or on the expansive outdoor deck that hosted a breathtaking view of the river.

As she looked at the library, Sammy had a thought. After seeing firsthand the many admirers who would probably attend on Saturday to meet Jane Johnson, she wondered if maybe she should move the book signing to the community room in the library. Community Craft might not be big enough to hold the crowd that would soon descend on the small town. Where would she set up the table for Jane? She would have to move a bunch of merchandise, that was for sure. She could move the racks along the back wall that housed the hand-sewn quilted place mats. Or maybe move the candle display? It would be tight at best. Another thing to add to her mental to-do list. As much as she wanted to sit and chat with the bestselling author today, she really did have a long list of tasks to tackle before the event. Hopefully she could put her mental list aside to live in the present. She didn't want to take this opportunity for granted, wishing to be somewhere else instead of enjoying this small moment in the spotlight. How rare a gift to sit and chat with and pick the brain of a bestselling author! Besides, she was sure she would be grilled by Ellie and Heidi for every last detail of the conversation upon her return, and she wanted to remember every last word. She smiled inwardly.

Sammy's mind wandered to her monthly book club. The reading group was so excited that she was hosting a bestselling author at Community Craft, the members could hardly contain themselves. In fact, because of the author's impending visit, the book club had gained serious interest in crochet, and the library was outgrowing the number of books available to lend now that the group had almost doubled in size. Maybe she could host a wine-and-cheese event to raise money for the additional craft books needed to fund the growing book club. Potentially, the event could be held in the community room, and then expand out on the outer library deck overlooking the beautiful floral display that the Beautification of Heartsford Committee had recently planted. The thought of friends gathering together, overlooking the colorful grounds while sipping a glass of pinot noir and chatting about the upcoming books they'd be discussing throughout the year, brought a skip to her step. She could almost picture the women wearing sundresses and the men casually dressed in polos and khaki shorts on a warm summer evening. The event seemed more inevitable by the minute. Sammy rarely dressed up, but she was surprising herself by wanting to do something a little outside her wheelhouse. Oh, and perhaps she could even convince Deborah to paint a few floral wine glasses to sell for the event! Any extra money raised could be donated back to the library in case any other literacy programs needed supplemental funding. She was sure Jennifer, the library director, would be thrilled. Sammy was convinced she was now going to organize this event. Just as soon as she got through her current event with Jane Johnson. First things first. She seemed to always be leaping one step ahead of herself.

Sammy noticed construction workers bustling about like busy bees in a hive across the street from the library. There were two seasons in Wisconsin: winter and construction. She didn't have a clear view from the river's edge; the library blocked most of the new construction site that was piquing her curiosity. Maybe Ellie's husband, Randy, would know what was being built? He worked for a mortgage company not far from town and seemed to know everything that was going on in town that had to do with real estate. There was often talk he'd even considered a change of careers to become a residential or commercial realtor, as he seemed uninterested in his current line of work as a mortgage lender. He was fascinated by the town's history and volunteered countless hours on the preservation of their town with the Historical Society of Heartsford.

The newly planted flowers along the riverbank swayed and caught her attention. The volunteer gardeners had done a beautiful job, as always, bringing pops of color after a long, gray winter and cloudy spring. Along the path, newly planted orange-and-yellow Gerber daisies pointed toward the sun. The white and blue hydrangeas that hugged the waterless side of the path held buds that were ready to burst open at a moment's notice, prepared to steal the show with their large-globed beauty. A few feet ahead, the small hill dropping to the river's edge had also been newly planted. Deep-red, soft-pink, and white fibrous begonias were sprinkled across the mulched flowerbed. By late summer, they would blanket the ground in one long multicolored wave. Sammy would have to call Kendra, the head of the Beautification of Heartsford Committee, to congratulate her for once again leading such a fine job.

The sound of the river rushing over the dam propelled Sammy forward. The recent rains provided ample water to cascade in a calming symphony. As she began to descend the large granite steps, the water roared louder. Sammy noticed the author, quietly seated on the wooden bench, facing the foot of the dam. She didn't want to disturb her rare moment of peace. Suddenly she felt a pang of sadness, for with this woman's success had come the huge cost of missing the simple things in life. The peaceful things that Sammy had most certainly taken for granted. The ability to come and go and live undisturbed. What might it be like to have people rushing at you all the time? Wanting to pose for selfies and asking for an autograph? Wanting a piece of you and presuming to know you when they really didn't know you at all? If she was being honest, she thought it would probably grow old after a while.

When Sammy finally reached the bottom step and turned toward Jane, it looked as if she might be reading a novel, as a book sat open across her lap. Though Sammy didn't remember her having a book in her hands when she left the store. A sudden chill started at the base of Sammy's neck and trickled down her spine when she noticed the bluish tinge to the author's hands, which were clutching the edges of the book. Sammy leaned over the novel to take a closer look. The words THE END were dug with thick ragged pencil across the open pages of a copy of the author's own work—the last book she'd published, *Hooked for Life*. The coffee dropped from Sammy's grip and the signature yellow Liquid Joy emoji cups crashed to the lower rocks. Sammy's alarmed eyes flew up to consider the now-vacant azure stare of the woman sitting in front of her. Jane Johnson, bestselling author and Queen of Crafts, was dead.

Chapter Three

*T*his *can NOT be happening.* Sammy frantically checked for a pulse on the author's neck as her cousin Heidi had once taught her. Unfortunately, she was already keenly aware there would be no pulse.

"Damn it!" Sammy uttered aloud.

Her hands flew to her back pocket, where her cell phone was most certainly *not* located. She hadn't brought it with her. Because never in a million years had she thought she would have to use it, and she had thought if the cell rang out with Adele singing "Hello" during the interview, it would come off as rude. Certainly, she could have turned the sound off, but she'd thought leaving the phone behind would leave no possible room for distractions. How could she have been so stupid as to not bring her phone? Her eyes darted around the immediate area to see if anyone was in earshot.

"Of course not," she muttered angrily. "When you need a phone, is anyone around? No!"

Sammy hated to leave Jane alone, but what other choice did she have? Clearly the author wasn't going anywhere. Sammy hoisted herself up the large granite rock steps two at a time even though her short legs could barely make the stride. By the time she was back on the footpath, she was already huffing and puffing and her heart thundered in her chest. It really wasn't the best time to think about it, but now she really wished she was in better physical shape. She couldn't deny the extra softness that padded her body, and it was more obvious to her now than ever. She could feel every last jiggle of pudgy bounce in places that should *not* be bouncing.

Sammy darted back past the flowers, this time not stopping to take in their beauty. Sudden thoughts flooded her mind. The book had said THE END.

Did Jane commit suicide? Or did someone do this? WHY would anyone do this? Oh God. The sudden exertion made her want to toss her lunch, but she didn't have time for that either. When Sammy reached the back parking lot of Community Craft, Heidi and Tim were luckily the first two people who came into view. They were leaning casually against Tim's patrol car, talking. When Sammy caught their eye, the two could obviously sense that something was very wrong and sprinted in her direction.

"What's going on?" Heidi placed a calming hand atop Sammy's shoulder.

"She's dead." Sammy stared back and forth between Heidi and Tim, then leaned over and braced her hands on her legs to hold herself upright and try to catch her breath. She couldn't remember the last time she had sprinted so fast and hard. Her chest constricted, making it hard to get a lungful of air.

"Whaaat? Nooo." Heidi looked as if she had just been splashed with a bucket of icy-cold water.

"Who's dead?" The veins in Tim's wide neck suddenly bulged in alarm. His strong meaty hands clenched together in fists by his sides. Sammy could tell by his body language that even he, who was accustomed to the call of emergency situations, was jolted by the news.

"The author, Jane Johnson," was all Sammy could sputter between her continued pants of heavy breathing. She turned and pointed a finger. "By the dam . . . the reflection bench. I'd say hurry, but I think it's already too late." Sammy stood erect and placed one hand on her heart. "No. I *know* it's too late."

Tim immediately called emergency services on the radio attached to his broad shoulder. Knowing it would take longer to jump into his patrol car and drive and park close enough to the water's edge, he instinctively turned to sprint in the direction of the dam. Heidi and Sammy galloped in close pursuit.

"Are you sure?" Heidi said as the two followed Tim, swiftly losing sight of him as he sped ahead with athletic ease to the scene.

"Dead sure." Sammy nodded and panted as she ran, desperately trying to keep up with Heidi's long stride. When it came to legs in the family, Heidi and Ellie had won that part of the gene pool. What little length Sammy did have came from her torso, not her legs, which at the moment wasn't at all helpful. Not in the least.

Before long, sirens blared. An ambulance. Added police cars. And the newest and only Heartsford detective: Liam Nash.

When the two cousins had reached the steps above the crime scene, Heidi's nursing skills had kicked into high gear. Sammy had sensed that her cousin already knew from the look on her boyfriend's face and the slow nod of his head that the author was indeed deceased. But Heidi persisted as she rushed to the victim to confirm the death for hospital records and then ran to await and greet the ambulance crew to let them know their services would no longer be needed. Instead, a call would have to be made to the coroner. Sammy stood at the top of the granite staircase, unsure of what to do while her legs pulsated and her muscles, unused to that degree of effort, twitched from the recent exertion.

Sammy hadn't seen Detective Nash recently. Even after all the time they had spent together to solve the previous murder in Heartsford. Their relationship had somewhat cooled since then. Which, if she were being honest, bothered her. Her feelings for him came in complex waves. She liked him. He annoyed her. And then, he would do or say something that would impress her or seem utterly charming. Sorting out her feelings for the new detective hadn't been easy. For whatever reason, it was complicated. She just couldn't decide which of them was the one with the complications. Him? Or . . . her? Sammy thought his heart seemed closed. Understandably so after the death of his fiancée, Brenda, who had died from breast cancer a few years back—just months shy of their impending wedding. Sometimes the detective came off as aloof or cocky. Sammy tried to explain away his behavior by comparing him to her notes from past psych classes she had taken at UW Madison. She saw his standoffish personality as textbook and something he often hid behind. When he let his guard down, which wasn't often, she sensed his tender vulnerability. Those were the times she felt wildly attracted to him.

Heidi, meanwhile, had strongly suggested that Sammy was

to blame for the two of them not coming together in a love connection. Heidi insisted that Sammy pushed people away if she really "liked" them for fear of anyone getting too close. Sammy too had battled loss. When her best friend Kate had died and she had returned to Heartsford to take over Community Craft, she too had had a lot of *stuff* to work though. Then there was another relationship she had lost through a rough breakup . . . Brian. A breakup that, at the moment, she did not want to relive in her head. No. She found it was much easier to suppress her feelings for the detective rather than act on them.

Sammy watched as Detective Nash stepped from his old silver Honda Civic with the rusted front bumper. He had mentioned the last time they'd spoken that he was thinking of trading the car in for a newer model. Interesting. Like her, he must not like change. Although, as he moved closer, she realized the extra beats in her heart were not from the recent exertion or finding Jane's lifeless body, but from the detective coming closer into view. She noticed his hair looked different, as if it had been recently cut. Now his formerly long, dark curls sat on the top of his head in a soft short wave, and the peppered portion at the sides had been tapered short above his ears. He was wearing a crisp white shirt with a brown tie that she imagined up close matched his eyes to a T. His khaki pants looked freshly ironed, as if he had just picked them up at the dry cleaner's. He couldn't have laundered them that neatly himself. Could he? Liam looked more like a banker than a detective, she mused. The officer must have caught her scrutinizing, as he returned her gaze with a grim smile and a shake of his head.

"Don't tell me," the detective said, a lopsided grin taking over his expression as the two stood at the top of the granite staircase leading to the water's edge.

"Tell you what?" Sammy asked innocently.

"Let me guess. You were the one to find my vic?"

"Your vic?"

"Victim."

"I know what you meant," Sammy retorted with a roll of her eyes. Like she didn't know what a vic was. He seriously underestimated her. She could already feel the annoyance seeping in. Brick one of her wall going up. She'd wait to see how quickly he could stack on brick two.

Detective Nash stood with one hand on his hip, waiting for her to confirm that she'd been the one who found Jane Johnson.

Instead of answering him directly, Sammy shrugged. While they stood silently in opposition, emergency personnel were rushing toward them.

"Nash," Tim called through cupped hands at the bottom of the stairs. Standing by the "vic."

Nash and Sammy turned to Tim as he waved a meaty hand for the detective to hurry closer. Sammy followed close behind like an annoying toddler grabbing at his pant leg. She wanted to see the details of the crime scene that she might have initially missed due to the shock of finding Jane Johnson no longer alive and breathing.

Heidi and the ambulance crew were also about to descend the stairs to check on Jane once again when the detective put up a hand to stop them at the top.

"Go ahead and call the coroner. Don't move her yet. I want to have a moment with the scene. Tim, you and the other officers fan out and canvass the area," he directed. "Someone had to have seen something." Liam's eyes then met Sammy's and held her gaze. "You really shouldn't be here."

To Sammy's surprise, he didn't adamantly push her away. Instead, he moved closer to the body to get a sense of what had happened. Sammy noticed a powdery white substance similar to talcum powder dusted across the author's navy blouse and pointed it out to the detective.

"What's that? There's something on her shirt that I promise you wasn't there before."

Detective Nash leaned in closer to get a better look. "Not sure. I'll have to send it to the lab."

"She also didn't have her latest book in her hands when I saw her at the store. Someone must have planted it there." Sammy pointed to the author's work sprawled across her lap with the heinous hand-scratched words THE END. "And who in the world uses pencil in this day and age? I doubt if I even own one, not to write with anyway, though I must admit I do use a pencil for different craft projects sometimes."

"Someone obviously has a vendetta against her. Look at the anger in the way those words are dug into the pages," the detective pointed out. "Where is that book sold?" A look of curiosity waved across his face. "We don't have a bookstore in town, do we? I'm not a huge reader, so . . . where would I find a copy of this book?"

"I've been selling them at Community Craft. Even though she's not a local author and I usually only carry local authors' work, we've been selling it because of her impending visit. Heck, a few places in town are selling them, knowing she was coming.

Liquid Joy, the library has a stack, even the new hair salon in town, I believe." Sammy's eyes left the detective and gazed back at the deceased author. It was then she noticed the ring of bruising around the victim's neck.

"What does the evidence suggest? Was she strangled? With what?" Sammy moved closer to get a better view.

Nash nodded. "Looks like it. I'm not sure what the weapon of choice was yet. Looks like someone may have choked her from behind with their hands. I'll have to let the medical examiner give us a detailed report. It's hard to say exactly what went on here. There's no blood."

"Give *us* a detailed report? You mean, you're actually going to let me assist you in the investigation? Are you really going to let me consult this time?" Sammy was shocked that Liam was including her and not pushing her away, which was his normal MO. Maybe he was warming to her after all?

"You were the last one to see her alive, correct? You never really answered me." He placed his strong, capable hands on his hips and eyed her with intensity. His brown eyes had the ability to go from dark liquid chocolate to hard as steel. Right now, he was bordering on steely.

"Actually, you asked if I found your vic. Not if I was the last one to see her alive," Sammy corrected.

Why would she have thought he would put her on equal ground? And allow her to consult? Because she had investigative skills? Heck, if it wasn't for Community Craft, she might even consider going back to school to become a private investigator! He so misjudged her . . .

"Are you going to answer my question?" His brown eyes bored into hers. No more melted chocolate.

"Yes. I was the last to talk with her, although Heidi mentioned passing her on the trail. Not sure if they spoke. You'd have to ask her yourself. The last place I saw Jane was at the back entrance to my store. I was meeting her here to share a coffee and do an interview for a book she's working on. I mean *was* working on." Sammy was going to have to get used to talking about Jane Johnson in the past tense. She shuddered.

"What time did you speak with her in your store?"

"I'm not sure of the exact time. Couldn't have been more than a half hour ago though. Actually, maybe a little longer. I did talk to Douglas at Liquid Joy for a bit. Could be more like thirty-five or forty minutes."

"Was that so hard? To answer a few simple questions?"

"What is your problem?" Sammy was growing increasingly annoyed. "I *am* trying to help you."

"It just seems suspicious that you seem to be the only one around town that's always finding dead bodies."

"Always? Try once. I've only found one. Well . . . two, now . . ." Sammy corrected.

"Either is too many, wouldn't you say?" The detective folded his arms across his lean chest.

"Are you calling *me* a suspect? Because you and I both know that will never fly."

"Everyone's a suspect until proven innocent. You, above all others, should know that." The detective winked, showing he was just trying to rattle her. And it was working; Sammy was irked. He smoothed it over, though, by giving her that goofy lopsided grin of his.

Sammy's eyes roamed the area beneath the bench to examine the scene, and nothing seemed disturbed, except for a few scuff marks on the dirt where Jane might have kicked her legs during the attack. Beyond that was a patch of grass where the killer must have stood and not left a footprint. "Looks to me like whoever strangled her came up from behind. She didn't even see it coming."

"How do you know the victim?" the detective asked sincerely.

"You can't be serious? You don't know who she is?" Sammy was flabbergasted.

"Should I?"

"Ummm. Yeahhh. Unless you live under a rock."

Nash stood pensively and stared at the victim for a few awkward moments. "Did you introduce me to her at some point? Has she been hanging out at my favorite bakery or something?" he asked sheepishly. Suddenly embarrassed, his face flushed red.

"No."

"Then why should I know her? So, you're selling her craft book. So what? She's a writer. I got that. Big deal." His eyebrows came together in a perplexed expression, and his gaze finally landed back on Sammy for an answer.

"*Big deal?* First of all, she's not just a writer. Jane Johnson is not only a bestselling author, she's also a huge celebrity in the craft world, that's why! *Was* a celebrity." Sammy looked at the woman and shook her head. "What a shame."

"Oh. Interesting." The detective tapped his chin with his index finger.

"Interesting? You think maybe you can expand a little more than *interesting*?"

"Our pool of suspects just got a whole lot larger if this woman's a celebrity. We're now looking at a high-profile case due to the nature of the crime and our victim. Did someone else want to replace her? Was this about money? A case like this could produce any number of motives and suspects." Nash blew out a frustrated breath as he squatted beside the river to see a puddle of liquid that had seeped into the ground and traveled to the water's edge. Sammy knew exactly what had caused the stain in the dirt and grass he was examining.

"Hey, I can help you with that. It's iced coffee. I dropped both cups when I found her." Sammy pointed to where she had been standing at the moment she had lost the cups from her grip. "Right here. See?"

The detective stood erect and intently took in the scene as if he was trying to commit it all to memory. A police officer from the Crime Scene Investigative Unit came up to them—"crime scene investigator" being a bit of a stretch, since the small town could come up with only two officers to alternate and take on the added duty. One of them was currently snapping photographs of the scene. As the CSI investigator was placing numbered markers and taking pictures, Detective Nash pointed out the unidentified white substance. "Don't forget to zoom in on her blouse. I'd like a close-up shot for the file."

Liam led Sammy by the elbow away from the crime scene and up the large granite steps. When they reached the top, he turned to her. "I'll need you to stop by the police station within the next twenty-four hours to give a formal statement, and I might have more questions for you, but for now, you're excused."

"*Excused?*" The tone of his voice made Sammy remember he had once been in the military in his younger years. She flipped him a mock salute, "Well thank you, Drill Sergeant!" Sammy then rolled her eyes and turned on her heel to head back in the direction of Community Craft.

"Sammy! Wait!"

Sammy turned and crossed her arms across her chest defiantly.

"I'm just trying to do my job." He held up his hands and shrugged. "What's got you so riled up?"

"I understand that you're doing your job, Detective. And as such, you are no longer interested in my input, and I may be *ex-cuuused*." Sammy enunciated every letter. She then nodded and turned back on the trail.

Nash shook his head in disbelief and watched as Sammy walked away from him. "Stay away from my crime scene," he finally shot back at her.

She could feel his eyes boring into her back, but she refused to turn back to face him. And to think, she had actually been happy to see him. Was he happy to see her? She really couldn't gauge. Heidi ran up from behind her as she walked and looped her arm through her cousin's.

"You okay?"

"He doesn't want my help." Sammy jutted a thumb in the direction of the crime scene.

"Oh boy. Here we go again . . ."

Not anxious to discuss the maddening detective, Sammy turned the conversation to the problem at hand. "Heidi, I can't believe this! Jane Johnson is dead. I have a huge event planned in a few days with people coming from miles around to see her. And now the woman we were all looking so forward to meeting is *gone*! Poof! Just like that . . . She's actually gone and died! How am I going to handle all of this?" Sammy shook her head and then placed her hands on top of her head, laced her fingers together, and groaned.

Heidi flashed a sympathetic smile. "Don't worry. Ellie and I will help you. Looks like this is a real job for the S.H.E. detective agency!"

Sammy smirked.

"I'm not trying to be crass, I'm trying to help you calm down . . . I'm actually worried about you." Heidi removed her arm from Sammy's and swung her cousin around briskly to face her. "You look kind of pale. I don't need you passing out on me. Let's take a seat over here to regroup before heading back to the store."

The two women stepped off the trail and moved onto a patch of lush grass underneath a large willow tree overlooking the river. After they took a seat on the shaded grass, Sammy heeded her cousin's advice and took a few slow, healing breaths and stuck her head between her knees while Heidi rubbed her back like a mother soothing a sick child.

After Sammy's breathing had returned to normal and the color had returned to her cheeks, Heidi asked, "You okay?"

"Yeah. I'll be fine. I know you're used to seeing death at the hospital. I guess I'm just still in shock. I still can't believe she's gone. I guess with all of this stress, I sort of flipped out on the detective for excusing me from the crime scene, too. I just want answers, that's all."

Heidi nodded and said, "Oh nooo. I didn't even think of that . . ." And then covered her mouth with her fingers.

"What?" Sammy had been watching a bird take a drink from the edge of the rippling river but now turned back to her cousin and eyed her directly.

"Now we're never going to know what she wanted to tell you in private."

"Oh, we'll know, Heidi. This is not over. We three S.H.E.s have to find out what Jane Johnson was so desperate to tell me about Kate . . . *and* if it has any connection to how the woman wound up dead."

Chapter Four

Sammy removed a nearby pebble lodged in the grass and tossed the rock into the river, making a widening ripple. The seriousness of the recent murder was evolving past the shock stage and slowly sinking into the ugly-reality stage. Heidi was right. Maybe now she'd never find out what Jane had wanted to tell her about Kate. The thought made her queasy. An eerie silence fell between the two cousins, neither of them knowing quite what to say about the recent loss of the craft queen—which didn't help ease the finality of her death either.

Heidi rose to standing and stretched her arms above her head. She often did this to release a kink in her shoulder that stemmed from a childhood injury following a fall from her horse on her family's farm. She claimed her shoulder had never felt right after that tumble.

After she aligned herself, Heidi caught Sammy's attention as she whispered, "What's that person doing across the river?" Heidi sank back to her knees to conspire with her cousin.

Sammy was instantly roused from melancholy to curiosity.

"I dunno? What *is* he doing? *Is* it a he? Or a she?" Sammy's eyes followed the person as he or she disappeared behind a tree.

"Hard to tell, but I think it's a *he*?" Heidi squinted one eye and closed the other, as if it would help center her vision.

Sammy's limited view was hindered by the distance across the water as well as a few mature trees, but it certainly looked as if a figure was hiding most of his (or her) stature behind a large oak and watching the bridge, seemingly the area where the police were still conducting their investigation below the waterfall. And it looked like the person was also using binoculars to get a closer look.

"Whoever it is . . . they're definitely watching the cops. Is he rubbernecking, or do you think he had something to do with the crime? Who else would hide behind a tree with binoculars watching a crime scene? That's insane."

Sammy stood and brushed the remnants of grass and soil from the backside of her jeans and pulled Heidi closer to her. "Let's go sneak up behind and see if we can get a closer look to see what he or she is up to. We'll have to go around, though. We definitely shouldn't go back over the bridge and send any alarm bells to Nash if he's still under the waterfall. Maybe at least we can get a description of the person before he spooks. Whaddya think?"

Heidi nodded in agreement. "Yeah, someone's definitely up to no good."

They didn't want to alert the suspect to their undercover work, so the two walked casually back to the footpath as if they were just taking a leisurely afternoon walk. Sammy tried desperately to keep a constant visual on the unidentified person who was spying on the crime scene, but it was difficult to remain inconspicuous. It would have been so much faster and easier if they could have used the bridge. Instead, the retreat back toward town, with an extended bit of backtracking between side buildings and two large manufacturing plants on the other side of the river, caused them to eventually completely lose a visual of the as-yet-unidentified person. When they finally made it to the other side of the river and were closing in on where the person had been lurking, the area behind the tall oak stood empty. Heidi made a sign for them to remain quiet as they tiptoed among the trees and darted between the oak and a maple tree to try to relocate their prey.

Sammy threw up her hands dramatically but quietly. "Now what?" she whispered as the two hid behind the trunk of the aged maple.

Heidi shrugged. "He has to be here somewhere; he couldn't just vanish into thin air!" She returned the whisper and then stepped on a twig, which made a loud snapping sound.

Sammy glared at her cousin, who returned a sheepish grin and mouthed the word *sorry*.

Sammy covered her mouth with one hand and then pointed a finger down the embankment. An elderly couple stood side by side, and the two had binoculars raised to eye a neighboring tree.

Heidi then walked over to a nearby bench, picked up a bird book that lay beside a picnic basket, and stifled a giggle. "Sorry. I guess my investigative skills are lacking. They're just bird-watchers."

The overwhelming tension and stress of the recent events caused them both to giggle, and then Heidi snorted, making them both bend over in laughter. This startled the elderly couple.

The older woman, wearing an old fishing hat to block the sun from her snow-white curly hair and pale face, turned briskly and sternly dismissed them. "You scared off the indigo bunting! What are you two hooligans doing? Get outta here!" she snapped.

This only made Heidi laugh harder. "I'm so sorry, ma'am. We didn't mean to scare the birds. Our deepest apologies."

"Tisk!" she snorted and waved them away with her hands.

"Wait." Sammy moved closer to the woman and asked, "Didn't you notice the crime scene over there?"

"Crime scene?" The man, who stood a foot taller than his white-haired companion, raised his binoculars and looked across the river to where Heidi was now pointing. "Oh, heavens no! I think they're taking away a body bag!" he croaked.

Sammy was hoping the aged couple had perhaps witnessed something of value, but by the sound of the man's astonishment, they obviously hadn't. She reached over to the older woman, who'd dropped the binoculars to her side in shock and remained silent. "May I borrow those?" Sammy reached over to release the field glasses from the woman's grasp, and she handed them over willingly.

Sammy raised the binoculars to her eyes and zeroed in on Detective Nash. She watched him turn his attention and zone in across the water on her. As she focused the lens clearer, she witnessed a stern warning glare from the officer. His two fingers pointed to his eyes and then out across the river as if to say, *I'm watching you.*

"Sorry. I think we'd better go." Sammy quickly handed the binoculars back to the older woman and then nudged Heidi to encourage their retreat.

The cousins fled back to the path in the direction of

Community Craft. When the two finally slowed and maintained a comfortable pace, they couldn't help but laugh at their ludicrous findings, both unwilling to cope with the seriousness of the situation they found themselves suddenly thrust in. After the laughter, silence hung between them.

As they meandered along the end of the path, Heidi grew serious. "We're going to figure this all out, Sammy. You know we will."

"You really think so?"

"I know so."

"I dunno about that. You should have seen the look Nash gave me when I saw him through the lens of those binoculars. I don't think he's going to be too keen on me nosing around another one of his investigations."

Heidi shrugged and gave her a grin. "Something tells me you're not going to give him much of a choice. Besides, truth is, I think you enjoy hanging around him anyway," she teased.

As the two cousins walked along, something glittery caught Sammy's peripheral vision and momentarily blinded her. She turned her head toward the embankment, where the water crested over a large rock before rushing downstream, and she swerved to walk off the path in the direction of the river.

"Where are you going?" Heidi asked.

"I think I may have found something."

The sunlight caused the object to sparkle once again. Sammy eased down the steep dirt embankment on her backside, careful not to fall, and shifted her weight against a substantial tree log that had fallen into the water after a recent storm. She climbed her way atop the log and held her arms outstretched, carefully taking steps as if she were a gymnast on a balance beam, then crouched down to her knees when she reached the end of the log.

Sammy reached her hand into the cool water and lifted out a cell phone cover. She flipped the pink iPhone case in her hand and noted the initials *JJ* bedazzled with rhinestones and turned her head to Heidi.

"Jane Johnson's phone case. It has to be." Sammy held the phone case up for her to see.

Heidi gasped.

"The killer must have dumped the case, thinking it would flow downstream, but it caught here instead." Sammy crawled backward on the log toward shore, gripping the case tightly in one hand. When she reached the shore, she turned her body, balanced on both legs, and reached for Heidi's outstretched arm to assist her off the broken tree limb.

"Where's the phone, then?" Heidi looked around the ground at her feet, searching.

"I doubt it's here. An iPhone without a cover looks much less conspicuous. I mean, look at this thing. I'm sure it was uber-expensive to have this kind of cover made."

"Do you think those are real diamonds?" Heidi peeked over Sammy's shoulder and pointed a slender finger at the twinkling gems.

"Well, if they are, the killer's motive certainly isn't money. This thing must be worth a fortune."

"Good point. Or the killer panicked and tossed it, knowing that having this type of case in their possession would link them to the murder. What should we do? I mean, shouldn't we call Detective Nash or something?"

"By the look on his face when I saw his warning through the binoculars, if he knows I'm still snooping, he'll have my hide." Sammy breathed deep.

"I've got an idea. Why don't you give it to me? I'll tell Tim I found the case, and I'll be the one to take the blame for removing evidence. I'll tell him the case would've been swept away downstream if I hadn't grabbed it. I can bring him back here and show him exactly where we found it."

Sammy handed the bejeweled cell phone case over to her cousin willingly. The thought of Nash getting up in her face about snooping this early in the investigation didn't sit well. She knew he'd then clam up, and the last thing she needed was to be cast out of the investigation entirely. She needed answers. Besides, Tim was like melted butter in Heidi's hands. Her cousin could get away with just about anything with a bat of her long eyelashes.

As soon as Sammy and Heidi reached the back parking lot of Community Craft, it was hard not to notice Ellie waving her arms frantically over her head for them to hurry up. They were met at the back door with dagger eyes. "Where the hell have you guys been? What took you so long?" Ellie hissed.

"Um, at a crime scene. I'm guessing you already heard the terrible news?" Heidi blew a large puff of air out her mouth, causing hair loosened from her braid to retreat from her face.

Ellie held a hand to her heart. "You have no idea what you're in for, Sammy." Ellie's anger morphed instantly to anxiety as she turned her attention to her sister. "I've been trying to call you on your cell, and then I hear your phone ringing out in the office. Why'd you leave me with no way to get in touch with you?"

Ellie had become much more fearful of everything since giving birth to Tyler. Over the last three years, since she'd become a mom, everything had seemed to make her nervous. It was an obvious change that both Heidi and Sammy had confided to each other they had noticed. At first, they'd attributed her personality change to postpartum hormones and thought it would dissipate after a while. But Ellie's anxiety only seemed to deepen with time.

"What do you mean, I have no idea what I'm in for?" Sammy stopped them from walking a step farther. She knew her sister couldn't possibly be upset with her for having to man the store a few extra minutes alone. There was more to it than that. She really hoped her sister was just having one of her mild panic attacks or overreacting to something minor, but the tone in Ellie's voice gave her definite pause.

"Satellite journalists from Milwaukee and the surrounding area have descended on our town like a flock of Canadian geese. The press has been busy setting up camp out in front of the store. And the crowd and the video equipment has grown substantially in the last fifteen minutes alone." Ellie wrung her hands nervously. "A few reporters came into the store and were looking for you. I didn't know what to do or what to say." Ellie threw up her hands in frustration. "I escaped to the restroom and texted Annabelle from my cell phone. Thankfully, she came right over and told them if they didn't leave, she would call the police for disrupting business. I'm sure she thinks she'll get some publicity from all this, as the Yarn Barn will be in the background shots and make the evening news too. I'm sure glad she came over, though. She handled the press, firm but controlled, just as I expected. She's really come into her own after her divorce. What a spitfire."

Sammy didn't move for a moment as she stood and pondered the recent events. When she finally took a step forward, she moved swiftly and directly to the office behind the cash register. Heidi and Ellie followed close on her heels until they were all in the safety of the small space.

"I'm going to close the store—at least until this all settles down. Considering the circumstances, I think our customers and local vendors will understand," Sammy said as she unlocked a desk drawer and pulled out her brown leather purse and cell phone. "But I don't want to close up yet. I need you guys to stick around for an hour or so if you can."

"Don't you think you should just address the press and get it over with? If they get what they want, maybe they'll leave you alone," Heidi suggested. "I mean, they know you were having the book signing here. I'm sure someone must have already leaked that you were the one to find her body. I'm also pretty sure you're not the only one they will want to interview."

"No, I've got another plan," Sammy said. "But I'll need help from both of you." Her eyes bounced between both, looking for their blessing.

"Absolutely! I'm in." Heidi thrust her fist out in front of her, their official sign signifying the S.H.E. club was now in session.

"I'm not so sure." Ellie rubbed her hands up and down her bare arms nervously. "What exactly do you have in mind?"

"I'm hoping you two can keep the press to wait here while I sneak out the back door. Hopefully none of the reporters has figured out I have a back entrance to the store yet. But I have to

45

hurry before they do." Sammy pulled her car keys out of her purse to ready herself.

"Where are you going?" Ellie raised a hand to block her sister from leaving the office.

"I'm going to Pine Haven Bed and Breakfast. If I address the press now, they'll start retracing Jane's steps, too. I've got to get over to where Jane was staying. I've gotta get there first, before the reporters beat me to it. If the press thinks I'm still on my way to Community Craft, maybe they'll hang out here and wait, and I'll have a bit of time. I have to find out what Jane uncovered about Kate during her research. What was so important that she wanted to tell me in private? You guys . . . *please*. I have to go. Now. Before the press and police make it to Pine Haven."

Ellie shook her head, defeated, then deeply inhaled. Concern sat like a mask on her face.

"Can you stay and manage the store and close up in about an hour, Ellie? That should give me a good head start."

"I guess. I'll call Randy and tell him he's on kid duty."

"What do you want me to do?" Heidi asked. "Besides babysit your sister?"

Ellie frowned and sent her cousin a laser-dagger look.

Sammy turned to Heidi. "Can you hang out in front of the store and see if any perps or anyone not from around here is lurking around? Someone that shouldn't be there? No bird-watchers, though." The two shared a smile before Sammy continued, "Maybe you can eavesdrop too and find out what the press knows, if anything. When you're both ready to close up the store in an hour or so, just tell the press I've changed my mind and decided I'm not coming back today."

"Perps? Who are you now? One of the investigators for the Heartsford Police Department?" Ellie said, her voice dripping with sarcasm. "You are a *craft* store owner. This could get dangerous." Her tone instantly changed to one of warning.

Sammy didn't acknowledge her sister's comment. Instead she said, "Let's regroup tonight for dinner at the Corner Grill. I'll meet you at our normal booth. I promise I'll call or text you guys if I'm running late."

"What about Bara?" Ellie pointed to the sleepy dog in his usual spot.

Sammy greeted her pup with a scratch of his head. "I really don't have time to bring him home. Any extra stops and I won't beat the press *or* the police to the bed-and-breakfast."

"I'll have Randy pick him up. Bara can spend the night at our house. Tyler will love it."

Sammy was surprised by the sudden generosity. Normally Ellie's home was completely void of dog hair. That's how, she had previously firmly declared, she wanted it to stay. But Sammy also knew her sister had a soft spot for Kate and would do anything to help find answers about what Jane Johnson might have wanted to share privately. "Thanks, Ellie."

"No problem."

"I'll give Tim a call and have him pick up the cell phone case, too," Heidi said.

Ellie looked at Heidi, perplexed. "Phone case?"

Sammy looked at her sister. "Heidi will explain everything. Okay, I'm out. I'll see you both at dinner." Sammy sprinted toward the back entrance and quickly rushed out the door. With keys in hand, she hit the fob and was almost in the safety of her white Chevy Impala when she heard her name being called from a distance.

"Ms. Kane? Ms. Samantha Kane?"

Sammy had already opened the driver's-side door when a reporter from a Milwaukee news station rushed to try to stop her from closing the door. Sammy recognized her from the evening news. The woman often worked satellite pieces in local communities surrounding Milwaukee, but Sammy doubted she had ever traveled this far into the farmland for a broadcast. It was rare, if ever, that Heartsford made the nightly news, and this was an explosion of a story. Suddenly, a cameraman was sprinting across the parking lot carrying heavy equipment on his shoulder, following the reporter. Sammy quickly closed the car door before the woman had a chance to stop her. She pressed the button to roll the driver's-side window down and addressed her.

"I'll be back very soon. Right now, I have an emergency I need to attend to. Please stay here, though, and I'll be happy to answer any questions upon my return." Sammy hit the gas and peeled out of the lot. As she looked in the rearview mirror, she saw the female reporter throw up her hands while the cameraman shook his head in defeat. As she turned out of the lot, she crossed her fingers that the reporter really believed she'd be back. And hoped the reporter wouldn't share the news of her departure with the other news outlets.

But Sammy didn't have a choice. If she didn't get to Pine Haven Bed and Breakfast first, she might not have a chance to get any relevant information before the place was crawling with police and press. She made a right-hand turn onto Sumner Street and headed south. The road took her out of downtown

Heartsford, past the local grocery store and the only Walmart for miles around. By the time she reached the patchwork of recently tilled and planted farmland, Sammy felt a tightness in her chest. She realized she had been holding her breath since she'd left Community Craft. For fear she might grow faint again, she breathed in and released it slowly.

What did she want to tell me, Kate?

Sammy often talked to her deceased friend and felt frustrated by the one-way conversations. The harsh reminder of the many things left unsaid. Never in her wildest dreams had Sammy thought she'd lose the best friend of her youth. So young. So unfair. She had taken for granted that Kate would always be there, like a safety blanket. They'd had plans to be each other's maids-of-honor when that day came for each of them. They'd agreed they wanted their future husbands to be close friends, too, so their children would get the chance to grow up together. They'd had it all planned out.

And then one day, a day that had started out like any other, it had ended in heartbreak. It was utterly amazing how the details could stay so vivid in the mind when tragedy struck. Sammy remembered exactly where she had been when she received the horrible news. She and her on-again, off-again boyfriend Brian had decided to "take a break" from their relationship . . . yet again. Sammy had finally decided to put herself first and go back to college to finish her degree. She had planned to stay in Madison that summer in a small apartment, in cramped living conditions with a few other roommates who also took classes part-time at UW Madison. She had arranged to stick around and take a summer class that wouldn't fit into her fall semester schedule, because it wouldn't be offered again until the following spring. She was working as a sandwich clerk at BJ's sub shop, walking distance from campus, when she got the dreaded call. She remembered vividly the tuna fish sub she'd been assembling for a customer. Her cell rang in her pocket, which had ticked off her boss. It was her mother calling. Then a text: CALL ASAP. Her mother never texted. To this day, Sammy couldn't stand the smell of tuna fish.

Her throat constricted. A tear ran softly down her cheek. She wiped it away quickly.

As she stopped at an intersection, she noticed a bumper sticker on the car in front of her that read KEEP CALM AND SHINE ON. She watched as the car took a left-hand turn off the main road. But the message remained.

Thanks, Kate.

Finally, Sammy caught sight of her destination when she reached a long line of jam-packed balsam fir and white spruce trees that flanked both sides of the road. The old Christmas tree farm had been left to overgrowth and converted to a haven hidden among the tall trees. A large, dark-green sign with gold letters pointed the way to Pine Haven Bed and Breakfast.

After turning left down the dirt road, Sammy rolled down the driver's-side window and breathed in the highly scented breeze that perfumed the canopy along the winding driveway. She hadn't been down this drive in many years. As a child, her family would pick their prize Christmas tree off this lot. But not since grade school had she taken the trip out here to the outskirts of town. A feeling of tranquility rushed over her as she drove through the dense trees, and she understood why Jane Johnson had decided to make this her place of refuge while staying in Heartsford.

Sammy pulled her white Chevy into a clearing, and the whole of the vast early-1900s farmhouse suddenly came into view. The stately, white, two-story home with a large wraparound porch stood proudly against the backdrop of aged pines. The clapboard siding of the home was in pristine condition, as if it had been recently repainted. Multiple aged whiskey barrels lined the drive, each overflowing with vibrant annual flowers in contrasting hues of yellow, purple, and red. Sammy parked her car on the crushed-stone parking lot in front of the building. All was quiet for the moment, and she was thrilled she had beaten both Detective Nash and the press to the location.

Sammy stepped from the car. A pungent smell of Christmas filled her nostrils as she closed the driver's-side door. She second-guessed herself and moved around to the passenger seat, where she had flung her purse. She dug into the glove compartment and was instantly relieved to see she had left an old pair of winter gloves. Finally, a rare occasion that she was happy for her disorganization and not cleaning out her old winter gear. She stuffed the gloves deep into her brown leather purse and swung the thick strap over her shoulder. As she walked up the wide porch steps, the inn's owner opened the front door to greet her.

"Samantha Kane, what a nice surprise!" The older woman moved toward Sammy with arms outstretched for an embrace.

"Mrs. Thatcher, so nice to see you." Sammy pulled herself from her fourth-grade teacher's comforting hug and held the woman at arm's length. The woman had aged gracefully. Her hair was most certainly dyed, but it was a warm shade of honey that made her friendly green eyes dance with delight.

"Mrs. Thatcher? Dear, no one's called me that since my teaching days. Call me Helen." She tucked her straight golden hair neatly behind one ear.

"I don't think I can," Sammy admitted easily. "I'm afraid I'll be sent to the principal's office if I call you that."

The two shared a laugh.

"What brings you to Pine Haven?" Sammy's former grade-school teacher gestured to a set of oversized red rocking chairs that sat empty on the porch, waiting for visitors and guests to sit and take in the view of the expansive property.

Sammy accepted the offer and took a seat. After dropping her purse to the ground beside her, she turned to Mrs. Thatcher and began to spin a story that she hoped would be forgiven . . . later . . . in her private prayers.

"Well, you know the members of the crochet group from Community Craft are so incredibly talented. Amazing group of artists. I *have* to call them artists. Their vision for designs, color combinations, and choosing the perfect skein of yarn for a project—well, they're simply outstanding. I was thinking maybe we could have a few of the ladies crochet a nice soft lap blanket or throw for each of your guest rooms?" Sammy paused for a brief moment and then took a breath before proceeding with her fib.

"And . . . well . . . possibly you might consider offering a few crocheted items for sale in your gift shop too? Wouldn't it be wonderful if some of your guests came to visit downtown, and they could stop in and meet some of the fiber artists from

Community Craft if they had interest? I was hoping for a quick tour of your beautiful bed-and-breakfast to see what might work for your decor. I don't believe I've walked through since you've finished with the renovation of this amazing piece of property."

The bed-and-breakfast owner eyed her carefully. "Interesting idea. And it just came to you today? Or was there another reason you might have stopped by?" Helen pressed.

She doesn't know about the author's death yet. She can't. Can she?

"Oh, I know Jane Johnson is staying with you this week. We've already met." Sammy tried to sound casual and steady her tone. "Actually, did you hear she had plans to interview me? Has plans," she immediately corrected herself. "Has plans to interview me," she repeated. "I can't believe it . . . such an incredible honor! Her next book is called *Behind the Seams: A Journey of Why We Love to Craft*. The book is very different than her normal craft and her bestselling crochet books. She's researching how handcrafted items are passed down from generation to generation, and I guess Community Craft piqued her interest because of our camaraderie and how we've made such a difference, bringing our community together. You know what I mean, how we don't just sell crafts and such but also assist those in need and offer a space for group classes. Did you know all the proceeds from those classes are used to help fund local nonprofits? This is apparently unique to our community. You must agree how special Heartsford really is. And yes, Jane is a very nice woman. Very nice indeed to be shining a light on our little town here."

Sammy laid her hands in her lap and pressed her fingers into her legs to help her shut her own mouth from continued rambling banter. "Actually, I'm killing two birds with one stone. Did

I not mention? While I'm here, I'm supposed to meet with her in her room for an interview." Sammy bit her lip. She hoped she wasn't going straight to hell with all her truth sprinkled with black lies.

"Now that you mention it, I think I do remember her telling me in passing that she was conducting research for a new project. I was so star-struck at first, it was hard for me to focus on everything she said initially. Our first conversations are a bit of a blur, to be honest." Helen smiled wide, showing coffee-stained teeth.

"I know, right? I had the same reaction. It's quite magical having someone of her stature visiting right here . . . in Heartsford!" Sammy slapped her hand a little too hard on her own thigh, causing a sting. "I bet you've been swamped with phone calls to see if she's really staying here. People wanting information. I mean, the townspeople can't imagine where else in town would be nice enough for a celebrity to stay. I'm sure the assumption is out there . . . the gossip train must be flowing."

"Yes. That is very true. I told my husband to let the machine take all our calls. Ms. Johnson booked the entire property for her visit. She's very private, so we have no need to pick up the booking phone this week. We've given her my husband Raymond's private cell phone number, in case she needs anything. We'd never get anything done around here if we stood at the booking phone trying to dodge questions. It'd be darn near impossible!"

"I totally understand," Sammy said thoughtfully. "It's been almost the same over at Community Craft. So many people wanting to talk about Jane Johnson and the upcoming event." She couldn't help but wonder who had come into Jane's path since she'd been in town, if Pine Haven wasn't allowing any other guests. "Has she held any other private interviews, then? I'm sure I'm not the only one that she's interviewing while she's here? I'm sure the press will be all over here too. That could prove great marketing for your inn . . . no?"

"Oh no. We signed a confidentially agreement with the author. We're not to disclose her location until after she leaves town. Every member of the staff has signed one as well. Our gardener, Ethan; our cleaning crew, Rose and Miranda; our food vendors—we're all sworn to secrecy. We signed it for her own safety and ours too, really. But we certainly can't help if the gossip train picks it up . . . We're doing our very best. Honestly, there isn't much more we can do."

"So does that mean you won't let me have the tour today?"

The innkeeper was pensive for a moment. "I suppose I don't see why not? I mean, she did tell you where she's staying and wanted to meet you here. I guess I don't see the harm?" Helen tried to decide while she justified the answer. "Plus it's *you*, little Samantha Kane. How could I not trust you?" The innkeeper didn't move from her seat but instead studied Sammy with knowing eyes.

Sammy could feel a sudden heat crawling up her neck. She hoped to God it didn't reach her face and give her away.

After several moments of silence between them, Sammy got a sick feeling in her stomach that she wasn't going to be able to snoop in Jane Johnson's room at Pine Haven Bed and Breakfast after all. Then Helen rose from her red rocking chair on the expansive front porch and Sammy mirrored her action.

The innkeeper then surprised her by saying, "I guess you're welcome to look around. The house is open. Go ahead and give yourself a tour. I was just on my way to meet Raymond in the barn before you stopped in. He's having trouble with the lawn equipment, and I need to bring him the credit card so he can hurry to the hardware store for parts to fix the rider. Ethan has been waiting all day to cut the grass. We can't have our houseguest traipsing through long grass; that would be totally unacceptable."

"Yes. That would be dreadful!" Sammy said a little too quickly.

"I'm really sorry I can't take you for a tour myself. But I have so much to do before our famous guest returns." Helen looked stricken, as if she didn't know which way to turn.

Sammy knew she could easily soothe Helen's worries in one swift comment: Jane Johnson wouldn't be returning. *Ever.* Instead she said, "Not a problem. Don't worry about me at all. I can find my way around quite easily." Sammy reached to pat Helen on the arm encouragingly and then directed her former teacher toward the wide plank front steps. "Go on ahead. I'll let myself inside."

Chapter Five

S ammy was running out of time. The police would be pulling into the driveway any minute, and then she would lose the opportunity to investigate Jane's room. She needed to hurry.

Helen reluctantly stepped off the top front step of Pine Haven Bed and Breakfast. Sammy knew the innkeeper's instinct was to turn around and return inside with her. But instead, Helen continued slowly down the steps and said over her shoulder, "Let me know if you need anything else. You can come out to the barn if you have any other questions."

"Thanks, Mrs. Thatcher," Sammy said as she turned abruptly and entered through the wooden screen door of the farm house.

The smell of orange and cinnamon welcomed her. Sammy wasn't sure if it was something the innkeeper was baking or a potpourri. Either way, the scent instantly brought to mind the feeling of walking into a candlemaker's workshop. She wondered if Abby, the vendor who created candles for Community Craft, could generate a comparable scent. She'd have to talk to her about it the next time she stopped in the store. The scent was lovely, and Sammy was sure it would fly off the shelves.

The wide entryway was blocked to her right by a narrow mahogany desk that sat in front of a large sitting room. Sammy presumed it was the reception desk. To her left, a long set of stairs covered with a deep burgundy–and–navy runner led to the second level. Behind the staircase, a library was fitted with floor-to-ceiling shelves tightly crammed with leather-bound books and a sliding oak ladder leaning against them. Sammy thought she should invite Mrs. Thatcher to their next book club meeting, as the members would drool over the prospect of a field trip to this dreamy room. If she'd had more time, she'd have loved to escape and peruse the various texts. A highly polished wide-plank pine floor led to the back of the house. Sammy assumed the hallway traveled to the kitchen. She didn't follow the hall-way and instead took the stairs located directly in front of her as quickly as her short legs would carry her. When she finally reached the top of the stairs, an expansive, white-subway-tiled bathroom anchored the hallway, which led in both directions. Sammy hesitated for a second before turning left. As she moved down the hallway, she noticed each door ajar, and the rooms looked as if no one had ever entered them. The vacuum marks on the beige plush carpet were still evident, and the beds were neatly made, with stark white coverlets and pillow shams. When she reached the end of the long hallway and the final bedroom, the door was closed tight with a Do Not Disturb tag attached to the knob. Sammy reached deep into her purse and plucked out one winter glove. She slipped it onto her right hand and tried to open the door. Locked. She should have known the private author would lock her room door. Sammy gritted her teeth. *Now what?*

Before she even had a minute to rethink her plan, the sound of heavy footsteps coming up the stairs sent a warning signal through her body. She slipped off the winter glove, jammed it deep into her purse, and then turned in the direction of the footsteps. Helen came rushing toward her with Detective Liam Nash and Officer Tim Maxwell close behind. "Samantha! Jane Johnson has been murdered!" Mrs. Thatcher's voice shrilled at a hysterical level.

Sammy plastered her best Academy Award–winning look of shock onto her face but remained silent. When Helen took her eyes off Sammy for a brief moment to eye the closed door, Sammy sent a warning glare at the detective and officer to not blow her surprise act at the news of the author's death.

The detective seemed to heed the warning and turned to Helen. "I'm going to need the key to this door. I'm assuming this is the room where Ms. Johnson was staying?"

"Of course," Helen said as her hands began to tremble. She was visibly shaken by the news. "I have the spares locked in a safe downstairs. I'll go fetch it right away." Helen turned to retreat down the stairs.

"Officer Maxwell, please accompany Mrs. Thatcher," Detective Nash directed, and then he waited until Helen's back was turned and moved down the hallway. He caught Tim's attention and then whispered a warning to the patrolman to not share with the innkeeper that Sammy had previously been aware of the author's death.

"Absolutely," Tim nodded before following Helen down the hall.

Neither the detective nor Sammy said another word until Helen had turned the corner.

"Samantha Kane. Why am I not surprised?" Nash stood with his hands on his hips, glaring down at Sammy.

"Before you go freaking out on me . . ."

He interrupted her. "You know you could be in serious trouble here. Am I going to have to arrest you for obstructing an investigation or tampering with evidence? You understand you can do jail time for those offenses, right?" His large frame bore down on her.

Sammy held a hand up to interject. "You don't understand."

"Oh, I understand. What? You think I didn't see you watching the crime scene from across the river after I excused you? I'm guessing this type of juvenile behavior is what I'm going to have to deal with throughout my entire investigation?"

Sammy shook her head. "No. You really don't understand." She really wished his eyes were back to their melted-chocolate state, but at the moment, things weren't looking promising.

The detective removed his hands from his hips and folded them across his chest. "I'm waiting . . ." He began to tap his right foot on the floor. The clicking sound of a shoe hitting hardwood. *Tap. Tap. Tap.* His black shoe continued to tap on the edge of the wood floor where the runner didn't reach the wall.

Sammy shook her head to remove the annoying tapping sound that now reverberated in her skull. "Jane mentioned she had to tell me something . . . about Kate . . . something, in her own words, 'that could change everything.'"

Nash dropped his arms, and his eyes narrowed and softened. The tapping foot stopped. Now she was getting somewhere.

"Why didn't you tell me this before?"

"Because you *excused* me from the crime scene. Did you not?" Sammy pursed her lips and flipped him a childish glare.

"I'm not going to debate semantics with you, Samantha. I don't have time for this nonsense. I have a murder to investigate." He brushed her aside, annoyance coloring his voice.

"Then let me consult on the investigation," Sammy pressed.

"Like I have another choice?" he said under his breath, and then blew out a puff of frustration. "*If*—and it's a really big *if*—I let you consult, you *must* follow my lead. You have to follow my rules. Do I make myself clear?"

"Very. Yes, very clear." Sammy nodded profusely, hoping he wouldn't change his mind and either tell her to get lost and go jump in a lake or throw her in jail for obstructing an investigation.

Helen topped the stairs and rushed down the long hall in their direction. "Here you go, Detective."

"Thank you," he said as he took the room key in his hand.

"Samantha dear, why don't you come with me?" Helen suggested. "We should give the officer his space." Helen once again looked stricken. "Sergeant Maxwell is waiting downstairs to ask me a few more questions; he may want to talk to you too?"

Sammy lifted an eyebrow at Detective Nash and waited for his approval.

"Actually, she can stay with me. She was the last person to talk with the victim, so I'd like her to stay to consult. Thank you, Mrs. Thatcher. You may want to go and warn your husband also. I have a feeling the press will be showing up here shortly. You might want to close the main gate to hold them off for a bit longer. Officer Maxwell can assist you, if you need.

Better yet, tell him not to let anyone past the main gate. On my orders."

"Oh dear, I hadn't thought of that." Helen's hand flew to her flushed face. "Right away, then." She nodded and left the two of them standing, holding the key to the author's room.

Detective Nash slipped the key into the lock, and the door opened with an aged creak. A somberness surrounded Sammy as she followed him into the room. How eerie to see a person's suitcase sprawled open on the bed, as if the author could return at a moment's notice! Beneath the suitcase, the bedsheets looked as if they had never held a sleeping body. The bed held only the remnants of the spilled clothing, as if Jane hadn't been able to decide what to wear.

"Did you happen to ask Mrs. Thatcher when Jane arrived in town?" Sammy wandered idly around the vast room. She wondered if this was the only suite at the inn. The large pine bed was covered in a pure-white coverlet with matching canopy. A seating area, across the room, in front of three large windows, held a window seat and fluffy emerald-green pillows. *The perfect place to read a book*, Sammy thought. Too bad Jane had never had the chance . . .

"Yesterday morning," the detective finally answered as he slipped on rubber gloves before beginning his search though the suitcase.

"I heard she came in a limo."

"The Crime Scene Unit is investigating a rental car in town. Apparently she was getting too many looks being chauffeured, so she rented a nondescript vehicle."

"I believe it. Not too many fancy cars and limos driving around through this part of the state, that's for sure."

Sammy moved past the window seat to a sliding glass door and peeked out of the white eyelet–curtained panels. She popped a lock, slid the door open, and stepped out onto the balcony to think. She thought if she gave the detective a minute to go through the author's things and be the first to find something, he might be more likely to share information with her. She needed to stand down and tread carefully. Right now, she was gaining more access into the investigation than she'd ever thought Nash would allow.

If Jane Johnson hadn't been murdered, the day would have been picture-perfect. The weather remained unseasonably dry and sunny, and a soft breeze moved past Sammy and ruffled the sliding door's curtain. The narrow balcony overlooked a newly planted vegetable garden and a henhouse in the distance, a view of simple Wisconsin country living. Sammy noticed Helen and a man she presumed was her husband, Raymond, talking with a younger man. Maybe in his late twenties? His arm was wrapped in a white bandage. *Must be Ethan, the gardener*, Sammy thought. Officer Maxwell was making his way to the main gate, obviously following orders. Her eyes traveled the property border, where the abandoned tree farm didn't allow viewing access to the neighboring soybean farm. The balsam firs had grown together, forming an impenetrable thick wood of privacy. Before turning back into the room, she noticed the gardener looking in her direction. She ducked back inside the bedroom before the rest of those gathered on the ground noticed her watching them.

"Find anything interesting?" Sammy asked as she sauntered over to the detective, who was carefully removing the author's clothing from inside the suitcase and neatly setting the contents aside on the bed. Sammy moved closer to investigate. A gasp caught in her throat and Nash turned to her, alarmed.

"What in the world?" Sammy leaned over the detective's arm to get a closer look. Inside the almost empty suitcase lay a red-and-white woven hair accessory. "Liam, look at that." She pointed a slender finger. "Kate and I made similar matching braided barrettes! *Years* ago. What is it doing in the bottom of Jane's suitcase?"

The detective removed the barrette from the suitcase and spun the red-and-white hair bauble between his gloved fingers, and together they eyed the braided satin ribbons. "Do you really think it belonged to Kate? How would that be possible? If so, what *is* it doing in the author's suitcase?"

"I don't know, but this is really weird. Kate and I each made a barrette exactly like that one for the homecoming parade. The red-and-white ribbons represented our high school colors. We were the only two people that had them. I promise you!" Sammy pointed to a clear bead clinging to the edge of the narrow satin ribbon. "The only thing different about this one is that it's missing the long beaded tails. I think I still have a matching one just like it in my closet at home."

Sammy couldn't believe it. She couldn't remember the last time she had actually laid eyes on her barrette. So many years had passed, and suddenly she was jolted back to the memory so clearly, she almost felt sixteen again.

"Why would Ms. Johnson have it?" The detective shook his head, perplexed.

Sammy plucked her cell from her purse and adjusted it to take a photo of the barrette while Liam held it in his gloved finger. "Do you mind? I'm going to compare it to mine at home. I'm ninety-nine percent positive this is the one Kate made. Gosh, it's been years since I've looked at it, and I'll have to compare it to mine to be sure. I hope I can find it in the back of my closet. I'm not even one hundred percent sure I kept it, to be honest."

"Go right ahead. You'll probably have better luck finding out why Ms. Johnson had it in her possession, knowing you," he said in a teasing tone.

Sammy smiled at his remark and moved her camera to both sides of the barrette as the detective spun it between his gloved fingers to take some close-up shots. "It doesn't make any sense. What the heck is Jane doing with Kate's barrette? And where are the long beaded tails?"

"I don't know." The detective placed it into a plastic evidence bag and tossed it on the bed beside the suitcase. "But we're going to have to find out. Maybe she met someone who gave it to her? Or maybe she met Kate years ago, before she was famous? I guess I'll add it to the list of things to investigate."

"I just don't get it. That makes zero sense. Those barrettes were something Kate and I made together. Who else would care? Even if Kate, by some miracle, did cross paths with Jane years ago, she wouldn't give her *that*." Sammy shrugged her shoulders and shook her head. "Did you find anything else?"

"Not really. No cell left behind. No real clues. Just a suitcase full of clothes."

Sammy didn't dare bring up the fact that she and Heidi had found what was potentially the author's cell phone case. Tim would handle it, so she'd let that slide for now. "This is so frustrating!" She huffed audibly.

"Welcome to my world. Killers don't just walk into the police station and offer up confessions of guilt. There's a lot that goes into my kind of investigative work."

Sammy nodded. "I can only imagine."

The detective moved the rest of the author's clothes out of the suitcase and revealed a small yellow legal pad tucked between a pair of black slacks and a mauve satin blouse. Sammy leaned over his arm to see what was written in ink on the yellow paper:

Highway 83
(24-14-5)

"What's on Highway 83?" The detective turned to Sammy.

"Miles of farmland, basically. Oh, and the newer industrial park that was built several years ago on the south end—a new steel manufacturing plant. But what's twenty-four, fourteen, five? Obviously it's not an address."

"Sounds like a combination lock to me," the detective answered.

"That doesn't make any sense. For what? There's nothing on Highway 83 that would require a lock?"

"No storage units?"

"Nope."

The detective shrugged and added the yellow legal pad to his growing pile of evidence. "Maybe the two notes aren't connected. She did write them on separate lines. Tell me again what Jane said to you before she left your store. Try to remember exactly."

"She just said she had something to tell me regarding the previous owner of Community Craft. And that it would change everything. Now I wish I could go back and force her to tell me what it was then and there. But she was adamant she would only share whatever it was in private. If she had Kate's barrette in her possession, maybe she wanted to prove to me that they spoke? I don't know. Now I'll never know, and it will haunt me every moment of my life."

Detective Nash removed his rubber gloves, lifted Sammy's chin sympathetically to face him, and then placed his hands lightly on her shoulders. His eyes returned to dark melted chocolate, and Sammy wanted to bathe in them. With a tenderness she hadn't heard him express previously, he said, "I won't rest until we find out."

Sammy broke her gaze from the immediate spark of intimacy that flew between them. This wasn't exactly how she'd pictured her first trip alone to the bedroom with Liam. She instinctively stumbled a step backward. Her eye landed on a box of computer paper next to the bedside table. She stepped past the detective, reached over, and flipped open the lid on the box, exposing the first blank sheet of paper. When she removed the top sheet, a gasp escaped her mouth, catching the detective's attention.

"What is it?"

"I think these are pages from her latest unpublished manuscript, the one she was currently working on. Are you going to let me read it?"

From the look on the detective's face, Sammy didn't think she was going to get the answer she was hoping for.

Chapter Six

S ammy didn't realize how hungry she was until she parked her white Chevy smack dab in front of the Corner Grill and her stomach growled in response to the scent of char-grilled burgers seeping from the restaurant. The owner of the eatery, Colin Chambers, who had taken over running the establishment upon his father's retirement, must have decided the evening was cool enough to keep the windows open and save on air-conditioning. The tantalizing smell wasn't hurting business either, Sammy thought as she entered through the heavy door of the restaurant. The small entryway was crammed with groups waiting for a table. An awkward line had formed in the small space, not quite indicating who was supposed to be called next.

Colin waved Sammy inside to the front of the line. "Your better halves are already in the corner booth." He smiled and plucked her by the arm to help maneuver her through the crowd.

"Thank you, Colin. I'm starving, and the smells emitting from this building are amazing!" Sammy sucked in a relieved breath when the room finally opened up enough to create a clear path for her to join Ellie and Heidi at their familiar table.

Sammy slid into the aged oak booth next to her cousin and opposite her sister. The two were both already nursing glasses of red wine and munching from a plate of various cheeses and crackers. Sammy wanted to reach out and kiss them both when she noticed a full glass of red wine already at her seat. She immediately took a sip.

"We thought you might be ready for that." Heidi winked as she swirled the wine in her own glass. She then gestured to the plate of snacks. "Did you notice? Colin's trying to make this old burger joint into a restaurant with classssssss?" Heidi giggled and held the *s* on class for an obnoxious amount of time. Sammy thought it entirely possible her cousin might not be on her first glass of wine.

"Hey, I'd eat just about anything right now. Fancy cheese? Bring it on," Sammy said as she popped a piece of herbed cheddar into her mouth and then washed it down with a sip of wine. "Sorry to keep you guys waiting," she added.

"No worries," Ellie said. "I was running late after dropping off Bara. Heidi made it here first, which explains her flush." Ellie widened her eyes and then winked at Sammy. "I think her old boyfriend might have given her a glass on the house before I arrived."

A look of disgust swept over Heidi's face. "Why did you have to bring that up? Good lord, it's ancient history. Was it freshman year or sophomore year?" Heidi looked as if she might hurt herself doing the mental gymnastics necessary to recall when she had gone on a handful of dates with Colin Chambers before they both realized, after an awkward kiss, that they were much better off as friends. "I hate to admit it, but I'm glad it didn't work out with us. Colin hasn't aged well. Have you noticed how much hair he's lost? He's practically bald! He's definitely not as cute as he was in high school. Not even close."

Sammy changed the subject for Heidi's sake, since she knew her cousin never said an unkind word about anyone, but the truth serum seemed to be taking over her words. Out of the three of them, she'd always thought Heidi was the kindest—after all, she nurtured the sick for a living. Sammy turned her attention to her sister. "Thanks for taking care of Bara. You don't know how much I appreciate it." Sammy reached for Ellie's hand across the table and gave it a light squeeze.

"I know how much you love that pup. Sometimes, I think he even trumps us." Ellie smiled. "You should have seen your nephew's face when he found out Bara was spending the night. Tyler ran around the room, giddy; I thought he was going to knock a baby tooth out, running into the living room coffee table." Ellie squeezed Sammy's hand, then released it quickly.

"You know, I really think you should get a dog. Tyler would be so happy if you did, and it would be really good for him. How about a rescue?"

"No way, uh-uh." Ellie waved her hand in defense. "I like having a clean house without dog hair flying everywhere and a yard where I can let my son run without landing in poo. Just wait until you have kids. I have enough mess to clean up during the day after my tornado of a son blows through. I don't need to be dealing with pets too."

Sammy was almost afraid to ask, but then decided she had to hear. "Speaking of messes"—she felt a twinge of guilt for leaving

the two of them to handle her mess at Community Craft—
"everything go okay with closing up the store?"

"No problem at all. The press pretty much dissipated when
they finally heard you weren't coming back. I told Randy to
DVR the news for us so we can catch it later too," Ellie said. "I
wanted to see if Annabelle actually made the final cut."

Heidi only nodded in agreement as she sipped her wine.

Ellie reached onto the open seat where her purse lay next to
her and pulled out a magazine. She slid it across the table for
Sammy and Heidi to view. "When I dropped Bara off at home,
Randy gave me this. He said he found it in the waiting room at
work. He brought it home because he knew you were having the
author at the store this week for a book signing. He hadn't even
heard that she'd been murdered until I shared the news with
him. Look at the front page." Ellie pointed.

Sammy set her glass of wine on the table and adjusted her
view to see the magazine. There on the front cover was a photo
of a man being physically restrained by a body guard, and a
very distraught-looking Jane Johnson. The headline read: Ex-
Husband of Queen of Crafts Slapped With Restraining
Order.

Sammy's eyes darted to the publication date. The magazine
was dated June 1st. "So, this is recent?" Her eyes darted from
Ellie to Heidi. "Had you guys heard of this? Seen it on TMZ or
anything?"

"I don't watch that junk," Ellie said.

"Me either," Heidi agreed, then downed the rest of her glass
of wine.

"We need to get more food into you. And no more wine; you're cut off until you eat something besides a measly nugget of cheese!" Sammy elbowed her cousin.

Heidi waved her off and, with slurred words, said, "I'm fiiiiine."

Ellie piped up, "Yeah, Tim is supposed to be picking her up from here after dinner. That's all we need is Mr. Police Dude blaming us for getting her drunk. You know he'll totally put this one on us." Ellie waved a finger between herself and Sammy as a wave of concern washed over her face. "He always sees us sisters as the troublemakers and is blinded by Miss Beauty Princess over there." Ellie smirked at Heidi, who responded with a flutter of her long eyelashes.

The waitress came and interrupted the three by attempting to hand out menus. Sammy stopped her with an uplifted hand. "Burgers and fries all around," she said as she circled her finger above her head like she was getting ready to toss a lasso.

Ellie interrupted, "Skip me. I'll take a salad, Italian dressing on the side, please."

The youthful waitress, who looked as if she was having a hard time keeping up with the crowded restaurant, nodded, causing her long dark ponytail to bounce up and down. She moved quickly away from the table without saying a word.

"Seriously, Sammy, I'm trying desperately to stick to my diet. Stop trying to sabotage me by ordering burgers every time we come here. You're a bad influence." Ellie's lip came forward in a pout.

"Sorry! It's not intentional." Sammy didn't want to torpedo

her sister's efforts, but she also didn't want Ellie eyeing her food with longing the entire meal.

But Heidi laughed out loud. A little too loud. Luckily, the busy restaurant was so noisy, no one even seemed to notice.

"What are you laughing at?" Ellie hissed.

"You're alwaysssss on a diet; give it a rest." Heidi waved her cousin off and threw her head back in open laughter as if she had said something hysterical.

"I really was hoping we could have a serious S.H.E. meeting here tonight about the investigation into Jane Johnson's murder, but I don't know if this one over here is even going to remember our conversation tomorrow!" Sammy jutted a thumb in her cousin's direction.

Heidi sat upright in the booth, saluted her cousin, and slapped her cheeks with her hands. "The wine really is going right to my head. I'm sorry, Sammmyyy." Heidi suddenly looked embarrassed.

"It's okay," Sammy said. "We've all had a pretty rough day." Although she couldn't remember the last time she'd seen her cousin borderline drunk. Tipsy? Yes. Drunk? No.

"You girls don't know the half of it!" Heidi confessed.

Instantly, Sammy and Ellie's attention flew to their cousin, the tone in her voice alerting them to something they'd both apparently missed.

"What's going on, Heidi?" Ellie asked, deep concern suddenly flooding her face.

Heidi held her breath to stop a sudden case of the hiccups.

Sammy couldn't understand her cousin's behavior. She

wasn't one to let loose too often, especially on a weeknight, but she seemed close to reaching that destination now. Something was definitely nagging at her cousin. And it wasn't just about the murder in their small town.

"Before all this stuff happened with the Queen of Crafts, Tim and I had plans for tonight. *Special plansssss.*" Heidi breathed out and then held her breath to once again try to stop the hiccups that were causing her whole body to shake.

"What do you mean, *special* plans?" Sammy eyed Heidi carefully.

"Tim bought me a new dress last week and asked me to wear it tonight. He said he was taking me into the city for a very special dinner." Heidi held her breath again. This time pinching her nose.

"The city? Midweek?" Ellie said. "Sounds serious."

The three of them knew that Tim hardly ever left the confines of their small town. He seemed just as happy after working all day at the Heartsford Police Department to stick close to home. Sammy wondered if next to his photo in the Heartsford High School yearbook, it read, *Most Likely to Stay a Townie.* She might have to peek into Ellie's copy and verify.

"You guysssssssss . . ." Heidi leaned in and motioned them to circle closer so they could hear her loud whisper. "I think he was going to ask me . . . something . . . reallllly important . . ."

Just then the waitress arrived, her arms carrying a full tray. As she lowered it from her capable shoulder, the three women leaned back in the booth so the server could place burgers in front of Sammy and Heidi. She then placed a salad in front of Ellie.

Ellie looked at the limp lettuce leaves in front of her and frowned. "You forgot my dressing," she said to the waitress, who nodded, held up a finger, and turned quickly on her heel. "Is she new?" Ellie pointed to the back of the waitress. "They seem to go through a lot of newbies in here lately. I wonder if Colin is a tough boss?"

Sammy and Heidi shrugged.

Ellie leaned across the table and plucked a french fry from Sammy's plate. Sammy scowled at her sister from across the table. Why couldn't she order her own fries? She did this all the time—ordered a salad, then picked from her sister's plate—and yet it was somehow Sammy's fault she sabotaged. Seriously? Sammy was growing annoyed.

"You think he was going to propose?" Ellie asked after swallowing her purloined fry.

"I don't know." Heidi placed her head in her hands. "Why else would he"—she hiccupped again before continuing—"why else would he want to go to Milwaukee? And buy a new dress for me? He doesn't even like to shop. He loathesssss shopping!"

"She has a valid point there," Sammy said.

"And now it's allllll ruined. Obviously, with everything that happennnnned"—Heidi held her breath to stop the hiccups before she continued—"he had to cancel our date tonight. Now I'm always going to wonder if tonight was going to be *the* night . . ."

"Would you have said yes?" Ellie asked.

Heidi didn't respond, and the three of them sat quietly for a few moments. Neither sister honestly knew how their cousin would have answered. Sammy and Ellie liked Tim, as a boyfriend, but as a husband? To them it seemed like he sometimes cared more about his physique than his intellect. Which, if Sammy were to be honest, didn't match her cousin's. Yes, they were good workout partners. But was that all they had in common? Great physique? Sammy and Ellie had kept their musings about the relationship to themselves. Their cousin seemed happy. Who were they to interfere?

"I think so?" Heidi finally said as she slumped forward in the booth, resting her arms on the table.

Sammy finally understood Heidi's unusual overindulgence that evening. Her poor cousin didn't know what to do. Or if she was even ready for that type of commitment. And now she had more than enough time to wallow in the decision. Maybe it was a good thing, Sammy thought. Heidi would really have time to weigh her options.

"You *think* so? You better not accept a proposal on *you think so*," Ellie said. "Hey, listen, I'm the only married one in this group, and marriage isn't all red and rosy all the time." She plucked another french fry from Sammy's plate, and this time Sammy tapped her on the hand to stop her.

"Whattaaayyyaa mean by that?" Heidi hiccupped.

Sammy was frustrated. This conversation wasn't going anything like she'd planned. She'd really hoped the three S.H.E.s would be putting their heads together to solve a crime. Instead, she was sitting next to her drunk cousin who might or might not even remember this conversation in the morning. Who might or might not want to marry Tim Maxwell. Who *might* or *might not* spend as much time with her if she were to indeed get married. Sammy selfishly wasn't sure she wanted Heidi to get married. That would mean she would be the only single one, and suddenly that feeling didn't sit well. She dug into her burger hungrily. She decided to keep her mouth occupied with food—while her sister devoured her fries—instead of fueling her frustrations and sharing the ugly truth that she feared she'd end up the only spinster.

But Ellie wasn't ready to let it go. "Marriage is hard. It takes give-and-take and a lot of work. Especially when kids are involved." She leaned back in the booth when the waitress came and placed the cup of salad dressing in front of her. "Thanks." She smiled at the server and then poured every last drop of liquid onto the salad.

After swallowing a large bite and taking another mouthful of food, Sammy interjected out the side of her mouth, "You've never said anything bad about Randy before tonight. Why now?"

"I'm not saying anything bad about my husband specifically. Randy is an awesome guy and the best partner for me," Ellie defended. "That doesn't negate the fact that marriage is complicated sometimes."

Sammy agreed. Randy was the best guy for her sister. She wasn't sure, however, if Tim was the best guy for Heidi for the long haul. But it wasn't her call.

"It's just hard sometimes . . ." Ellie continued. "Anyone married for any length of time will tell you that. Marriage involves a lot of compromise."

"Yeah, look at where it got herrrrrrr." Heidi pointed to the magazine on the table. "Looks like marriage might have gotten that chick killed."

Chapter Seven

Sammy rolled over onto her stomach and fluffed her pillow before laying her head back down on the bed. Sleep was not coming easy. She lifted her weary body once again and eyed the neon clock on the small white pine bedside table: 6:44 AM. Bara was still at Ellie's. If her dog had been home, she would have ended the sleep struggle right then and there and gone for a walk. With Bara gone, there was no other reason to get out of bed that early. But her mind was restless.

Sammy had hoped to show the photo of the barrette on her cell phone to Ellie and Heidi at the restaurant to see if they could provide any insight. She'd felt it would be a long shot that they would recall anything, though, which is why she hadn't pushed the issue. After all, her sister and cousin had graduated high school two years ahead of her. They certainly wouldn't remember how she and Kate had crafted matching barrettes for the home-coming parade. She still couldn't comprehend why and how Jane Johnson would have had it in her possession.

When Sammy had returned home after dinner, she had immediately rustled through the back of her bedroom closet to find the old shoebox of high school mementos and matched the photo to her barrette—which now sat underneath a milk glass lamp on her night table beside the clock. Sammy reached for the hair clip. She spun it between her fingers and rubbed her thumb along the red-and-white braided satin ribbons.

Kate. How did she get yours? Talk to me, Kate . . .

The familiar conversation ended with a vacant stare at the ceiling.

Sammy's mind searched the memory of their past. Even though so many years had passed, she vividly recalled the day of homecoming when they were curling each other's hair with a hot iron in preparation for the big parade. Kate's long blonde hair was coiled like tiny ringlets similar to Shirly Temple's. The soft ribbons on the barrette hugged her curls and blew in the breeze as the girls danced and laughed atop the float through the parade route. And then the memory snuffed out and Sammy's eyes returned to the vacant ceiling.

The barrette was perplexing, definitely an unusual find. Sammy didn't know of any connection between Jane Johnson and Kate Allen, or the town of Heartsford, for that matter. She might have to consult the mayor to see if the family had ties to the author that she was unaware of. Because if Jane had had this in her possession, there certainly had to be a reason.

Unable to make a connection, Sammy's mind wandered to her cousin. She wondered how Heidi was feeling and hoped she wasn't scheduled for the early shift at the hospital. Was Tim really going to propose? With all these thoughts traversing her mind, it was obvious that slumber was not in her horizon.

Sammy reached for the remote in the pull-out drawer

underneath the nightstand and flicked on the television that sat atop a tall white dresser across the room. The early-morning news lit the screen, so she turned up the volume to hear the broadcast. She reached for an extra pillow and plumped it behind her so that her head was upright, able to view the program. The police chief of Heartsford, Dean Geary, was addressing a crowd of reporters. The program had obviously been taped the day of the murder and rerun for the early-morning viewers:

". . . No, we don't have a suspect in custody at this time."

". . . This is an active investigation, we will not be sharing those details at this time."

". . . This is an isolated case of a high-profile victim. No, we don't feel the community is in any danger."

". . . We will update the public in a formal press conference when we have more information to share."

With everything that was going on and everything she had been thinking about, Sammy had totally forgotten about the reporters. They would likely be hounding her, and she wouldn't be able to avoid them forever. But what would she say? This was certainly not something she felt comfortable with. Addressing the press? Goodness. How had she found herself involved in yet another murder investigation? And this one so high profile. *I must be a magnet for this sort of thing*, she thought.

Oh no.

That wasn't the only thing that had slipped her mind. Sammy sat upright in bed. Her parents were flying into Milwaukee today! Ellie and Randy were picking them up from the airport at eight thirty AM. For an upcoming book signing later in the week that was no longer taking place. Since her sister and brother-in-law had assumed Sammy would be overwhelmed preparing for the big event, they hadn't even asked her to tag along for pickup. She doubted her parents would cancel their trip. Meeting the bestselling author wasn't the only reason for their visit; they had friends and relatives to catch up with too. Now Sammy would have both her mother and overprotective Ellie to contend with. That was almost too much to take. She loved her mother and sister very much, but the two seemed to handle tough news in an equally dramatic fashion. Not only that, but now she would have two mother hens trying to block her from digging into the investigation.

This day would require much caffeine. She clicked off the television, flung the blue-and-yellow star quilt aside, and rose from the bed. She padded down the darkened stairs barefoot and didn't flip on a light until she hit the comfort of her familiar kitchen. Mechanically, she placed the filter, coffee, and water into the machine and pushed the button. The overwhelming feeling of missing Bara hit her hard. Her morning was so quiet without him to share a morning greeting. She'd have to go pick him up on her way to work. Besides, Ellie was probably more than ready to be rid of her pet and vacuum the house to remove all remnants of dog hair before the arrival of their parents. Since Sammy was out of bed earlier than usual, she could possibly take a few moments and walk with Bara over to the farmers' market for fresh berries before opening Community Craft.

Sammy's cell phone, plugged in to charge overnight, was sitting inactive on the counter when it suddenly lit up with a text message. Sammy wondered if she was right and Ellie was tiring of Bara already or if she was up early to clean the house in preparation for their parents' visit. She reached for the phone.

GOT A MIN?

The message was not from her sister. Surprisingly, it was from Detective Liam Nash.

Sammy lifted the phone and returned the text: YUP.

Liam: MIND IF I STOP BY?
Sammy: NOW??

She instantly looked down at her pink ribbed tank top (bra-less) and pink pajama shorts with red hearts scattered all over. This would never do. It was barely seven AM. What was he thinking? And what made him think she was even out of bed?

GIVE ME A FEW MINUTES

Sammy rushed from the kitchen to the front of the house toward the oak staircase. When she reached the bottom step, instead of climbing upward to change clothes, she turned and instinctively moved into the small living room to the front window. She conspicuously peeked between the slats of the white wooden blind. The detective's car was already parked in her driveway. She dropped the blind and rushed up the oak stairs.

Sammy flung open the top drawer on her elongated white bureau, pulling the glass knobs hard, almost unscrewing the stripped knob on the left side. She thought about screwing it back on so it wouldn't fall off, but knew she didn't have time just then. She pulled out the first bra she could get her hands on. Sammy wrangled the pink tank top over her head and tossed it on the unmade bed. After snapping her bra shut in the front, she wiggled out of her pajama shorts and retreated to the dresser drawers to remove a clean white ribbed tank top and added a pair of faded overall jean shorts. She capped her head with a white baseball hat and pulled a makeshift ponytail out the back, tucking any remaining hair underneath. After blowing her breath into her hand, she rushed into the bathroom and brushed her teeth. One look at her reflection, and she frowned. *Not even close to presentable . . . especially for Nash.*

She reached into the mirrored cabinet above the sink and dug out crushed makeup that was almost empty. Inside the makeup case were barely a few crumbs of blush and an applicator that should have been dumped a long time ago. For the second time that week, she felt relief for her lack of organization because there was no time to run back downstairs to retrieve blush from her purse where she had left it in the kitchen. She had just enough blush to coat her cheeks rosy and added strawberry lip balm that was also on the verge of empty. The gel was down to the rim. She was able to dig out enough for one more application and then tossed the empty tube into the bathroom trash.

Sammy looked in the mirror again, adjusted her ball cap one last time, and then rushed back down the oak stairs. She flung open the front door, pushed through the screen door, and stepped outside barefoot. The early-morning sun was warm, but instead of a nice dry day, there was a hint of sticky humidity. She tapped on the detective's car window to gain his attention. He was leaning over his cell phone, enthralled in either a text or social media. He looked up and smiled.

Sammy stepped aside to give the detective room to open his car door. Instead of giving him a proper greeting, Sammy groaned, and a look of disapproval washed across her face. "I haven't even had coffee yet. What gives?" She laughed, then, to lighten the mood and show that she was teasing.

"If you start a brew, I'd take a cup." He grinned wide and then took hold of her shoulders and lightly pointed her back in the direction of her front door.

Even though Sammy loved the feeling of his soft touch, she shrugged him off and threw up her hands in defeat before the two retreated up the concrete stoop and through the dark-blue doorway of her rented Cape Cod.

"Well, I can already smell it. It seems to me the coffee is already brewing. How's that for investigative work?" Liam teased. "Where's the pup? I figured you'd be up early to let him out. That's why I took the initiative to stop by so early." The detective's eyes bounced along the floor in search of Bara.

"He spent the night at Ellie's," Sammy said over her shoulder as she led the detective into the kitchen. She reached into an overhead cabinet and pulled out two large mugs. The largest mugs she could find.

"I saw your light flick on. I knew you were up. Do you want the real reason I came over this early, though? I drove by your house this morning to scare off the press. They were scattered all over your front lawn ready to pounce. You're welcome."

"Oh? I didn't even hear a thing. Although I did have the television on this morning; I was watching Chief Geary. They replayed his interview for the morning crowd. Maybe that's why I didn't hear any commotion."

"Chief Geary was only the beginning. By the rumble of things I'm hearing, sounds like there will be several interviews; the press can't get enough of this story. They're perched all over town like hawks. That's why I took the initiative to drive by your house. There's another press conference scheduled outside the police station later this morning. Because of the high-profile nature of the crime, there'll be multiple news updates throughout the day. I'm sure it'll take a few days until this thing blows over. You really need to be careful not to get caught up in it. I wanted to be sure you didn't share anything with the news media—I mean *any* of our findings. It's very important you keep quiet. Mum's the word. No talking. Zipped lips."

"I got the message," Sammy interrupted him. She quickly turned around to face him squarely. "You really think I would do that?"

"Not intentionally." He must have sensed her growing agitation, because he moved closer, pointed to the mugs, and said, "Why don't you fill those first, and then we'll talk." He smiled wide enough to show that tooth on the bottom that jutted out ever so slightly.

Sammy shot him a glare but inwardly agreed. She could feel a tension headache building, and the day hadn't even started. She filled the two large mugs as directed, reached into the refrigerator for French vanilla creamer, and topped them both off. She handed him a mug and then lifted hers.

"Cheers," Sammy said as she blew into the steaming brew and took a much-needed sip. She felt the warm liquid instantly soothe her, but she held up her finger to the detective as if to say, *Just give me a few more minutes*, and took a few more sips, reveling in the silence between them. When she felt ready to speak, she said, "So . . . is that the only thing that brings you here? The press?"

"Of course not. Free coffee." He winked and raised the mug to his lips.

Sammy cracked a smile. "Good one."

"No. It wasn't just the coffee and the privilege of seeing your bright and smiling face first thing in the morning," he said teasingly as his smile widened.

Liam's smile sent a shiver zipping down Sammy's spine. She hated that she couldn't stop her body from reacting to his charm. There was just something about him. Something that made her want to stare into his sleepy bedroom eyes. Even when he annoyed her by showing up at her house before her first cup of coffee. He was quite obviously a morning person.

"You never came to the station to fill out the incident report like I asked. Twenty-four hours, remember? Most people forget important details after that. The more details you can provide, the better . . . for my investigation. I have the paperwork in the car." He jutted a thumb in the direction of the front door.

"It hasn't been twenty-four hours yet. I still have time," Sammy argued as she gazed at the antique clock on the wall that hung over the small kitchen table in the corner. "But I caught that. *Your* investigation," she teased, hoping to take his temperature and see how far she could push.

"Yes. *My* investigation," he confirmed as he nodded affirmation and smiled. Then the detective took a sip of coffee.

Sammy didn't fling back a retort. Although she wanted to.

Instead, she remained silent. Let him have his way, she decided. If he really thought she wasn't going to be doing any investigating of her own into the murder of author Jane Johnson, though, he was sorely mistaken.

"I'll have one of the officers or the chief address the press specifically regarding you and your lack of involvement in the case. I will also advise him to share the obvious, which is that your book event for Saturday has been canceled. Your best bet, if journalists continue to seek you out, is to say 'No comment.' After a while, they'll tire of asking and stop bothering you. Plus, if you stick to 'No comment,' there's no chance of leaking something that would jeopardize the case unknowingly."

"Okay." Sammy took a moment to absorb the message being conveyed. "I was actually thinking of posting the pictures of the barrette on Facebook to see if anyone recognizes it. Bad idea?"

"Very bad idea."

"May I ask why? I mean, I don't have to share *where* we found the barrette. We just have to find out where it came from. Someone had to have given it to the Jane. Maybe it would convince whoever it was to seek me out?"

"It may or may not be a link to the case. However, if it is, and you put that out on social media, you could potentially be encouraging a murderer to hide underground like a groundhog in winter."

"Oh. I never thought of that." Sammy took another sip of her coffee and considered. "Are you telling me I can't investigate why Jane had Kate's barrette in her possession?"

"No, I'm not saying that exactly. I'm just saying that it needs to be handled delicately. Listen, Samantha, I know your heart is in the right place. But when you get overzealous and jump into an investigation with both feet, I'm the one who has to rescue you from drowning. Just remember that . . . and think long and hard before you act." The detective leaned his arm casually on the white tiled countertop.

"I think you're confusing my sometimes impulsive behavior with overzealousness. I like to think of it more as tenacity, which can be a good thing, no?" she said to lighten the growing tension in the air.

"Yes . . . your tenacity just has to be channeled better," he said, with firm finality on that subject.

"Did you ask Mayor Allen if his family had any personal ties to the Queen of Crafts? Or if Kate'd ever met her?"

"I did. And the answer is no. I would also appreciate it if you don't poke the mayor about this, Samantha. If there *is* a possible link . . . This is his daughter we're talking about. We need to be sensitive."

"You're telling *me* to be sensitive?" Sammy's eyes narrowed in confusion as she jutted a thumb at her chest. "About *my* best friend and her family? I think I know how to handle myself, detective. *Especially* with the Allens."

"Yes, I know that. That's not really what I'm saying." He must have known he'd hit a nerve, because he paused before he continued with his train of thought. "What I'm trying to say is, I'm the one who has to make sure the person who is responsible for Ms. Johnson's murder is actually brought to trial and is ultimately convicted. If you mess with my investigation, I could lose important information that might solidify my case. I have to be sure all my evidence holds up through the rigorous judicial process. There can't be any flaws; it has to be a solid case to bring a perp to justice. Just consult with *me* first before you go snooping around and messing with evidence that you could taint and make inadmissible." He leaned his head back, emptied his mug, and then placed it on the counter.

The caffeine must have kicked in, because instead of feeling irritation at his comments, Sammy actually agreed that he'd made some valid points. Things that she might have not thought of. She agreed that she tended to be a bit on the impulsive side. Or tenacious. She liked to think of it as tenacious—a much better connotation.

"Will you help me draft the right message to use on the Community Craft Facebook page, to share condolences and announce the cancellation of the author's book signing event?"

The detective seemed noticeably pleased by her agreeable demeanor. "Sure. I'd be happy to do that."

"By the way, are you going to let me read Jane's unpublished manuscript?" When Sammy had discovered the drafted pages at the Pine Haven Bed and Breakfast, the detective had immediately covered the box, taken possession of it, and held it confined as evidence. Which had really pissed her off. There could be clues within those printed pages!

"I have to confirm that I can share it with you. This is my first high-profile case. I'm going to have to clear it with the chief, who probably has to clear it with Jane Johnson's agent. Things need to go through the proper channels and be handled delicately in this investigation. I will, however, put in a good word for you, and since you and your S.H.E. group helped with the last big case in town, he might consider it. But you'll probably have to read it at the station. I doubt if he'll let you take it home."

The detective combed his hand through his dark wavy hair and patted it down, even though it didn't need adjusting. His long curls that had recently been cut short stayed in place with a slight wave, yet he still ran his fingers through his hair as if he'd forgotten the curls were no longer there.

Sammy was pleased with his answer. The fact that he would put in a good word for her with Chief Geary gave her hope. Maybe he was warming to her help after all? The manuscript pages could bring a whole new insight into the investigation. "Did you take a look at it?"

"I scanned the first few pages. I wouldn't get too excited, as I doubt you'll find anything of interest or value . . . I certainly didn't. I didn't read it all the way through yet; the text revolves around the history of crafts through the generations, though. We did find a laptop in her rented car, but I had to give it to the computer lab since it was password-protected. She might have more written and just didn't print it all. Who knows?"

Sammy didn't think *he* would find anything within Jane's writings. He hadn't even known she was a bestselling author. But she was sure there was something of interest within those printed pages.

After finishing up the last drop of coffee, Sammy placed her mug next to his on the counter. "If you give me a minute, I'll go grab my laptop from upstairs. We can work on that social media post. Are you in a rush to get out of here?"

"I do have a meeting later this morning." His eyes glanced to the kitchen clock. "I have a little more time before I have to leave, though. While you get your laptop, I'll run to the car and get the paperwork for your formal statement." The detective raised himself from the counter and stood upright. He lifted his arms above his head, stretched his back, stifled a yawn, and then retreated to the front door. Sammy noted that she wasn't the only one who seemed sleep-deprived. Seemingly, he just had a better outlook in the morning.

Sammy rinsed the coffee mugs and set them aside in the deep farm sink. She then rushed from the kitchen and beelined up the stairs. If she were being honest, she wanted to quickly find out who had given Jane the barrette. She needed to talk to that person, since it seemed obvious that it must be someone connected with Heartsford. But if she had impulsively pursued that angle, she might have blown the whole case, as much as she hated to admit that. Maybe it was this impulsive nature of hers that was keeping her relationship with the detective from moving forward. Or . . . maybe now she was in a hurry to dive into a relationship before her cousin went off and got married and left her the only one in their tight group of three still single. Her head was spinning as she made her way to the bedroom. She reached for her laptop bag tucked beside the dresser, threw the thick black padded strap over her shoulder, and headed back in the direction of the stairs.

Sammy overheard the detective talking on his cell phone as she rounded the bottom step. She stopped dead in her tracks, trying not to creak the old floorboards, and held her breath so she could eavesdrop on what he was saying.

"The phone just pinged off a tower in Nebraska?"

Nebraska? How would Jane's phone be in Nebraska?

As the detective paced through the kitchen, he turned and noticed Sammy standing at the base of the stairs.

"Yeah, that's a great lead. Good. Yes. I'll be there shortly." Nash clicked off the call and looked up. "Oh hey. You're back," he said as Sammy grew closer.

"You want to tell me what that was about?"

The detective shook his head and smirked.

"Anything you want to share?" Sammy pressed again innocently as she placed the laptop bag on the kitchen island, unzipped it, and removed her computer. While the laptop was booting up, she leaned back against the kitchen island, folded her arms across her chest, and met his eyes directly. "Well?"

"We haven't found Jane's cell phone, but we've been scouring her phone records. The phone was turned off. We assume, according to the timeline, that was done shortly before the murder. Either she shut it off herself, or someone removed the battery. We're also following up on leads from her last incoming and outgoing calls."

"So the killer left Wisconsin? And is heading west? Interesting . . . What else have you found on her cell records? Who was the last person she spoke with? And how long did the call last?" Sammy lifted her back from the kitchen island and stood erect, her interest piqued.

"I didn't say anything about her phone being out west." He eyed her carefully. "I can't tell you that now. But there are a few interesting details I need to follow up on. That's all I'm going to say until I learn more and clarify a few things."

"Come on . . . *please?*" She hated to beg, but this was an interesting lead in the case. One of the biggest so far.

"No," he said firmly. "And don't think I'm not aware it was your cousin who found Ms. Johnson's phone case in the river. You really thought Officer Maxwell wouldn't share that information with me?"

Sammy ignored the detective's comment, as she'd known that information would probably find its way back in her direction and Tim would have to share it with Liam anyhow. Instead, she shook his arm to plead with him. "Who was her last call? Did she talk to her ex-husband? I bet her phone is on its way to his house. Doesn't he live somewhere in California or something? He couldn't have flown home; the airlines would track his flight and his escape would be a dead giveaway." Sammy didn't know where Jane's ex lived, only that they had been recently spotted together as she was leaving a boutique hotel off Hollywood Boulevard.

"How do you know so much about that?" The detective's eyebrows came together in a frown.

Sammy reached for her purse, removed the magazine Ellie had given her at the Corner Grill, and slapped it on the counter. "She's a celebrity. Everybody knows."

"I'm in the process of checking her ex-husband's alibi to confirm his whereabouts. He actually resides in Colorado, not California, so it's going to take a few days as we confer with the Denver Police Department."

"Do you think it was him?"

The detective shrugged. "We always check those closest to the victims first. You know that. But I'm not really sure if the guy was dumb enough to murder his ex-wife when his face is plastered all over that magazine. And besides, he'd have to know he'd be a prime suspect, with a restraining order filed against him. Time will tell. I have a feeling I'll probably be making a trip to Denver to interview the guy myself. Can I count on you to stay out of my investigation while I'm gone?"

He placed his hands on his hips and waited patiently while Sammy remained deathly quiet. She really didn't want to make a promise that she knew wasn't remotely possible to keep.

Chapter Eight

After retrieving Bara from Ellie's house and dodging the press in the back parking lot of Community Craft with Detective Nash's suggestion of 'No comment,' Sammy was finally ready to begin her workday. Immediately upon entrance to the store, Bara sauntered to his dog bed beside the register and curled up comfortably. Her nephew Tyler had noticeably worn him out on his overnight visit. Sammy stifled a yawn. The early morning and restless night of slumber had her struggling, too.

The tinkle of the back bell attached to the door caused Sammy to lift her weary hazel eyes toward the back entrance. She noticed the top of Deborah's familiar dark head as she struggled to juggle a large brown box and handful of keys through the door. Sammy rushed to her aid.

"Thanks. I brought new inventory. Since the other painted glasses aren't selling, I thought I'd swap them out. Hope that's okay with you." Deborah's voice sang out from behind the box as if the cardboard itself was speaking. Although Deborah's arms were thin, the petite woman had the strength of an ox due to her former profession as a ballerina. She gracefully set the box down and then wiped a bead of sweat that trickled from the side of her straight black hair parted perfectly down the middle. "Woo . . . It's getting hot out there." She removed a hair elastic from her wrist and gathered her hair into a makeshift bun atop her head, then fanned her face with her hands.

"Yeah, the humidity is rising, huh? Bummer. Yesterday was so nice; too bad it couldn't last. I can't wait to see what you brought!" Sammy clapped her hands together in delight like a small child about to receive a present.

Deborah smiled, popped open the box, and lifted out a bubble-wrapped painted wine glass. After removing the wrap, she held it in her right hand for inspection. "Palm trees. And I mixed hues to paint the bottom teal to look like tropical water. Hey, some of us landlocked homesteaders can dream."

"Those glasses are lovely! That design definitely makes me want to sit with a cocktail poolside." Sammy nodded. "Let's shelve them right away."

Deborah handed Sammy the unwrapped glass to carry and then retrieved the jam-packed box from the floor. The two turned toward the shelf that displayed the current inventory of painted glasses. As Deborah began to remove the outdated pieces, Sammy placed the wine glass that was in her hand onto the shelf as a replacement.

"I've been thinking about you." Sammy tapped a pointer finger to her lips. "I have an idea, and I want to pick your brain. I know I've got you crazy busy with leading the painting class, painting these beautiful pieces to sell here in the store, *and* working for me part-time, but I have an idea for something fun and uplifting for our community, too. I thought about it yesterday when I was walking along the river. Especially now with the latest catastrophe, Heartsford is going to need a refocus. We *all* are going to need something fun to look forward to. I know I definitely need a distraction."

"I was sorry to hear about that." Deborah instinctively reached a dainty French-manicured hand to Sammy's arm. "Are you okay? I heard you found Jane Johnson by the waterfall. How awful!"

"Yeah. Seriously hard to believe. I literally just met her, and then . . ."

The two shook their heads in dismay.

"She was so loved, too, had so much going for her. It's definitely going to be strange no longer having the official craft queen to aspire to! To be honest, Jane is the reason I picked up crafting. She really inspired me. Especially when my kids were little and I stayed home with them so much. Crocheting and painting have been my outlet." Deborah tucked a loose strand of hair that had fallen from her bun behind her ear.

"Yes. She inspired a lot of our artisans here." Sammy waved her hand around the store to highlight the vast selection of handmade items that beautifully surrounded them. "By any chance, do you remember if she ever wrote a book on how to make hair accessories? I mean, crochet brought her to the forefront of the craft world, but I know she published earlier books on other stuff."

"Now that you mention it, I think she did. Actually, I may still have it in my basement with a bunch of leftover stuff I moved from my mother's house when she went into the nursing home. Funny you should remember that. I forgot all about that hair accessories phase. Jane could take something plain like a hairpin and make it dazzle. Remember, she was the first one to start adding sparkle before that whole bedazzle craze? Everything now has a certain bling, but not back then. She really was a jack-of-all-trades. I think she gave Martha Stewart a real run for her money!"

"Do you think I could borrow the book? If you still have it."

"Of course. I'll look for it and bring it next time I stop in." Deborah adjusted another wine glass on the shelf and then bent back into the box to unwrap another from bubble wrap.

"Thanks." Sammy wondered if Kate had been inspired to make the braided hair accessory from one of Jane's early books, before her career really took off and she concentrated more on fiber art and crochet. Maybe that was how Kate had come up with the idea to make the barrettes for homecoming in the first place. It still didn't make sense, though, why the author would have the one Kate and Sammy had crafted together.

"I'm guessing you don't need me to help out Saturday since the book signing is officially *not* happening. Don't worry about it, Sammy. I don't really need the extra hours. Plus, with my boys out of school for the summer, I have my hands full."

"Oh, I hadn't thought of that. How are they adjusting to summer break?"

"Are you kidding? One week and they're already driving their mother crazy," Deborah laughed. "Can't you tell how frazzled I am? When does school start again? Luckily, my mother-in-law took them up north to the lake house for a few days, since I thought I'd be working overtime the rest of this week."

"Actually, I hadn't noticed. You? Frazzled? Not frazzled at all," Sammy said before the two shared a laugh. "Oh, wait, I never did tell you my latest idea. Let me tell you what I'm think-ing, and you tell me honestly whether you think it could work or not. If it's not doable, that's okay."

Sammy was just about to share her idea with Deborah when Marilyn from the Sweet Tooth Bakery rushed through the front door. She was carrying a carefully taped box the color of Pepto-Bismol, which Sammy thought she would probably need after diving in and gorging on the contents. Sammy knew what was inside, something tantalizing and sugary. Her teeth itched at the thought of it. If only her neighbor weren't so darn good at her job, Sammy's hips wouldn't be rapidly extending, and she wouldn't have to squeeze into her jeans. She looked down at her overall denim shorts that she hadn't changed out of due to her early-morning visit with the detective. She instinctively pulled the strap away from her shoulder. They were loose. She had room to binge.

Marilyn set the baked goods down on the polished pine cash register counter behind them and then thrust herself forward toward Sammy. The baker lifted her off the floor in a bosom bear hug and covered her with the smell of fresh baked goods. When Marilyn finally set Sammy back on her feet, she held her flabby arms out at length. *"Darlin'*, how do you always find yourself involved in such tragedies?"

The baker's overdramatic greeting caused Deborah to stifle a giggle. And she and Sammy shared a quick, inconspicuous smile.

Sammy placed her hand to her heart and turned to Marilyn after regarding the pink box by the register. "You brought treats for me? I'm fine. Really." Sammy did think it was kind of her work neighbor to always share her amazing talent. Even if it did add extra bulge to her waistline.

"Well, I brought you some cupcakes to sweeten your day. A little sugar will lift your spirits! With you finding more dead bodies and all, I thought you might need a treat, darlin'." Marilyn's stubby fingers moved to her overgrown hips. "Did they find out who killed her? I'm sure it's her ex-husband. Haven't you seen the goings-on between them on *Entertainment Tonight*? You know those restraining orders don't mean a darn thing to aggressive husbands. They keep on acting out and disregarding their wives like it's just a useless piece of paper. I just wish he didn't carry out his heinous act in our town! Disgusting. That's not how I wanted to be put on the map. It's bad for business! Now we'll always be known as the town where the Queen of Crafts died!"

Sammy and Deborah stood patiently as the baker rolled on endlessly about her opinions. When Marilyn finally wound down her diatribe, she looked at Sammy and said, "Well, did you?"

Sammy shook her head to get rid of the cobwebs. She had a way of instinctively tuning out some of Marilyn's musings. "I'm sorry, did I . . . ?"

"Yes, darlin'! Did you ask that cutie detective if the abusive husband has been detained? We need safety in this town. Not some deranged lunatic wreaking havoc upon our streets!"

"I'm sure the Heartsford Police Department has a handle on it. They're very qualified and will continue to keep the town safe, as they always do." Sammy tried to calm the overdramatic Marilyn but was pretty certain anything she said would fall on deaf ears.

"Well." Marilyn shook her head, disgusted. "I think you need your little S.H.E. team to gather and get this murderer out of our town!" She pointed her plump finger at the box of cupcakes.

"I hope you enjoy those. They *were* supposed to be the sample batch for Jane Johnson's book signing!" A cry caught in her throat. She wiped a tear from her eye. "I have to go, ladies . . . I have cinnamon buns in the oven." Marilyn turned abruptly and waddled out of the store.

Sammy and Deborah stood and looked at each other wide-eyed for a second. The overdramatic interruption had left both of them not quite knowing what to say. After finally getting her thoughts together, Sammy returned to the conversation they'd started before Marilyn's Academy Award–worthy appearance.

"I'm thinking of hosting a wine-and-cheese mixer on the library deck overlooking the flowers and the river. We could sell your hand-painted wine glasses for the event. I originally thought we could raise money for the Beautification Committee, but now I'm thinking we should do something to raise money for our book club. I was also thinking we should do something at the library in honor of Jane Johnson. Maybe our library director would consider adding a craft section, just for craft books. I've been bugging Jennifer about that for a few months now, especially since our club has expanded. Anyhow, could you create a special design specifically for the event? Maybe a floral pattern that could be more of a limited edition? You know, exclusive to the event? Exclusive products always make people bring out their wallets."

Deborah's eyes sparkled with delight. "I would love to create an exclusive glass!"

"You would?"

"Absolutely! And I love the idea of raising money in Jane Johnson's honor. I'd love to be a part of it! We certainly do need the funds for the book club too, since we've outgrown our loaned copies. I know a lot of members have been frustrated by the lack of renewals for books since we don't have enough copies; that hasn't been easy. I totally agree with you on that."

"It's settled, then. Let's plan this event. I can come up with another fund-raiser for the Beautification Committee. Maybe adopt-a-garden or something?"

"That's a great idea, and since we missed her book signing, the town can still pay homage to Jane and her great contributions to the craft book world."

"Exactly."

"Sammy, you always come up with the best ideas for the community to rebound out of tragedy."

"We have to set an example and show that the town of Heartsford can unite again even after this horrible tragedy. I'm sure Jane would have wanted it that way. Don't you think she'd want to be honored for her legacy to the craft world and not remembered for the horrific way she died?"

Deborah nodded in agreement.

"We could make the event casual dress. I'm thinking khaki shorts and polos for guys, sundresses for the ladies. We really need an occasion to bring everyone together." Sammy didn't share that she was also hoping this would possibly be a way to see Liam Nash, their newest resident, outside his detective role. He didn't seem to participate in the various community events outside of work, and she wanted to pull him out of his shell. Besides, he had seen Sammy dressed nicely only once . . . and that had been at Ingrid Wilson's funeral. Maybe if she was dressed to the nines, he would take notice of her?

"*Ohhh*, I've got an idea. How about live music, too? I'm sure we could find a local band?" Deborah's voice rose an octave with growing excitement.

"I like the live-music idea, especially if we host it in the community room and the doors are open to the outside deck. I'll ask my brother-in-law, Randy. I think his friend is in a band." Slow-dancing cheek to cheek with Liam Nash? Sammy's mind began to wander, but then she swiftly brought herself back to the present moment.

"This is going to be so fun!" Deborah clapped her hands together. "I'm already thinking of a new design. Maybe a rosebud? Or a hydrangea? Something summery, for sure. Thanks, Sammy; I have something to work on at home while the boys are away with my mother-in-law."

Sammy unwrapped the last two glasses from the box and handed them to Deborah. "Here's the last of them. If you don't want the box, I'll toss it in the workroom."

"Actually, I'll take it home. I can use it to pack glasses for our event."

"Good thinking." Sammy nodded.

While Deborah finished arranging the glasses, Sammy had a thought. "If the boys are up north, do you want to stick around a few hours now and work? I'd like to run an errand."

"Sure. No problem."

Sammy moved into the enclosed office behind the register and plucked her phone off the desk, revealing a text from her sister:

MOM AND DAD ARRIVED. DINNER AT MY HOUSE TONIGHT. JOIN US?

Sammy quickly texted back:

S<small>URE</small>. I'<small>LL BE THERE AFTER CLOSE</small>.

Sammy was glad to hear her parents had arrived safely and was looking forward to seeing them, even if her sister and mother's combination of anxiety-driven drama could reach insurmountable heights. Hopefully she'd be able to ease their worries after retrieving valuable information from the detective. She removed her oversized leather purse from a locked drawer, tossed her phone inside, and slung it over her shoulder. Before she left, she plucked the pink box off the cash register counter. She decided that instead of extending her own hips, she knew someone else who had a hard time resisting the Sweet Tooth Bakery's sweets: Detective Liam Nash. She was curious to see what other information he had learned since getting back to the police station. Maybe these treats would help him open up.

Chapter Nine

Sammy moved through the glass door of City Hall, where the town's municipal offices were located, balancing the cupcakes from the Sweet Tooth Bakery in one hand. As soon as she set foot in the lobby, she physically bumped into Heidi's boyfriend, Tim, and he caught the pink box like he was going for the winning touchdown.

"Whoa! That's not something you'd want to drop, little lady." He wiped his thick blond brow in jest. "Phew! That could have ended badly."

"Good catch. Sorry for the bump." Sammy rubbed her elbow where she'd collided with his rock-hard muscle. Obviously her elbow had done little to no damage on his end—he didn't seem bruised or injured in the least.

"Who are you sucking up to? The chief? Or Nash?" Tim smirked as he eyed the pink box in his hands. "I know it's unlike you to not rip that box open for your own guilty pleasure."

Sammy huffed audibly. Was she that transparent? Was it seriously that obvious? And *really* . . . had she gained that much weight that he assumed she couldn't resist a sweet treat?

"Well? Come on, which one are you trying to bribe with sugar?" Tim carefully handed the box back to Sammy and made sure she was holding it securely before he released his hold. "I know for a *fact* that box of sweet goodness isn't for me." He jutted a thumb at his chest. "You know I try to stay away from that place. You know sugar is like crack for your brain—it messes with you. I have to keep in shape for my job." He looked down at his fit chest. His uniform hugged a little too tight to his muscular arms as he flexed to show off his physique.

"Sure, but you can have a treat now and again. It's all about moderation . . . right?" Sammy didn't dare add that he was correct. Moderation hadn't been her discipline as of late. Although she'd never done "crack," she did agree that Marilyn's treats were hard to resist. "Just my way of thanking our law enforcement for serving and protecting our fine town. There are plenty of cupcakes to go around the station. I mean . . . depending on who's in the office today?" Sammy lifted on her tiptoes and peeked over his shoulder to glance inside the glass-enclosed police department within the municipal building.

"See. I knew you were looking for someone." Tim grinned. "Nash just left to pack a bag and head to the airport. He's following a case lead out of town. The chief is in a meeting with the mayor. And I'm on my way to pick up an early lunch to share with Heidi at the hospital."

"Oh." Sammy tried to not let her disappointment show as she sank back on her feet, but it was too late. Her cousin's boyfriend knew her too well to be fooled. "So, Detective Nash is on his way to interview the ex-husband? I'm guessing he's heading to Denver, then?"

Tim brushed her aside with one hand. Sammy quickly changed the subject so he wouldn't intentionally physically remove her from the building, back out the door and onto the sidewalk.

"How's Heidi today? I think we were a little loose with our drinks last night. Looser than normal, anyway. I am nursing a headache today." Sammy pressed her fingers into her forehead to ease the growing pain behind her eyes while balancing the box of treats in the other hand.

"She's fine. Working this morning. That's why I offered to drop off an early lunch. You guys went a little later than I expected at the Corner Grill, and we had a few things left to sort out last night." He placed meaty hands upon his lean waist. "But after leaving you two bad influences, she wasn't exactly in the talking frame of mind." His tone was a tease meant to poke fun, but Sammy could feel the underlying irritation in his words.

Ellie was right about one thing; it seemed Tim had plans in mind for Heidi and himself and viewed the two sisters as the endless cause of trouble. How wrong he was! Sammy's immediate reaction was to defend herself and her sister, but she held back. She decided not to push his buttons and get in the middle of their relationship issues or potential marriage proposal secrets. If Tim knew how much the three of them had actually shared at the restaurant, it might cause friction between him and Heidi, so she kept her opinions to herself and pressed on with her original reason for her visit to the station.

"Well, Liam mentioned that I could take a look at Jane's manuscript. He was going to talk to the chief about it. You know . . . he actually came over to my house this morning," Sammy stated, as if the two were in cahoots, which was of course a bit of a stretch. "Do you think I could take a peek now? It shouldn't take long for me to read."

Tim raised a hand from his athletic hips and placed it under his chin, then shook his head. "Sammy, Sammy."

"What?" Sammy looked up at the officer as innocently as a lamb. "He came to *my* house. Nash is the instigator here."

"You shouldn't be involving yourself in this investigation. Let us handle it. We're a little more than qualified."

Obviously, Tim wasn't buying what she was selling.

He then directed her eyes to his badge with a point of his finger. "I don't believe you wear one of these. This is a high-profile case, and *you* should be staying low profile. Catch my drift?"

Sammy groaned audibly and rolled her eyes. "You've been spending far too much time with that new detective. He's rubbing bad juju off on you. Listen, Tim. The famous author had something important to tell me about Kate. I have reason to believe the answer I'm looking for could be written within those pages you have in police custody. The early version of her newest manuscript could hold a significant message for me. This has nothing to do with the investigation and everything to do with Kate Allen, my dearest and incredibly missed best friend"—Sammy waved a finger between them—"who you and I both know meant a lot to this town." Her voice cracked with emotion.

She saw a look of compassion sweep across Tim's face. She knew she'd hit a nerve. *Everyone* loved Kate. Kate Allen was a huge part of the town's community spirit, and when she'd died, the lack of her presence had left a huge hole. Tim breathed in deeply and eyed her carefully.

To further convince him, Sammy added, "I'm sure, since the chief and the mayor are such good buddies, Chief Geary would want me to decipher any cryptic message about Kate. Especially since the message might be about the mayor's deceased daughter. Don't you think they'd want to know?" Sammy didn't dare tell him she hadn't been offered an actual *copy* but just a chance to read the pages. If Tim knew how valuable the early pages of a writer's manuscript were, he wouldn't dare let her peek. He wasn't much of a reader, though. What would he know about copyright laws and stuff? She doubted he had any expertise in the area of publishing.

After a moment of hesitation, he reached out for the box of cupcakes. "Give-y here, I'll take it to the staff room. Just wait here a few minutes." He held up a long index finger. "I'll see if I can get a copy made from the evidence pile if you're sure Nash said he was going to talk to chief about it. But despite my normal healthy eating habits, one of these little cakes has my name on it!" He licked his lips as she handed him the Sweet Tooth Bakery box. "Damn you, Sammy . . . you evil temptress," he said with a growing smile.

"Yeah, for sure, help yourself. Moderation is the key!" Sammy nodded.

She then remained tight-lipped as she watched Officer Tim Maxwell depart into the locked area of the police department. It really was amazing, the effect that Marilyn's sweet treats had on people. The tantalizing sweets could make people do just about anything . . .

*   *   *

With a copy of Jane's manuscript pages tucked deep inside her oversized purse, Sammy moved as rapidly as her short legs could carry her. She feared Tim would realize he might have made a colossal mistake, change his mind, and chase after her for the copied pages he had willingly handed over. When she reached the café with the "Deals of the Day" written on the sidewalk chalkboard sign, she ducked into the safety of Liquid Joy. The smell of rich dark coffee soothed her senses, and she breathed it in as she tried to catch her breath. Her eyes instantly met those of Douglas, the coffee shop owner, as she reached the coffee bar counter. He adjusted his dark-rimmed glasses and smiled.

"What can I get for you, Sam?" Douglas leaned his tall, lanky frame over the counter and wiped leftover spilled sugar into his hand with a wet rag. He then dumped the remnants and wiped his hands clean.

"Iced coffee and a raspberry-filled doughnut, please." Sammy tried to even her breath as she pointed to the pastry underneath the glass case. Since relinquishing her cupcakes to the police department, she was still jonesing for something sweet.

"What's got you out of breath this fine day?" Douglas reached for the sweet treat with a parchment-filled hand and carefully placed it inside a white paper bag.

"You know me. Always in a rush. Running here, running there." Sammy smiled wide.

"It's good to see you smiling after what you've been though." Douglas reached for the coffee and poured it over a cupful of ice.

"You heard?"

"Of course." He snickered. "Don't you know this is

Heartsford's gossip central?" Douglas pointed a lean finger around the room. "Best-of-the-best intel is right here."

Sammy nodded and smiled. "I see."

"I'm glad I got the chance to meet Ms. Johnson. You know, before . . ." His face twisted. It was obvious he was thinking about the murder. Douglas looked very uncomfortable at the thought of how the author had been found.

"Where did you meet her?"

"I delivered bagels and coffee to Pine Haven Bed and Breakfast the morning she arrived in town. She was sitting on the front porch with Ethan. A bit awkward at first, because it seemed I interrupted their conversation. But after a while, I was introduced. We spoke briefly. She tasted the coffee and said it was the best she'd had in a long time," he added proudly, and then smiled at the memory.

"She was sitting with Ethan? The *gardener*?"

"Yeah. They seemed deep in conversation when I pulled up to the house. Took a few minutes for them to acknowledge me when I reached the porch, to be honest. Actually, Ethan looked like he'd been crying. Totally weird." Douglas placed the iced coffee and paper bag atop the glass counter. Sammy dug into her purse and tried to inconspicuously move the manuscript out of the way to fish for her wallet.

"Did you happen to hear what they were talking about?"

"Sam, you know I tune out gossip. Rumors all around me, all the time . . . it gets old." He waved a dramatic hand across the emoji-painted walls. "When you only hear part of a conversation, you never get the full truth. For example, all I heard Ms. Johnson say was the word 'research,' and Ethan said, 'Yes, I was there.' What am I supposed to make of that? None of my business. And none of yours either. Best to stay out of it." Douglas nodded, causing his eyeglasses to shift. He pushed them back into place with his index finger.

"I suppose," Sammy agreed. But her mind couldn't help but wander. What would Ethan be doing with Jane Johnson? And what kind of discussion with a complete stranger could end in tears?

Chapter Ten

The afternoon passed swiftly within the confines of Community Craft as the customers' relentless bombardment with questions about the latest tragedy in the small town swung in and out of the establishment's doors and bounced around its walls. Sammy was thankful that her part-time employee had agreed to stay the rest of the afternoon to lend a hand. If nothing else, Deborah was a great buffer to help ease her through the trenches of town gossip. Sammy had the feeling that if she added up the actual sales that had been rung up that day, she'd be sorely disappointed. Yes, the store was busy, and the afternoon passed quickly. But, unfortunately, it wasn't for the right reasons. Sammy was resigned to the fact that Community Craft would probably be a revolving door for the next few days until news of the tragedy sank in; eventually the shock of the murder would fizzle out. From the chatter of the customers who passed through the store, evidently Detective Nash wasn't the only one following the story west. There was a leak somewhere, and journalists were chasing down the ex-husband for answers . . . even *before* the detective made it out of town.

At the end of the day, Deborah left Sammy alone to close Community Craft with a promise to return the next day, which eased Sammy's mind tremendously. At least she wouldn't have to deal with the chaos all on her own. After unlocking the office desk, Sammy reached for her purse and peeked inside longingly. She was eager to read the pages of the manuscript. Regrettably, the day hadn't offered a moment to think, let alone read. As she eyed the clock on the office wall, she blew out a frustrated breath because, again, it would have to wait. As much as she wanted to dig into the pages, she was running late for dinner with her family at Ellie's house, and it wouldn't be fair to keep them all waiting. After all, she still had to drop Bara off at home because she wasn't sure just how late dinner would go, and besides, she was sure that after Ellie had cleaned the house, her dog wouldn't be welcome to tag along. She flung her loaded purse over her shoulder and patted it, knowing that she would scan the pages later. Even if she had to stay up way past her bedtime.

"Come on, pup," Sammy said after she reached his dog bed, and Bara immediately obeyed. He stretched his hind legs before following her out the back door. "I don't think my sister is going to let you visit again, so I'm taking you home first." His ears flopped, and she swore it looked like his face had fallen because he wasn't invited to the party. "Next time," she said, which seemed to perk up his attitude.

The drive to Ellie's house didn't take but a few minutes, since her sister lived just on the other side of downtown Heartsford, off Monroe Avenue. The excitement of seeing her family reunited again began to build and brought a smile to her lips. They hadn't been all together as a family since Christmas. Sammy noted how, as she had grown older, time had seemed to pass rather quickly. How had six months gone by seemingly without a blink of an eye? Although she missed her parents at times, she had found comfort in the fact that they were enjoying their retirement in the warm air of sunny Arizona and didn't have to battle the endless Wisconsin winters. The fact that Heidi's parents had followed them and retired in Arizona too and lived only a few houses away was an extra bonus that seemed to tighten the extended-family bond.

Though Heidi's parents—Sammy's Aunt Beatrice and Uncle Bill—weren't expected to fly into Wisconsin and join Sammy's parents this particular trip. Aunt Beatrice had never had much interest in what she referred to as "the hoopla of Jane Johnson," and as a retired farmer, her interests lay more in horticulture, generational food recipes, and animals. *Anything other than crafts*, her aunt would have said. Since she spent endless hours canning vegetables from their garden, she never had leisure time to take up something as frivolous (in her mind) as crafts. There was talk that her aunt and uncle would be coming east to visit sometime during the summer months, but to Sammy's knowledge, no firm plans had yet been made.

Sammy pulled her car into her sister's driveway and noticed with surprise that Heidi's car was already occupying the right side. She watched as Heidi stepped from her recently purchased red two-seater Pontiac Solstice and fluttered her hand in a friendly wave. After turning off and exiting her much inferior vehicle, Sammy greeted her cousin with a quick hug.

"Hey, I wasn't expecting to see you here tonight. How are you feeling?" Sammy's eyes narrowed as she studied her cousin's expression carefully.

"What do you mean? Am I still hungover? The answer is no. A little ibuprofen and extra water throughout the day, and I'm good as new." Heidi elbowed Sammy's ribs playfully.

"No, I mean, did you work things out with Tim? Did you guys get a chance to talk over your early lunch?"

"How did you know about that?" Sammy didn't miss Heidi's look of surprise.

"I quite literally ran into Tim today inside the municipal building. He saved me from a near disaster. I almost dropped a box of Marilyn's cupcakes upside down." Sammy grimaced.

"Oh? And what were *you* doing there? And with treats, too?"

Sammy shook her head. She had a feeling she knew where her cousin was going by the tone of her voice. "No. No. No." Sammy waved a finger. "Liam is out of town, and we can talk about that lack of romance later. But right now, I want to talk about you. Is everything okay with you and Tim? You two good?"

"We're fine. Why would you ask?" Heidi's usual teasing nature turned suddenly serious.

"Don't you remember our talk last night about Tim possibly . . . you know . . ." Sammy lowered her voice and moved closer to Heidi's ear, even though no one was in earshot. "Proposing?"

Heidi's eyes suddenly widened, and she gasped. "We talked about that?"

"Boy, I guess you had more wine than I thought." Sammy stepped back, a bit surprised. She couldn't think of a time Heidi had lost memory from drinking. Had they seriously had that much?

"Yeah. I guess I did overindulge." Heidi's neck flushed, and then the crimson reached her ears. "I shouldn't have brought that up. I mean about Tim. I was totally overreacting." Heidi tried to downplay the entire episode, but to Sammy it seemed like a cover-up. Had she indeed been overreacting? Or was she trying to play it off like it was nothing so she could avoid the inevitable and not actually have to talk to Tim about it? Sammy was confused. One look at Heidi's face, and she decided to let her cousin sweep it under the table. For now. She hoped to get a chance to warn Ellie to not bring it up either, as it seemed a raw issue. It was unusual for their relationship, though. Sammy had thought she and her cousin confided in each other about everything; nothing had seemed off-limits until now, which gave her slight pause.

The burgundy front door of Ellie's two-story white Colonial swung open, and Sammy's mother came running out with arms flung open wide for an instant embrace. "How're my girls?"

Megan Kane wrapped herself in the middle of Sammy and Heidi in a death grip, and when she finally released them, she held the two lovingly in the gaze of her smoky-gray eyes. Sammy noticed her mother's hair had gained a few additional small clusters of gray where the original auburn hair had once waved naturally by her ear.

"Hey, Aunt Megs. Good to see you." Heidi smiled and wrapped an arm companionably over Sammy's shoulder. "I've been watching over this one. Not to worry," Heidi teased. "I've been keeping her out of trouble per usual."

Sammy sent a playful warning glare at her cousin.

Megan Kane at once bit at the comment by throwing her hand to her heart, a worried expression instantly washing over her face. "I'm glad to hear that, Heidi. My *daughter* needs to stop finding dead bodies. Especially the body of someone who is so high profile and adored! Tell me she hasn't involved herself any more than necessary in this tragedy!"

"Way to go, Heidi," Sammy muttered under her breath. They hadn't even entered Ellie's house yet, and it was already starting. "Mom, you say it like I chose to find Jane Johnson's body on purpose. Maybe this is happening because the universe knows I have a gift."

"A gift? For what? Morbid disaster?"

"No. A gift for seeking and finding the truth." Sammy defended herself with bright confidence. She was going to find out who'd killed the famous author and why. There was no doubt about it. She patted her oversized purse where the manuscript lay secretly waiting for her.

The garage door suddenly rolled open, nudging the three to maneuver through the parked cars and make progress up the driveway. Ellie stood just inside the garage's interior door. "Come in this way so you guys can leave your shoes on the doormat."

"See? Why can't you be more like your sister? These are the things a woman of your age should be concerning yourself with. Cleanliness. Not morbid disasters!" Megan nodded a head of approval at Ellie, who stood at the door watching to be sure Heidi and Sammy actually removed their shoes. Normally they chose to ignore Ellie and blow past her, but today Sammy's mother was paying attention, so they performed the shoe removal as requested.

"What? Obnoxiously clean and anxiously neurotic?" *And what was that crack about women her age?* Sammy wanted to add, but she remained quiet about that one.

"And . . . what's with the outfit, Samantha?" her mother asked with disdain. "Please tell me you did *not* go to work dressed like that."

Sammy absorbed her mother's disapproving stare as she tried to explain herself. "I had an early visitor this morning—the detective, actually. I didn't have time to shower." She self-consciously adjusted the baseball hat that had clung to her head since that morning and shoved the strands of hair that had frizzed and fallen during the humid day inside the cap.

Her mother gave her a disapproving shake of the head. "That's not the way you should be dressed at Community Craft. Even if it is your store. You should be setting an example for your vendors and employees. Just because you live in a farm town doesn't mean you should dress like you just came out of the fields. Look how pretty your cousin looks," she said, pointing a finger in Heidi's direction.

Sammy followed her mother's gesture. Heidi always looked cute. It didn't matter that she was dressed in a pale-pink sundress with matching slings. She could be dressed in a paper bag and look good. Sickening.

"What were you meeting with the detective about, anyway? Was he telling you to stop nosing around? Or does he think you were involved?" Megan Kane kept the pressure on like a tight squeeze.

"Seriously? Why do you always think the worst of me?" Sammy muttered under her breath. She couldn't believe how quickly her excitement to spend time with her family had waned. Was everyone's mother this difficult? Or just hers? Her mother seemed so much more loving when the relationship was handled across long-distance phone lines.

Heidi remained curiously quiet and didn't involve herself in the accusations flying between mother and daughter. Sammy was a little hurt. Wasn't anyone going to come to her aid?

As they entered the house, Sammy's father came to the rescue. "How's my sweet baby girl? Sammy!" Walter Kane brought his daughter in close for an embrace. She tiptoed up to reach the medium height of her father to speak in his ear, leaned in, and whispered. "A little help here with the missus, please?"

Sammy's father reached for his wife's arm. His chestnut-brown eyes narrowed. "You've already started with your criticisms, haven't you, Meg?" He rubbed his hands along his partially balding head. "Why can't you leave well enough alone? We hardly see the kids anymore; give it a rest already."

Megan stood aghast. "Oh, Walter. I'm the one who worries about our girls. Not you. You just act as if nothing bad is ever going to happen to them." She reached for her heart again and clutched it. "And how dare you say I'm critical? I'm just speaking the truth from my heart. By the way, Sammy has just informed us that she has a gift for finding the truth. Which she must have gotten from me." Megan then finally smiled a look of adoration toward her youngest daughter.

Funny how her mother could twist that in her favor. But Sammy realized that their time together was short. Soon her parents would be traveling back to Arizona and take with them the sometimes critical, often overprotective nature of her mother. Even though it could be frustrating and sometimes feel harsh, Sammy was perceptive enough to know that her mother's musings came from a place of fear and concern and not mean-heartedness. Sammy decided to play the peacemaker *this* time. Which was unusual for her. Usually she tried to defend herself. Maybe getting older did have its benefits. Picking battles. And maybe wearing earplugs.

The family gathered along a long handmade wooden table that Ellie's husband had recently built for the family's dining room. Randy had worked on polishing the gleaming salvaged barn boards in Miles Danbury's woodshop—Miles was a well-known woodworker in their town and a prized vender at Community Craft. Sammy couldn't help but drool at the craftsmanship.

"Randy, this turned out beautifully," Sammy acknowledged as she pulled out a metal folding chair, being cautious not to scrape their newly refinished hardwood oak floor, and carefully took a seat.

Randy smiled, the dimple on his chin caving, and he nodded his groomed head. His hair the color of golden platinum was always flawlessly trimmed thanks to Ellie's prodding. "Thank you. I learned a lot from Miles, and I'm anxious to get back in his shop to finish the benches," he added as he pointed to the metal folding chairs currently being used for the extra guests at the table. "Unfortunately, we'll have to improvise tonight."

Sammy's nephew Tyler ran to her, his reddish-golden curls bouncing, and he jumped in her lap with an animated expression. "Auntie Sam-eeee! I gots a new Lego from Paapaa!" Tyler suddenly thrust the plastic plane so close to her face it came dangerously close to her eye.

Ellie scolded. "Tyler. Be more careful! You just about took your auntie's eye out!"

Tyler responded with a pout of his lip. "Sowwy Auntie!" He jumped just as quickly from her lap and zoomed away from the table, propelling his new Lego plane up toward the sky with one arm in constant motion.

Ellie lifted her eyes and arms in frustration and huffed a breath. "Randy. Take care of your son."

Randy responded by saying, "Yeah. He's *my* son when he's acting out. He's *your* son when he's being a perfect angel."

Those who had gathered at the table joined in laughter. Heidi piped, "You married her, Randy! She's all yours!" Heidi winked at Ellie, who retorted with a scowl.

"Gee, thanks a lot, Heidi," Ellie said.

Sammy rose from the metal chair and gave her cousin a high five across the table.

Ellie then turned her scowl on her sister. "Seriously, you guys? You're supposed to be on my side."

Megan stood watching the antics and shook her head. "Isn't anyone else hungry? The aroma is making me want to eat, it smells so good. Ellie, dear, do you need any help in the kitchen?"

Ellie nodded. "Come on, Mom. I guess dinner is totally up to us. Let's get the food on the table."

The two walked off in the direction of the kitchen.

Sammy's father rubbed his protruding stomach that hung over his jeans and then took a seat at the table. "I, for one, am ready for dinner! Your mother doesn't make many home-cooked meals anymore now that we're retired. She expects me to fend for myself, if you can imagine."

Megan Kane's ears must have perked at the comment, and she yelled from the other room, "You poor, poor, poor man!"

Heidi's phone beeped a text, and she reached for it in her handbag below the table. She lifted her eyes from the phone and made eye contact with Sammy across the table. "Hey. You're not going to believe this. The police found Jane Johnson's cell phone and it was *not* with the ex-husband."

Chapter Eleven

"What do you mean, her ex-husband doesn't have the cell phone? Who else could possibly have it?" Sammy was astounded. She'd thought for sure that this particular part of the investigation into the murder of Jane Johnson would be pretty cut and dry. How else would the author's cell have escaped so far out west? *Someone* obviously had possession of it.

Heidi shrugged and slipped her phone back in her floral handbag under the table. "Beats me. That's all Tim sent in the text. I'll call him for the full scoop after we eat."

Sammy was sure it was against police policy to be sharing this kind of information. She was surprised Tim had sent that message to Heidi. Maybe he was just trying to impress her or get back in her good graces. Or maybe he felt obligated, since his girlfriend was the one who had found the expensive iPhone case. Either way, Sammy wanted whatever other information he had.

Ellie entered the dining room carrying a steaming lasagna, which instantly filled the room with an enticing scent. Her mother followed closely behind with a large glass salad bowl, which she carried carefully in both hands. "Ellie has outdone herself; hope you're all hungry," Megan said adoringly. "She already tossed the salad with a homemade Italian vinaigrette, and I sampled it in the kitchen. Personally, I think it tastes better than the Olive Garden; absolutely *divine*."

Sammy shared an eye roll with her cousin at her mother's constant praise of her sister.

Heidi leaned in across the table toward Sammy and whispered, "Eat fast, though, so I can make that call to Tim, because now I'm wondering what the heck is going on."

Sammy nodded and murmured conspiratorially, "Definitely."

"Call who?" Megan's ears perked to the whispers between cousins as she set the salad down and took a seat at the table beside her husband.

"Just Tim." Heidi smiled sweetly but didn't go any further for fear of getting her aunt riled up again about the case.

Walter rubbed his hands together in animated anticipation. "Supper smells divine, thank you, Ellie. Your mother used to make this all the time, but we haven't had lasagna in—gosh, I can't remember. It must be ages."

"Oh, and don't you look deprived and underfed. You poor dear," Megan snapped as she pointed to her husband's slightly bulging stomach that touched the edge of the table.

Sammy held her tongue. Her mother sure seemed a little over the top with her comments tonight. Maybe she was overtired from the flight or not feeling well. Or Sammy just wasn't used to being around her mother as much anymore.

Randy took a seat at the head of the table, and one by one, the family members passed him their plates as he cut a generous slice and loaded them up. "Dig in, everyone," he said finally when everyone's plates were filled with more-than-hefty portions.

Sammy blew on the food on her fork, then took a bite. Ellie had recreated their mother's recipe to a T, and the dish tasted exactly the same as it had in their childhood. "Nice job, Ellie. It's really good. Right, Dad?"

Walter closed his eyes and chewed slowly and thoroughly, enjoying the old family recipe as if he never wanted to wake from his dream state. "Just like I remembered. I want to enjoy this moment knowing my loving wife will never make it for me and I'll have to wait for our next trip back to Wisconsin to enjoy this state of euphoria again."

The whole table broke out in laughter, except for his wife, who merely rolled her eyes at his antics.

"I suppose you wouldn't be able to make this back in Arizona anyway, would you, Megs? We can't get flavorful cheese like this out in the desert. The cheese out there is absolutely horrid! Like eating plastic." Walter made a repulsed face.

"That's one thing we can agree about." Megan nodded her head in agreement. "If you want great cheese, you have to come back to the heartland. Tell you what, Walt. I'll pack some in freezer bags and tuck it in the suitcase for our return trip back home."

Walter looked at his wife affectionately. "You'd do that for me? Thank you, sweetheart."

Ellie was busy blowing on Tyler's food before the toddler could take a bite. "Me do!" he shouted at his mother, who gave up and handed him the spoon. She then cut up the rest of the food into miniature bite–sized pieces on his plate before touching her own.

As Megan passed the salad bowl to Sammy, she said, "I almost forgot. Guess who we ran into at the airport?"

Sammy waited for her mother to speak. After an obnoxiously long pause, she couldn't wait any longer and finally asked, "Who?"

"Bradley Schultz."

Bradley Schultz. Their neighbor from the old ranch house across town where the Kane girls had been raised, *and* the boy Sammy had crushed on all through her teen years. Sammy had desperately wanted to go on a date with him. But because they had grown up together, Bradley seemed to see her only as a sisterly neighbor and nothing more. Now Sammy fully understood her mother's distaste for her work wardrobe, she was worried Bradley would stop in at Community Craft and Sammy would look like farm help. Her mother seemed to think that she was quickly turning into an old maid. According to her mother, her pick of potential suitors for marriage was getting slim and soon she'd have to settle for divorcés or perpetual bachelors if she didn't get a move on.

"He's recently single. And boy, has he grown into himself. He is absolutely *gorgeous*," Megan added dramatically. "Right, Ellie?"

Ellie's face instantly flushed red, and then her eyes bounced to her husband. She shrugged it off, as if she hadn't noticed how gorgeous Bradley had gotten. But Sammy was sure she had noticed. She'd often thought her sister'd had eyes for their old neighbor, too.

"Anyhoo . . . I suggested he make a point to stop in Community Craft while he's in town. Bradley said he hadn't heard that you had taken over the store since Kate's death. He had no idea." Megan then took a small bite of food. "He's been working out east for a while now. His major in college was computer science. I think he mentioned he's a programmer?" she added between mouthfuls. "I guess he's making pretty good money."

"Thanks, Mom." Sammy wasn't exactly sure how she felt about seeing Bradley. Years had passed, and honestly, she had let him slip from her mind. Even though she scarcely dared admit it to herself, with Liam Nash in town, other men seemed to have recently squeezed out of her head. An interesting, tidbit, though to find out that her old crush was recently single.

Heidi's phone pinged, sending the eyes around the table looking in her direction. "Sorry. I didn't turn it all the way off." She leaned over, reached for it, and took a glance before turning the phone to silent. She then pushed out of her chair, stepped away from the table, and held the phone in one hand. "Sorry to be rude. This will just take a sec. If I ignore the messages, it'll just keep pinging until I respond. It'll be better if I just make a quick call."

"Is it the hospital calling?" Megan asked with concern. "Are you being called in for an emergency? Are they understaffed tonight?"

"Something like that." Heidi smiled and sent a look of warning to Sammy to not blow it, which meant it was probably Tim calling.

Even though the three S.H.E.s had grown to their midthirties, they still stepped around Megan Kane with kid gloves. Some things never changed. Sammy wondered how her mother had created that much power over them.

"Oh no. I forgot the dinner rolls!" Ellie said suddenly.

"No worries, my girl." Walter rubbed his full stomach. "I don't think we'd have room anyway."

Ellie shrugged. "I guess I'll save them for tomorrow's meal, then. Bummer." She slapped her hand to her forehead.

"I hope Heidi doesn't have to go. I was hoping we could all share dessert tonight out on the back patio while we catch up. I made a pie with the strawberries and rhubarb that Ellie picked up yesterday at the farmers' market," Megan said.

"Well, if she can't stay, I can eat her portion," Walter chimed in. "We don't get pie in Arizona either."

Megan took the back of her hand and slapped her spouse's arm. "That's enough out of you. You act as if I don't take good care of you."

Ellie and Sammy exchanged a smile. In an effort to rescue her sister and for a break from the parental banter, Sammy asked, "Mom, any chance you can watch Tyler tomorrow night? Ellie, Heidi, and I don't often get to hang out anymore, and I was thinking we could have a girls' night if you don't mind spending some time alone with your grandson?"

"Sure, I'd love to babysit. I only get to see my precious grandson a few times a year. Only if you're okay with it, Randy?" All eyes turned to Ellie's husband.

"I have my monthly meeting tomorrow night for the Heartsford Historical Society, and Ellie usually watches Ty while I'm gone. So that's really up to you folks to work out." Randy set his fork down and leaned back in his chair, satisfied. He turned his attention to his wife. "Great meal, honey. Thank you."

The rest of the table nodded in agreement with Randy's praise.

Ellie beamed at the compliment. "You're all very welcome. Sorry I forgot the rolls."

"If you will excuse me, I'm going to check on Heidi." Sammy pushed her empty dinner plate away from her and rose from the metal chair. Which caused her nephew to want to leave the table, too.

"Me play!" Tyler jumped from the table, and Ellie gave her sister a glare. "He wasn't done eating, Sammy. Why'd you have to rush?"

Sammy ignored her sister, left the table, and followed Heidi's voice out to the front step, where Heidi was talking on her cell phone. When Sammy arrived at her cousin's side, Heidi waved her away as if telling her not to interrupt the conversation. Sammy removed her socks, tossed them on the stoop, and then stepped barefoot out onto the grass. The shaded grass felt cool on her bare feet as she meandered over to a large oak, where Randy had built a tree swing for Tyler. Sammy sat down on the wooden slab and gave herself a light push. A soft breeze tickled her skin. She'd forgotten how much she loved to swing. As a child, the three S.H.E.s would spend hours at the neighborhood park plotting their next adventure as amateur sleuths. She smiled at the memory. She dug her heels into the compacted soil and gave herself a bigger push.

Heidi, now off the phone, ambled over to join Sammy and stood with a smile. "We had many a good day on those old swings off Highway 83, didn't we?"

"Yeah, you read my mind. Randy did a nice job on this . . . look how high I can go!" Sammy pumped her legs until she was soaring high above Heidi on the swing. "Whatever happened to that old park?"

"They tore it down when they built that industrial park a few years ago. Guess they didn't want kids traipsing around heavy equipment and stuff. And here I thought you'd be begging me for intel." Heidi laughed at her cousin's childish play.

"I'm ready to listen when you're ready to dish." Sammy kept pumping her legs as she teased her cousin. As if she didn't want the latest intel. Heidi knew her better than that, but if Sammy pushed, Heidi would clam up. Sammy was learning.

"Get off that thing so I can tell you. I think you're going to want to hear this."

The tone in Heidi's voice caused Sammy to slow the swing. When she came to a complete stop, she held on to the ropes and sat, waiting patiently. "Go ahead."

Heidi smiled. "Well, first of all, Tim is pissed at you."

Sammy didn't have to ask why. "Did he get in trouble?"

"Oh, he was reprimanded." Heidi flung a hand to her slim hip. "So, I had to use my girlish charm to get him to tell me what's going on, because he was more than hesitant."

"Why would he send you a text like that, then?"

"He did it on purpose. To get your goat. He knows I'm having dinner with you and the family. He also knew I would tell you about the text. He wanted to keep us hanging, but I threatened him to not play games with me. He knew the second he sent the text, we would call. Why would you do that, though, Sammy? You knew asking for a copy of Jane's manuscript would get him in trouble."

"That's not totally true. Detective Nash said I could see it."

"He said you could *see* it. Not have a copy! Anyway . . . did you read it?" Heidi's tone turned to one of curiosity. "Find anything interesting in those pages?"

"Not yet. I haven't had time. Work was insane with everyone coming into the store today to talk about the murder. I have it in my purse, and yes, I'm *dying* to read it. But I have to wait until I get home. You know Mom will freak if she hears I'm involving myself further. It's a lot easier to deal with her anxieties over the phone, not while she's here in the flesh. But it looks like she might watch Tyler tomorrow night, so you and Ellie can come over. We need to compile all of this information, put our S.H.E. heads together, and find out what the heck the author needed to tell me about Kate. Otherwise, I'll literally go insane. That's why I convinced Tim to give me a copy of the manuscript. Heidi, I need to figure this out."

"I know. Tim told me that's why he made a copy for you. I have a little nugget of information too that he shared . . ."

"Girls!" Megan stood at the front door, yelling across the front lawn to catch their attention.

Sammy thought it borderline hysterical that her mother still called them *girls*. If only . . .

Heidi and Sammy turned their focus to Megan Kane.

"Come back inside. We're going to grab dessert in the kitchen and sit out in the backyard. The weather is perfect, and Ellie just bought a new patio table she wants us to christen."

Heidi nodded, and Sammy stood from the swing. She reached out and held her cousin by the arm. "Tell me first. What have you got?"

"We'll be right there. Thanks, Aunty Megs!" Heidi turned

her attention back to Sammy. "Apparently they cleared the ex-husband. He had a solid alibi, so Nash is on a flight back to Wisconsin. They found the author's cell phone in Nebraska. The killer must have tossed the phone on a truck driving out of Wisconsin. When a delivery driver from Semco opened the back of the truck, the phone was lying there by the door. The guy turned it on, assuming it belonged to one of the Semco employees who had originally loaded the truck with equipment. That's why the phone was pinging off a tower out west. But the phone is password-protected, so he couldn't open it to see who the phone belonged to. When he called back to Semco in Wisconsin and talked to the guys on the loading dock, no one claimed the missing phone. Anyhow, being a good Samaritan and knowing it was the latest and greatest expensive iPhone, he dropped it off at the nearest police department, and voilà! Mystery solved."

"Yeah, one mystery. That only opens up more questions." Sammy let the information sink in. "Wait a minute. Semco is the large construction business on the opposite side of the river from the crime scene. I think they sell and distribute large equipment for paving or concrete. Do you think the killer worked at Semco and just ran back to work after he killed her? But then why would he leave her phone in the back of a delivery truck? Do you think he did it on purpose to have the police search in another direction while he made an escape? After all, we did find the phone case on that side of the river. Although it's hard to tell where along the river that case was dumped. Theoretically, it could almost have been dumped on either side and the water pushed it to land alongside that log."

"Why do you keep saying he? Do you think the killer is male?

What makes you think it's not a woman that killed her? Someone jealous over her success, maybe? I'm sure there's a lot of women out there who would *die* to be her."

"Girls! Come on!"

"I guess it's going to have to wait. Your mother's calling."

"Ugh." Sammy followed her cousin back to the front door. "Despite our age, some things never change."

Chapter Twelve

Sammy stepped out the sliding glass door leading to Ellie's backyard with a plate of pie topped with a dollop of fresh whipped cream in one hand and her cell phone in the other. Most of the family was already gathered around an elongated rectangular glass patio table shaded by an oversized aqua-colored umbrella. Except for Tyler, who was running in the grass attempting to kick a soccer ball back and forth with Randy. Tyler, mostly missing the ball every time his father kicked it toward him, chased the ball as fast as his precious pudgy little legs would carry him.

"What? No pie for my nephew?" Sammy took a seat on one of the brand-new matching aqua sling-back chairs and set her cell phone and plate on the table.

"He'll survive without it; he doesn't need the sugar. Grandpa bought him M&M's at the airport, which he devoured in the car this morning." Ellie shot a glare across the table at her father. "I don't know why my family insists on giving my son sugar. And even worse, first thing in the morning? I'm hoping Randy will wear him out so he sleeps tonight," she added before taking a bite of strawberry rhubarb pie.

"Beautiful patio set, Ellie. I really love the color." Megan's eyes bounced from the new umbrella above her head back to her husband. "We'll have to look for one when we get back to Arizona, right, Walt? The sun gets so unbearably hot, we don't sit out much. Especially in the summer months."

"I agree, I love the color." Sammy nodded. "Deborah recently displayed some new painted glasses at the store that would be perfect out here. The wine goblets are painted with palm trees, and the stem is pretty close to the color of this patio set. You'll have to look at them the next time you're in. They remind me of being on a tropical vacation somewhere exotic, just like your new patio set does."

This piqued Ellie's interest. "Oh? I'll definitely check them out next time I'm in. But don't tell Randy; we're trying to save money . . . but it's so hard!" she whined. "Especially when I love to decorate and play hostess."

"Maybe you should make decorating a side business," Megan suggested.

"Yeah, like I have time for that." Ellie flung a pointed finger toward the backyard, where Tyler and Randy were continuing their soccer game.

"That reminds me, I forgot to tell you my latest idea," said Sammy. "I'm planning a wine-and-cheese event at the library. Ellie, maybe you could help me with the decorations? Deborah is going to paint an exclusive wine glass for it. I can't wait to see what design she comes up with."

"Event?" Ellie asked. "When did you decide this?"

"Yeah? When is it? I'll definitely add it to my calendar. I like wine!" Heidi admitted easily. "And cheese, of course!" She laughed.

"Well, when I was walking along the river, I thought it would be nice to have an event that could both support the Beautification of Heartsford Committee and also serve as a fund-raiser to continue their work. But then after the heinous crime, I wanted to find a way to pay homage to someone who was so important in the craft world and will be deeply missed. Deborah and I were talking about the funding needs of our library and the adult book club again, too. If I host an event at the library, we can honor the memory of Jane Johnson and her literary legacy to the craft world. Deborah is going to create a special wine glass to sell, with a portion of the proceeds going to buy more books for our book club and a plaque to honor the former Queen of Crafts. I'm going to see if our library director would consider adding a craft section to the library, too; I've been bugging her about that idea for months."

"I think it's a great idea," Megan said. "Especially now, with the horrible tragedy that's tainted the town. Hopefully you can get some positive press and restore the happiness to this village. That's a very nice idea, Samantha. I hope you're planning it for sooner rather than later."

Sammy smiled. The first compliment for her out of her mother's mouth was well received, as the rest of the table agreed with nods of approval.

"That reminds me. I have to see if Randy knows of a band that might be interested in playing. Deborah suggested music would be a good addition. Isn't one of the guys from Randy's work in a band? Or karaoke? What do you guys think? Band or karaoke? We kind of decided if we had music, more of the husbands might show up for the event and not just the book club gals."

"Karaoke is always fun if you have the right audience. It depends on if you can get the crowd going and into the idea," Ellie said as she waved a hand and tried to get Randy's attention to return to the table.

"We could ask Colin. He used to have a guy lead karaoke at the Corner Grill. I think the guy's name is Dale," Heidi added. "When Colin hosted karaoke nights, it was so popular he would pack the house. I'm not sure why he doesn't do that as much anymore."

Randy jogged over to the table, and Ellie handed him her water bottle. He immediately put the water to his lips, emptied what was left, and then handed the empty bottle back to Ellie. "What's up?"

"We're looking for a band for an event Sammy is planning. Know of any? Isn't one of the guys at work in a band?" Ellie tapped the empty water bottle on the table as if she were playing the drums in a rock band.

Randy shook his head. "Nah, they dis-banded." He chuckled at his own pun. "Didn't have time to practice anymore. Everyone has young families."

Tyler came running up then and wrapped his arms around his father's leg. Ellie touched her son's red cheek, and his smile widened. "You must be thirsty, too." She ruffled her son's curls, which shone like strands of pure spun gold when hit with the sunlight.

Sammy reached into the center of the table for a full water bottle sitting in a bucket of ice and handed it to her sister.

"Thanks." Ellie unscrewed the top and handed it to her son, who took it willingly with both hands.

"I wish I could be here for this event. Sounds like it's going to be a good time," Megan said, deflated, as she placed her fork down on her empty dessert plate. "These are the times I'm bummed we live so far away."

"Well, we're here now, Megs. Just enjoy this time," Walter reminded her. "You forget the brutal winters here. Lest you forget what we really miss out on—long, snow-filled days where the sky and the ground are the same dirty white color, bone-chilling below-zero wind chills . . ." He shivered and poked his wife as he drove the point home. "Not to mention being cooped up with me." He laughed.

Megan waved her husband aside. "I know, Walter. You don't have to remind me."

Tyler handed Ellie the half-empty water bottle and then dragged his father by the hand to return to their soccer game.

Heidi took the last bite of her pie and placed her hand to her heart. "This pie is amazing, Aunt Megs. Tastes just like my mama used to make." She smiled wide.

"Well it should; I used her recipe." Megan nodded. "Beatrice always made the best pie. Remember those cherry pies she used to make back on the farm?"

"I remember," Walter added. "Blue ribbons at the county fair. My sister won best in the state, if I recall."

Heidi smiled at the memory. "Yes, but us three girls used to be sick by the time Mama pulled the pies out of the oven. We'd eat so many darn cherries while we were picking for her. Remember, Sammy?" Heidi nudged Sammy, bringing her wandering mind back to the table.

"Hey. Where'd you go?" Heidi asked.

Sammy smiled. "I'm right here." Although her cousin's instincts were correct. Her mind had definitely been wandering. And not about the upcoming wine-and-cheese event. Her mind unfortunately returned back to the brutal murder of Jane Johnson. Who had put the cell phone on that delivery truck? Why not just toss the phone in the river? Or had the killer just been trying to throw off police? And if the celebrity's husband hadn't killed her, who had? And why?

Sammy was trying to live in the present moment, but she desperately wanted to rush home and start reading the unpublished manuscript. She really hoped the detective was wrong and that between the written words left behind by the deceased author she might find a clue. If her mother hadn't been so irrational about her fears, she'd have brought the manuscript out right then and let them all have a look. She knew that would not go over well. Her mother would drive her insane about getting over-involved the entire visit, and she didn't want to ruin their small amount of time together.

"So . . . Mom. Are you for sure going to watch Tyler tomorrow night?" Sammy asked again.

"Absolutely. I thought it'd be the perfect time to take him shopping for a new toy."

"Not necessary, Mom," Ellie said. "The boy has plenty of

toys. I can hardly get inside his bedroom closet. Just a night of babysitting would be much appreciated. Besides, you already gave him the Lego set, which he's totally enamored of."

Megan pouted. "I only get to see my grandson a few times a year, Ellie. If I want to spoil him, let me. I want him to remember his grandma long after the plane takes off."

"Yes. Let us spoil our grandson," Walter agreed. "I'll go shopping too. I want to pick him out a remote-control car. Or maybe a drone?"

"Dad, he's three. I think you should wait on the drone idea." Ellie laughed. "Don't worry, he's growing fast enough. Soon enough he'll be chasing you around on a golf cart, wanting to go golfing with his papa."

"Hey, that's an idea! Megs, we can get him a set of mini golf clubs!" Walter's eyes lit in amusement.

Ellie shook her head and rolled her eyes. "Good grief. That's all I need is Tyler to have a long stick with a hard object on the end of it. Gee . . . I wonder what damage he could do with that?"

Sammy tried desperately to enjoy the time around the table with her family but couldn't. Her mind kept wandering back to the investigation, which kept her totally distracted. She reached for her cell phone and scrolled through recent photos. She stopped at the photo she'd taken of the barrette found in Jane's suitcase. Her mind instantly flew back to the day she and Kate had crafted them together. She could almost hear the sound of Kate's voice again: *Sammy-kins, we're going to be the hit of the parade! No one will have hair accessories like us. Just you and me . . . we'll be like twins.* The sound of Kate's contagious laughter that would bring them both to snorting and tears. After all the years without her, Sammy was losing the sound. The sound of her voice. The sound of her laughter. And it scared her.

"Hey, where'd you go. What are you looking at?" Heidi peeked over Sammy's shoulder, and Sammy shared the photo of the barrette with Heidi.

Heidi's radiant smile fell, and her face turned ashen. "Oh my God."

"You recognize this?" Sammy was astounded. The last thing she'd thought she'd see was her cousin turning deathly white at the site of a photo.

"Oh my God," Heidi said again, and then covered her mouth with her hand as if she was trying not to be sick.

"Talk to me!" Sammy cried out with such urgency, the family members at the table suddenly went quiet and all eyes flew in their direction.

Heidi moved her hand from her mouth to her heart and slowed her breathing to methodical breaths. "That was Kate's. What are you doing with it on your phone?"

Sammy's eyes narrowed. "Okay. Wait a minute. Back the train up for a second. How do you know it was Kate's?"

Heidi looked at her with such compassion, she thought her cousin was going to cry. "Sammy. That's what killed her."

Chapter Thirteen

"What are you talking about?" Sammy could feel her blood pressure swiftly rising to an unsafe level. Her heart began to hammer in her chest like the drummer from AC/DC, and her hands began to profusely sweat.

Heidi's color was slowly returning to her face. She took a sip of water before continuing. "You never wanted to hear the details of the accident. Are you sure you want to hear them now?" Heidi placed a comforting hand atop Sammy's, and her eyes filled with compassion. "We really don't have to talk about this. If you don't want to . . ."

"No. Tell me what I'm missing," Sammy said firmly. "Because it's quite obvious I'm missing something."

"The long ribbons . . . they got sucked into the tractor somehow. Kate had stepped out of the tractor cab to remove a stick or something from the combine, and the ribbons . . . those long satin ribbons . . . they got sucked into the tractor . . . Let's not talk about it."

The family members remained gathered around the table and fell eerily silent. Everyone was looking in Sammy's direction.

Even Randy stopped playing and held the soccer ball in his hands. Meanwhile, Tyler jumped to reach it, desperately trying to jar the ball from his father's sudden tense grip.

"We have to talk about it. We have no other choice." Sammy lowered her voice in hopes that Tyler wouldn't overhear the conversation. Randy took the subtle cue and kicked the soccer ball onto the far side of the backyard for Tyler to run and retrieve the toy away from earshot. "I thought the tractor rolled on her? That's all I remember hearing of the accident. I don't even remember who it was that told me what happened. I mean . . . I do remember you calling me, Mom." Sammy's eyes darted to her mother. "But I don't recall the conversation other than that she was . . . gone . . . the details escape me." Sammy sucked a breath. "The timing of that whole week is all such a blur. Such a shock . . . still is . . . sometimes even now . . . I can't believe she's really gone."

Heidi tapped lightly on her cousin's hand, as if to wake her from the awful moment yet again. "I'm so sorry you have to relive this. Yes. That part is true, the tractor did roll on her," Heidi explained. "Everything happened very fast. Kate's hair ribbons were sucked into the open belt guard on the combine, and then . . . well . . . the large tire . . . She didn't suffer, Sammy." Heidi let the words sink in.

"Why would she be wearing a stupid hair accessory that we made way back in high school, anyway? We made them so long ago, for the homecoming parade. That makes no sense whatsoever." Sammy threw up her hands in frustration.

"The event planned at the farm was to relive the past of our town. Everyone was supposed to dress in costume and wear something from their youth to show the heritage of the community and how things change over the years. Since you guys made them with Heartsford's high school colors, I'm not at all surprised she wore it that day. Even though it was only a day of tractor practice, she probably wanted to wear it to encourage others to dig through their closets and give them ideas for what they could use for a costume."

"But it still doesn't explain why you have a photo of her barrette on your phone," Ellie reminded her as she pointed to Sammy's cell phone. "Where did you take that photo?"

Great. Sammy had known she should have waited. Her eyes reached her mother's again, whose face was now the same ashen color as Heidi's. Why hadn't she waited to show Heidi the photo? She'd had no idea the impact showing the image on her phone would have on all of them. "I have it because the barrette was in Jane Johnson's suitcase."

Sammy heard a loud gasp, which diverted her attention back to Ellie, who had clutched her hand to her heart, matching their mother's pose exactly. "How is that possible?" she asked.

"You tell me. I was living out of town when Kate died. I don't know all the details, and Heidi's right. Up until now, I really didn't want to. But I certainly do now!" Sammy still sat in a place of disbelief. "If Kate was wearing the barrette when she died, how the hell did Jane get it?" Normally Sammy didn't use foul language in front of her parents. But at the moment she could not have cared less about her behavior or choice of words.

"Great question," Heidi said. "As far as I know, Jane Johnson wasn't in town at the time of Kate's death. In fact, before this week, I don't think the author had ever come to Heartsford. They didn't even know each other. Did they?"

"How about another great question? Why wouldn't Kate's barrette be in an evidence box at the police department?" Sammy's mind was now working overtime.

"Because it was an accident, Samantha," Megan said. "The police department doesn't keep evidence if the final ruling from the coroner is accidental death."

"Was it? How do you know? How do *any of us* know?" Sammy's questions raised prickles of suspicion to those gathered around the table.

She rose from the patio chair. A sudden burst of adrenaline kicked into overdrive, making her feel like she wanted to run. Run away from the past. Run away from the future. Uncertain of things she didn't know and wasn't sure she really ever wanted to know. Sammy leaned onto the table and pressed her knuckles hard on the glass to keep herself from bolting.

"And even if it *was* an accident, it still doesn't explain why Jane had Kate's hair accessory in her damn suitcase! How the bloody *hell*!" Sammy lifted her hands from the table and laced her fingers over her ball cap to help her think. It didn't help. Nothing gave her the answers to help her piece together the ragged pieces in her mind. She huffed a large breath and threw up her hands, defeated.

Those gathered around the table held their tongues, as no one knew quite what to say next.

After a long pause, Heidi suggested, "Maybe you could read the incident report on file at the police department. I didn't think you wanted to know the gory details of what really happened to Kate. But if you think you can handle all the details now, maybe you should ask to read the report? Maybe shine a light on something?"

"That's a good idea, Heidi." Ellie nodded.

Knowing her cousin and her inability to wait when it came to this type of information, Heidi said with finality, "I'll go with you."

Walter sent a warning look to Heidi. Wanting to protect his daughter from any more hurt, he said, "Are you sure this is a good idea? Maybe you girls should just leave it alone. Let law enforcement handle it. Instead, why don't you just tell the officers what you know? Let them take care of the rest. That's their job."

"Dad, I'm fine." Sammy stood and waved her father's comment aside. "I'll be even more fine *when* I get to the bottom of this," she assured him.

"When? Not *if*? You might be walking into Pandora's box, Samantha." Megan clutched her heart again out of fear.

"*When*, Mother. I will not let this go," Sammy said firmly, even though she wasn't really sure. She wasn't sure of anything anymore. She felt like she was falling into a deep abyss of uncertainty.

Heidi rose from the table and pushed her chair aside. "You might have better luck if I go with you, anyway. Tim is a bit upset with you at the moment, and it may come off better if I'm with you."

"Why is Tim upset with you, Samantha? What did you do now?" Megan's gray eyes narrowed, and her brows furrowed in concern.

"Not now, Mother," Sammy snapped, a little too harshly. Her emotions were rolling in overdrive. She noticed her mother sink back in her seat and close her lips in a grim line. When it came to Kate and anything having to do with her death, her mother should know better than to speak another word, because it would fall on deaf ears anyway.

"I'll clean up the dishes. You guys just go on ahead." Ellie began to reach for the dessert dishes and pile them in one stack.

"Thanks again for dinner, Ellie. The lasagna was amazing," Heidi said, and then waved a hand goodbye to Randy, who was back out in the yard keeping Tyler busy with the ball. "We'll see you tomorrow night? At Sammy's?" Heidi turned to wait for Ellie's response before she opened the sliding door, and Sammy numbly followed behind. She didn't wait to hear her sister's response. She was too busy reliving Kate's accident all over again in her mind.

Instead of leaving her car parked at Ellie's, Heidi made an executive decision to drop Sammy's car back at her house, and then the two would drive together to the police department in one vehicle. Sammy wanted to stop home and let Bara out anyway, so she didn't argue. Even though she didn't put the radio on for the short ride home across town, the ride was noisy due to the rumblings in her own head.

Talk to me, Kate.

Sammy tried to quiet her mind just long enough to hear from her deceased friend, but as usual, there was no response to her urgent call.

Heidi waited in her red convertible while Sammy parked, unlocked the front door, and moved inside to hug her furry best friend. After walking into the kitchen with Bara in close pursuit, she opened the back door leading to the small fenced backyard to let him out. While he was out in the backyard, she rinsed and refreshed his water. She then filled his food dish. By the time she finished putting out the food, Bara was back at the door panting to come in. He sauntered to his water bowl and slurped a drink. Sammy stroked along his long, furry back.

"I'll be home soon. I promise," she said, ruffling his soft golden head. She then returned to the front of the house, stepped out, and locked the door. Heidi was scrolling on her phone when Sammy slipped into the passenger seat.

"This is real fancy. Do you like your new sexy ride?" Sammy asked as she pulled the seat belt across her chest.

"Are you kidding me? I love it." Heidi grinned as she looked over her shoulder and pulled the Pontiac Solstice out of Sammy's driveway.

The two drove back toward downtown, the wind blowing Heidi's long blonde hair in the cool evening breeze. The sun was just beginning to set on the horizon, leaving a hot-pink hue across the western sky.

"Gorgeous night," Sammy bellowed against the noise of the wind as she pulled her ball cap down on her head so that it wouldn't blow out of the convertible.

"I thought this quick ride into town might relax you." Heidi turned her head from the windshield to Sammy for a brief moment. Before Heidi's hair could blind her, she tucked it behind one ear. "Something about the wind in your hair that calms the nerves and makes you feel alive!"

At any other time, Sammy would have enjoyed the convertible ride. Unfortunately, that night her mind was wound so tightly she couldn't fully enjoy the freedom of the moment. She remained quiet for the drive into town, her eyes catching things not normally seen when not driving in a convertible. She looked at the vivid color in the sky and wondered if her parents were still sitting outside at Ellie's, enjoying the sunset. Wisconsin might be subject to some of the harshest winters, but the sunsets in the summer almost made up for the bitter-cold months. They were spectacular year-round but too cold to view in the winter except from the warm comfort of inside, looking out a window.

Heidi pulled up alongside City Hall on Main Street and parked the car. She turned to Sammy and reached out to touch her lightly on the arm. "Are you sure you're ready for this? Once you read this information, there's no going back. All the gory details of Kate's death will finally be revealed to you, and you'll have to live with that knowledge."

Sammy shook off Heidi's concern and stepped out of the convertible. "I have to. What other choice do we have? Seriously? Especially if it might help Jane's case in some way." Sammy breathed the cool summer air deep into her lungs. "Let's go before I change my mind and lose my nerve."

She walked with purpose to the front door of the brick building and gave the glass door a large swing. Heidi rushed to catch up and made it through the door before it pulled shut on its own. The two stepped toward the long glass partition in front of the police department. Heidi lightly shoved Sammy aside. "Hey, Karen. Is Tim around tonight?"

A slightly overweight dispatch officer greeted them at the window. Her short dirty blonde hair was recently cropped short, as if a barber had cut it rather than a stylist. "He's out on patrol. Something I can do for you gals?"

"Actually, can I take a look at an incident report? From a few years back?" Sammy asked warily.

"That's considered public record, right, Karen? We can legally look at former incident reports?" Heidi added as she combed her fingers though her thick blonde hair to tame it after their recent convertible ride.

"You have to fill out a request form. It'll take a few days." Karen turned from the glass window and reached into a file cabinet beside a large desk.

"A few days?" Sammy groaned to only Heidi's ears, and Heidi shrugged in defeat.

After a few moments of digging in the cabinet, Karen turned back to the window. "Here you go." She slid a form underneath a small opening in the window. "You can pick the report up here in a few days, or if you decide you want it mailed, there's a charge for that," she added.

"Should I fill it out now?" Sammy asked.

"Sure. If you want. Or drop it off later. Your call," Karen said.

Sammy moved to a bench on the other side of the lobby and filled out the form while Heidi chitchatted with the dispatcher. When she finished filling it out, she returned to the window and slid the form back to Karen behind the glass. "Thanks."

"No problem. You gals have a good night," Karen said, officially dismissing them.

Heidi and Sammy walked out of the municipal building into a cool evening breeze. The sun had officially sunk into the horizon, darkness enveloped them, and Sammy's adrenaline rush waned, leaving her overwhelmingly weary. The two stepped back into Heidi's car and sank into the seats.

"Now what?" Heidi asked as she clicked her seat belt. "Sorry.

I was hoping Tim would be at the station and we could rush that process along."

"It is what it is," Sammy said, resigned. "Take me home, please. I don't know about you, but I'm beat."

"Sure."

Sammy leaned her head back on the headrest and looked at the indigo sky as they pulled onto Main Street. The stars were just starting to pop their brilliance. Sammy tried to absorb the limitlessness of it all. She wondered if Kate could see her. Could Kate hear her? But most importantly, could Kate help her find the answers she so desperately wanted? The knowledge that the red-and-white ribbons they had carefully woven together during their teen years could have led to her best friend's demise was almost too much to take. Accident or no accident. That information alone was almost unbearable. Sammy breathed in a deep, cleansing breath and let it out slowly, as if she were blowing up a balloon. A shooting star caught her attention, and Sammy immediately sat upright in the convertible. "Heidi, did you see that?"

"See what?" Heidi looked over at Sammy, who had a finger pointing above. "I'm driving, you goof. No. I didn't see a thing above us. What'd ya see?"

Sammy smiled at the confirmation she was so desperate to receive. "It's nothing. Never mind." But she acknowledged in her heart—Kate was listening and would show her the way.

Chapter Fourteen

Heidi offered to stay and comfort her, but Sammy knew her cousin had an early shift at the hospital and needed to get some rest, too.

"Really. I'm okay. You go along home and hit the hay, and we'll catch up tomorrow night when us three S.H.E.s meet. All righty? Don't worry about supper, either; come hungry. I'll throw together some cheesy nachos or something deliciously snacky. Hopefully Ellie won't mind taking one day off her diet. But I'll have a salad prepared for her just in case." Sammy winked.

Even though she was proud of Ellie for her continued hard work, sometimes she thought Ellie's unrealistic weight goal was ridiculous. Ellie shouldn't expect to fit into a favorite pair of jeans she had kept from the nineties in the back of her closet. Especially after having Tyler. Bodies changed, and besides, her sister was beautiful. She wished Ellie would just go with it.

Heidi looked at Sammy with such deep compassion, she thought it might make her weep. Sammy knew Heidi was keenly aware of her cousin's facade. Sammy was hurting, and her cousin knew how deep.

"Get going. I'll be okay. I promise," Sammy said with firm finality as she carefully closed the passenger door on the shiny new convertible. "Thanks again for going with me. And by the way . . . she's a really nice ride. Congratulations, girlie, you done good!" Sammy smiled, hoping her cousin would sense a lightness in her heart and that she would be okay—it might just take a little time.

"Yep. She's a beauty." Heidi ran her hand along the dark-colored dashboard. "What should I name her?"

"Scarlet."

"Hmmm. Scarlet. I like it!" Heidi grinned.

"Good night."

"Good night yourself. Get some sleep. See you tomorrow," Heidi said as she slowly backed Scarlet out of the driveway and waved a flowing hand goodbye in the breeze. And gave one last toot-toot to show off her new shiny horn.

Sammy smiled at the sound, returned the wave, and then turned toward the front door of her small, cozy Cape. She trudged her weary body to the front door and slipped in the key. Bara readily awaited, and she dropped to one knee to hug him close. "Hey buddy," she cooed as he licked the side of her face clean.

Sammy stood and reached over Bara for the leash hanging on a peg by the front door. She clicked the strap onto his collar and decided to take him for a brief walk up the road and back, even though it was dark outside and she was bone-tired. Bara stopped by the front oak tree for his familiar routine before sauntering onto the well-worn sidewalk at a comfortable pace. As Sammy walked her dog, she talked to Kate in her mind. *Thanks for the shooting star. I know you hear me. Please, I need your help. So much has happened down here. I need you, Kate . . . please talk to me.*

Bara stopped abruptly and turned to face Sammy. He looked up at her with those soft coal eyes as if to say, *I'm here. Don't worry. I'm here.* And then he turned and finished his lap as they strode along the sidewalk. Sammy smiled at her dog's tenderness and ability to understand her melancholy mood.

As soon as the two reentered the house, Bara curled himself on his dog bed in front of the unlit fireplace and laid his head down on his paws comfortably. Sammy followed his lead, sinking into a nearby recliner that groaned as her body hit the cool leather, and then leaned over to scratch the top of Bara's head. And then it came to her like a bolt of lightning. The manuscript! The abrupt memory jolted her upright in the chair. Sammy had actually let the printed pages slip her mind after the darn barrette drama. A quick rush of adrenaline pushed her body to a second wind. Her dog might be ready to sleep, but she suddenly found herself wide awake with curiosity. Sammy reached for her large leather bag and fished out the typed pages. Before reading, she removed her baseball cap, tossed it like a Frisbee to the nearby couch, and ran her hands through her matted auburn hair. After a deep breath, she reached for the wrought-iron floor lamp behind her, flicked on the switch, and began to read.

No offense to the author's writing, but now Sammy fully understood why the detective hadn't seen the point of reading through the rough draft for potential clues. The manuscript, although somewhat interesting, was like dry toast, and she was only on the second paragraph. Sammy didn't think this was even close to a finished manuscript—it was more like detailed notes.

She wondered how the author would feel about Sammy reading the raw version. Not too happy, she imagined. Sammy blinked her grit-filled eyes and laid the manuscript on her chest as she kicked back in the coolness of the leather recliner. She wiped her tired eyes with the back of her hand and tried to wake herself to read again, but as she lifted the pages back to her weary eyes, the words began to blur. She flipped off the light and closed her eyes for just a moment . . .

Sammy awoke to the sound of the cuckoo clock. She moved her hand across her chest, and pages fluttered to the floor like confetti. Her eyes squinted to read the clock in the early dawn light, but she couldn't make out the time due to the dimness of the room. Bara, awakened by the noise, wandered over and stood beside the recliner, looking almost as confused as she felt. "It's okay, pup. Go back to sleep."

Sammy snapped the recliner to the upright position and placed her feet squarely on the floor. She gathered the litter of pages and placed them neatly in a pile on the coffee table. Bara moved over to the table and gave the foreign pages an inspection, nudged the papers out of the neat pile with his nose, and then barked. Bara hardly ever barked.

"No, puppy. There's nothing there."

Bara barked again.

"*What?*" Sammy was tired and not in the mood for games.

But her dog didn't seem to want to let it go.

Sammy picked up the manuscript, tucked it all together in a perfectly neat pile, and held it in one hand. "Fine. I'll bring it up to my bedroom, then," she grunted at her dog.

Sammy trekked up the oak staircase, turned the corner into

her bedroom, and placed the manuscript atop her dresser. She took one quick look behind her to see if Bara had followed her up the stairs, but his presence was noticeably absent. Sammy moved over to her quilt-covered bed and took a seat on the edge. She leaned over and held her head in her hands before gazing over at the neon alarm clock, which read 5:43 AM. Too early to get up and too late to go back to bed.

"Ugh," she uttered aloud.

Bara came bounding into the room and seemed eagerly wide awake.

"I was wondering where you were. Fine. Let's go back downstairs. I'll let you out." Sammy lifted herself from the bed, while Bara moved over to her dresser to give the manuscript another sniff. Sammy laughed aloud. "You read it, then!" she said as she led him by the collar back toward the staircase.

Sammy plodded back down the stairs and immediately strode through the kitchen to the back door to let Bara outside alone. "Go on," she said to her dog, who simply raised one eye at her.

"Go!" She gave her dog a light shove toward the door, and he finally acquiesced.

"If this is a hint of what my day is going to be like, I'm going back to bed!" she said aloud to the closed door. Within minutes, her dog had finished, and Sammy reopened the door. Bara galloped past her, retreated into the living room, and curled on his dog bed and closed his eyes.

Sammy rolled her eyes and shrugged, headed to the kitchen counter, filled the nearby coffee pot, flicked on the machine, and waited for the smell of brewing coffee to rejuvenate her senses. As the coffee brewed, she went back upstairs. She decided a long hot shower might help.

The steam from the shower filled the tiny bathroom like a sauna. Sammy stepped out to wrap herself in an oversized purple towel that was held together with Velcro along the top. Dana, one of her many craft vendors, had sold them at Community Craft, and they were a huge hit as Mother's Day gifts. She would have to call Dana to see if she could sew more, as the stock at the store was running low. Sammy had a sneaking suspicion that the convenient towels would sell well for summer pool days, too; kids' sizes would be a great hit. She'd have to suggest that. Maybe Dana would consider whipping up a few and getting them back into inventory before the short Wisconsin summer flew by. She toweled off her hair and reached into the cabinet above the sink for her brush. After a quick blow-dry and a dab of makeup, she felt like a new woman.

Sammy padded to her bedroom and decided to take her mother's advice and dress a little nicer for work. After flipping through about a dozen hangers, she settled on a pale-blue sundress with a matching light sweater in case the air-conditioning at the store became too cool. Fancy shoes would not do, though so she finally settled on a pair of ordinary flip-flops bedazzled with clear beads. No one would see her feet behind the counter anyway.

Instead of walking to work like she sometimes did during the summer months, Sammy decided to take her car so she could pick up fixings after work for a makeshift supper for the three S.H.E.s as promised. Bara was sleeping so soundly by the time she was ready to leave, she decided to leave her dog home for the morning, too. Deborah was working the afternoon shift, and Sammy had already decided she would bug out of the store a little early to take an hour or two for herself.

The stress of the last few days had started to weigh heavily on her slender shoulders, and it was almost too much to handle. The loss of Kate, not ever far from her mind, was now visibly back front and center, and the details of her death were something Sammy hadn't expected to be rehashing. Ever. Not to mention finding the Queen of Crafts murdered! And the two events linked by a single barrette? *Were* the two deaths related somehow? Had the celebrity been at the wrong place at the wrong time and decided to return to Heartsford to make it right? So many questions flooded her mind. Questions that she would hopefully soon find answers for.

The sun shone bright in the sky as Sammy stepped out into the morning light and felt the warmth kiss her bare shoulders. She flung her leather bag and lightweight sweater onto the passenger seat of her car and placed her travel coffee mug in the cup holder before sliding into the driver's seat. Sammy fished her sunglasses out of her glove compartment and adjusted them on her face before backing out of the driveway.

The quick ride into town was uneventful, until she did a double take when she saw her father and Mayor Allen talking and laughing outside Liquid Joy. Sammy quickly pulled into a parking spot in front of the coffee house. She rolled her window and, to gain her father's attention, hollered, "Hey, Dad!"

Walter Kane turned his head in the direction of Sammy's car. Kate's dad also glanced over, smiled wide, and waved good morning. Sammy made the motion with her hand to encourage her father to approach the car. She saw her dad say something in Mark's ear, and then Mayor Allen threw his head back in laughter as he stepped inside the coffee shop.

"Good morning, Samantha darling. Gorgeous Wisconsin summer day . . . How's my girl?" Walter leaned his elbow on the driver's-side window to chat a moment with his daughter.

"Dad. Please tell me you didn't mention anything to Mayor Allen about our conversation around the dinner table last night?"

"Sammy. You've got to be kidding me. I wouldn't unduly upset Mark with no cause. We don't know anything, so why upset the man? He's in great spirits today; in fact, he just mentioned that Carter's taking a summer semester abroad. Can you believe it? Little Carter's not so little now! The young man is heading off to Europe tomorrow." Walter shook his head in disbelief.

Kate's much younger brother, who had instantly become Sammy's adoptive brother after her death, was growing into a fine young man. "Yeah, I heard that he was considering it. Wow. He finally made the decision, huh? Good for him! I'll have to call him later to say goodbye." Sammy smiled. "I didn't realize he was leaving town so soon."

"Speaking of soon, we're running a little late to golf, but Mark is treating me to some liquid heaven before we tee off! I gotta run." He jutted a thumb back toward Liquid Joy.

Sammy sat back in her seat, relieved. "Oh, I'm glad you're fitting in a game of golf. Dad, please don't say anything to him about all this digging I'm doing. Promise me?" Sammy pleaded.

Walter gave Sammy a resigned look "Samantha dear. Have a little faith in your father." He pointed a long finger to direct her.

"But *you* promise me something. When you do figure all this out, you'll come to me first, before your mother, so we don't have to deal with any more needless meddling. Deal?"

"Deal." Sammy smiled and reached her hand out the window to shake on it with her father.

"Now then. Have a good day at work, and don't forget to smile at your customers. You know, you're beautiful when you smile." Her father reached inside the car to hold her chin lightly in his hand. "And if you need me, call me," he added.

"Thanks, Dad." Sammy smiled, then shooed him away from her car so she could back out of the parking spot and escape before the mayor walked out and wanted to talk. She wasn't sure she could hide everything that was swimming inside her mind and heart from a man who would be absolutely devastated to find out his sweet daughter's death might not have been an accident. That alone would be harsh. But then add that it might be connected somehow to a celebrity death too? That would be too much for Mayor Allen and his entire family. A family Sammy would have taken a bullet to protect.

Chapter Fifteen

The morning moved swiftly at Community Craft as concerned citizens swirled in and out of the establishment, still trying to come to grips with Jane Johnson's murder within the confines of their small town. Deborah was hard at work manning the cash register and handling the many needless inquiries while Sammy took a few moments to escape and organize the stock room. Hiding in the back also gave her a moment of quiet and time to process the last few days' events in her own mind.

Sammy shuffled around the stock room, turned around, and took another deep breath. Empty boxes were piled at her feet. She crushed them into flat, manageable pieces and set them aside in a bundle. After that, she took a much-needed broom to the floor and piled the dirt and dust bunnies into one corner to gather later. The room was beginning to clean up nicely. Just as she was about to reach for the dust pan, Deborah caught her attention.

"Knock-knock."

"What's up?"

"Someone is here to see you." Deborah draped one delicate

hand along the door frame and half-blocked the entrance to the stock room with her tiny frame.

"Who?"

"Someone named Bradley?" Deborah's face held a question.

"Oh no." *Bradley Schultz.* He certainly hadn't wasted any time. Sammy looked down at her light-blue sundress, which was now covered in grime from the dusty floor. She desperately tried to brush the dirt away with her hands, but that only swept the dust into streaks of brown across the skirt. This was why she didn't dress up for work, she told herself inwardly. She was a mess. *Why* had she listened to her mother and rethought her wardrobe?

"Do you want me to tell him you're not here? By the look on your face, this guy must be *very* important to you."

Sammy shook her head. "Nonsense, you're right. I'm being silly." Sammy grimaced and then in a low voice asked Deborah, "Do I look that bad?"

"You're fine," Deborah assured her with a wave of her hand. "Who is he, anyway? Don't tell my husband, but he's quite dreamy. Reminds me of someone familiar. Hang on . . . give me a minute." Deborah tapped her finger to her temple and then ran her finger across her forehead. "Dang! I can't think of his name! I hate it when these senile moments happen to me. I'm way too young to lose my mind."

"We sort of grew up together. He's just a neighbor from Sunnyside Lane, the old neighborhood across town where I grew up."

"Oh wait . . . I think I remember the guy's name . . . hold on . . . it's on the tip of my tongue . . . Come on! I hate it when this happens . . . Remember the guy who's an actor, and he can sing too, on the Hallmark movies? Jesse *something*? Why can't I think of his last name?" Deborah slapped a delicate hand to her forehead.

"Jesse Metcalfe? That dark-haired hunk from the Hallmark movies?"

"Yes! Yes! Yes! Your friend looks just like him. *Gorgeous!*"

"You're kidding? Really?" Sammy remembered that Bradley was cute, but *Jesse Metcalfe* cute? Hmmm. That was a whole other scale of cute. This piqued her interest for sure.

"Definitely. But again, don't tell my husband I said that. Sure has been a while since another man had the ability to turn my head like that." Deborah jutted a thumb out the door. "But that guy certainly did. Anyhow . . . you comin' out of this dust bowl or what?"

"Yeah." Sammy brushed her hands along her dress one more time, to no avail. Water would be necessary to remove those dirt patches. She followed Deborah to the cash register, where Bradley leaned casually on the polished wooden countertop with both elbows. He was wearing tight jeans that fit his backside perfectly and a mauve polo that accentuated his broad shoulders. When he heard Sammy say his name, he spun in her direction.

His eyes widened in surprise. "Well look at you . . . *little* Sammy Kane?"

"In the flesh." Sammy could feel the heat rising in her cheeks as she self-consciously smoothed out her soiled sundress.

"Come on over here." He waved her closer. "Give your old pal a hug," Bradley said as he easily pulled her in close. He smelled of suntan lotion and manly perspiration. A beautiful combination. After their embrace, he stepped back a few feet to fully take her in.

"Well look at you. You've certainly grown up. You look amazing! What has it been? Ten years?"

"At least ten." Sammy smiled as she compared his looks to Jesse Metcalfe. Bradley's youthful features had disappeared, and those of a rugged man had taken their place. His weathered face with a dark tan caused his smile to shine bright white. His teeth were so white and straight they couldn't possibly be real. She did recall he'd worn braces as a kid, but he had to have bleached them. A light five o'clock shadow outlined his perfect lips. Sammy felt her stomach cartwheel. Deborah was right; he certainly had turned out gorgeous. She wondered what it would feel like to run her hand through his thick head of black hair.

"You okay?" Bradley asked. "Did I catch you at a bad time?"

Had she been staring that long? Sammy stuttered, "No. I mean, yes, I'm fine. No, you didn't catch me at a bad time." Her eyes darted to Deborah, who was watching this all unfold with pure amusement.

"I ran into your parents at the airport. They mentioned you had taken over Community Craft." He looked around the retail space and nodded his head approvingly. "Good for you. You were really close friends with the original owner? Kate. Right?"

Sammy nodded. "Yes. That's true. I'm trying to keep her legacy alive. She was certainly instrumental in bringing this town together, not only by selling their goods but also caring for each other deeply in community spirit. She is certainly missed and totally irreplaceable. But I'm trying my best."

"Oh, you're too humble. I hear you've done a great job! With all that's happened, though, I imagine it'd be hard. I actually met Kate a few times. Yeah, sweet gal . . . so sad what happened to her. She was so incredibly nice."

"You knew her?" Sammy cocked her head in surprise. "I didn't think your paths would have ever crossed, since you're a few years older than me." (And Sammy hadn't dared have Kate hang around her neighbor crush. Out of the two, he'd have been sure to pick Kate. Everybody had.)

Bradley laughed. "Not that much older. Come on now." His eyes twinkled, and he waved an amused hand of dismissal. "Only four years, right? Of course, when you're young and going to school, age really makes a difference, but now that we're all older . . ." He let the hint hang tantalizingly in the air. "I met her at the Corner Grill at one of those Friday night karaoke events. We actually sang a few songs together." He laughed at the memory. "I was really fond of her."

This took Sammy completely off guard. "You were living here when . . . ?"

"Yeah," Bradley interrupted, not allowing her to finish her thought.

"But I didn't see you at her funeral." Had he been there? The event was such a blur, she wondered if due to shock she could even name five people off the top of her head that had attended Kate's funeral.

"I had a final job interview out of town that week that I couldn't miss. I was competing with two other guys for the job. If I had missed the interview, I probably wouldn't be working at the company today."

"Oh." Sammy noticed customers starting to listen in on their conversation. The lack of privacy caused her to loop Bradley by the arm and encourage him to move to a private corner where the hand-quilted pillows and table runners were on display.

"Is there another place we could go and catch up? Would you mind taking this conversation over to the Sweet Tooth? I'm craving some of Marilyn's treats while I'm home." He smiled wide and rubbed a tanned hand along his flat abdomen.

Sammy could hardly call it a date, meeting at the Sweet Tooth Bakery. But after ten years of waiting for Bradley Schultz to ask her out, she'd have to take what she could get. "Sure. I'll meet you over there. Just give me a few minutes to settle things here with Deborah, and I'll be right over."

"Sounds good. I'll save you a seat at my table. See you in a bit." Bradley turned on his heel and strode casually out the front door onto Main Street.

As soon as he was out the door and out of earshot, Deborah rushed to her side and gushed, "Oh my word, Sammy. He's adorable! Find a way to keep that man in town, would ya? I'd love to see you find your soul mate." She winked. "Especially when he's that cute. A girl can dream . . . no?" She teasingly fanned her face with her hands.

"Seriously, Deborah, you sound like my mother!" Sammy threw her head back and laughed.

Deborah laughed along with her, then rushed back to the cash register when Sammy pointed out a customer waiting patiently to check out.

Sammy looked down at her soiled dress and decided a wet paper towel might do the job. She then noticed self-consciously that one of her bedazzled flip-flops was missing a few beads and truly was ready for the trash instead of barely surviving on her feet. With no other choice for shoes except a random pair of old tennis shoes she had left in the work closet (not happening), she rushed into the office to snag her makeup bag out of her purse and moved into the bathroom to clean up as best she could. The wet paper towel helped remove some of the grime—at least now the smudges weren't as noticeable. After a quick powder to add color to her cheeks and a wide comb through her hair, she felt presentable. She decided to skip the lipstick. The last thing she wanted was for Bradley to notice she had primped before walking next door.

"Deborah, I'll be back in a bit." Sammy waved goodbye as she adjusted the large leather strap of her purse over her shoulder.

"Take your time, Sammy!" Deborah smiled and turned her attention back to a customer.

Sammy stepped out of Community Craft into blazing sunshine. Since she was walking only a few doors down instead of searching for her sunglasses, which she had most likely left in the car anyway, she shielded the sun with her hand. Another group of customers entered the Sweet Tooth Bakery and held the door, so she slipped inside behind them. The smell of baked goodies wafted in her direction, and she breathed in the scent willingly. As she scanned the pink-painted room, she noticed Bradley in a back booth waving his hand to get her attention.

Sammy slipped into the red leather booth across from Bradley and laid her oversized purse at her side.

"I bought some cookies already. They're still warm, just out of the oven." He motioned to the table between them, where a pink box was flipped open and a glass of milk was half empty. "Sorry I couldn't wait for you," he admitted easily. "You know, my mom actually ships me a package of cookies every year for my birthday. That's about the only time I get to gorge. I really miss this place. I haven't found a bakery yet that can compare, and believe me, I've traveled far and wide." He chuckled.

"Yeah, it's seriously hard having a storefront so close to Marilyn's. A constant test of temptation. I've gained so much weight being her neighbor. The woman sure has talent in the baking department." Sammy smiled.

With a dismissive wave, Bradley said, "Samantha, I wouldn't worry about it. I think you look perfect."

Sammy instantly blushed. She had dreamed of going on a date with her neighbor for years, and here she was sitting across from him *and* he was complimenting her. Surreal.

"Did I embarrass you?" he teased.

"I'm just gonna go grab an iced tea to go with one of these cookies." She winked as she dodged the question coolly and slipped out of the booth.

Bradley threw his head back and laughed. "Sounds good."

Sammy strode to the counter, where the head baker stood waiting. "I see you over there with the Schultz boy. Hasn't he grown up into a handsome man. Oh, do tell!" Marilyn leaned forward on the counter and turned her ear expectantly.

"I can tell you this much—he's happy to be back in Heartsford, if only to have his hands on your chocolate chip cookies." Sammy winked.

"Well. You're too kind, darlin'! I heard that you brought my treats to the police department?" Marilyn's eyes filled with confusion. "Sammy, those cupcakes were for you, honey! Why did you do that?" she pouted.

"Honestly, I wanted to share your goodness. Everybody loves your treats, Marilyn, and I couldn't bear not to share them. The men and woman in uniform work so incredibly hard. I just wanted to spoil them for a moment. It's certainly not because I didn't want your delicious cupcakes, *believe* me."

This momentarily appeased Marilyn, and she smiled as she threw a puffy hand to her swollen bosom. "Well. That's mighty kind, darlin'. Any news on the investigation? You know I'm still havin' trouble sleepin' knowing there's a killer on the loose! I sure hope the police wrap that up soon. Are you helping them this time? I sure hope you are. What if the killer sat right here in my establishment? And ate one of these?" Marilyn held out her hands to showcase her collection of goodies. "These are the thoughts that go through my head." She pointed a pudgy finger to her temple. "Honey, this is keeping me awake at night!"

"I know what you mean," Sammy said. She had lost a few winks herself. Not for the same reason, though. Her loss of sleep was due to a restless mind about how Kate's accident could have had anything to do with the Queen of Crafts' murder. "Can I get an iced tea, please?"

"You sure can. Matter of fact, I'll bring it right out to your table in just a sec." Marilyn shooed her from the counter after Sammy paid for the tea. "You just get back over there. You're losing time with that fella. You need to get back over to that table and woo that cutie pie," she said, gesturing toward Bradley.

Sammy whirled from the counter, hoping Bradley hadn't

seen Marilyn pointing fingers at him. The last thing she wanted was for Bradley to know they'd been talking about him. When she slid back into the booth, she instantly grabbed a cookie and stuffed it into her mouth.

"Thatta girl!" Bradley said as he picked up another cookie and joined her.

"Do you mind if I ask you a little more about Kate?" Sammy asked between bites. She decided that, at the very least, perhaps she would learn more about the week her best friend died. "I was living in Madison at the time of her death, and there are a lot of details I don't know. You were living here, though. Do you remember the accident?"

After licking melted chocolate from the side of his mouth, Bradley clasped his hands on the table. Sammy noticed his grip was rather tight. "Are you sure you want to talk about this? Why now? Haven't you dealt with enough stress this week? Your mother told me that you found a famous lady murdered down on the river walk. By the waterfall?"

Sammy nodded. "I didn't think my mother would be the one to share the gossip right off the airport Tarmac, but I guess you'd have to live under a rock to not have heard that news around here anyway." For some reason Sammy felt the sudden need to defend her mother. "I guess she wanted you to know what to expect when you arrived in town. People are going a little crazy here due to this murder happening on their favorite walking trail."

"Yeah, she told me at the baggage claim after the surprise reunion. We were all so stunned to see each other there. Can you believe the stupid airline lost my luggage? The darn bag ended up flying across the country and back again. I saved the airline the trip and picked it up myself. As if I'd let them drive the bag to my mother's. Personally, I think they did enough damage losing it once; I didn't dare give them the opportunity to lose it again. Anyway, your mother is just worried about you is all. Go on. There must be something specific you want to ask me."

"I have reason to believe that the woman I found murdered may have uncovered something about Kate that possibly got her killed. I don't know . . . I'm sensing a weird connection."

Bradley's eyes narrowed. "What do you think she uncovered that had anything to do with Kate? Help me out; I'm totally confused."

"I really don't want to go into too much detail." Sammy hadn't seen Bradley in years, and here she was spilling her guts. Perhaps she should learn to do less talking and more listening. But it was like the years had easily slipped away between them and she was instantly transported back to the old neighborhood, back to their innocence, and back to their youth.

"You always did have an active imagination. I kind of forgot about that," he teased, and then a lopsided grin formed on his adorable face.

"What do you mean by that?" Sammy mirrored his expression.

"You were always a curious kid. Looking deeper into people's motives. Don't you remember the time you almost got old man Thomas into trouble for luring kids to his yard? The man pretended his house was haunted to keep kids *out* of his backyard. And you said it was just a hoax?" He laughed.

"It *was* just a hoax!" Sammy exclaimed. "I was right, was I not? Didn't that just make us kids even more curious to hang out by his house? Now that I look back, I still think he was some kind of creepy predator. I'm glad he finally moved out of Heartsford."

Bradley laughed harder until his eyes watered. "Oh, I remember the times we spent spying on the old guy with you and Ellie. A couple of loony kids hiding up in the trees, acting like no one could see us. Good times . . . good times." He slapped a hand on the table.

Sammy smirked. "Okay. Even if I do have an active imagination, there are real clues in regard to this case. I'll *prove* it to you. For example, Jane left a sheet of paper with the combination '24-14-5' and 'Highway 83' in her suitcase. Those notes have to mean something. You can't just disregard information like that or act like I'm exaggerating," she defended. "How would that information have anything to do with researching anything about crafting? It doesn't, does it?"

"Sammy, Sammy . . . some things never change." He rolled his eyes and hung his head.

"At least indulge me on this. Tell me about Kate's accident. I wasn't here, and I have to know . . ."

The mood instantly grew serious. "Well, you know she died in a tractor accident, right?" he asked, lowering his tone.

"Yes, of course. I just don't know a lot of details, and I wasn't in the area at the time to hear all the gossip flying." Sammy leaned her arms on the table and steepled her fingers while she waited.

"I don't really want to rehash the accident per se. I can tell you some of the gossip that was flying around town at the time, though."

Sammy encouraged him to continue with a nod.

"I heard her hair got caught in the combine belt because the cover was open or something like that, and then she was rolled over by the tractor wheel. I'm not sure? The memory is a bit cloudy on that." Bradley must have noticed Sammy's grimace, as his tone grew soft and compassionate. "I'm so sorry, Sammy. Maybe we shouldn't talk about this."

"No. It's okay. Seriously, I can take it." She waved a hand to encourage him to continue talking. "Anything you can remember. I really want to know."

"I do remember *something*. Do you want to know what always sort of bothered me?" Bradley chewed the side of his mouth. It was almost like he was doing that to stop himself from saying something he might regret.

"What's that?" Sammy sat up straighter in the booth and leaned in closer.

"Well, it's probably nothing. Water under the bridge now." He shrugged. "And anyway, nothing changed, so I guess it wasn't important."

"What do you mean, *nothing changed*? Spill it!" Sammy said, a little louder than necessary.

Bradley scanned the room to see if anyone was listening to their conversation. When he felt confident they weren't going to be overheard, his voice lowered. "Kate mentioned that she wanted to clear her father's name. Something was going on down at City Hall, and she felt like her father was getting a bad rap."

"Really?"

The seriousness of her voice caused Bradley to tenderly cover her hands with his. It was at that moment that she saw the shadow of Detective Liam Nash standing over their booth.

Chapter Sixteen

S ammy's hands flew to her lap and Bradley looked across the table, stunned by the jolt of sudden movement. Detective Nash stood at the end of the booth, hovering over them as he cleared his throat. "Please excuse me for the interruption."

Sammy's eyes met the detective's directly. "Hey, what's up?" She tried to sound casual, but her voice cracked like a croaking parrot.

"I need to speak with you when you have a moment. Preferably sooner rather than later. Do you possibly have time later today?" Nash's eye twitched.

Was that jealousy? Sammy couldn't gauge. Again, Liam displayed his customary poker face. She wondered whether, if Nash was ever tortured, he'd crack. Probably not. He was that good.

"No problem; I'll make time. Have you met Bradley Schultz?" Sammy directed his attention to her *very good looking* friend from the old neighborhood. "Bradley, this is the detective who replaced Stan Oberon when he retired from the police department. Meet Detective Liam Nash." Sammy gestured her hand toward the officer. For some reason, the introduction of the two men amused her. Perhaps it would be nice for Liam to see her sitting across from someone as attractive and well-groomed as Bradley Schultz. Maybe, just maybe, it would force his hand a little?

Nash held out a hand to shake. "Are you related to Barb Schultz?"

Sammy's pencil-thin eyebrows furrowed. How the hell did he know Barb?

"Yes, Barb is my mother." Bradley smiled as the two shared a handshake. They pumped hands as if they were old war buddies reuniting after a long, drawn-out battle.

"How do you know Barb?" Sammy blurted. She could no longer wait to hear the connection, and finally the words came out of her head for them all to hear.

"I helped shovel her driveway a few times this past winter." Liam's eyes swiveled to Bradley. "Your poor mother was out there struggling one morning in a large snowdrift that was darn near taller than her. I couldn't drive by; I had to stop and help her out. After that, when we'd get more than a few inches of snow, I'd drive by to check on her. What a sweet woman. She would always bring me a homemade meal packed up in those plastic containers. I swear she watched the weather, and when the snow was coming she'd make a special dinner for me as a token of her appreciation. Great home-cooked meals, too. I loved every single one of them. I almost looked forward to the snow; we had a real good bartering system going." He laughed. "Although now I have more than enough plastic containers to fill a recycling landfill."

"You're the one? Wow. Great to meet you, man. She mentioned that a nice gentleman helped her this winter, but she failed

to tell me you work for the Heartsford Police Department."
Bradley smiled.

"Yup, I'm the one." The detective mirrored Bradley's smile.

"Man, I really appreciate that. That's why I made the trip
back to Heartsford. The handyman list has gotten way too long
on that old house. Replace the missing shingles on the roof, fix
the fallen eaves, patch the concrete driveway, the list goes on and
on. I'm trying to convince my mother to move into a condo
before another harsh winter hits. Summer is the best time to
sell, and I'm anxious to persuade her to get her house on the
market."

"That would be wise." Nash nodded. "A house like that is a
lot of upkeep for an older woman."

The detective's willingness to aid another by shoveling Barb's
driveway impressed Sammy, but the two men connecting like
brothers? Sammy wasn't exactly sure how she felt about that. On
second thought, she knew exactly how she felt about it—she
didn't like it one bit. Sammy cleared her throat, which caught the
detective's attention. Where was Marilyn with her tea? She
looked over at the counter, where the baker was deep in conversation with another customer. The dried cookie in her throat was
about choking her. She reached across the table, stole Bradley's
milk, and took a sip.

"Samantha, if you can stop by the police station when you're
through here, I'd really appreciate it. I believe we have a few
things to discuss."

"Is she in trouble? This one's a tough one to corral." Bradley
chuckled as he directed a finger at Sammy, who smiled and shook
her head at the comment.

"You might say that." The detective chuckled, too.

"Yep. She's a real piece of work. We grew up together over on Sunnyside Lane," Bradley confessed. "Oftentimes she'd come home muddier than me. You should have seen her as a kid— rough-and-tumble, I tell you. I'm actually surprised she didn't grow up to do something like your line of work at the police department. The craft world seems a little tame for you, Sam." Bradley laughed heartily.

"Oh, I'm fully aware." Liam played along, throwing back a laugh.

Sammy did not appreciate the sudden camaraderie between the two men. Quite frankly, it was ticking her off. She slid out of the booth and stood upright. Bradley caught her with one hand on her wrist. "Hey? Where ya going?"

"I have work to do," Sammy said curtly. "And it seems I'm wanted at the police department today for a meeting. I'm going back to check in with Deborah to see if she needs anything at the store, and then I'll be over." She directed her final statement to the detective. *Screw the damn tea*, she thought.

Sammy bid the boys adieu and darted out of the Sweet Tooth Bakery with the sensation of eyes following her exit. She thought she might've heard one of the men say, "What's that all about?" But she refused to turn to see which one of them had made the comment. She had probably blown any chance of a romantic connection with either one of them now, but at the moment she could care less. She was more interested in getting to the bottom of two possibly connected deaths: her best friend and a celebrity. She didn't have time to waste dealing with those two idiots who were now apparently the best of friends. Why did it bother her so much? She guessed it was because she had wanted the detective to be jealous. And clearly, he was not. As far as Bradley was concerned, she'd never thought she had a chance with him anyway.

Sammy moved with purpose back to Community Craft, and when she reached the front door, she flung it open wide, nearly throwing her arm out of the socket. Completely frustrated, she stomped—as best she could in flip-flops—over to the cash register, where Deborah was standing cutting six-inch curling ribbons to be used to adorn the customers' bags.

Deborah must have seen the steam coming out both her ears, because she asked Sammy tentatively, "Hey? You all right?"

"Men!" Sammy huffed.

"Oh boy."

"You got that right."

"It didn't go well with the Jesse Metcalfe lookalike, I take it?" Deborah bit her lip. "I was hoping and praying for shameless flirting." Deborah set the ribbons and scissors atop the filled basket and then tucked it underneath the counter.

Sammy blew out a breath. "Now that's funny! Apparently, Bradley still sees me as a tomboy from the old neighborhood. Who knew?"

"You certainly don't look like a tomboy today. In fact, this is the most dressed up I've seen you in, well, forever." Deborah pointed to Sammy's dress. "The dress looks nice on you, too, if I didn't mention that already today. You look very pretty."

"Yeah, the dirt stains really adds to the look," Sammy grumbled.

"Whatever." Deborah threw up her hands in defeat. "I think you look great."

"I'm probably overreacting. In fact, I know I'm overacting. I'm stressed. I'm overwhelmed. Honestly, Deb, I'm just tired. The last few days have sucked, haven't they?" Sammy slumped against the counter. Since Bara was at home, she had the sudden urge to crawl into his dog bed beside the counter and fall asleep. Even that was tempting.

"Hey, you've had a rough week. Cut yourself some slack. Why don't you just get out of here for the rest of the day? Take a break and regroup?" Deborah suggested. "I got this."

"I think I might. I have another appointment now, anyway. I certainly wasn't planning that for today," Sammy huffed.

"Appointment?"

Sammy stood erect but ignored the question and instead redirected. "You sure you can close for me tonight? I don't have to come back?"

"Nope. Take the rest of the day. Trust me, I've got this. Someone's trained me well." Deborah smiled as she pointed in her direction. "Plus, we've finally hit a lull. I think the gossip train is finally back at the station. Pretty quiet here the last hour."

"Well, that's good news, about the gossip retreating. Not the lack of sales, though. That part is a bummer. But I'm not going to concern myself with sales; I have enough on my plate today," Sammy said. "Thanks, Deborah. I'll see you later."

"Yup, no worries, Sammy. Take care of yourself, okay? You've witnessed a traumatic event. Maybe you should go talk to someone? Like a professional?" Deborah nudged.

"I'm fine. You're sweet for asking, though. Nothing that a hot bath won't cure." Sammy dismissed Deborah with a slight wave of her hand. "Thanks again for closing."

"You bet. Get some rest," Deborah said, before turning her attention to the rack of hand-dyed silk scarves that needed adjustments after a customer had left them in disarray.

Sammy stepped farther away and retreated out the back door of her store into the parking lot. The rising humidity caused her sundress to cling to her legs like plastic wrap. She pulled it away with one hand. Then she remembered she had left her sweater in the office. *Ah well. It's too sticky for a sweater anyway.*

Even though the police department was within walking distance from Community Craft, Sammy decided that since she wouldn't be returning to the store, she would make the drive around the block. The loop around town was so quick, she barely had time to get the engine running before she was exiting the car again. Sammy was frustrated by the detective's interruption of her conversation with Bradley. What was Kate upset about that she had confided in Bradley? And why hadn't Kate ever mentioned Bradley's name in any of their many long-distance phone conversations? There was something about the lack of mention that felt odd. What did he mean, there had been something going on at City Hall? Had there been a target on the mayor's back? If so, why? She wondered if her dad could provide any insight into that. Although she knew her father never shared much about his relationship with the mayor—unless, of course, it pertained to golf. She'd have to probe him later.

Sammy stepped into the cool municipal building, where the air-conditioning seemed to be running overtime. A sudden chill swept up her bare arms, and she brushed the goosebumps away with her hands. She walked over to the police department window, where Karen stood, shuffling papers.

"Hey, Samantha. You're here to see the detective, right? He told me to buzz you in as soon as you arrived." Karen leaned over and hit the buzzer to unlock the entrance into the police department. Sammy walked through the door, and Karen accompanied her to the office of Detective Nash. The small office was empty, and Karen encouraged Sammy to take a seat on a chair beside the desk. "He'll be right with you. I'll check to see if that police report that you requested is ready. If so, I'll go and grab that too while you're here. Can I get you a water or something while you wait?"

"Nah, I'm good, but thanks." Sammy took a seat on the metal chair. The air-conditioning had chilled the chair like an ice cube, and the cool discomfort crept through her light sundress, causing her to shiver. Now, as visible bumps rose on her bare arms, she wished she had brought her sweater along.

Detective Nash entered the room almost immediately, stepped past her, and took a seat on an aged wooden chair behind the wide desk. He shuffled a few papers atop his desk and finally said, "I don't even know where to begin with you, Samantha Kane." His voice sounded like that of a school principal, and she felt as if she had stepped into the school office to be reprimanded. "I really don't appreciate you waltzing into this department while I'm out of town and telling people I offered you a copy of the author's manuscript." He cleared his throat. "Which, by the way, is considered evidence in this case."

Sammy held up a hand to stop him. "Wait just a minute," she defended. "I didn't tell anyone that you offered me a copy. I just said I had permission to see the document. That's all. I'm not trying to cause trouble."

"You're not trying to cause trouble, but you *are*, Samantha. I told you to wait for me. I asked you to not get ahead of yourself. To let me take the lead here." He folded his hands neatly on his desk. Sammy wondered if he did it to restrain himself, so he wouldn't jump over the desk and strangle her. As an officer of the law, she was certain, he had more self-control than that. Although, clearly, he was pissed.

Sammy tried to warm him from another angle. "Hey, what you did for Barb Shultz was really sweet. You're a good guy, Liam. I know that. But you have to remember, I too am very dedicated to this town and the people who reside here. Heartsford is my heart and soul. I was born and raised here—this town is my lifeblood. I made a promise to Kate after she died that I would continue what she started. Which is inspiring a loving sense of community and keeping that flame alive in this town."

The detective shifted in his chair. "Although I appreciate your kind words, that doesn't give you the right to stomp all over my investigation. And insinuate yourself in places where you don't belong."

"Listen. I understand if you feel emasculated," Sammy said, and as soon as the comment left her lips, she knew clearly it was the wrong thing to say.

"Get over yourself. It's not about feeling emasculated! It's about you tainting my investigation." The detective pointed a finger at her. "Why can't you see that?" He stood from the chair, gripped the side of the desk, and leaned toward her. "You need to back off. I'm serious. You're not trained for this type of work. Besides the fact that you're too impulsive."

Sammy was no longer cold. In fact, she was now approaching

red hot. At least mentally. "Well. You can forget that. I will not. Back off, that is," she said defiantly as she crossed her arms across her chest. At least her crossed arms would help keep her from shivering in this frozen, forsaken office.

Karen stepped into the room, and her eyes darted between them. "Everything okay in here?" The dispatcher handed her a form, which Sammy assumed was a copy of the police report she had requested. *Great timing, Karen*, she thought. Wait until he found out she had requested Kate's accident report. That news might just send him to the moon. She was completely within her rights, though. Of that she was sure as she gripped the sheet of paper with both hands.

"Everything's fine, Karen. Thanks." Nash waited until the other officer left the room and then inquired with a lift of his head, "What's that?"

"An incident report that I requested. And . . . by the way . . . as a concerned citizen of this town, I can request this document if I wish. It's all within my civil rights. So please excuse me one moment while I check something." Sammy's eyes flew to the page, eager to read the notes in the narrative portion of the report, which read:

Witness 1: Duke Reed

Narrative:
At approximately 1400 hours, I was on the scene of a fatal car accident when I received the call. I radioed my backup Sgt. Walters to dispatch to the scene of the tractor accident. After I finished with the car accident I

Immediately responded and met with Sgt. Walters at the location on Hwy 83. Kate Allen was found unresponsive at the Reed family farm where she allegedly was learning how to drive a tractor for an upcoming town event.

According to the witness: Duke Reed
The subject: Kate Allen and Duke Reed were both inside the enclosed cab of the tractor. Kate wanted to learn how to operate the controls. Duke asked her to step out of the cab because he wanted to remove a branch that had lodged in the corn combine. The tails of the subject's barrette were flowing in the breeze due to the windy conditions. Earlier in the day Duke had removed the belt cover on the left side of the combine to adjust the tension and he remembered he didn't put the cover back on because he wanted to make sure he solved the problem. As Duke saw the subject's hair flowing he grew concerned that her hair could potentially get caught in that belt. He believed that's exactly what happened because when Duke rose up from the seat and took his foot off the clutch the tractor lurched forward pinning the victim, Kate Allen, underneath and the long ribbon tails of the barrette and a chunk of her hair were never recovered from the scene.

Sammy's eyes scanned the document to find the name of the reporting officer listed on the bottom of the page: Stan Oberon. Who was now retired and, last time she'd heard, living in

Clearwater, Florida. Along with another officer name: Sergeant Walters. Sammy didn't know who that was. Clearly he was no longer with the department, because Sammy knew everyone who currently worked for the Heartsford PD.

Detective Nash had abandoned the chair behind the desk and stood over Sammy's shoulder, casting a shadow on the page. "What are you doing with that report? Who is it for?" He squinted his eyes to try to read the paper in her hands.

Sammy laid the sheet of paper on her lap and eyed the detective squarely. "I have some information that I think is going to blow your mind."

The detective breathed deeply as if to compose himself. "What now? Obviously, there is no way I'm going to keep your nose out of my investigation. That would be impossible, wouldn't it?" he said under his breath as he moved a small step backward, took a seat on the only corner of his desk that wasn't covered in random sheets of paper, and set his hand in a closed fist and stared at her.

"You've got that right, Detective; I'm not going anywhere." Sammy's eyes met his as if a duel were going to take place. If he thought for one second she was going to back off, he was dead wrong. He'd have to toss her in a jail cell and throw away the key. "I'm guessing you cleared Jane Johnson's ex-husband of the crime when you were out of town?"

The detective must have sensed not to push. He knew she had something, information he needed, so he softened. "You guessed right. I checked his alibi. It's solid."

"Did you ever find out what that white substance was on Jane's blouse at the time of her death?" Sammy cleared her throat.

"No. Not yet. I had the shirt sent out to the lab. You do remember we're a small town? We don't have a back-office toxicology lab at our fingertips. Now. What've you got?" He rested his flat hands back against the desk and crossed his ankles casually.

"You ready for this one?" Sammy lifted a thin eyebrow. "The barrette that was in Jane's suitcase was the barrette that Kate was wearing in her hair the day she died. As a matter of fact, the barrette is what *caused* her death." Sammy handed the incident report to Nash, who sat up at attention and immediately scanned the report with his own two eyes. "And now we find that hair accessory in the author's suitcase? Explain that, Detective."

After a few moments, he shook his head in disbelief. "Wow. Okay. I wasn't expecting this. A little out of left field. I'm chasing another lead that might just be leading me down the rabbit hole, and now this?"

"What do you mean by that?" Sammy asked.

Nash put up a hand in defense. "Not now, Samantha." He stood up from the desk, his eyes not leaving the page until he finished reading. "Interesting. What do you know about this Duke Reed?" He asked as he pointed to the name on the report.

"Honestly? Not much. I know he used to farm. That's about all I know of the guy. I don't even know if he still lives in town. It's not like he hangs out at my craft store selling handmade items." Sammy added with a hint of sarcasm. "*Oh my gosh.* Wait. Duke owned a farm on Highway 83. We just confirmed that reading the police report. Remember the author had Highway 83 written on a yellow pad? The one you added to the evidence pile?"

The detective shook his head in disbelief. "What is going on here?" He laid the paper on his desk and looked toward the wall, contemplating it as if it held the answers he was looking for.

"You tell me, Detective. How did Kate Allen's barrette, that she allegedly wore the day of her death, end up in Jane Johnson's suitcase? And why was the author interested in Highway 83, the location where Kate's accident happened? On Duke's farm."

His eyes left the wall. "Are you *sure* she only had one barrette? Maybe Kate made more?"

"Positive. We only made one each, and I have the other one at home sitting on my bedroom dresser at this very moment. I'd be happy to bring it in for you to confirm," she added.

"That won't be necessary. Wait here." He held a hand out to encourage her to stay seated. "I'll be right back."

Sammy couldn't believe what she had just read in the report. Reading and rehashing the details from her best friend's last moments on earth wasn't easy. With no other choice, she'd have to try to set her emotions aside in order to get to the bottom of this. Should she share with the detective what Bradley had told her about the mayor? If Nash hadn't barged into their conversation, she might have learned more from Bradley. She'd wait on that little nugget. Maybe she could probe Bradley a little further. She looked up when the detective reentered the room.

Nash held an evidence bag in one hand. He dropped it to his desk and then rolled on a set of rubber gloves. He removed the barrette from the evidence bag and held it between them. "You're telling me she didn't make more of these—possibly after you left or any other time? You're absolutely sure there are only two in existence and you have the other one?"

Sammy stood from the chair to examine closer. "Yes. Do you wanna know how else I'm sure?"

He nodded for her to continue.

"The ribbon company stopped making that color red." Without touching the hair accessory, Sammy pointed to the deep-red satin ribbon. "We wanted a specific color to match our school colors, you know? You'd think that would be easy, but it's not. Some red ribbons are more on the orange spectrum and some reds lean to more of a burgundy hue. You catch my drift? We wanted a very specific red. And we used the entire roll. We were going to make more for her cheerleading team later that week, and we couldn't find a roll of that color ribbon anywhere. The company stopped making the color; it's that simple."

The detective spun the hair accessory in his gloved fingers and held one end for her to examine closely. "Look there," he said as he pointed to the ribbon that had been obviously cut clean. "If this was sucked into a machine, it would be frayed. Not cut. This clearly was cut by a sharp object. Scissors or a knife, perhaps?"

Sammy picked the incident report up off his desk and reread the narrative. "It says here Duke was concerned that the barrette *might* get caught due to the wind and Kate's hair blowing. Which caused him to jump off the seat inside the cab. But it doesn't say on the report what happened to the evidence. And why are the long ribbons cut off? How did the ribbons get cut so clean? And if the barrette actually *was* part of the accident and the ribbons were sucked into the belt, why wasn't the barrette brought in for further investigation when Stan Oberon was reviewing the accident?"

"Keep reading; it should state that information."

"Oh wait, here it is. It says: 'No barrette was recovered from the scene. Officer reports that he believed it might have gotten caught under the belt and been impossible to remove.' How is that possible? They didn't do a thorough search for the evidence of what supposedly killed her? Wouldn't they need that to rule it accidental death?"

"I don't know, Samantha. According to the report, Oberon was at a fatal accident when he got the call. Maybe he knew the victim that died at the scene and it shook him up a bit; then he gets a call about Kate? Hey, we're all human. But let's keep this information between the two of us. Do you understand? Just you and I." He motioned his finger between them. "We're really going to have to tread lightly, because this is the mayor's daughter we're talking about. And if word gets out that something else might be going on here . . ." He let the words linger, but more than anyone, Sammy knew the implication.

"You have my word," Sammy said as she crossed her heart and hoped to God she could keep that promise. How in the world would she keep from spilling this information to her sister and cousin?

"Meanwhile, I'll try to get ahold of this Sergeant Walters, who no longer works here. Maybe he can help us fill in a few blanks."

Sammy liked what she heard. He was finally using the word *us*.

Chapter Seventeen

Sammy rolled through the supermarket checkout with the receipt in one hand. Corn chips, salsa, jalapeños, green onion, taco seasoning. Turkey meat, because her sister was convinced ground turkey was healthier, as it had fewer calories than beef. Was she forgetting anything? She was having a hard time concentrating after the day's events. Detective Nash had seemed to calm down after they had put whatever differences aside and instead put their heads together into the ongoing investigation of Jane Johnson. At least now they seemed more on the same page. There might be a connection between Kate's so-called accident and Jane's murder. Although the detective was a bit tight-lipped and seemed to have other information that he hadn't shared. Were there other suspects that had no connection to Kate? Sammy didn't think so. She couldn't get past the fact that Kate's hair accessory had been found in the celebrity's suitcase. *Why?* It made no sense whatsoever.

Sammy stepped out of the supermarket into the late-afternoon sun. The humidity had diminished and the rays were hiding behind a large cloud, sending a chill on the light breeze. She moved with purpose to her car and popped the trunk, loading up the grocery bags. When she was finally tucked behind the wheel of her car, Sammy's mind, preoccupied with the recent events, lost focus, and she came dangerously close to backing up into another car that was dodging through the busy parking lot. Her foot slammed on the brakes, and she clutched her heart. The near miss scared the hell out of her. She leaned forward and rested her head on the steering wheel. Her throat constricted as she tried to hold back tears. But to no avail. Fat tears began to form in her eyes, making them blur. Sammy's tough exterior began to crack, and soon her body was convulsing with deep sobs, as if she was reliving Kate's death all over again. Grief swept over her like a tidal wave, the undertow grabbing and reaching, threatening to overtake her. She wept until she was empty. Sammy knew she would always struggle with questions, some of which would never be answered. Why would God take Kate, a lovely shining light in the world, so early . . . so young? Some unanswered questions would have to wait until she met her maker. Some, however, she would investigate until she learned the truth. The tears were cleansing, and when they finally sub-sided, she felt like a load had been lifted. Only then did she real-ize she was still half in and half out of the parking spot. With the back of her hand, she wiped her eyes, and then she cautiously pulled out of the spot, out of the parking lot, and back onto the road leading to the comfort of Bara and home.

To keep her mind focused on the present moment, she tried to turn her attention to the familiar landmarks as she drove. The old farm beside a rusty abandoned steel shed that was heading for demolition to give way to the growing industrial park. The fields had changed so much since she was a child. Miles of corn and soy replaced with large commercial manufacturing plants. The place where the three cousins had played their S.H.E. games innocently in their youth. The park flattened and now long gone. Sammy passed a place she and Kate had hung out before it too had been demolished and replaced by a Walmart—an old five-and-dime store that sold penny candy. The girls would ride their bikes from town to the store and buy pieces of bubble gum for a penny. They'd purchase a whole quarter's worth, and their jaws would ache from the hours of chewing twenty-five pieces in one day. She and Kate would have bubble gum–blowing contests, letting the bubble explode all over their faces, and the two would succumb to laughter. Sammy smiled at the memory.

Her mind then returned to Bradley. Sammy had never known he had seen her as a *rough-and-tumble* girl. No wonder he had never asked her out. He probably saw her more like a sister or annoying pest rather than someone he wanted to date. Certainly, it wasn't the way she had hoped or expected him to remember her. Although, in his defense, she had chased him a lot and thrown mud pies at him any chance she could. Or the occasional snowball during the winter months. Not because she was *trying* to be boyish but because she had childishly wanted his attention.

At that moment, she decided to take a sharp right onto Sunnyside Lane, through the old neighborhood where the Kane girls had grown up. When she arrived close to the old homestead, she noticed a car parked in the driveway at Barb Schultz's house that she assumed was a rental from the airport. Impulsively, she pulled her car in behind it. Her eyes darted to the blue neon digital clock on the dashboard. She had a little time. She briefly looked at her eyes in the rearview mirror to be sure there was no evidence of her recent tears before getting out of the car.

Sammy rushed from her car, jogged across the overgrown lawn up to the front door the best she could in her flip-flops before she lost the courage, and rang the doorbell. Her heart skipped a beat as she waited.

Bradley answered the door, instantly turned his head toward the inside of the house, and yelled, "Mom, it's little Sammy Kane." He then turned to her and smiled wide, sending Sammy's stomach to lurch again like she was doing gymnastics.

"I was just driving through the neighborhood . . . I was hoping to find a mud pie to throw your way, but unfortunately the old fields have all been turned into manufacturing plants."

Bradley smiled, showing his perfect white teeth. "You're kidding? You're going to go with that one?" He laughed heartily, "Maybe I should try and make a run for it."

Sammy chuckled. "No . . . you caught me." She flung her hands out to prove they were empty. "No mud pies today. I'm clean."

His smirk grew at the comment. "Gosh, I almost forgot about that. I used to walk down the street looking over my shoulder. You really had quite an arm back then," he teased.

Sammy grinned and lifted her arm to show her small muscle. "Still got it!"

"Hey, listen." Bradley turned sincere. "About today. I hope I didn't upset you at the Sweet Tooth . . . you know, I was only teasing. I really felt bad after you left."

"Oh, not at all. I'm tougher skinned than that. *Believe* me."

Sammy adjusted her flip-flop on her foot, as it had come loose during her traipsing across the lawn. "Let's just say the new detective in town and I have had our ups and downs."

"Are you two dating? I didn't know."

The question took her completely off guard. "Ah . . . no. Nope. Not at all." She laughed a little too hard as she held a hand to her chest.

"Do you want to come in? I'm sure my mother would love to see you." Bradley gestured his hand indoors, and Sammy shook her head no.

"I can't. I have company tonight. Girls' night, actually, or I'd invite you to come along."

Bradley cocked his head to one side. "You don't want to come in? Why then, may I ask, *are* you here?"

"Oh. I was just at the grocery store and . . . I was driving by . . . I don't have your phone number. But I really wanted to continue our conversation, especially about Kate. Any chance you can meet for coffee tomorrow morning? How about some Liquid Joy while you're in town? Douglas has added a few breakfast sandwiches to the menu. I'm sure you'd like them; everybody does. Like them, that is." Oh God, she was getting anxious. She hated that she rambled when she got nervous. "Let me take you to breakfast." Sammy hoped she wasn't being too forward, but she guessed age really did have its benefits. She'd never had the courage to ask him out in her teen years, but look at her now.

"Yeah, sure." He nodded agreement. "What time?"

"The earlier the better for me. Otherwise I can check and see if Ellie can watch the store if it's later than nine." *Did he actually say yes to breakfast?*

"I'm an early riser. How about eight?"

"Sounds good. See you tomorrow morning, then? And please give my best to your mom. I'd step in and say hello, but I really must run." Sammy jutted a thumb toward her car, which was probably melting her ice cream at that very moment. Looking into his hazel eyes, which held a hint of emerald sparkle, was certainly making *her* melt.

"Great. See you tomorrow, then." He smiled again. That near-perfect smile. Sammy turned and walked quickly back to her car and slipped into the driver's seat. Hopefully now she'd be able to dig a little deeper into his relationship with Kate. He definitely had more knowledge than she did of what had been happening in the town of Heartsford at the time of her death. And it was up to her to jog the guy's memory. Staring into Bradley's gorgeous hazel-green eyes? Well, that would just be an additional perk.

When Sammy finally turned into her driveway, she was surprised to see her cousin's red convertible already parked on the right side. The convertible top was down, and Heidi looked like a model leaned back on the driver's-side headrest with her eyes closed and face pointed to the sun. She turned her head and shielded her eyes with her hand at the sound of Sammy's engine pulling up next to her.

Sammy stepped from her car and popped the trunk. "You're early. Sorry I kept you waiting. Had I known you were here already, I would have rushed along. You could've texted."

"Yeah, I could have." Heidi sat up in the car. "It's no problem; I was enjoying the sun. I wanted to catch you before Ellie arrives. I need to talk to you. But before I get into it, how are you holding up? You doing okay, hon?" Heidi stepped out of the convertible and moved to help snag a few grocery bags from the open trunk.

Sammy's eyes softened. "I'm hanging in there. I lost it in the grocery store parking lot, but to be honest, I think a little boohoo did the trick. I actually feel a little better," she admitted. "But what's up with you? What did you want to talk about that you don't want to include Ellie in? Does it have to do with the investigation?"

"Let's just get these groceries inside and then we can chat. It's really nothing too important; I just want to bounce a thought or two off you," Heidi said as she juggled a bag in each hand.

The two walked up the narrow concrete path leading to Sammy's front door. She slipped in the key, and Bara about knocked the two over upon their entering. Sammy held her dog back with one hand so Heidi could get inside. She then encouraged Bara to follow her to the kitchen so she could drop the shopping bags on the kitchen counter and then immediately open the back door to let her dog out into the fenced yard. "Sorry about that."

"No problem. You know I can't resist your puppy even when he's rude." Heidi laughed.

Sammy fished the ice cream out of a grocery bag and immediately put the melting dairy inside the freezer. "I bought your favorite, cookies and cream, for dessert." Sammy smiled.

"Oh, how I love thee," Heidi said dramatically as she turned and air-kissed Sammy on both cheeks.

Sammy peeked in the grocery bags to see if anything else needed immediate refrigeration, plucked out a block of cheese, and put it in the refrigerator. She fished out the remainder of the perishables and then left the rest to unload later.

"Hey, come upstairs with me. I've gotta get out of this stupid sundress!" Sammy reached to remove each flip-flop and then flung them by the back door. Even though the shoes really belonged in the trash, she had decided she wasn't quite ready to part with her old faithfuls just yet.

"Yeah . . . what's up with that? Your mom's comments are influencing your attire now? A *dress*?" Heidi laughed as she followed Sammy toward the front of the house and up the stairs. "I've never seen you wear a dress to work."

"Umm, yeah, major mistake too." Sammy turned abruptly to show her the smudges of dirt still evident on her sundress. "Look at that. I'll probably never get that stain out."

"Hey! I've got an idea," Heidi said as they trudged up the staircase.

"What's that?" Sammy asked over her shoulder.

"How about asking one of your vendors to make Community Craft T-shirts? And then you could make them your work uniform and wear one every day. You'd be like a walking billboard." Heidi laughed.

Sammy stopped midstep and turned to her. "That's actually a brilliant idea!"

"Hey, I'd buy one. Community Craft is the hub of Heartsford. Why not have shirts to solidify the theme of community spirit even more?"

"I love it. I'm definitely going to put that on tomorrow's agenda. And to think, I'd never have to worry about what to wear to work again."

As soon as the two topped the stairs, Heidi moved toward the bathroom. "I'll be just a sec."

While Heidi was in the bathroom, Sammy ripped the sundress over her head and tossed it into the hamper. She knew she should probably soak the stain but at this point she figured *screw it*. She'd almost rather toss the darn dress in the trash along with her flip-flops. She slipped on a comfortable pair of gray sweat shorts and an oversized Green Bay Packers T-shirt. Perfect for girls' night. She might even consider losing the bra by dusk. She stepped out of the bedroom, met Heidi in the hallway, and the two made their way back downstairs. As Sammy headed into the kitchen and began to unload what was left in the grocery bags, she said, "All righty now, spill it."

Heidi's demeanor grew pensive, and she took a deep breath. "I wanted to tell you why I was so 'off' the other night." She raised her slender fingers in air quotes. "I could tell you thought I was acting out of character. I *know*. I definitely had a little too much to drink."

Sammy, noting the seriousness in Heidi's voice, stopped removing the groceries from the bag, and her eyes met her cousin's.

"I also know I mentioned some things about Tim possibly proposing. I mean . . . I don't really remember, but you told me that's what I said, and I believe you. Honestly, the whole proposal thing has me a bit freaked out. Which makes me wonder . . . why?" Heidi looked at the ceiling and contemplated.

"Go on." Sammy let the groceries wait. Heidi needed her full attention. She was glad they were finally having this conversation, because it was unnatural for her cousin to ever hold back from her. And it had seemed like there was a bit of a crack between them that she couldn't pinpoint. Now she knew—Heidi just needed time to process.

"If I love him, then why am I freaked out? Shouldn't my response be excitement . . . not cold feet already? Isn't everyone our age in a rush to the altar? Why not me?" Heidi threw her hands up in frustration before placing them on her slender hips.

Sammy wasn't exactly sure how to respond. She didn't even know how she felt about marriage for herself, never mind for her cousin. But at least Heidi had better odds, considering she was currently in an *actual* relationship.

"You love him . . . right?" Sammy finally asked.

"Of course. That's not the issue at all. Maybe I'm just being ridiculous." Heidi chewed on a fingernail while she considered.

"No, you're not being ridiculous. These are your feelings, and your feelings are valid. Don't say that," Sammy corrected with a pointed finger. "You have to trust your gut. What does your gut say?"

"Ah, I'm hungry?" Heidi grinned.

"Seriously, not about food . . . what does your gut *really* say about Tim Maxwell?"

Heidi's smile faded. "My gut says I don't want to lose him, but I'm not sure I want to marry him, either. Is that fair? Or am I leading the poor guy on?"

Sammy nodded in understanding. "So, are you concerned that if you tell him you aren't quite ready, then that would end the relationship?"

"I don't know," Heidi said flatly. "Maybe that's what I'm really afraid of. I don't want to lose him."

"Well . . . Tim hasn't asked you yet, right? So, I mean, you still have time to think it through and weigh your options. Maybe you'll be surprised; maybe he wouldn't treat a proposal like an ultimatum. I think you're more afraid of hurting his feelings—or his pride. Am I right?"

Heidi nodded sadly.

Sammy hugged her cousin tight. When they finally stepped apart, she said, "You've always been concerned for everyone else's feelings, but in this regard, you really have to consider your own. I have a feeling you'll figure it out. As a matter of fact, you may already have the answer in your heart. You just have to listen to it."

Heidi smiled. "Okay, Buddha. You are sounding so wise these days. What I'm hearing you say is I need some quiet time to really hear my inner voice and not worry about hurting Tim."

"Exactly! However, you also know I'm here to talk anytime. You didn't have to shoulder this alone. You're my best friend, Heidi. I'm here for you always; I hope you know that. Is there a reason you don't want to share all this with Ellie, though?"

"First of all, your sister is already married and seems to handle the whole 'ball and chain' thing quite nicely, but second of all, she'd rush straight into wedding-planning mode and miss the point completely."

"I guess you don't remember what Ellie said at the Corner Grill about marriage, then."

"Huh?"

"Never mind."

"Plus . . . you know how your sister can be. Her anxiety would only add to my already-growing stress, and honestly, I don't think I could handle that. I guess I didn't do a good job covering up my fears, though. I ended up getting all drunk and stupid."

"Nonsense. We all have those moments sometimes. You're not stupid." Sammy rested a hand on Heidi's shoulder. "I just wish you would have come to me if you needed an ear. I know you're independent and strong, but it's okay to need people. That includes me," Sammy added gently.

"Yes, and it's okay for you to need people too. People like Nash?" Heidi hinted.

"Okay, how did we get so off course?" Sammy laughed. "We're talking about you now!"

"We *are* getting older. Maybe we do need to start settling down and getting serious about life. Look at your friend Kate, and how young she was, and how she never got that chance." Heidi paused. "I'm just not sure if Tim's the *one*. Like, for the rest of my life, wake up every morning, the *one*. I do know he wants kids. What if I don't? I don't know. I'm really confused. I'm having a really hard time figuring out what I want out of life, you know?"

From Sammy's perspective, it was out of character for Heidi to reflect so deeply on her life. This was new to Sammy. Heidi was always the carefree one, the fun one, the spontaneous one out of the three of them. Sammy and Ellie were the overthinkers, not Heidi; she was Little Miss Sassy. Nothing could stop her. Until now.

Sammy didn't know what to say, so she reached for her cousin to give her another hug.

"I don't have the answers for you, Heidi," she said finally when they stepped apart. "But you can *always* come to me. No matter what. Do you hear me? At the very least, you can use me as a sounding board. Right?"

"I know." Heidi nodded. "But you had just experienced a pretty traumatic event. I didn't want to add to your stress load. I guess my concern for you trumped telling you what's been going on with me. I won't let it happen again."

"Typical Heidi, putting her needs after everyone else's," Sammy nudged with a smile. "Promise me you'll come to me when you're struggling with something."

"Promise."

Sammy paused to drive the point home.

"I swear, I promise!" Heidi held up scout fingers.

"Okay then," Sammy said as she reached to unload the remainder of the groceries. She began to assemble the items needed to make an improvised supper on top of the kitchen island. A super-large plate of nachos for the three S.H.E.s to share seemed like the perfect idea.

"What can I do?"

Sammy directed Heidi to the cabinet. "Can you look in there to see if I have a can of black olives? If not, no biggie," she said over her shoulder. "Olives aren't a must-have."

"Sure." Heidi moved to the cabinet and popped her head inside. After removing a can of olives, she said, "So, do you want to bring me up to speed on the investigation? Are you ready to compare notes? And by any chance is Kate's incident report ready at the police department yet?"

Sammy turned to face her. "We have to wait for Ellie . . . but just wait until I tell you. You won't believe what I found."

Chapter Eighteen

Sammy and Heidi laid out all the nacho fixings in an organized fashion atop the kitchen island, and together they assembled each layer of goodness. Just after they had topped off the dish with shredded cheddar cheese and placed it in the oven to melt, they could hear Bara's excitement at the front screen door. Ellie had arrived, and when Sammy went to greet her sister, Ellie had already stepped inside and was petting her dog.

"You have no idea how thankful I am to you for this break. I mean, I love Mom and Dad, but the bickering is going to send me through the roof! And they've only been here a day, Lord have *mercy!*" Ellie huffed as she shifted a brown paper bag to her other arm and headed toward the kitchen. "I brought leftover lasagna."

"What? I can't believe it. Uncle Walter must be totally pissed. How did you pry those leftovers from your father's hands?" Heidi said in amazement.

Ellie laughed. "I had to. Mom was yelling at him to stop eating it. According to her, Dad's cholesterol has been running high. That's why he hasn't had her famous lasagna in a while. It's a lot easier, I guess, keeping him off the cheese in Arizona since he doesn't like it there. He keeps telling me over and over how it tastes like plastic. I'm like, I know, Dad, you keep telling me that. I get the message! Meanwhile, he's eaten every last curd of cheese left in my refrigerator. He's worse than a mouse, I tell ya."

Sammy rolled her eyes. She was so glad Ellie was hosting their parents and taking the brunt of the visit. Small chunks of time were all she could manage with everything else going haywire around her.

"I actually packed a bag. I left it in the car. I told Mom if we're drinking wine, I was spending the night. I may just spend the night whether we're drinking or not! I'm not really looking forward to going home. Especially when Dad returns and finds the lasagna gone."

The three laughed aloud.

Ellie added, "And mom told him she was going to pack more cheese to bring back to Arizona? What a joke! I think she just said that to appease him."

"You're more than welcome to spend the night. You guys will have to draw straws to see who gets the other bed, though. That's for you two to decide," Sammy said as her eyes pinballed between the two. Sammy's rental had only one spare bedroom upstairs, which usually worked out as the three didn't slumber party too often. Especially after Ellie had gotten married, sleepovers had been fewer and farther between.

"No worries. I'm not drinking tonight. More than likely I'll be heading home. Early shift in the morning," Heidi said with a yawn. "You get the extra bed, Ellie."

Ellie turned, unwrapped the lasagna from the paper bag and

then tucked it inside Sammy's refrigerator. "Did I miss anything regarding the investigation? You guys didn't start the S.H.E. meeting without me? Did you?" She placed her hands on her hips accusingly.

Sammy was glad Ellie had directed the conversation back to the investigation. "You didn't miss a thing. We waited for you so I could bring you guys up to speed together. There's a lot of information to sift through, and I'm really glad you guys are here to help sort it all out. I'm more and more convinced that Jane's murder may be connected to Kate's so-called accident somehow. I know that probably makes no sense whatsoever"—she waved a hand dismissively—"but when we talk about everything, I have a hunch you guys will feel the same."

The oven timer buzzed, and Heidi raised a hand. "I'll grab *los nachos grandes*," she said dramatically with a poor attempt at a Spanish accent.

"Where do you guys want to eat?" Sammy eyed her tiny table in the corner with two ladder-back chairs that didn't give them much room to spread.

"How about the backyard? It's a nice night," Ellie suggested. "We should enjoy every summer night while we have the chance. You know how fast the season always goes. The snow will be flying before you know it."

"Okay, but my weathered picnic table doesn't compare to your gorgeous new patio set," Sammy said with a sigh. "But you're right. We might as well enjoy the nice weather while we have it. Just be careful not to get a splinter," she teased with a chuckle.

Heidi balanced the hot tray of nachos with hot pads while

Sammy held the back door open for her. Bara bounded out of nowhere, almost knocking Heidi off her feet. "Gee whiz, dog, you're going to be the death of me tonight!"

"Sorry *again*." Sammy winced.

"Bara's just about as impatient as his master," Ellie said, laughing as she reached for a stack of paper plates and napkins to bring outside to the picnic table.

"Touché." Sammy had to agree with her sister's quick wit. Ellie was so right.

"Hey Sammy, the one positive about this picnic table is that I can put the hot pan right on the table, right?"

"Go for it." Sammy nodded. "Are you guys up for margaritas, or are we skipping the alcohol tonight?"

"I think I'm going to pass, but thanks anyway," Heidi said after placing the nachos on the picnic table and taking a seat on the attached wooden bench.

"Figures. The one night I could really let loose, and you guys aren't up for it?" Ellie pouted.

"Hey, *you* can if you'd like," Heidi teased. "Don't let me stop you," she added, eyes wide, bouncing her eyebrows.

Sammy stood by the door and waited for her sister's decision. "Well, don't take all night. Otherwise, I'll go grab a pitcher of ice water."

"Well . . . are you going to have a margarita, Sammy?" Ellie asked.

Sammy shrugged. "Nah, wasn't planning on it." She really wanted the group to stay clearheaded so they could put their brains to action, but she hesitated to tell her sister that if Ellie really wanted a drink. She knew her sister didn't get out as often as she'd have liked.

"Fine. Grab the pitcher of ice water," Ellie huffed.

"Oh, okay, twist my arm. I'll join you for one; just give me a few minutes to put it together. Do you want salt on the rim? Or sugar?

"Salt, please." Ellie smiled victoriously.

Sammy retreated to the kitchen, grabbed a bottle of water out of the refrigerator, opened the door, and tossed it to Heidi, who caught the bottle with two hands. Then she returned to the kitchen, where she added strawberries, ice, tequila, lime juice, and margarita mix to the blender and gave it a whirl. She wished she had bought the strawberries from the farmers' market and not the grocery store, as they were far superior. Oh well; next time. Before she poured the cold mixture into the glasses, she wiped a cut lime around the rims and then dipped them in salt.

When she returned, Heidi and Ellie were already digging their hands into the nachos like scavengers, as if they hadn't eaten in days.

"This is amazing!" Ellie said between bites.

"Sorry. I know this doesn't fit into your diet plan," Sammy confessed as she placed the glass in front of her sister and straddled the seat of the picnic table across from Ellie. "But I did make the nachos with ground turkey, if that helps."

"At the moment, I don't really care. I'll take my sorry ass for a run later," Ellie said hungrily as she reached for another chip covered in melted cheddar. "I brought brownies, too. I'm going all out tonight. No diet tonight for me. No-sir-eee!" Ellie reached for her margarita and lifted it in cheers.

"Yeah, you do make the best nachos, Sammy," Heidi agreed, licking the salsa from the side of her finger. "I don't know what it is. I try to make these at home and they never compare. Since I helped make the dish tonight, maybe, just maybe, I'll have a better shot next time I try."

"I guess this is one of my only specialties." Sammy laughed heartily. "Ellie's really the better cook between us sisters." Sammy gave the deserved accolades to her sister, whose meals always turned out the best. "You seriously brought brownies?"

"You bet I did." Ellie nodded. "And I added chocolate chips. Do you have ice cream?"

"Yeah, I bought some. Hopefully I got it back in the freezer in time. It may have melted a bit while I was talking to Bradley."

Ellie's and Heidi's eyes flew in Sammy's direction.

"Ohhh, lookie who's holding back? I've been here almost an hour and I'm just hearing you've already met with Bradley *Schultz*? Do tell!" Heidi batted her eyes and puckered her lips. "Is he as cute as you thought he was back in the day?"

"OMG! He's bea-u-ti-ful!" Sammy admitted with a giggle.

"He did grow into his looks, didn't he?" Ellie agreed.

"Oh Ellie. Come on, now. You know he was a cute kid, too . . . don't even try to deny it. I know you crushed on him. Admit it." Sammy nodded. "Bradley turned out to be one hunk of a man!"

"Well, well. This is certainly interesting news," Heidi teased.

"What does this mean for the newbie detective in town? Sounds like Liam Nash might have a bit of competition!"

The three giggled like schoolgirls.

"Nah, I'm pretty sure Nash hates me," Sammy said as she lifted a corn chip filled to the brim with toppings, stretching the cheddar cheese until it broke.

"Oh no, he doesn't hate you. On the contrary, I think he's rather fond of you. Tim told me," Heidi admitted easily.

"What?" Sammy said with a stuffed mouth. "Hold on a minute." She held up her finger and nearly choked on her food. She grabbed a napkin and wiped her mouth. When she could finally speak, she sputtered, "He's *fond* of me?"

"Yes. He most certainly is," Heidi said as she fluttered her eyes yet again to confirm.

This came as a complete surprise to Sammy. She'd really thought he saw her as a nuisance. Especially recently.

"What did Liam say to Tim? Like, *exactly*?" Ellie asked, nudging her cousin with her elbow. "Give it to us word for word."

Sammy leaned into the table across from Heidi to hear. "Liam Nash said he finds Sammy attractive and captivating. This is according to Tim, so I'm not one hundred percent sure I'm getting the exact lingo." Heidi grinned.

"Is that all he said?" Sammy asked. Minorly intrigued. Okay . . . a little more than minorly intrigued.

"Well, no." Heidi admitted.

Sammy waited for the rest.

"He said you're a firecracker."

"Oh. So I get it. I'm explosive." Sammy's frown deepened.

"Or sparkly?" Ellie encouraged. "Fireworks can be quite beautiful."

"Well, either way, I'm sure his impression of me has changed as of late. That was probably how he felt *before* I stole the manuscript from the police department."

"You did *what*?" Ellie put the food back on her plate instead of into her mouth.

"Oh, you didn't hear how she conned my boyfriend into giving her a copy of Jane Johnson's book? Your sister is a master manipulator when she wants to be," Heidi razzed.

"Master manipulator is taking it a bit far, wouldn't you say?" Sammy defended. "I was told I could look at it anyway . . ."

"Yeah, but not take a copy home!" Heidi reminded.

Clearly Heidi was defending her boyfriend, and these were dangerous waters for her and Sammy to swim. "Yes, I may have overstepped a little," Sammy flatly agreed.

"Ah, yeah. You're lucky he didn't throw you in jail," Heidi continued.

"But did you find anything? Something must be written in those pages that could help us figure this out!" Ellie reached across the table to touch her sister's hand to redirect her attention.

"Honesty, I haven't read it all yet."

"*What?*" Ellie was beside herself. "Wow. This is a first for you, Samantha. Not reading through potential evidence related to a murder victim? I'm utterly shocked!"

"Ellie, the manuscript is upstairs on my dresser if you want to read it. I really didn't find much in the first few pages. Mostly notes about how crafts originated and stuff like that. A dry read for sure; I actually fell asleep reading it. And it's not like I have a store to run or anything! You act like I have all the time in the world to read." Sammy rolled her eyes.

"You had time for Bradley Schultz," Ellie said as she rose from the picnic bench.

Sammy sent her sister a look of disapproval. "Really?"

"Where are you going?" Heidi asked as her eyes followed Ellie.

"I'm going upstairs to go get Jane's manuscript off Sammy's dresser so we can review it. Obviously, you two are slacking in the investigation. Which, by the way, blows my mind!" Ellie said as she left the two sitting alone at the picnic table.

The sun was deepening in the western sky, and a cooler wind came with the lack of sun.

"I'm going to get a sweatshirt. You want one?" Sammy asked as she rose from the picnic table and shivered.

"Nah, I'm good. The breeze feels nice."

"Suit yourself." Sammy shrugged as she stepped inside the kitchen, moved to the entryway, and plucked a gray zip-up from a nearby closet. After she covered her chilled arms, she retreated outside and noticed Heidi looking pensive.

"What's going on in that head of yours?"

"You know, Ellie did have a point. You had time for Bradley. Pretty unusual for you, Sammy. Especially during an investigation of mass proportions for someone like Jane Johnson, *the* celebrity craft queen. Something like this would normally take top priority. Above all else." Heidi eyed her cousin carefully. "You *like* him!"

"I can't believe you guys!" Sammy held up her hands in

defense. "There was nothing in the pages of Jane's manuscript that stood out. Even Nash said so. At least that's what he told me before he reamed me out. And besides, you didn't let me finish. The reason I met with Bradley in the first place is because he mentioned something about Kate, and I wanted to hear his take on the subject." Sammy crossed her arms defiantly across her chest.

"Hmmm. Well, did you learn anything from Bradley, or did you just make goo-goo eyes at the dude? Let's play truth or dare, shall we?" Heidi's manicured eyebrows rose, and she tapped a finger to her lips.

"Truth? You want the truth?"

"You bet I do."

"I would have learned more if Nash hadn't shown up at the Sweet Tooth and interrupted our conversation! So I'm meeting Bradley tomorrow morning at Liquid Joy for breakfast."

"A date?"

"A meeting."

"Ahhh," Heidi said with amusement as Ellie returned with the manuscript in her hands.

"Sammy?"

"Yeah?" Sammy turned her attention to her sister.

"Did you read the second to the last page?" Ellie asked, huffing as if she had run a race from Sammy's bedroom, down the stairs, and back out to meet them.

"No. Like I said, I started reading it and fell asleep. Why?"

Ellie paused and then said, "Well, since you mentioned you read it from the beginning, I skipped that part and flipped through the final pages. Which is where I found something really interesting. There were some indentations in the page. It looked like Jane wrote a note *on top* of the manuscript, and her writing dug into the page beneath. I darkened it with makeup from my purse because I couldn't find a pencil upstairs to save my soul. Jane wrote something in the margin about 'research into Kate's death—potential negligence.' I think she had plans to interview the mayor to find out what happened. She annotated, 'Make appointment with the mayor to discuss city council.'"

Sammy gasped. "How did I miss that? How did Nash miss that?"

"It was lightly dug into the page. I can easily see how you all would've missed it. I had to squint my eyes and darken it by powdering it with my blush brush to see it. Hey, maybe the detective does need S.H.E. on his team? A little makeup isn't used to just 'pretty up' us girls," Ellie answered, and then a smile of satisfaction curled her lips.

Sammy reflected on the night she'd read the manuscript and remembered Bara's reaction to her setting it aside. Maybe her dog was more intuitive than she was.

"Wait, how could it be dug into the page if Tim gave you a copy?" Heidi looked at her cousin accusingly.

"Hey, don't look at me," Sammy answered innocently. "I asked for a copy; if he gave me the original, that's his bad!"

"You are going to get Tim in so much trouble," Heidi warned with a finger wag.

Sammy disregarded her cousin, "You know what, you guys? I don't think Kate's death was an accident. Remember what Kate's ex-boyfriend told me the last time I saw him? 'I know you think Kate's death was an accident. It wasn't!' I'm starting to think maybe Gary was right. I wonder if *he* knows something that he's not sharing. I can't tell you how many nights sleep I lost over those words." Somewhere deep inside of her, Sammy thought maybe she had always known that Kate Allen's death had been no accident. But she hadn't had the courage to test that theory . . . until now.

"Why would you believe anything that idiot said? He just said that to you to get your goat. You should know that, Sammy," Ellie said. And Heidi agreed with a nod of her head.

"Yeah, I wouldn't entertain the idea of paying him a visit. Let him rot. He'll just get under your skin and take you for an emotional roller coaster ride. If there is something that proves Kate's death wasn't the result of an accident, then we'll find the truth without the likes of him," Heidi said as she shooed a mosquito that was buzzing annoyingly by her ear.

"Hey, Sammy?" Heidi gently added. "I know you think you want answers to all this, but maybe you don't. Rehashing all of this is not going to bring Kate back."

Sammy looked at Heidi and Ellie with deep resolve. "I have no other choice . . . I can't let this go."

Chapter Nineteen

The fireflies were just starting to pop their neon glows of brilliance in the blackening sky. The luminosity bounced around the backyard grass and bushes as if the fireflies were putting on a private light show for them. The three S.H.E.s huddled together around Sammy's backyard picnic table with the pages of the manuscript spread between them. Remnants of dried coagulated cheese and corn chip crumbs littered the bottom of the baking dish, evidence of a well-eaten nacho platter.

"Why would she want to meet with the mayor and talk about the city council?" Sammy's eyebrows furrowed.

"That's all I found before hitting the final page of the manuscript. The note reads exactly as I told you: 'Meet with the mayor—city council and research into Kate's death—potential negligence.'"

"Okay, I'm totally lost. Because it seems to me we're looking at two separate events that may or may not be connected here. Let's back up for a minute. I say we start from the beginning," Heidi said as she tucked her blonde hair to hang over one shoulder and combed it though with her fingers.

"Yeah," Ellie chimed in. "What do we have so far? Sammy, take us back to the day you found Jane. I remember the last thing she said to you was that she had to tell you something that could change everything, right? Do you think maybe she wanted to tell you something about the mayor or something to do with the city council?"

"No, Jane specifically told you she wanted to tell you something about the previous owner of Community Craft, right?" Heidi said as her eyes left Ellie and traveled to Sammy.

Sammy weighed her words before speaking. "Yeah. I dunno . . . I can't help but wonder why she's referring to the mayor. Kate's *father*? And the city council—what does that have to do with Kate?" Sammy took a deep breath and let the air out slowly. This was a big one to swallow. Mayor Mark Allen was like a second father to her. She couldn't fathom having to bring up his daughter's death or question him at all about the accident. She wasn't the only one who loved the mayor dearly, in fact, the entire town adored him. He would do anything for anyone at the drop of a hat. Sammy wouldn't allow herself to think she might have to tell him his daughter's accident had been the result of foul play.

"Listen," Heidi said. "You have no idea what Jane wanted to tell you. We shouldn't really make assumptions at this point." She must have sensed the feeling of dread that had washed over Sammy.

"Yeah, I agree, Sammy. Let's not fill in blanks that we don't know yet. It could be totally unconnected, although I don't know why Jane would even concern herself with anything going on in this town," Ellie said. "Take us back to the beginning, and maybe together us three S.H.E.s can figure some of this out."

"Okay." Sammy nodded and waved Heidi and Ellie closer,

even though there was no one else within earshot. "What I know so far about Jane's murder is this." She began to use her fingers to tick off each clue. "First, she was strangled from behind—the poor thing didn't see her attacker coming. There wasn't much defensive bruising or scratches on her body except where she was strangled, at least from what I could tell. Only a few scuff marks beneath the bench where her feet rubbed against the ground. Second, her last published book was in her hands and had THE END scratched in pencil across the page. Third"—Sammy tapped her third raised finger.

"Wait!" Ellie interrupted. "The *end* of what? The end of Jane Johnson? Or the end of something else?"

"I don't know. Good question. Let's marinate on that." Sammy nodded and then continued, "She had some kind of white powdery substance on her navy blouse that stood out, but Nash said the toxicology report isn't back yet. And fourth"— Sammy pointed to her pinkie finger—"she must have had her cell phone stolen at some point, because we know the phone ended up out west."

"Yeah, but who's to say she had her phone stolen at the time of the murder?" Ellie interjected.

"Wouldn't she have reported it stolen if her phone was missing before she was attacked?" Heidi suggested. "Let's face it, nowadays people can't last five minutes without their phones. Could you?"

"That's a good point," Ellie said, nodding her head in agreement.

"Okay. That gets us through the scene of how you found Jane. But let's go over again why you think this has any connection to

Kate's accident." Heidi leaned her elbows on the table, laced her fingers, and leaned her chin on her closed fist.

"I no longer believe Kate's death was an accident," Sammy admitted. "Something just isn't sitting right. And negligence, to me, sounds like foul play. And that's not even taking into account what Gary said."

"Okay . . . and what is the glaring realization that makes you connect Kate's death to Jane Johnson's?" Ellie licked her finger and then dipped it into the empty nacho platter, picking up left-over corn chip crumbs. She then licked the salty crumbs from her finger.

"Really, it comes down to the barrette," Sammy said. "How the hell did Kate's hair accessory—which, by the way, she wore on the day of her death—get inside Jane's suitcase? Someone must have given it to her. There's just no other explanation."

"Okay. Who?" Heidi asked.

"And why?" Ellie added.

Sammy threw up her hands in frustration. "I dunno . . . You guys tell me!"

Ellie idly tapped her fingers on the table as the three sat silent. Bara sauntered next to Sammy and nudged her hand for her to pet him. She was surprised he wasn't chasing the fireflies like he normally did when let out at dusk. His soft fur felt warm and comforting to her touch.

"Do you have anything else?" Ellie asked. "Or are we looking at *just* the barrette as the connection between Kate and Jane?"

"Well . . ." Sammy hesitated. "Oh my God, Nash is going to kill me," she said under her breath and puffed a burst of air, sending her auburn bangs momentarily away from her eyes.

"What?" Heidi's hands flew up dramatically. "You're not going to pull the I-can't-tell-you-because-of-Liam-Nash card? I think we're waaaaay past that. Don't you?"

"Okay, but if this leaks out . . . you guys just happened to look at the police report on my coffee table or something. Don't go blabbing that I shared all this information willingly. This S.H.E. meeting never happened." Sammy waved her hand across her throat. "You hear? In fact"—she rose from the picnic table—"I'll go and grab the police report so you guys can read it for yourselves to see what is blaringly obvious."

"Yeah, no problem, you have our word." Heidi nodded. "Right, Ellie?"

"Absolutely. Hey, Sammy, hit the outside patio light when you go in. It's getting harder to see out here. And grab me a jacket too, will you? I'm getting eaten alive; these bugs are horrendous." Ellie slapped her bare forearm to squash a pesky mosquito.

Sammy returned with the police report in one hand and a light jacket for her sister in the other. Heidi reached for the report willingly, and Sammy tossed Ellie the jacket.

The three sat quietly while Heidi scanned the document. When she finished, she said, "Okay? So . . . they never recovered the barrette. I get that. But other than that, Sammy, what's blatantly obvious?" Her eyes left the page and met Sammy's directly.

"If the police never recovered the barrette, *someone* did. And when we find that *someone*, we find our killer."

"Or whoever had possession of the barrette knows something?" Ellie suggested.

"Exactly." Sammy nodded. "Not only that, but the barrette ribbons were cut. If you look at the police report, the ribbons couldn't have been cut clean by the tractor; that would be literally impossible. If they were sucked into a belt as Duke described in the police report, they would be gnarled, greased, and chewed up. And the barrette would have been sucked into the machine never to be found again. But that's not what happened." Sammy pointed to the report. "This proves Duke was lying. The question is, why?"

"What do we know about Duke Reed?" Ellie's eyes pinballed between Heidi and her sister.

"I know my parents and the Reeds helped each other out now and then when farm equipment broke down. I think that was more with Duke's father though; nice family." Heidi answered.

"Duke Reed? You guys already knew Duke Reed was at the scene of Kate's accident, didn't you?" Ellie asked. "I mean, even before reading the police report?"

"He wasn't the only one, though. There were a bunch of people at the farm that day. They were all practicing for the upcoming fund-raiser. Kate was just getting a lesson on driving the tractor when the accident happened. They were over the hill, out of sight," Heidi defended.

"Doesn't it say something about Highway 83?" Sammy rose from the bench and began to pace on the small back patio. "Heidi, look at the police report again."

"Yeah? Again, sooooo? You guys know where the accident happened. Right? They were at Duke Reed's farm—on Highway 83! A farm that's no longer *there*. And to be honest, I think everyone in the town is glad the farm's gone, so it doesn't remind us of where Kate died."

"Jane not only had Kate's barrette in her suitcase; she also had a small yellow legal pad where she had written 'Highway 83.' The location of Duke Reed's farm, the farm that used to be there before it was flattened and turned into the industrial park. And it just hit me now. Maybe that's why Jane had 'Highway 83' written down. Maybe she had connected something to the Reeds' farm. Maybe she uncovered something about Kate's death that got her killed . . ."

"What are you getting at, Sammy?" Ellie asked.

"Why did they sell it? Maybe there's clues there. Something we're missing . . ."

"So, you're saying that the Reeds didn't sell the family farm as a result of the accident? That's what I was told. That the Reeds had to move. They couldn't live there anymore because of the horrible memory." Heidi's expression fell.

"I know a way you can find out." Ellie held up a finger to interrupt them. "Bradley Schultz."

Sammy's head spun in her sister's direction. "What?"

"While you were living in Madison, Bradley worked on the Reed family farm. He used to pollinate the corn or something like that. This was right before he moved out east. I know for a fact he worked there, at least part-time, because I remember when Mom told me he'd no longer have time to cut their grass. That was the summer dad broke his leg, remember? To be honest, there was a rumor going around that Bradley was fired from the job for stealing something from the farm, or something to that effect."

"Seriously? He was fired? Huh . . . he doesn't seem the type of guy to be fired from his job, never mind steal anything."

Sammy hadn't thought it possible, but now she was even more excited for her breakfast with Bradley Schultz.

Chapter Twenty

The next morning, Sammy rifled through her closet for the third and final time and threw up her hands in defeat. Her mind waffled between her typical pale plaid blouses (of which she owned a spectrum of pastel colors) or something different. Deciding what to wear to breakfast shouldn't be this difficult. She was glad her sister and Heidi hadn't spent the night, because if they had, they'd have been teasing her about the insane amount of time it was taking her to get ready. The pressure she was putting on herself was crazy ridiculous. Another sundress was out of the question, but she didn't want to dress too casually either. She finally settled on a pair of khaki capris and a crisp white three-quarter-sleeve button-up blouse. A small wooden disc essential-oil necklace that a new vendor at Community Craft had created completed the look. And smelled good too. A calming blend of lavender, sweet wild orange, cedarwood, and frankincense wafted from the necklace. She breathed it in willingly. Sammy tastefully applied her makeup, adding a bit of light brown shadow to her eyes, blushing her cheeks, and finishing with a hint of lipstick. She pulled her hair back loosely in a neat but still casual ponytail. She stole a last-minute glance in the bathroom mirror before heading downstairs, where she slipped on a newer pair of brown leather sandals she had forgotten about that were hidden in the back of her coat closet.

"I'll be back later to pick you up, Bara," she said to her dog as she patted him on the head after she'd made sure he had everything he needed. He responded with a sad face that tugged at her heart. "I *promise*," she added, before persuading him back inside the house and then closing the front door. She skipped down the front steps and slipped into her car for the quick ride into town.

Sammy suddenly realized it was Saturday. The day she was *supposed* to have been hosting a book signing for the Queen of Crafts. How quickly her life had turned upside down from the unexpected turn of events. She decided to momentarily tuck the thought aside because she didn't want to be depressed. Not on the day she was going to meet her old teen crush.

The hayrack baskets that hung from the lampposts as she entered downtown caught her attention. The colorful flowers always made her happy and brightened her mood. This year, the Beautification of Heartsford Committee had overloaded the baskets with trailing ivy and deep-purple, pale-pink, and white petunias. They were so pretty, Sammy mentally decided she might stop by the greenhouse after work to create a new flowerpot to place by her front door at home. She was very good at keeping Community Craft seasonally decorated, but not so much her house. She wondered if she never really felt settled because she lived in a rental property. Maybe she should just go ahead, take the leap, and purchase her own property. Although it was small, she felt comfortable in her cozy rental. Maybe her landlord would consider selling it to her? She mentally added *pick Ralph's brain to see if he'd be willing to sell* on her list of things to do. At the very least, she should figure out her options.

Sammy pulled into the last available parking spot in front of Liquid Joy. Bradley was sitting on an outdoor bench in front of the coffee shop awaiting her arrival. His arm was casually draped across the top of the bench and his tan muscular legs were crossed at the ankle. He too was wearing khaki shorts. And a pale-green polo, which she imagined made his eyes pop like emeralds against his dark tan. He waved when he noticed her pulling up.

Sammy stole a glance in the rearview mirror to remove a pesky eyelash that had fallen into the corner of her eye. She smeared the soft brown eyeliner evenly after removing the irritation. She was pleased with her reflection. Taking the extra time to primp had been in her best interest, as she actually felt attractive and confident, more so than usual. She stepped from the car to greet Bradley.

"You look so comfortable basking in the sun, I hate to move you," Sammy chuckled.

"Beautiful morning. Beautiful girl. Boy, it doesn't get better than this, does it?" He shaded the sun with his hand and smiled.

Sammy instantly blushed at his charm.

Bradley rose from the bench, and his lips softly brushed her left cheek with a light kiss. She hadn't been expecting that.

"Mornin', Samantha," he whispered as he stepped past her to open the door of Liquid Joy and held it open for her as a gentleman would. Her thoughts immediately flew to Nash and how he never held a door for her. This surprised her. Why was she comparing Bradley to the detective? She slipped under Bradley's arm, through the door, and instantly breathed in one of her favorite morning scents: coffee.

"Where would you like to sit?" Sammy asked over her shoulder as the two scanned the crowded, cheery room for an open table. The emoji-painted walls seemed to be encouraging smiles and inspiring patrons to be in a jolly mood. The room rumbled with happy chatter.

"There's one." Bradley pointed to a white table for two beside the front bay window where they could look out onto Main Street.

"Perfect."

Sammy maneuvered through the filled tables, waving to familiar faces and greeting people with smiles and hellos as she went.

When they finally settled at the table, Bradley said, "Boy, you must know just about everyone in here, don't you?"

Sammy smiled wide. "Yeah . . . well . . . that's what I get for working across the street."

Sitting across from Bradley was almost too good to be true. The man was beautiful. He smiled back at her with such gleaming bright teeth, she almost needed sunglasses.

"You must recognize a few familiar faces?"

"Yes. Some do look familiar," Bradley agreed. "Actually, I'm surprised at how many don't." He frowned. "This town is certainly growing and changing."

Even when he frowned, he was gorgeous. Sammy wanted to pinch herself. "Do you want to try one of those breakfast sandwiches I was telling you about? I have to order them at the counter because Douglas hasn't hired additional waitstaff or anything.

This breakfast addition is a new thing he's trying out. He said he's gonna give it a go for a few weeks and see if it's popular with the patrons. By the look of things, he may have to hire additional help. This place is packed today."

"Sure. But only if you let me buy." Bradley leaned to one side, pulled a silver money clip out of his pocket, and handed her a twenty-dollar bill. "Is that enough?"

"You don't have to buy." Sammy waved him off casually, but he caught her by the hand and held it a minute before releasing her. "I insist." His eyes met hers, and her heart leapt to her throat.

He pulled another ten-dollar bill from the clip. "This should more than cover it. No?"

She resigned to his offer and plucked the cash from his hand. "Thanks, this should definitely cover it. Coffee with cream, too?"

"Sure. Sounds perfect."

"I'll be right back." Sammy lifted herself from the white wooden chair and maneuvered her way back to the counter, where she stood behind a few people waiting in line.

Officer Tim Maxwell walked into the coffee shop and stepped directly in line behind her. "Look at you, Miss Fancy Pants." He nudged Sammy's arm playfully.

Did she really look that different? She must, if Tim had apparently caught on. "What are you talking about?" Sammy turned and frowned at him.

"Oooh. Makeup and all, too. Lookie you." He continued to tease as he reached for the bottom of her ponytail and gave a light tug. "Are you here with Nash?" Tim's eyes scanned above her head and then across the room, looking for the detective.

"Nooo, keep your voice down," she hissed. Tim could really be a thorn in her side sometimes. "Where's Heidi?" she asked, and then remembered her cousin had an early shift at the hospital. "Never mind." She waved him away like she was trying to rid herself of a fly. But she was going to need something stronger to get rid of this bug. He was so annoying sometimes.

This only caused Tim to throw his head back and laugh.

Then it was Sammy's turn in line. "Hey, Cara, I'll have two of those new ham, egg, and cheddar breakfast sandwiches and two coffees, please. You don't have to pack it to go. I'm eating in house today."

The barista nodded, her blonde ponytail bobbing in response. "I'll get the coffee right away and call your name when the sandwiches are ready." She turned to the coffee machines, and Tim bent over to speak directly in her ear. "Eating for two? See, I knew you were on a date! Who *are* you with?" He craned his neck to scan the entire space. "Wait until I tell Nash you were on a date with another guy," he added out the side of his mouth.

Sammy swatted him with her hand, causing Tim to smile wider. "I'd hardly call breakfast with an old friend a date. And besides, what's it to Liam what I do, anyway?"

"The lipstick is a dead giveaway that this isn't just breakfast," Tim argued as he pointed out her ruby-tinted lips. "Well? What old friend? That guy?" Bradley, one of the only people sitting alone, was faced toward the wall away from them, making it impossible for Tim to recognize who she was with.

"Gosh, you're nosy! Bradley Schultz. From the old neighborhood," she finally acquiesced.

"No way! Schultz-ie? I used to play baseball with him." Tim

stepped out of the line. "I'm going to go over and say hello. Grab me a coffee, will ya?" He pushed his way through the crowd away from her.

Sammy made eye contact with the barista, and Cara said, "I got it. I'll add Officer Maxwell's to your order."

"Great," Sammy huffed under her breath.

"Don't worry, we don't charge members of our police department. Their first cup of coffee is always on the house."

"Oh no. I wasn't worried about the cost, more the company," Sammy added in a teasing tone with a roll of her eyes. "I can see why Tim's always in here, though, if the coffee is free." She laughed.

"Douglas says it's the best way to support our women and men in blue. If they want food or extras, though, they pay for that." Cara handed her a tray with three smiley-faced emoji cups and lids and individual creamers on the side. "I didn't put your cream in today; since you're eating in, I'll let you add it. These new breakfast items are keeping us hopping. I'll call your name when yours is ready."

"I think that's a very nice gesture for those who protect and serve us. Thanks, Cara." Sammy smiled as she turned with the tray and tried to balance three steaming coffees in her hands without bumping into someone from the expanding crowd. Word must have gotten out about the growing breakfast menu, she thought as she maneuvered her way back to the table. Tim was sitting across from Bradley, and the two were laughing and carrying on without a care in the world. Sammy set the coffee tray down on the table, and the two guys willingly removed their cups. She waited for Tim to get the hint and remove himself from her chair, but instead he said, "Pull up another seat," and returned to their conversation.

Sammy was growing even more irritated. She turned around to look for an empty chair she could add to the table. There wasn't one. "Seems to be a full house," she said, and then secretly glared at Tim while Bradley added the extra money left on the tray back into his money clip.

"Ah. I better get going anyway. Duty calls." Tim capped his coffee with a lid, rose from the chair, and then held it out for Sammy and waved his hand dramatically as if she were a princess and he her servant.

"Great to see you, Tim-bo," Bradley said.

"We should get together again while you're in town," Tim said, and Bradley agreed with a nod of his head. "Toss the ball around or something," Tim added.

The two men shared a mock salute, and Tim turned from the table and began maneuvering back through the tables.

"Goodbye to you too, Tim," Sammy added with a cupped hand, and then Tim's hand shot up in a backward wave.

"What's wrong? Don't you guys get along okay?" Bradley nodded his head toward the officer, who was now stepping out of Liquid Joy. "Seems you have an interesting relationship with those in law enforcement here in town. Something you want to tell me?" His dark eyebrows lifted.

Sammy threw her head back and laughed. "No worries! All good, I promise. Tim is dating my cousin Heidi. He treats me like an annoying sister, but I know somewhere deep down he loves me." She winked.

"Sammy Kane," a male voice called out.

Sammy turned her head in the direction of her name to see Douglas behind the counter placing a tray with their breakfast atop the counter. "I'll be right back."

Sammy retreated through the crowd to reach Douglas, who was adding napkins and plastic cutlery to the tray of food. "Breakfast is served, milady," he said with a wide smile.

"Thanks. I can't wait to try this." Sammy reached to retrieve the tray.

Douglas waved Sammy closer to the counter. "Hey, wait. Did you go and talk with Ethan yet? Over at Pine Haven?" he asked conspicuously.

Sammy's eyes narrowed. "No. Was I supposed to? I believe you told me to stay out of it? Or something along those lines," she added in a teasing tone, her eyes crinkling in a half-moon smile.

"Well . . . I thought maybe you'd gone and done your typical snooping thing anyway." He waved a lean finger. "Especially after I told you I'd seen him crying the day I met Jane Johnson. I just want you to know Ethan came in here yesterday all bandaged up, acting real anxious. Weird, I tell ya. *Really* weird. Word on the street is that he's been acting this way since the murder." Douglas's voice grew serious. "I mean . . . what if we have a murderer living among us?" His eyes grew wide behind his dark-rimmed glasses.

"I don't know, Douglas," Sammy said. "I saw him at Pine Haven after the murder. Would he return to work if he committed the crime?" Then again, if she'd had time to drive over to Pine Haven, Ethan could have also made it back there in time.

Douglas shrugged. "I dunno, but this murder sure has me

creeped out. I wish the police would arrest someone and put all our minds at ease."

"Yeah, I think we all want the same. Thanks for the intel," Sammy said as she lifted the tray and a patron came dangerously close to hearing their private conversation.

"No problem. Keep me posted." He nodded, keeping his mousy-colored brown hair in perfect place.

Sammy walked back to the table, balancing the breakfast tray and hoping she wouldn't drop it while her mind was spinning out of control. *What does Ethan have to do with any of this? He's much younger than I am. How would he connect to Jane Johnson? Would he have known Kate too?*

When she made it back to the table, she knew she had to focus.

"Here you go, Bradley." Sammy took a seat across from a man she had fantasized about all through her teen years. How could a man be so darn beautiful? Life seemed suddenly unfair. All of his facial features were perfectly balanced. She instinctively touched her nose and wondered if it was the right size for her face.

"You know . . . you don't have to call me that." He shook his head and awoke her from her daydream.

"Call you what? Bradley?"

"Yeah. Only my mother calls me that. People in the real world call me Brad."

"Oh? The *real* world?" Sammy chuckled. "As if Mayberry here isn't the real world?" Her smile widened.

"My mother's pretty stern about calling me Bradley. She said if she had wanted to name me Brad, it would be written on my birth certificate. She named me Bradley and she'll call me Brad-ley," he said with a laugh. "But seriously, everyone out east calls me Brad."

"That's certainly what I remember. I can still hear your mother now," Sammy agreed, "Brad-ley, come in for supper!" she said with a pretend holler.

"Yep. Good times." He nodded with a smirk and then took a bite of the breakfast sandwich. His eyes met hers, and he gave a thumbs-up. "Ohhh, this was a good call," he said between bites.

"How is your mom?" Sammy shifted in her seat. "You think you'll be able to convince her to sell the house?"

"I'm working on it," he said with a hint of frustration. "But the more I push, the more she seems to push back. I'm not sure what it'll take to get her to sign on the dotted line."

Sammy agreed the breakfast sandwich was a good call. The melted cheese and smoked ham were a great combination with the fried egg. She nibbled on it daintily in Bradley's presence, though. If she were with Heidi and Ellie, the egg sandwich might have been gone by now, she thought inwardly.

"Tell me more about Kate," Sammy urged. "I was really sur-prised to hear you knew her."

"I really don't have much to add, honestly. I wish I could help you out, Sammy, but I really can't think of anything more that could possibly help. I couldn't sleep last night thinking about it. Unfortunately, Kate died before she could share more about her concern for her father. At times she certainly did cross my mind over the last few years. I mean, what else was going on here in Heartsford that she didn't share? And did it have meaning?" His voice lowered. "Especially when she died on Duke's farm. I mean, geez, I worked for the guy. The whole thing made me uncomfortable. I was glad I was offered the job to move out east and get away from it all."

"I heard that." Sammy self-consciously licked her lip to remove what she thought might be melted cheese. "That you worked for Duke, I mean."

"Yeah, it was tough. Living here at the time of Kate's death. The whole town was in shock and mourning. She was such a light in this town . . . and so young . . . so much life left to live. Kate sure had a way with people, didn't she? The type of person that would give the shirt off her own back."

Sammy nodded and tried desperately to keep her emotions in check. She wanted intel, not emotions. She took a discreet deep breath and sipped her tepid coffee. She had forgotten to add the lid, and the morning brew was already growing cold.

"So, tell me. Did Duke sell his farm *after* the event, or was the sale already in the works? What I'm getting at is, I was told he sold the farm as a *result* of the accident. That the family couldn't stand to live there after . . . you know . . ."

"Ah, I don't think so. That's not how I remember it." He set down the coffee cup and looked over his shoulder before whispering, "The land was taken by eminent domain. He didn't want to leave, but his family had no other choice. The land was sold so the new manufacturing plant could be built. After the fund-raiser that Kate was organizing—it was the last event that was ever held on their land—the Reeds were forced to move. The closing was to take place after what would have been the last community gathering on the farm."

"Didn't the county compensate the family for the land? It's

not like they were evicted and received no compensation, right? They must have been paid a fair deal?"

"Not what the Reeds thought it was worth. This is a generational farm we're talking about. At the time, corn prices were low. I think Duke thought it should have sold for more, but I don't think he sold it willingly. I think he blamed the Allens, to be honest, especially the mayor. I bet he thought Mayor Allen was bending the common council's ear." Brad wiped his mouth with a napkin. "Prices of corn and soy fluctuate. He was having a bad year all the way around. And sometimes he would hold off paying us. He just didn't manage the funds very well year to year, I guess. Actually, I hated him as my boss."

"Huh. Interesting." Sammy shifted in her chair and then asked, "Do you really think the mayor could have stopped the farm from being sold? Maybe that's what Kate was going to tell you? That Mayor Allen was involved somehow?"

"Maybe?" Brad shrugged.

The two sat silently for a moment, Brad eating his breakfast sandwich and Sammy deep in thought.

"Just curious—what kind of work did you do on the farm?"

Brad smiled. "Anything that was needed, really. The last summer I worked there, I pollinated corn. You know, detasseling corn is a long process. Long and boring." He rolled his eyes.

"Why detassel corn? Seems a bit counterproductive. I mean, why would a farmer do that by hand?"

"Each plant has a male and female flower. The tassel at the top produces the pollen, which shakes loose and falls on the silk. The pollen makes its way down the silk to create a seed. When done naturally, a corn plant will pollinate itself. But if you want a hybrid seed, you have to detassel the top. So then you have male and female rows to pollinate into a new seed."

"So, you have rows that you have to detassel the top?"

"Exactly. Corn pollinates from the wind, so if you detassel one row, *ba-da-bing*"—his eyebrows lifted—"new baby seed."

"Wow. Learn something new every day." Sammy smiled.

"Yep. Fields are planted with three or four rows of female to one row of male. Just think about that for a second when you look at the size of a field." He laughed. "That's a lot of detasseling. As I said, long and boring and hot too in the humid Wisconsin summer heat. Blah! I sure don't miss it," he admitted easily.

"Crazy." She nodded, then took a small nibble. "Not to throw salt in an old wound, but I heard you were let go from that job. Is that true?"

Brad's demeanor changed as he sat upright in the chair. "That rumor is still flying around, huh?" Brad lowered his voice so only she could hear. "The guy was a complete ass to work for. Duke accused me of stealing some old tools he had hidden inside the barn. I think his ex-wife must have taken them before she skipped town, thinking they were antiques or something. Maybe she thought she'd get some money for them. Unfortunately, I was blamed, and everyone in town seemed to believe Duke. He completely smeared my name across Heartsford. Obviously, there was no proof that I stole anything, so he couldn't press charges against me. I was so glad to move out of this town, but I guess the rumor is still haunting me."

"Nah." Sammy waved a hand of dismissal. "I think you may be overreacting a bit. People talked after his wife took off. They insinuated the couple had marital problems, and no one understood why she didn't take her son with her. Or at the very least visit. That I'll never understand; how does a mother just drop a kid, just like that? Anyway, I'd just heard you were let go from the farm—that was all I heard. I seriously think anyone in town would consider it old news."

A look of relief swept across Brad's face. "I wouldn't want you to think differently of me, Sam."

Sammy reached across the table and gave his hand a squeeze as an act of encouragement. "No worries there."

He returned the smile, and Sammy couldn't help but think Deborah was right. The man resembled a movie star.

Brad finished the last bite of his breakfast sandwich and sat back in the chair, satisfied. "That was good. I already foresee coming in here again while I'm in town. Might have to bring my mother along next time."

"How long are you in town for?" Sammy wasn't at all ready for him to leave Heartsford.

"Few more days. I can work from my laptop. My boss is pretty lenient that way, as long as I get my work done. He's giving me some flexibility."

Sammy leaned into the table and waved Brad closer. "Whatever happened to Duke? Do you know? What does he do for work now that the farm is gone?"

"Last I heard, he was working construction. I'm not sure, though. Why?"

"He doesn't work for Semco?"

"Nah, don't think so. Wait a minute . . . Now that you mention it, he might."

"Huh. What about the rest of the family? Did he remarry? Kids?"

"I know his son took a landscaping job over at Pine Haven."

A sudden chill zipped down Sammy's spine.

"Are you okay? Your face just went pale." Brad reached a hand across the table.

"Yes. I'm fine." Sammy took a breath. "Ethan is Duke Reed's son?"

"Yeah. Why?"

Chapter
Twenty-One

"Hey? Did you hear what I said?" Deborah waved her hands frantically in front of Sammy's face to gain her attention. "Hellooo. You in there?"

"Huh?" Sammy turned to Deborah as they stood at the cash register counter at Community Craft reviewing the schedule of upcoming classes for the interior craft room.

"You are so *not* with it today," Deborah said as she pointed a French-manicured finger to the paper on the counter. "I just asked you if I could move my painting class as long as the students are okay with it. Thursday evening would work much better for me over the summer months. My husband is usually around on Thursdays and can help with the kids instead of having to get a sitter."

"Yeah. Sure. If everyone in your class is in agreement and the craft room is available, you certainly can move the day and time. Whatever you need." Sammy nodded.

"What's going on with you? You're so distracted today." Deborah's dark eyes narrowed as she placed a hand of concern on Sammy's arm.

"Sorry." Sammy smiled and shook her head to rid it of the cobwebs. "I had breakfast with Bradley—I mean Brad—this morning, and I'm just rewinding our conversation over and over in my head. Not to mention, we were supposed to be hosting Jane Johnson for her book signing today. I guess I'm just a little weirded out." Sammy moved her long auburn bangs away from her eyes with her hand. She really needed a haircut. Or to let her bangs grow. This in-between look was ridiculous.

Deborah released her arm and refocused on the class schedule. "Yeah, definitely not how we thought this Saturday was going to go, huh?"

"Yep." Sammy blew her bangs away again with one large puff of breath. "Not. At. All."

"Okay, so let's not talk about the elephant in the room, since it's creeping us both out. Let's talk about something else. You two had breakfast? And now you're calling him *Brad*?" Deborah teased as she rewrote the time for her painting class and then moved from behind the counter toward the craft room to tack the new schedule to the window. "I'm glad to hear you two made up. The other day, things weren't looking too promising. Better now, I hope?" she added over her shoulder.

"All good. All fine," Sammy said as Deborah turned, retreated, and headed toward the office.

"That's all you're going to share, huh? All good? All fine? All right, I'll let it go for now. I'm going to grab my purse and then I'm off."

"Sounds good. Thanks for your help today." Sammy's mind was whirling. She really wanted to leave Community Craft and run over to Pine Haven Bed and Breakfast to see if she could corner Ethan with a few pointed questions. Unfortunately, she had no one to cover the store, and she didn't dare ask Deborah to stay late again. That wouldn't be fair.

Deborah left the office and slung the slim black leather strap of her purse over her shoulder. "By the way, I started painting those glasses for the fund-raiser. I love how they're coming along, but I'm not sharing them with you until the event. I want it to be a surprise. You're okay with that? Right?"

"Huh?" Sammy turned to Deborah, and the two made eye contact.

"Gee, you're really not all here today. I'll see you later." Deborah chuckled and turned toward the back door. "Oh, one more thing. I left that book you were after on your desk. The one Jane Johnson wrote on hair accessories," she added over her shoulder, and then walked toward the back door.

"Thanks! Have a good afternoon," Sammy yelled after her. After her coworker left the store, she chastened herself for not keeping her mind more focused. She decided to check out that old craft book. She quickly headed to the office and picked up the book. She fanned the pages until she saw the instructions for braided satin barrettes. Just like the ones she and Kate had made. The year of publication certainly fit the timeline.

So, this is where Kate got the idea.

Sammy wasn't really sure if this meant anything. This puzzle was growing more perplexing. If Kate only knew that the author of this book was supposed to be doing a book signing in that very store, that very day. *Bizarre* was the only way Sammy could put it. She could hear customers talking out on the shop floor, so she abandoned the book on her desk and went back to work.

After a while, the store quieted down to a few random shoppers. Maybe the obvious, the fact that Jane Johnson's book signing had been canceled due to her unforeseen death, was keeping patrons at bay. No one wanted to address the noticeable hole in the schedule. In between the sparse customers who actually approached the counter to purchase something, Sammy decided to call Dana to see if she could sew a few more of those popular spalike Velcro towels to sell for the summer months. She also called Abby to suggest a new scent for her candles, the scent that had greeted her when she entered Pine Haven. And then she decided to go ahead and make the call to Kendra to share her adopt-a-garden idea. Then she remembered Stacey and the T-shirts she had made for a past fund-raiser and phoned her to ask if she'd be willing to create a Community Craft T-shirt like Heidi had suggested. After all the phone calls were made, the feeling that she had done something productive for the store took the place of the tumultuous feelings that had been lying heavy on her heart.

By late afternoon, Community Craft had hit a definite lull. The store was quiet and empty. Everyone must've had their fill of the murder gossip. Although there was much Sammy could organize and work on in the store, her mind wouldn't allow it. She removed her cell phone from her pocket and made a phone call to her sister.

Ellie picked up on the second ring. "Hey! How are you doing this gorgeous summer day?"

"Is Mom with you?"

"She sure is. You want her?"

"No. I want you."

"Huh?"

"I was hoping Mom could babysit and you could come work a few hours here at the store?"

"Oh. Now? Actually, we were just talking about stopping in to see you. Dad wants to see the improvements you've made to Community Craft, and Mom wants to shop for something she can bring back to Arizona that would remind her of home. Why? Where do you have to go right now that you need me to come in and work?"

"Never mind." Sammy realized she was being too impulsive. She should be spending time with her parents this week instead of chasing down leads. Although the curiosity was killing her, she'd have to wait. "Do you want to work tomorrow morning instead? While Tyler is in preschool?"

"I was having him skip preschool this week so he could spend time with Mom and Dad."

"Oh."

"But I can come in tomorrow, first thing. I'll open. How does that sound? I'm sure Mom wouldn't mind making breakfast for Tyler. We can let him sleep in, too. He's been up so late with all the grandparental excitement."

"Perfect."

"Okay, we'll all be over to Community Craft within the hour."

"I'll be here." Sammy's glazed eyes looked around the empty store. Wishing for escape.

"All righty. Bye." Ellie hung up.

Sammy decided her time would be better spent making a work list for the upcoming fund-raiser instead of daydreaming.

If she didn't get moving on planning the event soon, it might never happen. Since Ellie and Heidi had offered to help, she could divvy up the responsibilities into four sections if she also included Deborah. By the time she had made out her list and called the library to lock in a date to reserve the outer deck and community room, she heard commotion at the back door. Tyler weaved between the racks and rushed toward her.

"Aun-tie Sam-eee!" The toddler opened his arms wide, and Sammy took him in willingly and spun him in a circle, careful not to knock over any merchandise. When she set him down, he looked up at her wide-eyed. His reflective blue eyes filled with wonder. "Lol-lee?"

"Ah, not this time!" Ellie rushed over before Sammy could lead her son into the office where the lollipops were stored inside the locked desk drawer. "We're going to have dinner soon. Nice try, Tyler."

Tyler's lip came out in a pout. "You can go ahead and put that away," Ellie said to her son as she placed her finger to his lip. He then looked around for Bara, who was missing from his dog bed.

"Bara's not here today, Ty," Sammy said over her shoulder as she greeted her mother with a hug. "I lost track of the day and didn't have time to go and pick him up."

"Well don't you look pretty today." Megan Kane looked at her daughter adoringly. "Was it something I said?" she teased. "Certainly a big improvement from the other night."

"Ah, no, Mom," Ellie interjected. "Your daughter met Bradley for breakfast this morning."

Sammy sent a quick dagger look at her sister.

"Is that so?" Megan eyed Sammy inquisitively. "And how was that?"

"Now, Meg, leave Sammy alone." Walter shooed his wife away. "Go do that shopping that you were so adamant you needed to do. Not like we need another thing," he added under his breath.

"I just want to know if *my daughter* is interested in pursuing our old neighbor," Megan snapped at her husband before giving up and perusing the store, with Tyler rushing to her side to be lifted.

Ellie pried Tyler from her mother's leg. "Tyler, you come with me. Let Grammie shop." She picked up her son, and he popped his thumb in his mouth. Then he removed it and squealed again. "Lol-lee!"

Ellie rolled her eyes.

"Just let him have one," Walter said.

Sammy smiled victoriously at her father, knowing her sister would give in rather than fight a tantrum this late in the day or argue with their father.

"Fine," Ellie huffed, as she carried her son in the direction of the office.

"Key's on my desk," Sammy yelled to her sister, who was already rounding the corner to the office entrance.

Sammy was left to stand alone with her father, who said, "The store looks great. Very organized. How about showing me around? Since you mentioned all these changes you were planning over the phone, I'd like to see them in person."

"Sure."

Sammy led her father to the back of the store, where she and

Deborah had hung a long expansive shelf to hang the blankets for sale. The shelf had multiple dowels attached where each blanket could be individually showcased. As her father studied the shelf and how it had been designed and assembled, she leaned toward him and said, "Dad, I need to talk to you."

Walter lifted his scrutiny from examining underneath the shelf to meet his daughter's gaze. "Sounds serious." His voice lowered. "Is this about what I think it's about?"

"Yes." Sammy nodded, then craned her neck to see if her mother was in earshot. Megan was in the far corner of the store contemplating a throw pillow that had the state of Wisconsin stamped on the muslin fabric.

"Did you find out anything new?"

"When Kate passed away, you and Mom were still living here. I'm just curious. Did you attend any of the council meetings regarding the new manufacturing plant that went up on Highway 83?" Sammy removed a few crocheted lap blankets and put them in a pile on an empty shelf. Later, she would box them up and bring them along to Pine Haven. The throws would provide an ample reason to pay Mrs. Thatcher a return visit.

"No. Why?" Walter ran his hand along his partially bald head.

"What if Duke Reed losing his land to eminent domain had something to do with Kate's death? Help me out. Do you know Duke? Or his son Ethan? What was the buzz around town at the time?"

Sammy's father took a measured breath. "I don't know the family personally. I did hear there were some domestic situations going on over there. In fact, I felt bad for the guy; the kid's mom took off and left Duke to raise him on his own. And then they had to leave the farm. Ethan's his son's name, you say? I did hear rumblings that the Reeds weren't happy with losing the farm. Who would be? That farm had been in the family, I think, three generations. But from what I heard, they were well compensated. Why?"

"Just to confirm, then. They were already losing the farm *before* Kate's death. They didn't move because of the accident. Right?"

"Yes. The ball was already in motion," he confirmed.

"Don't you think that could be motive for murder?"

"What are you saying? You think that one of the Reeds murdered Kate? What would she have to do with anything? That's quite a stretch, Samantha." He rubbed his bald head nervously. "You know, digging all this up isn't going to bring Kate back. Are you sure you want to open up this can of worms? The Allen family would be greatly affected by that type of news. You don't think it was just a bad accident? Is that what you're saying? *Why* would Duke kill her? To get back at the mayor for selling his land? By killing his daughter?"

"Yeah, I'm not gonna lie; the thought crossed my mind."

"That's quite an accusation to make. You'd better really know for certain before you go spreading that kind of rumor and causing even more trouble." He warned with a finger. "I wouldn't go casting blame, no? The mayor wouldn't take the full blame for the Reeds losing the farm anyhow. The Common Council would've voted for or against the land to be used for the new manufacturing plant. The zoning law change from agriculture to industrial takes a long time. That industrial growth was planned out years ahead of time. Years before the mayor's time, too. Guess Duke should've killed the whole town, then. The community wanted the manufacturing plant built because it brought in a ton of jobs. With more jobs came more money. Win-win for everyone. Except, as you're implying, the Reed family."

"I'm not trying to throw around baseless accusations . . ." Sammy closed her mouth when Tyler ran toward her father and landed between his legs. "Pa-pa!" He pointed to his lolly stick and smiled triumphantly.

"Ellie!" Sammy cried out. "At least I don't let him run through the store with lollies in his mouth!"

"He got away from me." Ellie threw her hands up in frustration. "This kid is making me crazy today, I swear."

"Hey, don't blame me. I tried to give you a break. You could have worked this afternoon," Sammy razzed.

"Yeah, if I wasn't so hungry I'd probably take you up on it." Ellie nodded and then turned to her father. "I'll meet you and Mom at the restaurant. I'm already tired of corralling this kid around the store."

"We'll be over in a few minutes. Go ahead and order the pizza if you want. Tell them to be generous with the pepperoni," Walter said as he smiled and patted his grandson's curly head.

Ellie turned to her sister. "I'll definitely open the store tomorrow morning. Take your time coming in. Matter of fact, I might be here all day." She nodded as she wearily dragged Tyler by one hand toward the front door.

Sammy turned to her father. "You guys headed to the Corner Grill for supper?"

"Yeah. I'm trying to hit all our favorite spots before we head back home. Besides, I can only get real cheese on the pizza here. At home it tastes like—"

Sammy interrupted with one hand raised. "I *know*, plastic." She wondered if her father was going senile.

Megan rounded the corner of a merchandise rack and said, "There you two are. Where're Ellie and Ty?"

"You didn't see her leave? She's already headed to the restaurant to get a table." Walter pointed toward the front door, where they noted Ellie wrestling with her son and his candy through the glass window. Sammy knew she was secretly trying to get the sugar away from him. Good luck with that plan.

"Well, she didn't give us much time to shop, now, did she?" Megan frowned.

"I think she's overwhelmed with motherhood today." Sammy smiled.

"I can see why." Megan nodded. "He's my grandson and I love him dearly, but he's certainly a pistol . . . what a hyper child."

"Well, it could be all that sugar you two are pumping him with. Ellie says he really reacts to sugar," Sammy defended her nephew.

Megan shrugged and adjusted her purse strap on her shoulder. "Well that's just what grandparents do, I guess. Wish you could join us for dinner, sweetheart." She placed her hand on Sammy's cheek.

"Yeah, well. This is my life." Sammy sighed and then smiled. "I love Community Craft, I really do. It's just hard at times like these when I have to miss out . . ."

"What, no merchandise?" Walter gave his wife a look of superior surprise after noting her empty hands.

"Oh, I'll come back. I'd like to shop more now, but we're always in such a rush. I do think I may pick up one or two pillows. We'll see, I guess." She rolled her eyes. It was at that moment Sammy realized where she and Ellie had gotten their consistent eye rolling tendencies. Her family left the store, removing the raucous volume, and a quiet hush ensued. Only one thing remained on Sammy's mind. She needed to talk to Duke Reed.

Chapter
Twenty-Two

S ammy inched her Chevy along the gravel road. The crunching sound beneath the tires seemed to echo within the confines of her car. She checked her phone again to verify the Google map, even though it seemed the long snaking driveway led to nowhere. The overgrown trees slapped the side of the open windows, threatening to scratch her as she edged closer to a field where a tall deer tree stand stood erect from the overgrown grass. Finally, up ahead, a small gray clapboard house appeared in the distance. A man, bent at the waist, was reaching for a tool and then retreated under the hood of a truck to tinker with something. Sammy thought the man might have heard her car approach the acreage. She really hoped she wouldn't startle him.

Sammy put the car in park in the middle of the gravel driveway and stepped out. In case she felt she needed a quick exit, she kept the engine running. She took a deep breath before the man noticed her. He wiped his hands with a rag hanging from his faded jeans pocket and walked toward her.

"You lost?" he asked. "A little early in the day for a social visit." The man looked like he was in his late fifties. His brown hair was receding and slicked back as if it had just been washed. The rugged leather-looking skin on his arms was dark from the early summer sun and he was muscular, as if he'd already worked a lifetime outdoors in manual labor. He pulled a soft pack of cigarettes from his short-sleeved plaid shirt pocket, shook one loose, lit it, and took a long drag.

"Duke?"

"Yeah, who's asking?"

"I'm Samantha Kane. I work in town . . . at the craft store. Sorry to show up so early in the morning; I was hoping to catch you before your day got started." She shifted her weight wondering, a little late, if she should've driven out to his house alone first thing in the morning. Why hadn't she waited and taken Ellie or Heidi with her for backup? Or Bara even? She hadn't expected the man to live in the middle of the boonies.

"Well, looks like you took a wrong turn," he chuckled. "I'm not much into artsy stuff."

"No, I kinda figured." Sammy smiled. "I own Community Craft, on Main Street. I took it over after Kate Allen died." Sammy waited and watched as Duke's demeanor changed in front of her eyes from a slight smile to suddenly serious.

Duke took another long, hard drag on his cigarette and let it out slowly. "That was an awful day, the day that girl died," he stated before flicking the long ash.

"I'm here because I want to know what happened. Kate was my best friend, and I was living in Madison at the time of her death and I need to know how she died."

"Gosh, it's been a few years . . . terrible accident," he said before taking another drag of his cigarette. His eyes squinted through the smoke. "Woman was full of youth," he added.

"You were driving the tractor?" Sammy asked tenuously.

Duke visibly stiffened. "I'd really rather not talk about this. Enough time has passed, and rehashing that day ain't gonna bring her back. I think it'd be best if you leave it alone now." He pointed to her car and said, "You can turn around right here. I'm not concerned about driving over the grass."

It was then that Sammy noticed the gray T-shirt beneath his unbuttoned plaid shirt adorned with a Semco logo. She sucked in a sharp breath. With her heart in her throat, she continued fearlessly, "Why won't you talk to me?"

"Nothing to be said. I think it's best if we're done here." He turned on his heel, dismissing her.

With her heart pounding and her hands shaking, Sammy didn't have any other choice than to leave. She watched Duke's image grow smaller and smaller in the rearview mirror but didn't feel relief until she finally turned the corner out of his long winding driveway.

*   *   *

As Sammy drove closer to the Pine Haven Bed and Breakfast, her father's comment echoed in her head.

Are you sure you want to open this can of worms? It's not going to bring Kate back . . .

It was the same thing her sister had said at their S.H.E. meeting. Why couldn't anyone understand the importance of finding out the truth? Perhaps if it was their best friend who had died, they'd all think a little bit differently. Not to mention the fact that the killing clearly hadn't stopped with Kate. Somehow this was all connected to the murder of Jane Johnson, too. Like a tight knot in a ball of yarn, and Sammy was going to do everything in her power to unravel it. She just hoped she could somehow ease the burden and protect the Allen family from the awful news she might uncover. A fleeting thought of Nash crossed her mind too. Boy, he wouldn't be happy with her little excursions this morning. Not a chance.

Sammy tried desperately to clear her mind and set everyone else's opinions aside for the time being. She needed to do what was best for her. And right now, what was best for her was solving this mystery she had found herself deeply entrenched in. With the car windows rolled down, she breathed deeply the wooded pine scent as she turned left turn toward the bed-and-breakfast. Her slick palms were sliding down the steering wheel. Heat of the humid morning? Or nerves? She couldn't decide which was a greater cause of her perspiration. If Duke wouldn't share anything about the accident with her, maybe his son would be able to shine some light on it. She'd known Duke was hiding something the minute she caught sight of his Semco T-shirt. The same company on whose truck Jane Johnson's phone had just happened to be found. Things were not looking good for Duke in Sammy's mind.

The gravel kicked up a cloud of white dust as she raced, probably a bit too speedily, into the parking lot in front of the expansive property. Her eyes darted out the open window to see if she could gain a visual of Ethan working out in the gardens or somewhere on the extensive grounds. She finally found him far in the distance, creating perfect patterns of cut grass that mimicked a basket weave from the sharp blade of the riding lawnmower. She breathed a sigh of relief that he was on property grounds. How she would get to him and poke him with a myriad of questions was another story.

Sammy jammed the car into park and then hastily stepped from the vehicle. She popped the trunk with her fob and removed a large box with both hands. The oversized box was jam-packed with crochet throws in a variety of patterns, textures, and colors. After balancing the box between her leg and one arm, she closed the trunk, took hold of the box with both hands, and trekked to the front steps of the wide porch. Mrs. Thatcher, deadheading flowers from a nearby flowerpot, dropped the withered leaves in a pile on the porch and rushed toward the front door to hold it open for Sammy to enter.

"How nice to see you, Samantha. I didn't think you'd be back so quick. You sure are a savvy businesswoman, that's for sure." Helen smiled and reached to help set the box down once inside the foyer. "I'm guessing you brought the blankets?"

"Yes." Sammy sighed and wiped her beaded brow with one hand. "Hot one today. Or I'm out of shape. Could be a bit of both," she laughed. "Certainly is nice and cool in here with the air-conditioning running; that humidity is awful thick today. I also thought I'd stop in to personally invite you to the next library book club meeting. Have you ever thought of joining? I couldn't help but notice your impressive library—you must love to read, and not just texts from the ole teacher days."

Helen laughed. "Although I appreciate the offer to join the

reading group, evenings are terribly hard to break away from the inn. I do thank you, though, for thinking of me. Maybe in the future when we settle in with our schedule and I can depend on Raymond to cover for me. I'll keep that in mind, though."

"Well, we'd love to have you."

"You certainly didn't have to drag those blankets all the way out here. I could have stopped by Community Craft to take a peek. Besides, as hot as it is, we probably won't be needing heavy layers anytime soon, at least not until the fall season."

"Hmmm. That may have been a smarter idea." Sammy agreed lugging the box of crocheted blankets and removing them from the store display probably hadn't been wise. If that had been her real reason for stopping over, that is. "I thought you might want to see one draped beside a bed or chair, perhaps? You might have a better feel for how beautiful they would look if we give one a try. Besides, these lapghans aren't heavy; they're hooked with a lightweight yarn, perfect for the air-conditioned summertime. For the winter stock, a few of my fiber artists use a heavier-weight yarn. These summer lapghans are more of a thin pretty coverlet for when the air-conditioning is necessary but still feels a bit chilly."

"I see." Helen nodded. "You have a point. Seeing them displayed on a chair or draped at the bottom of the bed as opposed to just viewing them in the shop might make a difference, too. Plus, I don't have any guests now anyway since . . . well . . . you know . . ." She laid a hand beside her cheek, which was covered in heavy makeup unevenly applied. Or matted from the humid weather.

"I understand." Sammy leaned over the oversized box and

popped it open with her fingers. "The murder of Ms. Johnson has been tough on all of us in the community. Such a total shock." Sammy lifted one of the blankets to show the bed-and-breakfast owner, hopefully as a distraction, while she grilled her with a few pointed questions. "How's your staff handling all of this?"

"My staff?" Helen's brows came together in concern.

Sammy held the lapghan between two extended arms to show the design and hide behind it. "Yeah, I'm sure this has been tough on them too? Ethan especially. Wasn't he out here working the day Jane died? I thought I remember seeing him when I arrived . . . and then of course we got that awful news." Sammy poked her head around the side of the blanket, waiting for an answer.

"Not that I remember, although I'm still not functioning properly after all that's happened." Helen shook her head. "Ethan wasn't here until the afternoon. I didn't have the staff work the early shift, so I could give Ms. Johnson her complete privacy. Yes, he was here when we got the news, of course. But by that time it was afternoon, no?"

"Oh," Sammy said, deflated. And again, she tried to redirect Helen into thinking she was visiting for one purpose and one purpose only. "What do you think of this design? Do you like the colors?" She folded the blanket and held it out draped on her arm for Helen to inspect.

"I think it's very pretty. I'd have to agree with you. I'd like to try it on one of the beds to see how it looks. Do you mind? I have the perfect room that would fit those sage-green colors."

"Not at all. That's why I'm here." Sammy smiled and lifted the blanket just enough to carry it in her arms and not drag it on the floor. She followed Helen up the staircase into one of the smaller guest rooms.

When the two entered the small room that was just large enough to walk around a queen-sized bed, Helen reached to help unfold the blanket and said, "Let's just try it draped over the corner of the white coverlet." When they adjusted the blanket to cover the corner of the bed, Helen stood back and studied it. "Love it." She nodded.

"I had a feeling you would. Really adds a handmade cozy feeling to the room, don't you think? Especially with the white-painted paneling you have on the walls." Sammy turned to Helen, who continued to slowly nod her head in agreement. She was beginning to sound like Ellie with her home decor talk.

"Yes. I was thinking we were going to repaint this wall, but now with the blanket, we might not even have to. It's a real nice addition." Helen placed her hands on her hips and studied the room intently.

"Hey, I have a question a bit off topic." Sammy waited for what she thought would be the perfect opportunity to dig further.

"Yes?" Helen's eyes left the bed as she turned to Sammy.

"Do you know Bradley Schultz?"

"Can't say I do. The name is familiar, though. Why do you ask?" Helen dropped her hands from her hips and reached out to smooth out a wrinkle in the blanket.

"I thought you might've had him as a student. Well, *anyhoo* . . . he's back in Heartsford for a few weeks. Trying to sell his mother's house. She's aging, and the house is a lot of upkeep. You understand."

"Okay?"

"He mentioned needing a landscaper. Just for the time being. You know, to spruce up the yard before selling. Does your gardener happen to do any side work, or do you keep him hopping around here? It would only be for a few hours. Do you think I could talk to him while I'm here?" *Oh God*, Sammy thought. *I'm going straight to hell with my continued white lies. And more lies to my grade-school teacher, no less.* She could feel the heat rising from her neck to her face.

"Yeah. He's quite busy here at Pine Haven, but you're more than welcome to ask him. I don't mind if he finds the time. On his days off, of course."

"Yes. Absolutely. I just want to talk to him and see . . . you know . . . a favor . . . for a friend." Sammy could feel her mouth going dry.

"Samantha, I'd love to add these soft cozy blankets. Is it okay if I talk to Raymond about how many we could afford to start? I'm not sure we have the funds right now for all the rooms. We might just start with a few and add more as funding allows. Also, you mentioned having a few here for sale at my gift barn? I really love that idea, too. I would give you a cut, of course."

"Not necessary." Sammy waved a hand of dismissal. "I like to help my vendors out whenever I can. If you want to sell blankets here, too, that's perfectly fine. You could also send customers my way if they want a different color than you have on hand. Or a different size. Fair?"

"Sounds like a plan." Helen thrust out her hand toward Sammy, and the two sealed the business deal with a shake.

"The name of each fiber artist is pinned in the left corner of each blanket." Sammy flipped the corner of the blanket to show Helen what she was referring to. "As long as you keep track of whose sell, we can compensate the artist. I'll leave the box here for a few days if you'd like, and you can put a few in your gift barn or some in your rooms. Whatever you don't want in stock, you can always bring back to Community Craft, and I'll sell them back at the shop. Or better yet, give me a call and I'll stop back out. There're only five blankets in the box; it was all that I could fit. I love coming out here. Your place is so peaceful," Sammy added sincerely.

"Thank you. We try really hard to make our guests feel comfortable." Helen brushed her hand across the handmade lapghan to feel the quality of the soft acrylic yarn.

"I think you're doing a great job." Sammy moved to the other side of the bed and patted Helen on the shoulder gently.

"Better than when I was your teacher?" she asked, hinting for approval.

"Of course not; you're multitalented. You were an amazing teacher too," Sammy encouraged. *Except you forgot to teach me about lying and ethics*, she thought inwardly, sending a new flush of heat to her face. "Don't forget, these blankets I'm leaving behind are from the spring/summer collection. Many of our fiber artists use a wool blend or a heavier yarn for the winter collection, so if you are looking for a warmer blanket in a few months, keep that in mind. I personally like the lighter ones, as they fit nicely in the washing machine because they're not so bulky."

"Better yet, maybe I should take a crochet class? Then I could make a few of my own. Although I don't know where I would find the time. I can't even join you for book club." Helen put a hand on her cheek.

"We do offer classes at the shop; all you have to do is sign up. Actually, in the fall we'll be offering a morning class, if that tempts you." Sammy smiled, and then her smile faded. "Speaking of time, though, I probably should hurry along. Especially if I'm going to stop and talk to your gardener. I need to get back to Community Craft." Sammy jutted a thumb toward the door.

"Oh nonsense, catching Ethan should take you but a minute."

If she only knew.

Sammy eased past the bed and said over her shoulder, "I'm a phone call away if you have any further questions. Thanks, Mrs. Thatcher."

"Helen," she corrected, and Sammy smiled as she rounded the corner out the door and retreated down the long staircase.

Sammy opened the front screen door of the bed-and-breakfast, and the smell of fresh-cut grass drifted toward her with the warm thick breeze. She couldn't hear a lawn mower engine, nor could she see one in the distance. Her eyes traveled the vast property in search of the gardener. She noticed him step inside a nearby work shed, so she hurried down the wide porch steps and dashed in the direction of the shed as if her pants were on fire. Just before arriving at the shed door, she stopped a moment, laid her hand on her chest, and tried to catch her breath. Her heart was racing from the exertion and possibly the sudden rush of adrenaline.

Ethan stepped out of the shed carrying a gas can. He startled when he near bumped into her.

"Sorry, ma'am. I didn't see you standing there."

"No, I'm sorry. I didn't mean to surprise you."

"I can count on one hand how many times someone has been near my work shed." He lifted his left hand, which was wrapped in a white gauze bandage from the tips of his fingers all the way to his wrist.

Sammy's eyes flew to his bandaged hand. She smiled weakly. "You must be just the man I'm looking for, then, if this is your work space." Although *man* would be a stretch. He stood lanky and lean, and the freckles still evident across his nose and face made him appear more boy than man. "You're Ethan?"

"Yep." He set the gas can on the ground.

"What'd you do to your hand?" Sammy pointed out the large bandage, and her thin brows came together in a frown.

"Work accident," he said with his eyes to the ground. "Can't hardly get my work done. I'm about handicapped trying to use my right hand."

"Oh." Sammy noted the scratches on both forearms, as if he'd been scratched by a cat.

Or a person trying to defend herself from strangulation?

The sudden shock of Sammy eyeing the dried scrapes and scabs caused a slight pause between them, and Ethan leaned over, plucked a large reed of grass beside the shed with his non-injured hand, placed it in his mouth, and gave a slight chew. Without removing the reed, he asked, "You mind telling me why you're here?"

"You don't remember seeing me the other day? Out on the balcony?" Sammy gestured behind her toward the main house.

She watched his expression turn from confusion to unease.

Sammy decided just going for it was her best approach. Especially if Helen had followed or her husband Raymond was lurking around the property, she might not have much uninterrupted time with the boy. "I know you talked with Jane Johnson before she died. Please, can you tell me what you talked about?"

"You the po-lice?" Ethan eyed her carefully.

Sammy threw her head back in mock laughter. "No. Absolutely not. I own the craft store in town. You know the one, on Main Street—Community Craft? I took it over after the original owner, Kate Allen . . . well . . . after she died," Sammy added, hoping to catch a reaction similar to his father's, and she did. He flinched.

Ethan grew fidgety, and began chewing the reed in his mouth, like he was chewing gum. "Yeah, what do you want with me?" he said, obviously already feeling accused of something. "I ain't into no crafts," he added.

"I just want to talk with you," Sammy said quickly, trying to ease the young man's mind, but he was growing increasingly anxious as he shifted his weight from foot to foot. "I know you met her, though. Not Kate, the celebrity–Jane Johnson. You met her?"

"I don't know nothing."

"I know you talked to her and I know you were crying. Talk to me. Please?"

"I'm not a crybaby," he spat, removing the wet reed and tossing it to the ground.

"That's not what I said."

This clearly wasn't working. She'd have to soften her words or this conversation would end badly. And soon.

"Okay, I'm not actually here to talk about Jane Johnson's murder. I want to rewind this conversation and talk to you about my best friend, Kate Allen. You were there, weren't you . . . at your family's farm . . . the day that she died?"

"I don't know anything. And my dad didn't neither. He's a good dad. I was just a kid; how'd you expect me to remember anything?"

A trickle of sweat crawled down Sammy's spine as the full realization that Kate had been murdered was confirmed by Ethan's choice of words. Why would both he and his father say they didn't know anything unless they were most certainly hiding something? Kate's death was no accident, but intuitively Sammy had already known that. Her face must have echoed her private thoughts.

"I was just a little kid. Tryin' to protect everyone—especially my dad."

"But you were there, weren't you? With your father? The day Kate Allen died. He was driving the tractor," Sammy pushed, but her voice grew soft and soothing. She reached out to touch his arm and he flinched.

Ethan hung his head.

"You don't have to protect him anymore. I saw the police report; I know Duke was driving. Tell me the truth; it wasn't an accident, was it . . . ." Sammy pleaded.

"I'm tellin' you it *was* an accident. I was there, and that's *one* thing I do remember." His eyes blazed.

Sammy knew instantly she had pushed a bit too hard and wished she could rewind her words.

"I gotta get back to work." He shoved past her and turned for the nearby gas can. And then winced in pain when he realized he had tried to grab it out of habit with his injured left hand.

"You gave Jane Johnson the red-ribbon barrette, didn't you? The piece that was cut, the long tails—where are they? Where are the tails? They didn't get sucked into the combine, did they?"

She knew from the shocked look on his face that she was right.

"What do the numbers twenty-four, fourteen, five mean? A combination lock, perhaps? Jane had it written in her notes. Along with Highway 83. The road where your family farm used to be. Jane uncovered something, didn't she? Something about your family that no one knew."

Sammy knew she had taken it too far. Ethan lifted the gas can with his right hand and stomped off in the direction of the lawn mower. She threw her hands up in frustration. She had learned nothing. Other than the fact that she was closing in on *something*.

Chapter
Twenty-Three

The return ride to Community Craft was unbearably hot with the air-conditioning no longer blowing cool air inside Sammy's Chevy. "Time to trade in this crap car," she said aloud as she reached for a water bottle that had rolled away from her on the passenger seat. She stretched her arm as far as she could reach and nearly ran off the country road with the car veering dangerously near the ditch. Luckily, she wasn't in traffic, or she potentially could've caused an accident. She opened the water bottle, took a swig, and nearly spit it out, the water near boiling. Using her knees to steer the car, she recapped the bottle and tossed it to the passenger floor. Her cell phone rang, and she spoke through the Bluetooth.

"Hey. Where are you?"

"I'm on my way back, Ellie."

"You'd better hurry. Detective Nash is waiting in your office."

"What?"

"He wanted to know where you were hiding and didn't believe me when I said I didn't know."

Sammy's lips came up in a smile. "He's interrogating you?"

"I told him to call you directly, but he said you wouldn't tell him where you were if he asked anyway. You'd just lie."

Sammy laughed aloud. "Well, I guess he's got me pegged."

"Where are you anyway? You heard me. Don't make any stops. Come right to Community Craft."

"On my way," Sammy said, and then abruptly ended the call.

Sammy peeked out the upper windshield after she turned left onto Sumner Street. A storm was brewing. The cumulonimbus clouds were forming and moving at a rapid pace across the darkening sky. A storm was probably brewing inside her office too, she thought.

Sammy pulled into the back parking lot behind Community Craft just as fat drops plopped on the windshield, making the sound of tiny pebbles hitting glass within the confines of her car. She quickly rolled up the windows, her arms instantly soaked from the heavens opening in a deluge of rain.

Great.

Sammy could wait it out or make a run for it. She decided on the latter. The cool rain pelted her sticky skin. The humid air thickened, and the rain caused her soaked clothes to hang on her like an unwanted hug. As she opened the back door of the shop, she combed her soaked, matted hair with her fingers and shook it loose. Since her bangs were long, the wet strands blocked her vision. She swiped them to the left with one hand. Ellie gasped at the sight of her as Sammy moved closer to the cash register counter.

"You look like a drowned rat!"

"Gee. Thanks. Love you too." Sammy shook her shoulders to

rid them of the wet streams that had made paths from her hair down to her arms.

Sammy moved past Ellie where she stood behind the counter and stepped inside the office.

The look of shock on the detective's face was an understatement.

"Looks like the rain started? Or did you get pushed into a swimming pool with your clothes on?" The detective stood from the chair to greet her, but she restrained him with one hand.

"Just hang on a sec, please; go ahead and take a seat. If you don't mind, I'm going to need a moment." Sammy reached for a nearby shelf, where an old gray sweatshirt was balled up in the corner. Although it wasn't cold, between the air-conditioning and her wet skin, she was starting to shiver. She moved out of the office into the restroom. She stripped her wet top off in one swing and replaced it with Carter's old Heartsford basketball sweatshirt, which hung near to her knees. She looked in the mirror to find paths of eyeliner streaking down her cheeks. She washed her face with hand soap and patted it dry with a paper towel. It was then that she realized her makeup bag was in the desk inside the office.

Great.

His timing is impeccable for catching me at my worst, she thought. What other choice did she have? She pinched her cheeks until at least they gave a rosy glow, combed her hair one more time with her fingers, stepped out of the bathroom, and retraced her steps back into the office.

"Seriously. Where've you been?" The detective's eyes followed her as she entered the room, and he held her with his steely-eyed gaze. His teasing tone was officially gone.

"I'm in no mood for an interrogation right now. Why do you dislike me so much?" Sammy asked pointedly as she took a seat behind the old desk and removed her cell phone from her wet pocket to let it dry out.

Nash shifted in the metal chair beside the desk. "I don't dislike you."

"Then why give me such a hard time?"

"I'm tired of having to chase you. To protect you." His eyes softened. That dark melted chocolate was back. "You're like reliving Brenda all over again . . ." he said under his breath.

"You told me your fiancée Brenda died from breast cancer. You couldn't save her from that," Sammy added softly. "Unfortunately, in life we don't get to pick and choose when we leave this earth."

"I know. And I can't protect you either."

And there it was.

That trickle of vulnerability that made her heart swell in deep understanding. He was afraid to get too close to her for fear of losing someone else in some kind of horrible tragedy. The mere possibility kept him at arm's length.

"Let's start again. Where'd you go this morning?" Nash leaned across her desk on one elbow with casual ease. The casual demeanor that made most people open up like a flower. She wasn't most people. His immediate switch back to business bothered her for some reason. She wanted to linger in his openness, as it helped lower her guard to him even more, but the moment had dissipated like smoke.

"Is that why you're here?" She sat back in her chair and crossed her arms across her chest defensively. Maybe she could turn this conversation and she could be the one to interrogate *him* for a change.

"No. I have information to share. I actually came to collaborate with you. I was just surprised to find you not working at the store this morning." He shifted so both elbows rested on the desk and steepled his fingers. "I was hoping you could help me."

Sammy's cell phone vibrated, and Adele sang out "Hellooo" on the desk, stealing both their attention. Bradley's name showed up in neon glow. Sammy's heart leapt, but she waved the call aside. "It can wait."

Sammy knew by the look on his face that Nash had noticed who was calling.

"Let me take you to dinner tonight," he blurted.

Sammy's eyes widened in surprise. She hoped the surprise wasn't that obvious on her face. Suddenly self-conscious, she combed her hands through her damp hair again. This guy was hard to read. No, impossible to read.

"That depends," she finally said after a long pause.

"On what?"

"On whether or not you're going to share with me the latest on your investigation."

The detective threw his head back and laughed. "You're unbelievable."

"Well?" She uncrossed her arms and set her hands flat on the desk.

"The toxicology report came back. The substance on Jane Johnson's navy blouse was a mixture of sand, rock, and cement."

"Sand?" Sammy paused a moment and then said, "There's no sand over by the river walk that I'm aware of. Dirt, yes. Sand, no." Sammy adjusted and sat up in the chair.

"I know. I just walked the crime scene before coming over here and couldn't find anything similar that made sense. I even went across the river to check out the nearby manufactures. They don't work near or around cement, and the parking lots are asphalt. Luckily for me, I checked it out before the downpour." He regarded her wet hair again, and she ignored it.

"Huh. That's strange."

"Yeah, sure is. Now tell me what you've got, because I can tell from the look on your face you've uncovered something. I feel like I'm actively watching you piece together a puzzle."

"All I know for sure is that someone is hiding something." Sammy resigned herself to the fact that she might have talked directly to a killer. Not just Jane Johnson's killer but Kate Allen's as well. The thought made her want to gag.

The detective took a deep breath and sat up in the metal chair. His interest was piqued. "Go on." He waved a hand for her to continue and remained quiet.

"I spoke with Duke Reed this morning . . . and Ethan. Separately, of course."

Nash flew to his feet, alarming her with the sound of the metal chair scraping across the floor. "Samantha Kane." His eyes grew instantly dark. "What are you thinking? You think one of these men might be involved somehow and you go and 'talk' with them?" He gestured his long fingers in air quotes and then placed his hands firmly on his slender hips, demanding an answer. "That's the last thing you should do."

Sammy had known this was coming. Letting him vent might be her best option. She honestly felt she kind of deserved it, so she kept her mouth shut.

A long pause ensued before the detective asked, "Aren't you going to say anything?" His face was growing beet red.

"I know. I shouldn't have gone, but please . . . hear me out . . ."

"I'll hear you out, but after that I may just have to cuff you and arrest you for impeding my investigation." Nash stood gripping the back of the chair and waited.

He wouldn't do that, would he?

"I'm waiting, Samantha."

Sammy breathed deeply and then began, "The one thing that doesn't add up for me is the fact that they're both lying. Ethan insists Kate's death was accidental. But something doesn't make sense. His demeanor was weird at best. It's like he's trying to protect something or someone . . . his father, maybe? He was just a little kid. I mean, I know sometimes when you're a kid it's hard to recall everything and your mind picks up what adults tell you to fill in the blanks. Ethan was *adamant* that Kate's death was an accident, but his body language said otherwise."

The detective ran his hand through his wavy hair in frustration. "Maybe Ethan doesn't know what's in the police report? After all, he was young; most likely he's never seen it."

"I know. The lies or lack of information are making someone look awfully guilty, in my opinion. But who?"

Sammy shook her head and dropped her eyes to the desk until he finally sat back down on the metal chair and waited for her to speak. She could feel her throat constricting and her eyes holding back tears. The emotion from potentially confirming that Kate's death hadn't been an accident but rather an intentional, heinous act suddenly hit her hard. Otherwise, why would these men lie?

"I'm sorry," she finally squeaked out. She swallowed hard, trying to moisten her mouth to speak. "Ethan's been acting strange around town, too. His arms are covered with scratches, and his hand is injured—could they be defensive wounds? And he's a gardener. No doubt *he's* working around sand, building something at Pine Haven Bed and Breakfast. His family lost the farm when the manufacturing plant was built out on Highway 83. When I asked him about the barrette, he visibly flinched. He definitely has some connection to all of this, or at the very least knows *something* that he's not sharing."

Sammy laid her head on top of her arms, facing down on the desk.

Nash stood, reached over, and touched her arm. "I'm going to go. Text me later if you want to meet for dinner," he said.

Sammy raised herself from the desk chair. "Where are you going?"

"I'm going to investigate this further. I'll head over to Pine Haven first," he said over his shoulder as he exited the office.

As soon as the detective was gone, Sammy slumped back into the chair and covered her face with her hands when Ellie rushed into the room.

"Sammy? You okay? I heard raised voices, but I couldn't make out what was being said."

Sammy lifted her head from her arms and made eye contact with her sister. "I dunno."

"What happened?"

Sammy relayed everything she had learned from her conversations with Duke and Ethan, and also the chat with the detective. Ellie's facial expression mirrored exactly how she felt: crestfallen. Sammy rose from the chair, and her sister approached with arms wide, ready for a hug.

"I don't know what else to say except I'm sorry. I wish someone would just tell the truth." Ellie's tone was thick with empathy.

Sammy fell into her sister's arms for a tight embrace. When the two parted, Sammy said, "I just don't know how the Allens would take this kind of news. How are Mayor Allen and Connie going to feel if they find out their daughter was possibly *murdered*? And Carter? How is he going to feel? I thought I would feel better, but honestly it just renews my grief to the core. A senseless act that stole my best friend's life? All the hurt and pain that could have been avoided for those who loved her? Not to mention the thousands of lives she touched with her open and giving heart. Honestly, the whole thing sickens me. And I feel like taking Duke and Ethan by the throat myself for not sharing what they *clearly* know." Sammy pressed her fingertips to her forehead to stop a tension headache that was quickly forming. "Did I say that out loud?"

Ellie touched her sister's arm tenderly. "Yes, you did. You're angry, and you have every right to be." She nodded. "I know you didn't mean it. You wouldn't harm anyone, and that includes them."

Heidi popped her head inside the office and surprised them both.

"Hey *chicas!*" Heidi took one step further into the office. "What's going on?" Her smile instantly faded.

"Sam just came from Pine Haven Bed and Breakfast. She thinks Ethan is hiding something. So's his father."

Heidi's manicured eyebrows furrowed, "Really? Ethan?"

"Yeah, when I talked to both of them this morning, their demeanor was really off. I think they're *both* lying. Even Douglas mentioned Ethan was acting weird when he came into Liquid Joy. I don't know if you've seen him, but his arms are covered in scratches and his hand is banged up. He definitely looks like he's been in a fight. But with who?"

"Ethan . . ." Heidi repeated.

"Why do you keep repeating the kid's name? What are you thinking?" Ellie eyed her cousin carefully.

"He's so wiry and young. Could he really do it? What's his motive?" Heidi stepped backward and braced a hand along the doorframe as she shifted her weight to one hip.

"Well, I'm sure he was going to inherit the farm someday. Now he's stuck working at Pine Haven," Sammy thought out loud. "I'm not really sure what his motive for Jane Johnson would be, though," she added thoughtfully. "We'll let Nash figure that one out."

"Also, Sammy mentioned that Nash said the toxicology report came back and the substance that was on Jane's blouse was sand and cement used to make some kind of mortar substance. We figure Ethan would probably come across that somewhere on the bed-and-breakfast property."

"Umm. Hellooo? You *guys*. Are you sure about that? I think you're missing something kinda important here. Duke Reed is a laborer for a local contractor. He pours concrete for B&S Concrete for a living."

Sammy's eyes flew to her cousin's. "You're kidding. Why didn't you say something the other night when we all met?"

"Honestly, I didn't think it was relevant," Heidi admitted.

"You know what? I just thought of it now. How could I be so stupid?"

"What?" Ellie and Heidi said in unison.

"Duke pours concrete. Semco is a manufacturer supplier for B&S Concrete, I bet, because Semco fabricates different types of industrial equipment. He was wearing a T-shirt with the Semco logo today. And I totally neglected to share that detail with Nash. Remember Jane's phone? It was found on a Semco truck. That has to be connected."

Sammy began to pace the room. "The day I was meeting Jane at the River walk?"

"Yeah?" They both nodded.

"There was construction going on behind the library. What if Duke Reed was pouring concrete that day? That places him directly at the scene. Duke has motive, opportunity . . . *and* cement-covered hands."

Chapter
Twenty-Four

"Ellie, can you stay and handle the store?" Sammy slid both hands nervously through her matted auburn hair, which was now starting to dry, albeit gracelessly.

"Where are you going?" Heidi asked.

"I need to get back to Pine Haven Bed and Breakfast." Sammy continued pacing back and forth a few steps despite the small office. "If I just call Liam on his cell phone, he probably won't pick up if he's in the middle of an interrogation. Don't you think? Plus, he'll just tell me to stay out of it. I have to go over there. I started this mess and I need to finish it."

"Don't you think you're overreacting? I'm pretty sure Nash wouldn't come to any conclusions based on your hearsay."

Ellie nodded in agreement.

"I forgot to tell him that Duke was wearing a Semco shirt. I feel like I need to go and follow through on this. I have to tell him and see if he uncovers any other new details. Otherwise I won't sleep tonight, and I'll drive myself insane wondering."

"Go," Ellie said. "I've got the store. Just go." She jutted a thumb toward the door.

Sammy's eyes pinballed between her sister and her cousin. "Thanks, you guys, for everything. Supporting me in all this. You know, we make a great team, us three S.H.E.s. I love you guys." She smiled weakly, waved a hand, and rushed past them out the office door.

The sound of rushing water gushing from a nearby rain gutter reached her ears as she swung open the back door of Community Craft. Steam from the cool rain hitting hot asphalt sent a visible vapor into the air. En route to her Chevy, Sammy clicked the fob to unlock the doors and race to the safety of her car, dodging wide puddles along the way. But instantly, the shower returned full force and soaked through Carter's high school sweatshirt. She adjusted the heavy, wet garment before clicking on her seat belt. She thought again of calling the detective on her drive over to Pine Haven Bed and Breakfast but instead spent most of the car ride trying to decide how she was going to explain herself. Had he taken her at her word? Or was he just following up on other leads that he hadn't shared? If she'd been a little more transparent with him from the beginning, maybe he would've included her more in the investigation. Why did she have to do everything so impulsively and on her own? What *was* that about? Did she have something to prove? Why didn't she trust him?

The windshield wipers on full speed barely kept up with the deluge of rain. A dribble of water seeped into the interior of the vehicle where she noticed that she must've neglected to raise the windows all the way. She quickly pressed the button to close it. The air inside the vehicle was stuffy and uncomfortable, especially wearing the oversized wet sweatshirt. And there was no air to be found. Sammy thought if she'd had to drive a longer journey than the ten-minute ride to the B and B or be stuck in the car for any amount of time, she would surely suffocate to death. The thought of Jane Johnson having hands around her throat, constricting her breath, sent a sudden uncomfortable feeling through her body. She wondered if that's how the author had felt in her last moments on earth. Sammy pressed on.

When she had almost reached her destination, the sound of sirens blaring rapidly came up out of nowhere from the rear, forcing her to move. She carefully maneuvered the car to the side of the road and let the emergency vehicles pass. An ambulance and a police car raced in front of her, their blurred, distorted lights dancing amid the rain through the windshield. *Where are they going?*

Sammy gasped when she saw the vehicles turn into Pine Haven Bed and Breakfast.

"Oh God. No."

Her mind instantly rushed to places it shouldn't. *Did Ethan attack someone in his defense? Did my action of sending the detective to search for Ethan cause him to act out? Did he hurt Liam? Does someone on the property have a medical emergency? Is it Helen or Raymond Thatcher? Are they hurt? Did Ethan attack them?*

Was this all her fault? Everything in her head screamed, *Yes! It's all your fault with your impetuous rush to judgment!*

Sammy followed the emergency vehicles to the parking lot of the bed-and-breakfast, careful to give them ample space and not get too close for fear they might send her away. She saw Officer Maxwell jump from the patrol car and sprint toward the large hay barn. The rain was making a clear visual of the scene near impossible. Detective Nash's Honda Civic was parked in front of the farmhouse, and Sammy pulled her car alongside and shoved the gear into park. She waited a moment before deciding what to do. Her impulse left her no other choice. She opened the car to the pouring rain and stepped into a deep puddle, soaking her foot clear through to the sock. She made a wet dash to follow Tim toward the barn. Her throat constricted and her heart beat wildly in anticipation of what was behind the door. When she finally got the courage to step inside and survey the scene, she felt her knees grow weak. Tim was standing over Ethan, partially blocking her view. But she saw enough to know that the gardener was lying faceup on the dirt barn floor. Quick eye contact with the detective and a nod of his head confirmed her assumption. Things were not good.

Sammy dropped to her knees. "Noooooo." She heard a moan come out of her own throat—a strange sound that was unrecognizable to her own ears.

Detective Nash rushed across the large space from where Ethan's unresponsive body lay and came to her side. "What are you doing in here?" He said it as more of a statement. Not with an angry tone, but rather as a comment spoken out of deep compassion.

Sammy put her head in her hands and rocked back and forth on her knees.

"It's okay. The paramedics are working on him. They think it's just a surface wound." The detective leaned over and rubbed his hand on her back in small circular motions.

"You don't understand," Sammy cried as she stopped rocking back and forth momentarily and looked up at him.

"No. Really . . . it's all going to be okay. He left a suicide note, Samantha. We got him."

A deep groan escaped Sammy's mouth.

The sudden agonizing realization that Kate's death really hadn't been accidental was simply unbearable.

"Here. Read this. I think it will answer a few questions for you." Nash handed Sammy a lined yellow sheet of paper.

"I don't know . . . if I can," Sammy admitted with a sniffle. She wiped her nose with the back of her hand. She hadn't even realized it was running.

"Up to you, but I think this will answer the questions you've been searching for about your friend." He held the paper out for her to grab. "Take it," he encouraged.

Sammy seized the paper in her hand, closed her eyes for a moment, and took a measured breath to prepare herself. Then she held the sheet of paper with both hands as she read the penciled words through blurred tears distorting her vison:

Mayor Allen should have stopped the Common Council from stealing my family's land. He probably paid those council members or haggled some kind of deal to agree with him. Made them all vote against my family. He's a disgrace to this town! I had no other choice than to steal something that belonged to him. Something that was as precious to me as my heritage. My family's land for his daughter. Then some fancy celebrity author was going to pronounce to the world what a great community leader Kate Allen was? That she cared about the people of Heartsford? She didn't care! If she did she wouldn't have let her father steal my land! No way would I let the mayor's daughter be memorialized in some book! Mayor Allen has sold out this town to big industry. Heartsford has taken everything from me. And that's why I choose to end my life. This book is over! THE END

Sammy placed the paper in her lap and began to sob. Deep, gut-wrenching sobs that had been buried deep since the day her life had forever changed. The day she had learned of Kate's death.

The detective genuflected down on one knee and wrapped his arm around a sobbing Sammy. He let her cry until she was depleted of tears. "It's okay now," he repeated soothingly. "It's all going to be okay. I promise."

"Who found him?" Sammy asked after her sobs quieted.

"Raymond Thatcher. He came out to the barn to look for Ethan and found him lying over there." Nash pointed across the room. "Little did he know I was already pulling into the parking lot. He's back at the main house consoling his wife. I told him not to let her come out here. No reason for his wife to have to see Ethan like this. Paramedics think he'll make a full recovery; thankfully, Ethan just grazed the top of this head."

"What do you mean?" Sammy glanced over to where Ethan Reed lay on a stretcher being wheeled across the hard-packed dirt floor. Tim was still blocking her view, and the distance was too far to see with the naked eye.

"He attempted a gunshot to the right temple. But luckily for him, he has terrible aim. We found the revolver and the shell casing from the weapon used. Case closed."

"Oh, that's awful." Sammy paused. "Wow." She raised her

hand to her heart. The same way her mother and sister did when unwelcome news struck. Only this was bad. Real bad.

The detective nodded. "I'm just glad it's over and we can wrap this one up." And then Officer Maxwell waved for the detective to return to the scene where Ethan had just been removed. Nash raised himself off the floor and stood and was about to walk over to join the officer when Sammy grabbed him by the arm.

"Wait."

"What's wrong?" He looked down and met her eyes.

"Which hand did you say you found the gun in?" Sammy's eyes narrowed as she tried to picture how Ethan could possibly have accomplished a gunshot to his right temple.

"His right hand."

"That's impossible."

"What?" The detective's eyes narrowed.

"There's absolutely no way he tried to commit suicide. That was attempted murder." Sammy rose to her feet and pointed in the direction of the body on the stretcher. "Ethan Reed is left-handed."

Chapter Twenty-Five

"*A ttempted murder?*" Detective Nash repeated. He laid a protective hand on Sammy's shoulder. "Stay put," he ordered, before moving over to Tim, who was waving from the area where Ethan's injured body had recently been moved to a stretcher.

Sammy didn't obey his direction. She leapt to her feet and followed the detective to the other side of the large barn, closer to where Ethan had previously lain in the packed dirt. She knew she couldn't unsee whatever they were going to come upon, however gruesome, but she had to know. Could someone else really have tried to kill him? Sammy suddenly reviewed the conversation she'd had earlier with the young man as she followed Nash across the room. There was no question in her mind that the suicide note had been written by someone who used better verbiage. Ethan didn't speak proper English; how could he possibly write it?

When they approached the scene, Sammy noticed something very shallow written in the packed dirt. Almost invisible to the naked eye. She elbowed Tim for use of his pen flashlight that she knew he carried in his belt. He handed it to her unwillingly.

Sammy shined the beam of light on the ground. Scratched into the dirt were what she thought could potentially be the numbers *2* and *4*. The best Ethan could do with his bandage-covered hand. *2 and 4*. 24.

Sammy gasped. "Nash!"

The detective's eyes left the side of the barn, where he was examining a bullet hole, and flew to Sammy's. He must have caught the serious tone in her voice, because his response was immediate.

"Please come over here for a second!" She waved him closer.

Nash moved from the edge of the barn to where Sammy shined the beam of light to illuminate what she had discovered.

"Doesn't that look like the number twenty-four scratched in the dirt?" Sammy asked. "I mean, he did the best he could, considering the hand he used for writing is busted up, but doesn't that look like numbers to you?"

"I believe it does. Unfortunately looks like he couldn't get out the rest."

"So, you're thinking what I'm thinking?"

"I'm thinking Ethan left us a message. The first series of numbers written on the handwritten notes we found inside Jane Johnson's suitcase. We have to find out what that combination lock belongs to. I think we need to see what's inside." Sammy's eyes met the detective's, and for the first time she thought she saw a glimmer of praise. Reassurance for her *not* to back off the case. "I'm sure we'll find that lock, Samantha," he said. "And when we do, it'll answer a lot of unanswered questions. Did the ambulance leave yet?" As the detective looked up for confirmation, they heard loud sirens, which confirmed the emergency vehicles' departure. "I was hoping to see if Ethan was coherent enough that I could ask. I guess it'll have to wait."

"Well, let's just hope Heidi's working in the ER tonight and not still subbing for her friend on maternity leave. Heidi's an amazing nurse; she'll have him bandaged up and healed in no time."

"Officer Maxwell," Nash directed. "Call in the Crime Scene Unit and let's start canvassing the area. Look around the barn for footprints. Hopefully the mud will help us out tonight. Looks like we've got an attempted homicide investigation on our hands."

"Yes, sir," Tim said as he called in backup on the radio attached to his shoulder.

The detective then returned his attention to Sammy. "You come with me. We're going to interview Raymond and Helen Thatcher to see if they saw anything unusual they can think of. Maybe finding out their gardener didn't take his own life will trigger their memory to something minor they might have overlooked."

"Hey, Maxwell?" Nash called out as Tim was exiting the barn. "Let me know when CSU arrives. I want them to be meticulous in handling this scene. We've gotta get this perp."

"What are you thinking? Are you going to look for another suspect? Or do you think Duke's responsible?" Sammy asked.

"I definitely need to have a conversation with Duke Reed, but I'm not ruling anything out at this point."

"It has to be Duke. He's the one who lost the farm. He must have killed Kate out of revenge. He probably thinks the mayor could have stopped the sale, just like the fake suicide note said."

"Yeah? What about the author? You think it's like the suicide note suggests? He didn't want Kate memorialized in some book?"

"Yeah, I guess, maybe? I also noticed Duke was wearing a T-shirt today with a Semco logo. That certainly ties in with the author's phone ending up on a Semco truck. Things aren't looking good for the guy, in my opinion."

"Hey, it's not what we *know* at this point . . ."

"But what we can prove," Sammy said, finishing the detective's train of thought. After a pause, she added, "How could Duke attempt to kill his own son? That I'll never understand."

"Do you know how many investigations go unsolved because we don't have the evidence we need to convict? It's one thing to know who committed the crime. It's another to bring the perpetrator to justice, and not just on circumstantial evidence. We need everything we can get to prove our case."

"That's why you're always frustrated with me."

The detective cocked his head in question.

"Because even though I may have an indication of who committed a crime, I sometimes get overzealous and contaminate substantial evidence to convict. I also tend to jump to conclusions."

"I think you're finally getting it." The detective smiled wide and placed an encouraging hand on her shoulders to direct and escort her out of the barn. "Just remember that when we go in and question the Thatchers. Let me take the lead; don't offer up too much. Deal?" He flung his hand out to shake, and she took it willingly.

The heavy rain had subsided, and a foggy mist had materialized. The two walked over to the main house and up the wide front porch steps that were still wet from the rain.

The detective instinctively reached for Sammy's arm to keep her from slipping, which made her smile inwardly. She noticed the subtle change from the man who had never so much as held a door for her in the past.

Helen opened the door of the bed and breakfast after the detective rang the doorbell.

"Samantha?" The surprise on the bed-and-breakfast owner's face was obvious. "What are you doing here?"

"Well . . ."

"She's consulting on the case," Nash interjected.

Helen didn't hold back the surprised look on her face.

"Can we come in?" the detective asked.

"Oh, forgive my manners, I'm sorry. Of course." She opened the door and held it wide. "Please come on in."

Raymond rushed toward them as they entered. "Everything okay?" His eyes darted nervously between Detective Nash and Sammy.

Sammy had never met Raymond Thatcher, and the man seemed much older than Helen. She couldn't decide if it was because of his thick gray beard or his balding head. Either way, he seemed to be at least ten years Helen's senior.

"You mean, did Ethan make it? He's still alive, right?" Helen corrected her husband and looked to the detective for confirmation.

Instead of answering the question, Nash said, "Why don't we all sit down somewhere?" He then removed his wet loafers and tucked them on the welcome mat beside the door. Sammy decided she'd better follow suit and removed her wet sneakers too. After removing her Sketchers, she looked down and decided to remove her wet socks also and tuck them inside. For a brief moment, she self-consciously curled her wet toes.

Sammy and the detective followed the Thatchers into the kitchen, where they all gathered around a large round table in a floral-wallpapered breakfast nook. The rain streaked down the floor-to-ceiling bay windows, hiding what would normally be a stunning view of the expansive back pines.

"Would you like some coffee or tea?" Helen asked after they had all been seated around the table.

"That's okay; no need to put yourself out," Detective Nash said as he folded his hands and set them on the table.

"Not at all. You both look cold. I'll put on a pot of coffee." Helen rose from the chair and moved toward the tall oak kitchen cabinets.

Between the wet clothes and the air-conditioning, Sammy would have been surprised if her lips weren't turning blue. She set her clammy hands in her lap and then tried to stop herself from visibly shaking while she waited for the coffee.

"Is he alive?" Raymond asked, and Helen turned with a mug in hand and paused, waiting for the answer.

Sammy could tell the detective wanted Helen to be sitting down with them at the table before he shared any news. It was too late. By the long pause and the stoic look on Nash's face, the bed-and-breakfast owners assumed the wrong the message loud and clear.

"Oh nooo . . ." Helen whispered.

"We kind of already thought that he didn't make it," Raymond finally said. "I mean, I pretty much knew when he was lying bleeding on the ground. I was just hoping the EMTs could do something to revive him. I felt so helpless . . . I was so shocked . . . I wasn't capable of doing anything, never mind saving the kid's life." He nodded his head and dropped his eyes sullenly.

"I can't make any promises. I'm not a doctor, but the paramedics thinks it's just a surface wound and he'll make a full recovery," Detective Nash interjected.

"This is all so sad. If he was hurting, I sure wish he would've let me know. I didn't know . . ." Raymond shrugged his shoulders. "I didn't know . . ."

"Me either," Helen added. "I thought he was a happy young man. He wasn't depressed at all. I just don't understand it. He loves working here. At least that's what he always told me. He's like a son to us." Helen plucked a tissue from a nearby Kleenex box, dabbed her eyes, and then tossed the soiled tissue into the trash can.

"What happened to his hand?" Sammy asked, and then noticed the detective giving her a slight warning glare for jumping ahead with questions and not allowing him to direct the conversation.

"Oh that?" Helen asked over her shoulder. She went back about her business, bringing mugs to the table and filling the coffee machine with water while she spoke. "He injured himself out fixing the door on the chicken coop. His hand caught on a metal wire and ripped his skin pretty deep. I personally thought he should have gone to the hospital for stitches. His hand bled like crazy. I've been constantly running after him with antibiotic salve so it wouldn't get infected."

"And the scratches on his arms?" Detective Nash asked. "Same injury?"

"Oh, no. That was last week when he was trimming back the

raspberry bushes. Those darn bushes are so overgrown and they're full of thorns. I told him to wear long gloves for protection, but he didn't listen. Ethan has a bit of a tough streak in him. My goodness, I can't believe he's injured himself this way." Helen pushed the button on the coffee machine and then returned and took a seat with the rest of them around the table. She reached for the nearby Kleenex box, plucked another tissue to dab her watery eyes, and placed the box on the table, knowing more might be needed.

When Helen was finally seated comfortably, Nash said, "We have reason to believe Ethan did not try to commit suicide."

"What?" Raymond nearly snapped his neck as he swung his head to face the detective directly.

"But what about the letter he left?" Helen asked. "Raymond mentioned there was a suicide note." She ran her hand through her hair nervously and then finally tucked it behind one ear.

"We believe the scene was staged to look like a suicide. Do you know anyone that would want to harm Ethan? Anyone at all you can think of? If so, please share it now." The detective leaned into the table intently to hear how the owners of the bed-and-breakfast would respond.

Helen, visibly shaken, covered her mouth with her hand.

"You mean, Ethan *didn't* try to kill himself?" Raymond asked with bewilderment.

"We have reason to believe otherwise," Sammy said, and then realized she had again spoken out of turn. When was she going to learn to keep her mouth shut? She might have to ask Mrs. Thatcher for some Elmer's glue from her old grade school days. Maybe then she could seal her lips shut.

"Anyone that would want to harm Ethan?" The detective steepled his fingers and held them tight to his lips. Sammy wondered if this was his discreet message for her to remain quiet.

"I can't think of anyone." Raymond shook his head and shrugged. "You, Helen?"

Helen sheepishly shrugged, and then her watery eyes dropped to the table.

"What is it, Helen?" Raymond asked, voicing what they all knew to be true. Helen Thatcher seemed to be holding back.

"Well, I know he didn't get along with his mother. That's no secret. She abandoned her child years ago when I taught Ethan back in grade school. That's why Raymond and I sort of took him under our collective wing. But I can't imagine a mother actually doing something so heinous to her own child . . ." Helen reached for the Kleenex box again, dabbed her now full-fledged streaming tears, and then blew her nose with a tissue.

"What about his father? Did Ethan get along well with him?" The detective shot Sammy a warning glare for opening her mouth yet again.

"Duke has been a good father." Helen nodded. "Done the best he can as a single parent, in my opinion. He's had a hard life too . . . losing his farm was a hard transition for them both. They're salt of the earth, good folks, you know."

"Before going into the barn, Raymond, did you see, hear, or smell anything that you can think of? Nothing is too small a detail." The detective unsteepled his fingers, folded his hands on the table, and waited patiently. "Let me take that a step further. Go back to the moment before you entered the barn. What did you see? Anything unusual? Lights on or off? Anything?"

Raymond began to chew his lower lip and shook his head. "It was raining pretty hard. Honestly, I didn't see much."

"Did you see anything on the ground? Any footprints? Wheel prints? Any images on the ground as you were walking over to the barn?" Detective Nash pushed.

"Actually, now that you mention it, I did see what looked like a bike track in the mud, or better yet an imprint of one of those fat wheels for all-terrain bikes? Like you see people ride in the winter? Yeah . . . like a trail bike." His eyes widened in surprise at remembering something.

"Does Ethan own a bike like that?" Sammy asked, and then realized her Elmer's glue wasn't working *again*.

"I don't think so? Helen?" Raymond's eyes sought out his wife's for confirmation.

"As far as I know, Ethan doesn't have a bike on our property," Helen said with a sniffle.

Detective Nash's cell phone rang, disrupting them. "Excuse me a moment." He held up a finger to keep them quiet when he answered the phone. "Nash," he said abruptly. "Great. Send CSU over here. I want to direct them to check on something. Thanks."

After the detective finished the quick call, he said, "Officer Maxwell just informed me that the Crime Scene Unit has arrived. Raymond, I'd like you to show them where you may have seen those bike tracks. Hopefully they're not all washed away from the rain. They're on their way over to the house right now." The detective rose from his chair. "If you'll come with me, please." He directed Raymond to follow him to the front entrance, where a member of the Crime Scene Unit was already knocking on the front door.

After Raymond had stepped outside and was all settled with CSU, the detective returned to the table and took a seat beside Sammy.

"Anything you can think of, Helen? Anything at all?"

The detective folded his hands and waited patiently.

Sammy, feeling restless and impatient, asked the question that had been burning in her mind during the entire conversation, "Mrs. Thatcher, do you know what the numbers twenty-four, fourteen, and five mean?"

"Well, of course I do. That's the combination to our garden shed."

Chapter
Twenty-Six

"Helen, I request permission to search inside your garden shed." Detective Nash leapt to his feet and waited for the owner of the bed-and-breakfast to acknowledge his request.

"Yes, of course, permission granted. Why, though? What are you looking for?"

"I don't really want to explain yet. But I certainly will when I sort all this out. If you can please direct me to where the garden shed is located on your property? Since you have multiple buildings on your land, I want to be sure I'm headed to the right structure."

"But the coffee? If you wait just a few moments, it should be ready." Helen gestured her hand toward the coffee machine that was percolating and scenting the room with a lovely aroma. If Sammy hadn't been so curious as to what was inside that garden shed, she'd easily have taken the offer of rich dark java.

"No thanks. Maybe I'll grab a bit after we're through, if you want to save me a cup?" Nash nodded his head efficiently and returned to his usual all-business manner.

Helen followed the detective to the front entrance of the bed-and-breakfast, and Sammy shadowed closely behind. Helen opened the front door, stood just outside, and pointed with an extended arm to exactly where the garden shed was located on the spread-out multi-building property.

Sammy removed the damp socks from her Sketchers and tossed them aside in a ball. She scrambled in haste to shove her feet inside her wet sneakers and follow the detective outside to the garden shed. If she didn't hurry, she was afraid he'd leave her behind.

"Wait here, Helen. We'll be back." He moved with purpose off the porch steps with Sammy quickly following behind, desperately trying to catch up.

When she finally caught up to his long stride, she said, "Wow. You didn't ask me to wait back at the house with Mrs. Thatcher. Talk about a shocker!"

The detective hung his head and nodded as if to say, *Sammy, Sammy, Sammy*, but he remained silent.

With the rain officially subsided, the air felt less humid, and although it was late in the day, the sun was finally pressing to make an appearance. Typical Wisconsin. It could rain all day, and then the sun would come out just before it was time for it to lower itself deep in the western sky, Sammy noted as the two made their way across the wet grass toward the garden shed. On their way, they passed the chicken coop where Ethan had allegedly injured his hand. Sammy felt a pang of regret. Detective Nash was right. She *did* rush to justice. She really could have destroyed important evidence with her impulsiveness. Here she had thought at times that the detective was just being an ass, when really it was she who needed to work on her behavior. She huffed a breath.

"You okay back there?" Nash asked over his shoulder as she fell a step behind his long stride.

"Yeah. I'm okay." Sammy pushed the long, soggy sleeves of Carter's high school sweatshirt up her arms as best she could.

The detective abruptly stopped midstride and turned around to face her. "What's on your mind?"

"Nothing. I'm just berating myself as I always do," she said under her breath. "Let's just hurry up." Sammy rolled her shoulders and cracked her neck. "Please . . . go on," she added when he didn't move.

The detective didn't argue. He turned on his heel and moved in the direction of the garden shed, which looked like a small red painted barn with a contrasting white door. A metal rooster cupola ornamented the top of the roof. When they finally arrived at the locked door, he turned to her. "You ready for this?"

Sammy answered with a deep breath and a nod of her head.

Nash turned and clicked the combination back and forth on the lock and then gave it a swift pull.

Sammy peeked around the detective's arm, but all she could see were garden tools lining the walls on both sides of the shed. The detective ducked his head and stepped inside. The low ceiling caused him to stoop down, as it was far too short for him to stand straight.

"Please let me in!" Sammy exclaimed.

"There's not a lot of room to move in here."

"Make room."

"Good grief, you're a bossy woman!"

The detective maneuvered behind a large rake, leaving just enough room for Sammy to squeeze into the shed beside him.

"What are we looking for you think?" Sammy asked.

"Something that doesn't belong. Or looks out of place."

Sammy's eyes darted around the space, and all she could see was garden tools. Rakes, brooms, shovels, snippers. Buckets, flower pots, watering cans . . . she didn't see anything out of the ordinary. "Over there." She pointed to a shiny red toolbox tucked in the corner. "Do you think something is hidden inside the toolbox?"

He shrugged, reached into his jeans pocket, and handed her a rubber glove. "Go take a look."

Sammy squeezed by a leaf blower and knelt down to open the toolbox. She slid on the rubber glove and opened the lid with her gloved hand. A hammer, wrench, socket set, blah blah blah. After sifting through the tools and searching through various compartments, she came up empty. "Nothing." She blew her long auburn bangs away from her face. She looked to the ceiling in frustration.

Talk to me, Kate.

Immediately she noticed a latch on the ceiling. "Liam, look up. What's that?"

The detective craned his neck to see. He then slipped on his own rubber gloves and pulled the latch. When he did so, an old-fashioned cigar box landed in his hands. "Whoa. Wasn't expecting that to pop out," he said, his eyes wide in surprise.

"Open it!"

The detective opened the cigar box, took a peek, and then held the box for Sammy to view.

Inside were two long red satin ribbons with clear beads sewn on the ends.

Sammy sucked in a sharp breath. "The other half of Kate's

barrette . . . the *ribbons*." Her eyes immediately began to moisten at the sight of them.

"We were right. They were cut clean, and not sucked into the combine as the police report suggested. Looks like Duke did lie on the police report." When Nash's eyes left the ribbons, he looked at Sammy, who wondered if she had visual smoke coming out her ears, trying to piece together the puzzle.

"Now we know with complete certainty it wasn't an accident that caused Kate's death. Otherwise, these ribbons wouldn't be here, right? Why would anyone keep them?" She searched the detective's face for answers.

Liam didn't answer. He just looked at her with deep compassion.

"Ethan must've found these and kept them hidden in the shed. Otherwise, why would he have tried to share the combination in the dirt when he was shot? Either way, I suspect Ethan knows a lot more than he's saying. Looks like he's protecting his father," Sammy said as a single tear traveled down her cheek.

After a long pause, the detective removed a glove, leaned over, and lifted her chin into his hand so their eyes would meet. "I'm sorry, Samantha. I'm so very sorry. For all of this."

Sammy's cell phone rang in her pocket, startling them both. She dug into her jeans pocket and plucked out her phone. Bradley's name popped up on the screen. She'd forgotten to return his call earlier, and now he was calling again. She quickly looked up to see the detective studying her phone. She shoved it back into her back pocket.

"Aren't you going to get that?"

"I can call him back later."

"I know this is probably a bad time to ask, but I suppose going to dinner tonight is out of the question?"

Sammy smiled at his attempt to lighten the heavy mood. Liam tried to adjust his height by cocking his neck in the uncomfortably small space. "You can actually think about food right now?" She wiped the sticky tears from her face with her soggy sweatshirt sleeve.

"Hey. A guy has to eat."

"Rain check? I'm personally ready for a hot bath, a glass of wine, and a soft bed," Sammy said resignedly as she moved from her position on the floor to stand. She had one advantage with her height—the ability to stand inside small spaces.

"I understand. Actually, Samantha, why don't you go and do just that. Get home, get some rest. Personally, I've still got a lot of work here. I need to get to the bottom of this investigation. I'm going to touch base with CSU and Officer Maxwell and see what they've come up with and if it leads me closer to this perp. Then I've got to go back and talk with the Thatchers again. Sounds like Duke has some explaining to do, and hopefully Ethan will be awake at the hospital later and I can find out who attempted to gun him down. Looks like I've still got a very long night ahead of me. No reason for you to stay, though. Go on and get outta here. I'm sure you need to open the store tomorrow morning. You need your rest."

He stepped out of the shed and rocked his head side to side to remove the kinks in his neck. He then handed Sammy the cigar box and stretched his arms to the sky for one long stretch to readjust his back from being misaligned inside the tight garden shed.

Sammy followed him out the shed door and onto the wet grass. "Are you sure?" She was suddenly weary, and it was the first time she hadn't envied his job. She was more than ready to abandon the crime scene and leave the investigation up to the professionals. And run as fast and as far away from there as humanly possible. The emotions and rushing adrenaline from the past week had her feeling completely depleted. Her legs felt like two wobbly rubber bands.

"Yeah, I'm sure. As long as you're not ditching me to have dinner with someone else." He raised an eyebrow in question.

"Is that jealousy I'm hearing?" Sammy teased.

"Nah." He dismissed her with a wave of his hand. "Thanks for your help, Samantha Kane," he said sincerely as he padlocked the door and double-checked that it was locked. He then reached for the cigar box. "I'll need that for evidence."

Sammy handed the box over willingly. "I'm sure when you talk to Ethan, he'll explain why this was hidden in his work shed. And maybe you can save them for me. When all this is over, I think I'd like to have them back, if that's okay."

Detective Nash nodded and turned toward the crime scene to walk away, but then turned abruptly. "Do you need me to walk you to your car? It's getting kind of dark."

"No. I'm good." Sammy smiled. "But thanks."

"No problem. Get some rest, kid," he said, and she watched him walk away.

The sun was setting in the western sky, and Sammy came to the realization that she had left Ellie at Community Craft to handle the store. She plucked her phone from her back pocket and immediately dialed her sister while she walked to her car.

"First of all, I'm so sorry," Sammy said as soon as Ellie answered her call.

"No problem. I figured things were a bit crazy or else you would've called sooner. I'm closing up the store a few minutes early, if that's okay. I'm ready to head home. Is everything okay? I've been trying to hold Mom off—she's pretty worried since I'm not back at the house yet. I've been making excuses for you so she doesn't freak out. Heidi ended up getting called in to the hospital. You may want to text her also and let her know you're okay. She's been a little concerned too."

Sammy was grateful to hear that Heidi was at the hospital. As soon as she was off the phone with Ellie, she'd text her cousin for information on Ethan's condition.

"Can we talk about all of this later? I promise to fill you all in . . . later." Sammy was afraid that if she admitted all that had gone down, her whole family would be on her doorstep when she arrived home, and there was no way she had the energy to face that just then. "I think we're all exhausted. Thanks for closing up for me. There's no way I could make it in to the store at this point. I'm pretty tired," Sammy admitted easily.

"No problem, Sammy. You get some rest . . . love you."

"Love you too. And thanks again for covering," Sammy said, and then ended the call. She opened the door of her car and sank into the driver's seat. After clicking on the seat belt, she started the engine. She texted Heidi regarding Ethan, knowing her cousin was busy and it'd be awhile before she'd hear a reply. When she was back out on the open road, she adjusted her Bluetooth to play her voice messages:

Hey Sam, it's Brad. Give me a call.

Next message:

Hey Sam, it's Brad again. I was hoping to talk with you. I'm headed back east because I have a work emergency. Mom's dragging her feet on the house sale anyway. I was hoping to see you before I left, but you didn't return my call. Hope you're doing okay. Take care.

Sammy's heart sank. Could this day get any worse? She'd hoped to spend more time with her old neighbor, but she resigned herself to the fact that the timing apparently wasn't meant to be. Maybe it never had. Sammy's mind wandered to Mayor Allen, his wife, Connie, and Carter too. With Carter abroad at school, she hoped his parents' sharing what she had uncovered about his sister's death wouldn't cause him to want to come home. What would that kind of news do to his psyche, especially while he was so far away from Heartsford? She wondered if she had made the right decision to get involved. Did ignorance really mean bliss? She didn't think so. Knowing Kate's death wasn't an accident didn't make it easier, though. Would bringing the murderer to trial bring Kate back? Certainly not. Or Jane Johnson? They deserved justice though and young Ethan deserved justice for his injuries too. The carnage! She needed a mind break.

Sammy decided on a whim to try to return Bradley's call. The phone went straight to voicemail: "Hey, Bradley, um, I mean . . . Brad. That feels weird on my tongue. Anyway, have a safe trip. Catch you on the flip side! Bye!"

Catch you on the flip side? What an idiot. Sammy slapped her hand to her forehead.

The dark wet road and lack of overhead lights on the county highway made visibility on the ride home tough. Without warning, Sammy saw something dart across her path just beyond her headlights. She swerved and skidded the car to avoid the large animal, but as she continued driving, she quickly came to the realization it wasn't an animal she had narrowly missed, but a bicyclist.

What the hell is someone doing out in the dark on a bike at this hour? And without reflective clothing? What an idiot!

And then it happened.

She noticed the oversized fat tires on the bike . . . trail tires. Her heart thundered.

Sammy's eyes flew to the cyclist, who was wearing a dark helmet and pedaling hard. Her eyes narrowed in on the letters on the back of his gray T-shirt, which reflected the name SEMCO in bright white letters. Duke! The adrenaline rushed through her veins like a cresting river. Her immediate instinct was to hit him. She could do it right now . . . and no one would blame her. *I could say it was an accident.* Everyone would believe her. She'd never done anything to hurt anyone in the past . . . but that was then. That was before Kate's killer had flashed right before her eyes.

Sammy shook her head as if to waken herself. She was appalled at the vulgar darkness that had clouded her thoughts. Thoughts like that made her no different than the killer, in her mind. The thought made bile rise in her throat.

But she had to stop him! He must have known she had slowed the car to follow him, as his riding path changed. He jerked the bike into the median, kicking up wet stones, and pumped hard along the grass, waiting for a break in the thick brush to escape. He was within feet of an opening where the brush met farmland, and then he could easily squeeze through. She couldn't let that happen. With seconds to spare, Sammy lurched the car into the median to follow the fat-tired bike and bumped the back tire, just enough to cause the man to fall. She could have run him over. Right then and there. But she slammed on the brakes and skidded inches from his body. Immediately she texted Detective Nash a 911 text with instructions to leave Pine Haven. Surely he'd find her on his way back toward town.

Sammy leapt from the driver's side and sprinted to the front of the car. The man was groaning, but he was alive. He rolled over onto his side, and Sammy knelt down to remove his helmet. And the blow hit her hard.

"Bradley?"

Sammy stood and took a half step back, unable to comprehend who it was that lay on the ground at her feet. She kept shaking her head and uttering, "No, no, nooo, no," as she slowly backed away.

"Sammy, wait . . . listen to me," Bradley groaned through clenched teeth. "I think my leg is broken."

"I could give a crap if I broke your leg. You're lucky I don't break your neck," she spat. "Where did you get that T-shirt?"

"I'm lying here on the ground and *that's* what you ask me? How about you apologize for running me off the road? So . . . I lied to you, I'm not heading back east yet."

Sammy stepped forward and wagged a warning finger in front of his eyes. "Oh, you're *never* going back east again, you bastard! You called and left a message on my phone to solidify your alibi? You *used* me! You piece of crap! Now tell me where you got the T-shirt."

"This isn't about the shirt, is it?" He moaned again and reached to clutch his injured leg. "Duke gave it to me; his company uses Semco as their business supplier. I told you I worked for him; you know, we're still friends. We decided to let bygones be bygones."

"Liar!" Sammy screamed.

"Sammy. What is wrong with you?" Bradley's face was twisted in pain.

"I know you killed her. I know you did." Sammy shook her head as if this were all nothing but a bad dream. No, a nightmare, and she could will it all away with a shake of her head.

"I didn't kill Jane Johnson . . . I wasn't even in town yet . . . remember? I saw your parents at the airport."

Sammy paused to collect her thoughts. "I was talking about Kate, not Jane!" she shrilled. "But now that you mention it . . . you didn't fly in that day. You went to baggage claim to pick up lost luggage, which means you were in town before the author died! You killed her too!"

"I didn't. And Kate . . . it was an accident."

"You were there. Weren't you? At the farm when Kate died." Sammy's eyes were laser-sharp.

Bradley didn't respond.

"Admit it," Sammy shrieked. "You killed my best friend!"

"No. I didn't . . . it was an accident. But Duke had Ethan

convinced that I did. He brainwashed that kid since the time he was knee-high. Why do you think his wife left? Well, he wasn't great with his employees too, namely me. He was going to bring charges against me. They're all *lies*, Sammy. I promise . . . all lies. Duke's trying to set me up because he's still convinced I stole some antique thing from his barn. I'll never be convicted of a crime he can't prove. Not to mention, I didn't take his old crap; his ex-wife must have when she took off! By the way, I don't blame her for leaving. That guy's a jerk. Duke has been a thorn in my side for years!"

Sammy's eyes lasered in on him. "So you tried to kill his son."

"Who? Ethan? No . . . he killed himself."

"Wrong! Try again, Bradley. You're an idiot. You put the gun in the wrong hand."

"Huh?" Bradley looked at her, confused.

"Yes, you idiot. The boy was left-handed. I know you tried to kill him and then tried to get away." She pointed to his method of escape. "Bad news for you, Bradley . . . looks like you have terrible aim!"

Bradley's face flushed red. "I had no other choice. Duke had Ethan and the author convinced that I killed Kate. Duke Reed was trying to set me up. He's been blackmailing me ever since I started my job out east . . . a high-paying job! But Sammy, it was Duke who was in the tractor cab that day."

"Try again!" Sammy hissed. "Duke *was* driving, but it was no accident. And you made Duke take the blame! Why, Bradley? Why!"

"I loved her! But she didn't love me back!" he finally spat.

And then his story unrolled like a sordid dream. "She was

flirting with me and then was hanging all over Gary Dixon that day! How could she do that to me? Lead me on like that? What a slut."

Gary Dixon . . . so he wasn't lying . . .

"So, you just go and kill her?" Sammy wailed as she flung her arms out in exasperation.

"Nooo, it's not like that . . ."

"What the hell?! Because she didn't succumb to your boyish charm?" Sammy venomously spat.

"Everything happened so fast, Sammy. Honestly, it was a knee-jerk reaction. Yes, I pushed her in anger, but I didn't *really* mean it. Duke didn't know that I pushed her, though. He said, 'It's okay, you couldn't save her from rolling under the tire, it was an accident, it's not your fault or my fault her hair got caught. It was Kate's fault for wearing that stupid barrette!'"

"Let me get this straight. Duke—the guy who you've been talking smack about actually covered for you?"

"Well, he wasn't *exactly* covering for me . . . you really want to know what happened?"

"Damn right I do!"

"Duke yelled from the tractor window for me to come over and help Kate get the branch out of the combine and to get those damn ribbons away from the open belt, so I cut the ribbons with my switchblade, and then she got all pissy with me and said I should have let Gary help her instead, and then I pushed her. That's how it went down."

"So that's why the ribbons were cut so clean off the barrette . . ."

"Duke figured I'd been through enough, being there when

Kate died, so he left me out of the police report, didn't tell anyone I was there. But then he had to go and find the damn barrette and the ribbons and then he knew the truth. He knew her hair hadn't actually gotten caught. I never thought he'd be stupid enough to keep the damn ribbons! I thought he was just bluffing!"

"Wait, so how did you get her barrette? I'm confused."

"I cut it off with my switchblade and stuffed it and the ribbons in the pocket of my vest. I had borrowed Duke's reflective vest because I was parking cars that day too. I *had* to make it look like they got sucked in the combine. After the tire rolled over her, I quickly realized her hair would have been caught too, so I cut the barrette out of her hair as well. That was the last I ever saw of them . . . until I heard recently that Ethan found them. I didn't *mean* to push her, Sammy; it wasn't my fault that she tripped and fell backward when I pushed her. But she ticked me off that day with her behavior. You have to believe me."

"Whoa." Sammy held her hand to her heart. Her world was spinning dangerously out of control. "And Duke didn't see all this?"

"Umm, have you seen the size of those tractor tires? He honestly thought I was trying to save her! I didn't realize Ethan would find the ribbons at Duke's house and blame his father for killing Kate. Who keeps a damn reflective vest that long? Duke wanted me to come clean with his son, but I wouldn't. I just wouldn't . . . Ethan confided in that stupid author lady who was digging up the past. He asked her to find out the truth. Things just got so out of hand. I didn't mean for all this to happen."

"But it did happen. You killed Kate, and that was no accident.

You could have saved her, but you didn't, did you? It's not just an oopsy you can take back! Then you go and kill Jane Johnson to cover your tracks because she was bringing it all back up. And then you nearly kill poor Ethan? You're a sick man, Bradley Shultz! As long as I live, I swear, I'll never forgive you!"

"Sammy, you have to *understand* . . . I couldn't lose my job. I couldn't . . . I've worked so hard . . . With that author and Ethan gone, Duke had no way to blackmail me anymore. No one would believe him."

"*Understand?* Are you kidding me? I understand none of this! Why didn't you just kill Duke, then? Huh? At least have the decency to tell me that! What? Was he next on your list?"

"Because everyone in town knew Duke fired me. Everyone would automatically blame me if Duke was the one killed. Everyone *knows* how much I hate the guy!"

"And knowing what a curious kid I was, you led me to follow all the clues in the wrong direction. You used me! You sick bastard!"

Sirens and lights were suddenly upon them. Detective Nash had barely put his car in park before he leapt from his Honda Civic and run to stand next to Sammy. When he saw who was lying on the ground clutching his leg, he gasped. "Whoa. What the . . ."

Sammy nodded at the detective. "Didn't see this one coming, did we?"

Chapter
Twenty-Seven

They say time heals. A few weeks had passed, and Sammy wasn't sure if that statement rang true. Maybe she just needed a little more time. During the event, she was choosing to set aside the sting in her heart and focus on the moment. A wine-and-cheese social to bring the community of Heartsford together was just what she needed. The library director, Jennifer Hawthorne, was so incredibly touched by the outpouring of love and support their community was providing for the town's library. She had chosen to take Sammy's suggestion and use the donated funds to create a special "craft corner." The new section of the library added a collection of crafting books, comfy leather-back chairs, and a few donated lapghans from Community Craft. Of course, the throw blankets had been lovingly crocheted using one of Jane Johnson's patterns in memory of the craft queen herself. Jennifer's face expressed humble gratitude as she addressed those who gathered around the microphone during the first few moments of the fund-raiser. You could feel the outpouring of support in the air as the joint applause erupted after her welcome speech to those who had gathered.

Sammy's eyes searched the crowd. There were swarms of people but only one she was in search of: Liam Nash. She wasn't sure if he was planning to come to the event or not. Socially, he didn't come out of his cocoon much. She was hoping tonight would be different. How would he treat her outside the latest investigation?

Deborah maneuvered her way through the crowd to find Sammy and lead her by the elbow to a place where they could hear each other over the roaring chatter.

"Are you ready to unveil the design?" Deborah asked excitedly as she smoothed her long, dark hair on her shoulders.

"I'm a little nervous; this crowd is so much larger than I ever imagined," Sammy admitted.

"Oh, you'll do fine. Just be yourself." Deborah dismissed her remark with a wave of her dainty, manicured hand.

"Do I look all right?" Sammy looked down at her floral sundress and smoothed it nervously with her hands. She then lifted her hand to check her hair to see if it was still all coiffed in that fancy updo she'd had specially done at the new Live and Let Dye hair salon in town.

"You look ah-mazing." Deborah put one hand on each of Sammy's shoulders. "Everyone loves you here, girl; you have nothing to fret about. Now, go sell those glasses and let's make some money for our library and pay homage to the craft queen by honoring her with a new craft section."

Deborah's intense dark eyes searched Sammy's for the real meaning of why they were there. Her coworker knew the exact button to push to give Sammy the courage to act. This was not about her. This was about helping the library fund the new craft section and memorialize Jane Johnson for what the notably creative woman had accomplished over her lifetime to inspire her many followers. She needed to get up on that platform and address the crowd. She just hoped she wouldn't pass out from the nerves. She took a deep breath. "Okay, let's go before I chicken out. But you're going with me."

"Uh? Wait a minute? I don't think so." Deborah shook her head in disagreement.

"What?"

"I'm not going up *there*." She pointed to the platform, where a microphone stand waited. "This crowd is getting huge!" Deborah instantly grew agitated. And she waved a slender finger back and forth in refusal. "Nope. No way."

"What about the little pep talk you just gave me? Oh, you are *so* coming with me." Sammy nudged her arm and spun Deborah in the direction of the makeshift stage where the karaoke would be set up later in the evening. She had to hurry before they both completely lost their nerve.

When they reached the stage area, Deborah hesitated. "You really don't need me, Sammy. This was your idea. Go on ahead. I can wait back here."

"You're not getting out of this; the glasses are your handiwork, after all." Sammy smiled as she dragged the two of them in front of the microphone.

The crowd *was* even larger than Sammy had initially thought as she looked out at the sea of faces. She focused in on Marilyn talking in a corner with Annabelle and Miles. The mayor and Connie were sipping wine and talking with the police chief and his wife. Members of the book club were peppered among the guests. Douglas was waving his hands dramatically in deep conversation with Randy and Kendra. Ellie was behind them, standing in front of a long table filled with boxes of painted wine glasses ready to be sold. The whole town of Heartsford seemed to be there. Except for the one person she was searching the crowd specifically for. The roaring chatter was so loud that no one seemed to care that she and Deborah were standing there waiting for everyone's attention on the platform.

Deborah took a step backward in one last meager attempt to escape, so Sammy instead sucked a breath, tapped the microphone, and said, "Thank you, everyone, for coming. May I have your attention?"

The rumble of the crowd started to dissipate, and eyes . . . *so many eyes* . . . were suddenly upon them.

"Thank you, everyone, for coming," Sammy said again. "If you were here at the start of tonight's event, you had the privilege of hearing from our library director, Ms. Jennifer Hawthorne." Sammy searched for her in the crowd but couldn't find her in the sea of people. "Oh, there she is." Sammy pointed out the library director, whose fluttered hand rose above the crowd as all eyes turned to her momentarily. "Anyhow, we'd like to thank you for coming out to support our library, to unveil the new craft corner and also pay respects to the late Queen of Crafts, Jane Johnson, who really paved the way and had such an impact on a lot of our own local handcrafted artisans. In order to raise money for the new craft section here at our library"—Sammy put her hands on her coworker's shoulders—"Deborah has designed a new exclusive spring floral hand-painted glass for purchase." She directed Deborah to a nearby table to take the sample glass and hold the goblet up for the crowd to view. "These glasses are exclusive to this event and are absolutely stunning! Aren't they? When you purchase a glass, bring it to the bartender for one free drink. All proceeds will go directly to the library. And let us raise a glass in remembrance to the great Jane Johnson. Thanks for coming out tonight. I look forward to hearing you all sing karaoke later. Let's have some fun as we raise money for our community!" Sammy pumped a fist high in the air.

A ripple of clapping ensued. Sammy turned to Deborah, stepped away from the microphone, and said, "We did it!" She held a hand to her rapidly beating heart. The electricity in the room was palpable.

Deborah was visibly shaken. Her hands were trembling, and beads of sweat lined her forehead. "That was awful! Did you see how many people were looking at us?"

"But Deborah, you used to perform all the time when you danced professionally. How is this different?"

"I never saw faces in the crowd! It just looked like a sea of dark faces, and I pretended they weren't there. Here, I actually *saw* people." Her eyes widened into saucers.

Sammy threw her head back and laughed. "You were right, though. This wasn't about me. When I took the focus off myself and my own nerves, well . . . what you said back there gave me the courage to speak. Thanks for the pep talk; I really needed the encouragement." She leaned in and gave her coworker a half hug, and Deborah almost passed out in her arms.

"All right, well, I'm going to go freshen up in the restroom and then try to find my husband out there somewhere in this massive group. Danny can help me relieve your sister at the glass sale table. I told her we could take shifts, so we can all participate in the fun tonight too. Every hour a new person shifts. How does that sound?"

"Sounds perfect. Please thank your husband for me. I'll try to catch him at the table later to offer my gratitude, but if I miss Danny in this crowd, will you please pass on the message?"

"You bet," Deborah said as she stepped off the platform to make her way through the swarms of people.

Sammy noticed Dale, the owner of Show-Off Karaoke, setting up his equipment. She headed over and thanked him for his donation. When Dale had heard the proceeds of the event were going to help the community, he had donated his time and equipment for the entire evening.

Heidi came up behind them. "There you are! What a crowd, eh? This is an amazing turnout, Sammy. Incredible, don't you think?"

"Look at you!" Sammy eyed her cousin, who was wearing a simple white sundress with a fresh purple flower attached to her spaghetti strap. The white reflected off her deepening summer tan, and her hair was lifted from her shoulders in a braid that went across the side of her head and held a matching purple flower. "Gorgeous girl! You could wear that dress if you're maybe considering having a lake wedding, or better yet maybe some exotic beach wedding." Sammy lifted her pencil-thin eyebrows in a question.

Heidi replied with a smile and no comment.

Sammy wondered if Tim was going to move forward and ask for her cousin's hand. According to Heidi, he had seemed to drop the subject entirely, causing her cousin to flip in the direction of now *wanting* a proposal. She guessed she'd just have to be patient and wait and see. Something it seemed she wasn't very good at: patience.

After a brief pause, Heidi leaned over and whispered in Sammy's ear, "She'd be proud, you know."

"Who'd be proud?" Sammy asked.

"Kate. She'd be proud you kept her heart alive, Sammy. You do it again and again . . . every time you hold an event like this." Heidi's eyes scanned the crowd that surrounded them.

Sammy replied with a hug, then asked, "Where's Tim?"

"You mean, where's Nash. Let's just be honest here."

"Huh?"

"I know you think if I tell you where Tim is, Nash will be close behind." Heidi eyed her carefully.

"Nonsense," Sammy disagreed.

Heidi smiled. "Sure. I believe that."

"I should go check on Ellie. She's been great tonight. She handled all the food, decorations, helped Deborah unload the glasses from her car, and now she's selling them. I feel like I'm dropping the ball a bit here."

"Nah, Ellie loves this stuff. Besides, we'll all take turns at the table tonight selling glasses. Take a moment for yourself. No worries; we have a long night ahead."

Sammy took the final step off the platform where she had given her speech and then had zero view. Her height made it impossible for her to see anything or anyone in the crowd. All she could see were body parts.

Tim came up behind Heidi and slipped his arms around her, then spun her around as if to show her off like they were contestants on *Dancing With the Stars*.

"Hey Tim-bo. Look at you. Rare to see you out of uniform. Let's see . . . what are you wearing?" Sammy tried to break the pair from their close proximity to see what Tim had come up with to wear. She was secretly wondering if Heidi had dressed him.

"I'm wearing Louee-louee Vuitton," he said, and then took a dramatic bow like he had just met the queen of England.

"Louis Vuitton? Seriously? Where on earth did you find that in Heartsford?" Sammy rolled her eyes and laughed.

"I dunno." He shrugged and then looked at Heidi. "What am I wearing? You bought it for me." He looked down at his navy polo and khaki shorts. "I like how these new shorts show off my muscular legs, don't you?" Tim extended his leg and flexed his muscle.

"Yeah, beefy," Sammy said with a teasing, sarcastic tone.

"All right, you guys," Heidi said. "Who's going to start the night off singing?" She batted her eyelashes.

"Hey, don't look at me. I'm not doing it." Tim put up his hands and retreated a few steps before bumping into someone and saying, "Pardon me."

"I already put my name in," Heidi said. "I'm singing Pink!"

"What? Pink?" Sammy smirked.

"Yeah! Raise your glass! Perfect, right?" And just as Heidi said it, Dale called out her name and held a microphone in expectation.

"Here I go!" Heidi said as she displayed her famous jazz hands. "Wish me luck!"

Sammy smiled. "Go get 'em, girl."

The music started, the wine was flowing, and Heidi was singing.

Tim retreated into the crowd and was instantly swallowed among the people.

"Are you next?" Sammy heard in her ear, and then spun in the direction of Detective Liam Nash.

"Next?"

"To sing." He nodded his head in Heidi's direction.

"Hardly."

"This is quite an event you put on here. Congratulations. I think the whole town is here tonight."

"Thanks. This is what we do in our community. We help each other." Sammy smiled and nudged him playfully with her elbow.

"I'm sorry, I can't hear you in here." He held a hand to his ear, and a look of confusion crossed his face. "Do you wanna step outside for a breath of fresh air?" Liam offered.

"Actually, that sounds perfect."

The two maneuvered through the crowd and made their way to the outdoor deck overlooking the river walk and gardens. As soon as the cool breeze tickled her skin and the scent of lilacs filled her nostrils, Sammy felt refreshed. The sun had about a half hour left in the western sky before it would morph into a brilliant magenta sunset.

Sammy turned to Liam. Her eyes discreetly checked over his appearance. He was casually dressed, though not in shorts like most of the men in the crowd. He wore a white short-sleeved buttoned shirt and black pants. He kind of looked like a waiter at a fine restaurant. Sammy chuckled inwardly. He was about as bad as she was when it came to attire. But his cologne was another story . . . *that* was divine.

"I'm surprised to see you here tonight, especially since you said you're not much of a reader. And yet here you are, at the local library. I think I'd fall over if I ever saw you join our book club meeting."

"Hey, I support my community . . . and you." His lips curled upward.

The detective's smile sent a shiver down her spine.

As a way to deflect from the sensations cursing through her body, she asked, "So, do we have the investigation wrapped up tight?"

"You want to talk shop? Tonight? Why doesn't that surprise me?" He laughed heartily.

"I just want to know that you have enough evidence to get a solid conviction," Sammy said innocently.

"After interviewing Helen Thatcher further, she admitted to watching Ethan hand Ms. Johnson Kate's barrette on the porch. She had no idea the significance of the hairpiece; she thought it was just something he had made for a girlfriend or something based on one of the author's old crafts. Helen said she never saw Ethan crying and had left them alone on the porch to fetch lemonade."

"How could she know?" Sammy agreed. "Hey, I'm really sorry. You were right . . . I'm far too impulsive," Sammy said sheepishly. "I can't believe I shared the combination lock with the killer. I guess one of the last things Ethan was pressed for before he was shot was where he was hiding the ribbons. I can't believe Brad never found them in the shed."

"Yeah, when I paid a visit to Ethan at the hospital, he told me that when he found the ribbons at Duke's house after the farm was sold, he thought for sure his dad really had hurt Kate. He was so young when it happened, he couldn't really remember—and Bradley had him convinced by filling in the blanks in his mind. That's why Ethan gave the barrette to Jane. She was digging around asking Ethan how the family felt after losing the farm, because as you and I both know, Bradley had people around town believing all kinds of lies he was spreading. Ethan was hoping to find the real truth and clear his father's name. Duke kept those ribbons all this time as proof to keep Bradley in line and under his thumb. Little did he know, keeping those ribbons almost cost him his son's life."

"I know, but if Duke hadn't kept them, we might never have found out the truth. If Duke was so unhappy with Bradley, though, why did he lie on the police report and keep the ribbons in the first place? Why didn't he let Bradley be arrested for Kate's death back then?"

"Because he really thought Bradley was trying to help Kate, *at first*. The only explanation he could come up with is that her hair was caught in the combine and Bradley was trying to cut her loose. He couldn't fathom that Bradley had actually pushed her. It wasn't until after he sold the farm, when he found the ribbons in one pocket of his vest and the barrette in the other, that he began to question everything. When he saw the two pieces cut and how there was no apparent damage, he knew something wasn't right; he came to the same conclusions we did when we initially read the police report. Instead of coming to the police with the truth, which he thought would only compound the hurt to the Allen family, he decided to blackmail Bradley. Someone was bound to crack sooner or later."

"I honestly never in my wildest dreams would have thought Bradley could be a murderer. Never . . . not in a million years . . ."

"I've told you before, Samantha. Everyone is capable of murder if pressed into the right circumstances. You'd be surprised."

Sammy sighed. "I know, I have a lot to learn."

"We just have to corral your inner impulses a bit," he said gingerly with a growing smile.

She wondered if that included her inner impulses of attraction. On this topic she would definitely remain silent, for *now*, so she quickly changed the subject. "What will happen to Duke? I kind of feel bad for the guy."

"Duke Reed won't be charged for lying on the police report, because when he initially wrote the report he believed the barrette was the reason for the accident. He didn't add Bradley's name to the report, as he thought it would just lead to further investigation and confusion. The mayor and his family have decided it best to let it go. They feel bringing it all back up doesn't serve a purpose or bring honor to Kate's memory. Duke is still convinced Bradley stole antiques from his old property. He's ecstatic that the guy will finally be brought to justice, especially with regard to his son. The lack of gunshot residue on Ethan's hand will prove he didn't try to kill himself. Plus, according to the hospital, he's going to make a full recovery and be able to testify. We got him, Samantha."

"Good. That's really good news," Sammy said, although her heart sank at the reality of everything that had happened and the lives that had been lost.

"I'm still waiting on the toxicology match to show that the concrete from Bradley's mother's house, where he'd patched the driveway, was the same as the dust that was found on Jane's blouse, but you and I both know . . ." He waved a slender finger between them.

"It's a match," they said in unison, and then laughed.

321

"And Kate?"

"If Bradley had come clean years ago, this wouldn't have snow-balled so far out of control, and more lives wouldn't have been damaged in his need to cover it all up. In a lot of ways, I'm sorry you found out the truth. I'm sure it's not an easy pill to swallow." The detective handed Sammy a glass of red wine.

"Where's yours?"

"I'm an idiot. I thought you already had a glass. I'll go grab another one."

"You don't have to." Sammy reached to hold him back, but he had already backed away from her.

"I want to." Liam's eyes turned to dark melted chocolate. The kind she wanted to savor. "I'll be right back."

Sammy strolled over to the metal railing along the outer deck and gazed out over the gardens and the river that snaked through Heartsford. She raised her glass to the sky in remembrance of Jane Johnson and her dear friend Kate and then took a sip of wine. Her thoughts turned to the haunting events that had taken place over the last few weeks. Recently, this had happened quite often in quiet moments. A heaviness that she desperately wanted to leave behind for this one night hovered over her, poking expectantly at her heart. She leaned over the railing, holding the glass of wine with two hands. A monarch butterfly swooped up and landed on the rim of her wineglass. It stilled its rapidly fluttering wings and breathed.

Thanks, Kate.
Sammy looked up and smiled.

Kane Family Lasagna

Ingredients

9 lasagna noodles
½ pound hot Italian sausage
¾ pound ground beef
1 medium onion, diced
½ of a green pepper
3 garlic cloves, minced
2 cans (one 28 ounces, one 15 ounces) crushed tomatoes or
    2 quart-sized mason jars of Aunt B's stewed tomatoes
    (drained)
2 cans (6 ounces each) tomato paste
⅔ cup water
2 to 3 tablespoons sugar (helps reduce acid)
1 teaspoon dried oregano
2 teaspoons dried basil
¼ teaspoon salt
¼ teaspoon coarsely ground pepper
1 large egg, lightly beaten
16-ounce carton ricotta cheese
4 cups shredded part-skim mozzarella cheese
¾ cup grated Parmesan cheese

Instructions

1. Preheat oven to 375°.

2. Cook noodles according to package directions; drain. Meanwhile, in a large pot, cook sausage, beef, and onion over medium heat 8–10 minutes or until meat is no longer pink, breaking up meat into crumbles. Add garlic; cook 1 minute. Drain.

3. Stir in tomatoes, tomato paste, water, sugar, seasonings, salt, and pepper; bring to a boil. Reduce heat; simmer, uncovered, 30 minutes, stirring occasionally.

4. In a small bowl, mix egg, ricotta, and a dash of basil.

5. Spread 2 cups meat sauce into an ungreased 13×9-inch baking dish. Top with with 3 noodles, additional sauce to cover, and a third of the ricotta cheese mixture. Sprinkle with 1 cup mozzarella cheese and 2 tablespoons Parmesan cheese. Repeat layers twice. Top with remaining meat sauce and cheeses (dish will be full). Bake, covered, 25 minutes. Bake, uncovered, 25 minutes longer or until bubbly. Let stand 15 minutes before serving.

Urban Ripple Lap Blanket

Materials

Crochet hook, size 4.5
Yarn (any worsted-weight yarn [4] will work—I used Hobby
 Lobby's Yarn Bee, Urban Chic)

Directions

Row 1: Ch 122, sc in 2nd ch from hook, *ch 3, dc in same ch as previous st, skip 2 ch, sc in next ch. Repeat from * to end. Finish last repeat with ch 2, dc in last sc, turn.

Row 2: Ch 3, sc in the next ch 3 loop, *ch 3, dc in same ch loop space, sc in next ch loop. Repeat from * to end. Finish last repeat with ch 2, dc in last sc, turn.

Row 3: Ch 1, sc in first st, ch 3, dc in ch 2 loop, *(sc, ch 3, dc) in next loop. Repeat from * to end, finishing last repeat with a sc in the top of the turning ch, turn.

Repeat Rows 2 and 3 until piece measures 38 inches or desired length.

Edging: Sc crochet around all sides, working 3 sc in each corner.

Jamie Hans created the Urban Ripple Lap Blanket pattern. You can find her on Facebook as EllieJane Crochet (www.facebook.com/elliejanecrochet). She is also the owner of the Bee's Knees Homestead (Brookfield, Wisconsin), where you can find many of her finished crocheted items to purchase.

Acknowledgments

I always thank my readers first, because without you I wouldn't be here, and I'm very aware of that fact. So, from the deepest part of my heart, thank you for choosing this series to read and journeying through the town of Heartsford with me . . . and also for sharing your reviews online. This greatly helps series like mine continue. I'm humbled!

Thanks to Jamie Hans, owner of the Bee's Knees Homestead, who created a special blanket pattern for you readers!

My deepest thanks to Sandy Harding; you're amazeballs, and don't think I don't know it. I owe you the world for nurturing my craft.

Thank you, Faith Black Ross. I'm the luckiest gal alive to have you as my secret weapon. Your edits are spot on and you give me the confidence to push harder and the desire to seek perfection.

Deep gratitude to the entire team at Crooked Lane Books: Jenny, Sarah, Ashley (whom I constantly bug), and those behind the scenes as well.

Thanks to cover artist Ben Perini, whose cover designs are loved by our cozy readers, especially those who belong to "Save our Cozies" on Facebook.

Thanks to Chloe Christiaansen, who handled a first-draft

Acknowledgments

read under stiff time constraints with grace and ease. I know you have a long way to go, but I wish you much success in this industry should you choose to work in publishing after you graduate.

Thanks to the real Jennifer, who often lets me pop into her office for human contact and smiles and is the *best* library director a town could be blessed with. And to the JRML book club and our amazing leader (and friend) Patti, it's an honor to share the love of reading with you all.

Thanks to Chief David Groves, who started the Hartford Citizens Police Academy many years ago (it's been both enlightening and fun!), and our local brave men and women in blue.

Wendy, Jason, and Zoey . . . aww my peeps, my chosen family . . . you won my heart.

Heather and Karl, what a blessing . . . we're finally all in one state! And Conor, please visit often as we love and miss you! Love you all.

Last but certainly not least, thanks to my sweetheart of a husband, Mark. I really do love you *more*. See, it's in print now (ha-ha)! And to my grown children, who are finally happy Mom has something better to do than to bug them. (I'm pretty certain they're begging you to keep reading so Mom keeps writing!) ☺